A Harvest of Lies

THE SECRETS OF STONE BRIDGE
BOOK TWO

JEN TALTY

JUPITER PRESS

This book is a work of fiction. Names, characters, places, and incidents are products of the author's imagination or used fictitiously. Any resemblance to actual events or locales or persons living or dead is entirely coincidental.

Copyright © 2025 by Jen Talty All rights reserved.

No part of this work may be used, stored, reproduced or transmitted without written permission from the publisher except for brief quotations for review purposes as permitted by law.
This book is licensed for your personal enjoyment only. This book may not be re-sold or given away to other people. If you would like to share this book with another person, please purchase an additional copy for each recipient. If you're reading this book and did not purchase it, or it was not purchased for your use only, please purchase your own copy.

Book Description

Lies run as deep as the vines.
And in a town built on secrets, trusting the wrong
person could be deadly.

Devon Boone has spent his life at Stone Bridge Winery, working the land alongside his family and enforcing the unspoken rules that keep the valley running. Old rivalries, public smiles, private grudges—Devon knows how quickly they can turn dangerous. Bringing Emery Tate to Stone Bridge was a calculated risk. Letting someone target her on his watch isn't an option.

Emery Tate refuses to let one betrayal define her future. Once a respected name in the world of fine wine auctions, she's rebuilding her career piece by piece—and someone is determined to tear it down again. The sabotage is deliberate, personal, and escalating, aimed at reminding her she's not welcome. Emery won't retreat. Not now. Not again.

In Stone Bridge, standing your ground has consequences—and losing your heart might be the most dangerous one of all.

Book Description

Book Description

Lies run as deep as the vines.
And in a town built on secrets, trusting the wrong
person could be deadly.

Devon Boone has spent his life at Stone Bridge Winery, working the land alongside his family and enforcing the unspoken rules that keep the valley running. Old rivalries, public smiles, private grudges—Devon knows how quickly they can turn dangerous. Bringing Emery Tate to Stone Bridge was a calculated risk. Letting someone target her on his watch isn't an option.

Emery Tate refuses to let one betrayal define her future. Once a respected name in the world of fine wine auctions, she's rebuilding her career piece by piece—and someone is determined to tear it down again. The sabotage is deliberate, personal, and escalating, aimed at reminding her she's not welcome. Emery won't retreat. Not now. Not again.

In Stone Bridge, standing your ground has consequences—and losing your heart might be the most dangerous one of all.

For Bart and Julia... thanks for the tour of Napa!

THREE MONTHS AGO…

Devon Boone hadn't planned on staying for the entire wine auction but watching Emery Tate get publicly eviscerated by her boss had been like witnessing a car accident, impossible to look away from.

He'd been nursing a glass of overpriced Bordeaux in the back of the Terroir and Gavel Auction House with his Operations Manager, Gabe Maxwell, when Harold Pemberton, the owner of Terroir and Gavel, had taken the microphone and announced that "irregularities in authentication" had been discovered. Emery had stood frozen at the front of the room as Pemberton detailed her alleged crimes with theatrical flair, her face growing paler with each accusation. The crowd had shifted from polite attention to a gossip-hungry gathering, and Devon clenched his jaw watching her endure it.

She'd walked out with her head high, but he'd caught the tremor in her hands.

Now, three hours later, he found her exactly where he'd expected—drowning her sorrows at the Rusted Rail, the kind of establishment that didn't ask questions and poured drinks strong enough that a patron would forget their name.

Emery sat alone at the far end of the bar, still wearing her auction house uniform of black blazer and pearls, though the blazer was now wrinkled and the pearls slightly askew. Her dark hair had escaped its professional style, and she was staring into a rocks glass like it might hold the answers to life's mysteries.

"I'm surprised to see her out in public," Gabe said. "I can't believe she made such a grievous mistake."

"Regardless, Harold didn't need to hang her for all to see."

"I don't know, man," Gabe said. "Collectors dish out a lot of money for unique bottles, and they need to trust the person authenticating them, and Harold had the proof in hand. Hard to argue with that."

"I struggle to believe she'd make such a blunder. For two years, we've both seen her work at different auctions. She's a perfectionist, and she's diligent in her research." Devon stared at the sexy woman at the end of the bar. "She deserves the benefit of the doubt."

"You're going to go have a chat with her, aren't you?"

"I am." Devon couldn't let it go if he tried. For the last month, he'd been doing all that he could to banish her from his thoughts, but she haunted his dreams and occupied his daily thoughts. When she'd returned to Napa Valley two years ago, he'd kept a safe distance. She wasn't the kind of woman he typically went for. She was intellectual, elegant, and somewhat shy, which he found endearing. Only, in the last few months, since he'd gotten to know her better, he'd learn she wasn't shy... she was reserved.

"No offense, but considering Winston and Callie are sitting in the back booth, I think I'll pass on that nightcap."

Devon glanced toward the booth in question. It hadn't surprised him to see his family winery's biggest rival at Terroir and Gavel. Winston constantly bragged about his collection. But seeing them at Rusted Rail, well, that was different. Callie believed the bar was beneath her, and Winston thought it was where the poor folk hung out.

Guess they decided to see how the real world lived.

Gabe checked his watch. "And I told my wife I wouldn't be too late."

"I'll see you tomorrow." Devon slapped Gabe on the back before Gabe turned and slipped out the door of the tavern.

Devon strolled across the bar, boots crunching the peanut shells covering the floor, his gaze locked on Emery. She'd always been the prettiest girl in any room, even when she looked like the most miserable, as well.

"Hey there." Callendra "Callie" Callaway stepped in front of him, blocking his path. She wore a tight pink top with a low V-neck, a black mini skirt, and knee-high boots with heels at least four inches. Granted, Callie was only five foot four, and she'd always been sensitive about that. But he couldn't fathom how she didn't topple over between the new breasts and the stilts for shoes. "Want to throw down a drink with the competition?" She leaned closer. "Maybe you and I could catch up back at my place?"

Devon tried not to laugh. He really did, but it proved to

be impossible. However, it came out more like a half-grunt followed by a mangled snort.

"Aww, come on. Still think I'm too much for you?"

"You're definitely too much of something, and I'm still too old." He ran his fingers through his hair, staring over the top of Callie's head while Emery ordered another drink.

That worried Devon.

"You know, that might have flown when I was a freshman in college. But not last year." She lowered her chin and batted her eyelashes. "Or are we still pretending that one didn't happen?"

"Not pretending, nor am I denying, just saying we're not a good match." He lowered his gaze and smiled. It was impossible not to. Callie wasn't the worst person in the world. Misguided. Immature. Spoiled. But she also had a sweet side. She was kind. Considerate. And often generous with her time and even her money. She volunteered and organized many charitable events, and she was damn good at it. Devon's mother had to admit that Callie had skills in that department, and she'd even co-hosted an event with Callie.

Now, that was a big deal. Not just because it was Callie.

But because she represented Callaway Wines—their biggest competitor in the space.

And rumor had it they were also about to enter the premium wine market.

But as nice and adorable as Callie could be—she had two fatal flaws—at least in Devon's eyes. The first being that while she had a role at the family business as a manager of their tasting room, both in town and on-site, as well as running private tours, she didn't seem to have any ambition outside of finding a husband who could take care of her—which was a problem since the idea of walking down the aisle made Devon twitch.

The second flaw—and probably the biggest of the two—because who was he to judge a person and their life choices when it came to family, was that she had a touch of crazy. Callie knew how to hold a grudge, and when backed into a corner or pissed off, that woman came out swinging.

Callie reached out and traced her finger along his jaw. It was so quick, he barely had time to react. But fast enough to be unnoticeable. He glanced at Emery in time to see her pursed lips and rolling eyes.

Wonderful.

"You say that, and perhaps long haul could be tricky, but we always did have a good time between the sheets," she said.

Christ. Sometimes he and his brother sure knew how to pick them. "You're a nice girl. Go find yourself someone who has the same interests," Devon said, leaning closer. "Now, if you'll excuse me."

She grabbed his forearm. A little too forcefully. "Where are you going in such a hurry?"

"To talk to someone who's had a rough day," Devon said.

Callie's eyes narrowed as she followed his gaze toward Emery at the end of the bar. "Always playing the hero. You know that's going to bite you in the ass one day."

"Not playing anything. Just being a decent human."

"Is that what you call it?" Her grip tightened and her

perfectly manicured nails dug slightly into his skin. "You've got a soft spot for strays. Always have. But sometimes people's problems are their own making."

"What's that supposed to mean?"

"It means maybe you should think twice before getting involved in drama that doesn't concern you. This valley's a small place. Reputations matter—yours, your family's, your winery's." She leaned closer, her voice dropping. "Don't go making things complicated for yourself."

Devon pulled his arm free, irritation flashing through him. "I'll take that under advisement. Now, if you'll excuse me."

"Just remember, I warned you," Callie called after him, but he was already walking away.

Devon pushed that entire encounter out of his mind and approached slowly, sliding onto the barstool beside Emery. "Mind if I join you?"

She looked up. Her green eyes were glassy but still sharp enough to recognize him. "Why, Devon, did you get bored, or did Callie turn you down?"

"That's not even a good joke."

"I thought it was hilarious." She fiddled with her glass. "What are you doing here?"

"Same thing you are, I'd guess. Wondering how the hell that auction house stays in business selling overpriced wine to people with more money than taste." He signaled the bartender for a whiskey. "Though, I'm guessing your evening went considerably worse than mine."

Emery let out a bitter laugh. "Understatement of the year." She took a sip of her drink.

Devon's beverage arrived, and he raised it slightly. "For what it's worth, I thought Pemberton's performance was over the top."

"Performance." She said the word around like she was tasting it. "That's exactly what it was. Complete with dramatic pauses and everything." She studied him over her glass. "So, tell me, Devon Boone, Stone Bridge High's golden boy, you didn't bid on a single bottle of wine. Nor did you have a conversation with Harold. That makes me think you went out of your way to see me. I thought we agreed that what happened was a one-time thing."

"Research. Not to mention I've been known to lurk around these things before." He grinned. "And I believe you have me mistaken me for my little brother when it comes to being the golden anything."

"Didn't you both date homecoming queens?"

"Only me. But she thought I was too busy working the harvest to give her the attention she deserved." Devon took a draw of his whiskey, studying her profile. Even disheveled and drunk, Emery Tate was strikingly gorgeous, not to mention the most intelligent person in the room. She'd been that way in high school, too—the smart girl who sat in the back of AP classes and made teachers rethink their lesson plans.

"Everyone noticed Hilary Letchworth. Even I noticed her and big freaking boobies." Emery waved her drink, her pinky sticking out slightly as a bit of the dark liquid sloshed over the rim. "And then there's Callie Callaway." Emery lowered a shoulder, and then her chin, as if that hid the fact that she was glaring at Callie. "Her breasts are way too big for her frame—although hers are fake—but I think you'd know a little something about that. I always thought she was too young for you."

"I'm never going to live that one down." He sighed. Callie was five years younger, so not a big stretch. However, when he first dated her, she was nineteen and he was twenty-four. His father had been furious. Probably less about the age, more about her last name. The relationship lasted all of four months. "At least I didn't marry her like Bryson did with Monica." But of course, Devon, being Devon, he'd done what he'd always done, and he and Callie had gone back for round two about a year ago. No one knew. At least, not while they were—whatever they were doing—because it wasn't a relationship. It had lasted for six months, but they hadn't been exclusive.

Only, Callie had gotten jealous. Really jealous. Threw him for a loop. He'd never expected her to go all *Fatal Attraction* on him, but she'd come close.

She'd eventually calmed down, and now things were... normal-ish. For them.

"Yeah, that wasn't the brightest move on your brother's part."

"Nope, it wasn't," Devon said. "And he's the smart one, like you."

She glanced at him sideways. "I don't know about that." She gestured vaguely at the bar around them. "Smart enough to spot forgeries but apparently too stupid to realize my mentor was setting me up to take the fall for something I didn't do, and I have no idea why."

Something twisted in his chest at the defeat in her voice. "Did you talk to Harold after the auction?

"There wasn't anything to say. I spent the last two years building cases against suspected forgeries, researching the history of vintage wines, and preparing them for auction. I was good at my job. I can't explain what happened, and Harold didn't give me a chance even to try." She shrugged. "Instead... well, you saw what he did—and he had my authentication documents right there in his hands for everyone to see. There's nothing I can do."

"You said he set you up. If you get the paperwork and it shows that something's off, it'll exonerate you."

"My signature. My stamp. His word against mine." Her shoulders slumped forward. "Those bottles were fakes. I got a good look at them while he was humiliating me. It wasn't easy to see it, but they were swapped with the originals."

"What about the authentication paperwork?"

"Didn't get a good look at that because Harold's hands were flapping about like a bird learning how to take flight. But it doesn't matter. They'll be filed, and it's cause to fire me on the spot."

The bartender refilled her glass without being asked, and Devon frowned. "How many of those have you had?"

"Not nearly enough." Emery raised the fresh drink in a mock toast. "Here's to the beginning of a distinguished career going up in flames before it ever really got off the ground."

"Here's to new beginnings," Devon countered, clinking his glass against hers before she could drink. "The best is yet to come."

That earned him a genuine smile, the first he'd seen from her all evening. "You always were too nice for your own good."

"Was I? I don't remember us talking much in high school. And you've been avoiding me since you spent the night."

"Maybe, but we both know I've always noticed you." The admission slipped out with the casual honesty of someone several drinks past her usual filter. "You were different from the other kids. Quieter. More..." she waved her hand, searching for the word, "...substantial." She leaned closer. "And sexier."

Devon felt heat creep up his neck. "Did Emery Tate just admit to having a crush on me?"

"Past tense," she said quickly, though her cheeks flushed pink. "Very past tense. Ancient history."

"Ah, yes, a month ago is ancient history," he agreed. "So, what's next for you? Besides drinking the bar out of top-shelf whiskey?"

Emery's expression darkened. "Honestly? I have no idea. Harold will make sure I'm blacklisted from every major auction house on the West Coast. I'm living in an Airbnb, and my savings account is looking about as promising as my career prospects."

"There are other places to work in wine."

"We both know my reputation is ruined. Word travels fast in this industry. But you already know that." She took another long sip. "I left the art history world two years ago and reinvented myself. Now, at thirty-four years old, I'm starting over. Again. My mother always said I should have been a teacher like my sister."

"Your mother clearly doesn't know you very well."

"We slept together once, and you think you know me?"

"I know you spent senior year writing a paper on terroir

that made our agriculture teacher rethink everything he knew about soil composition. I know you got into Stanford on a full scholarship and graduated summa cum laude with a degree in art history and chemistry. And I know you turned down three job offers from major museums to work in wine authentication because you wanted to combine art and science in a way that mattered."

She stared at him with parted lips and wide eyes. "How do you possibly know all that?"

"Small town. I've heard things."

"People talk, or Devon Boone paid attention to something other than ESPN?"

"Maybe both." He met her gaze steadily. "The point is, you're brilliant at what you do. Harold is a snake who threw you under the bus to save his own skin. That doesn't erase everything you've accomplished."

Emery was quiet for a long moment, swirling the liquid in her glass. "You know what the worst part is? I actually loved that job. Every morning, I got to touch history. Hold bottles that were crafted by people who died over a hundred years ago. Authenticate pieces of liquid art." Her voice cracked slightly. "And now, every time I look at a wine label, all I'll think about is fraud and forgery and failure."

"That's the alcohol talking."

"No, that's reality tumbling from my lips. The alcohol is just making me honest about it."

Devon watched her drain her glass and signal for another. She was well past tipsy and heading toward genuinely drunk, but underneath the alcohol was real pain. The kind that went deeper than professional embarrassment.

"Come on," he said, standing and dropping money on the bar. "Let's get you some air."

"I'm fine right here."

"You're drunk, it's getting late, and I'm not leaving you alone in a dive bar to make decisions you'll regret tomorrow."

"Who says I'll regret them?"

"The same smart woman who just told me she's lost everything she cared about. That woman deserves better than waking up in a strange place with no memory of how she got there."

Emery looked up at him, and for a moment her defenses dropped completely. She looked young, lost, and scared. "Why do you care what happens to me?"

The question hit him harder than it should have. "Because someone should. And because watching Harold humiliate you in front of that crowd made me want to punch something."

"My hero," she said, but there was warmth in her voice rather than sarcasm.

"Your designated driver," he corrected. "Let's get you home."

"This place I'm renting is ridiculous. I thought if I went with expensive, I'd be telling the universe I was successful and that would force everything to fall into place." She fumbled in her purse for a key. "Last night of luxury before I start shopping for cardboard boxes."

Devon helped her off the barstool, steadying her when she swayed. "Lots of places to rent in this town. Lots of job prospects, too."

"You really are too chipper."

The walk to her Airbnb took twenty minutes, with Devon keeping a careful hand on her elbow as she navigated the sidewalk in heels that had clearly been chosen for standing, not walking. She kept up a steady stream of chatter—about wine, about Harold's terrible toupee, about how she'd always imagined her life turning out differently.

"You know what I thought I'd be doing at thirty-four?" she asked as he took her key. "Married to some respectable museum curator with a house in the suburbs and maybe a kid or two. Very predictable. Very safe."

"Sounds boring."

"Boring sounds pretty good right now." She leaned against the wall. "What about you? What do you want?"

"Exactly what I'm doing." Devon hit the button for the fifth floor. "Working with my family, making wine, trying not to screw up the legacy."

"The good son."

"That would be Bryson—even when he married what's her name and then divorced her. I'm the careful son. There's a difference."

Her one-bedroom condo was elegant, with all cream colors, soft lighting, and furniture that cost more than most people's cars.

"Well," Emery said, turning to face him in the doorway. "This is me. Thank you for the escort service and the pep talk. Even if I don't believe a word of it."

"Get some sleep. Things will look different in the morning."

"Will they? Will Harold suddenly not be a lying snake? Will my career magically resurrect itself? Will—"

Devon stepped closer, close enough that he could smell

her perfume underneath the whiskey. "Will you still be the smartest, most capable woman I've ever met? Yeah. That part doesn't change."

Something shifted in her expression. The brittle humor faded, replaced by something vulnerable and raw. "Don't look at me like that." She took a few steps backward, into the kitchen.

He followed. "Like what?"

"Like you believe what you're saying."

They stood there in the doorway between her kitchen and bedroom, the space between them charged with possibility. Devon could see the exact moment she made her decision, could see her defenses crumble completely.

"Stay," she whispered.

Every instinct told him to walk away. She was drunk, devastated, and not thinking clearly. But the word hung between them like a plea, and he found himself stepping into the room instead of backing away. "Emery—"

"Don't get all noble now. I know I'm being pathetic, and this is a terrible idea. But it's not like we haven't done this dance before." She kicked off her heels and sank onto the edge of the bed. "I don't want to be alone tonight. I don't want to lie here and think about how I've thoroughly destroyed my life."

Devon closed the door behind him and leaned against it. "You haven't destroyed anything. You've had a setback."

"A setback." She laughed, but there were tears in her eyes now. "My mentor betrayed me, my reputation is ruined, and I have nowhere to go. But sure, let's call it a setback."

He moved to sit beside her on the bed, keeping a careful distance between them. "Stone Bridge is your home."

"I can't stay here after what happened. I could move in with my sister. She's in Portland with her husband and kids. Or go back to Arizona with my parents." She wiped her eyes with the back of her hand. "But no way in hell could I stay here."

The words hit Devon like a physical blow. He'd never not had a home, never questioned where he belonged or whether there was a place for him in the world. His family's land was in his blood.

"There's so much opportunity in Stone Bridge," he heard himself say.

Emery looked at him like he'd suggested she sprout wings and fly. "And do what? Pour wine at the local tasting room? Teach high school chemistry?"

"You could work for us."

The words surprised them both. Devon hadn't planned to say them, but now that they were out there, they felt right.

"Work for Stone Bridge Winery? Doing what?"

"I don't know yet. But we're expanding, looking for people who understand wine from different angles. Someone with your background in authentication and provenance..." He trailed off, studying her face. "This isn't pity. This is recognizing talent when I see it."

Emery swayed slightly, exhaustion and alcohol seemingly catching up with her. "I can't think about any of this right now. My brain feels like it's swimming through molasses."

"Then don't think. Just sleep." Devon stood and pulled back the covers on the bed. "Come on."

She looked up at him with glassy eyes. "You're really going to stay?"

"Yes, but you're going to sleep, and I'm going to make sure you don't do anything you'll regret in the morning."

"Like what?"

"Like calling Harold and telling him exactly what you think of him. Or booking a flight to somewhere with no extradition treaties." He helped her stand and guided her toward the bathroom. "Go change. I'll be right here."

When she emerged fifteen minutes later in pajamas, her makeup scrubbed off and her hair in a messy bun, she looked younger and more vulnerable than ever. Devon had turned down the lights and was sitting in the armchair by the window, having put as much distance between himself and the bed as the room allowed.

"You don't have to sleep in the chair," she said softly, climbing under the covers.

"Yes, I do."

She was quiet for a moment, then, "Devon?"

"Yeah?"

"Thank you. For tonight. For not letting me drink myself into oblivion alone."

"Anyone would have done the same thing."

"No," she said, her voice already thick with approaching sleep. "They really wouldn't have."

Devon watched as her breathing evened out, watched the tension finally leave her face as she drifted off. Only then did he allow himself to really look at her—the curve of her cheek against the pillow, the way her dark hair spilled across the white sheets, the peaceful expression that replaced the devastation he'd seen earlier.

He settled back in the chair, knowing he wouldn't sleep much. But that was fine. Someone needed to make sure she was okay, and apparently, that someone was him.

When morning came, things would be different. Clearer. But tonight, he'd keep watch over the most intelligent woman he'd ever known and try not to think about how right it felt to be the one she'd asked to stay.

Consciousness crept in slowly, accompanied by the kind of headache that felt like someone had taken a sledgehammer to her skull. Emery kept her eyes closed, afraid that opening them would make the pounding worse, and tried to piece together the previous night through the fog of whiskey and humiliation.

The auction house. Harold's betrayal. The bar afterward, where she'd apparently decided that drowning her sorrows was a viable life strategy. And then...

Her eyes snapped open.

Devon was asleep in the armchair by the window, his long frame folded awkwardly into a space clearly not designed for someone his size. His dark hair was mussed, his button-down shirt wrinkled, and there was something endearingly vulnerable about the way he'd managed to fall asleep sitting up.

What the hell had happened last night?

Emery sat up carefully, but that didn't stop her head from spinning. She remembered Devon appearing at the bar like a guardian angel. Remembered walking back to her Airbnb with his steadying hand on her elbow. And she definitely remembered asking him to stay. However, the specifics of that conversation were frustratingly hazy.

Had she thrown herself at him? Please God, she hoped she hadn't thrown herself at him—again. The last thing she needed was to get tangled up with Devon. He was a nice enough man. Maybe too nice, and that meant trouble. She knew that to be a fact. While she wouldn't label him a player, he wasn't the kind of man who had *future husband* tattooed anywhere on his body. His reputation for breaking hearts had kept her from pursuing him for the last two years.

That was until last month when she'd found herself strolling past his tasting room and decided to go in for a glass. One turned into two, and the next thing she knew, she'd spent the night at his house down the street.

She looked down at herself—at least she had on pajamas, which was something. But the fact that Devon was still here, that he'd apparently spent the night watching over her...

"Oh God," she whispered, burying her face in her hands. The last time she'd been with Devon hadn't been under such dire circumstances, but alcohol had been involved.

"You're awake." Devon's voice was rough with sleep, and when she looked up, he was stretching in the chair, obviously working out the kinks caused by his improvised bed.

"Please tell me I didn't make a complete fool of myself last night," she said.

"You were hurting." He stood, rolling his shoulders. "You needed someone to make sure you were okay. End of story."

She studied his face, looking for any sign that he was lying or sparing her feelings. But Devon had always been direct, even in high school. If she'd done something mortifying, he'd tell her.

"I'm sorry," she said finally. "For putting you in that position. For making you sleep in a chair. For whatever I said that convinced you to babysit a drunk stranger."

"Stranger? We've known each other since grade school." Devon moved to sit on the edge of the bed, seemingly keeping a careful distance between them. "And you don't need to apologize. You had a shit night."

The memories of yesterday came flooding back—Harold's public humiliation, the whispers of the auction crowd, the devastating realization that her career was over. In the harsh light of morning, with a splitting headache and the taste of lies in her mouth, it all felt even worse.

"God, what am I going to do?" The words slipped out before she could stop them. "I can't stay in Stone Bridge. I can't face my colleagues or anyone who witnessed that disaster."

"Yeah, well." He pulled out his cell. "Unfortunately, that disaster has found its way to social media."

"You're joking, right?"

"Unfortunately, no."

"Wonderful. I'm an internet joke and I'm apparently unemployable in the only field I have any real passion for and I don't want to go back to the museum in San Fransico with my tail between my legs."

"You don't have to. There are so many options for you in this industry right here in Stone Bridge. Or anywhere in Napa."

"Who the hell is going to hire someone with that kind of reputation? Especially when..." she snagged his cell. "Jesus. That's way too many views. I'm so screwed. I'll never recover from this."

He leaned forward slightly. "I meant what I said last night about the job opportunity."

Emery stared at him, her pulse rattling in her throat. "I'm pretty fuzzy about the details of that."

"Good thing I was sober and remember it exactly."

"I appreciate the gesture, but—"

"It's not a gesture. It's business. And this is an opportunity." His tone sharpened slightly. "What happened doesn't change your qualifications or your expertise."

"My expertise in spotting forgeries? In authenticating and developing a creation story for a historical vintage? The same expertise that apparently collapsed when I failed to catch massive fraud, and... never mind."

"Your expertise in wine history, chemical analysis, provenance research, and market evaluation would be assets to our business development team."

Emery felt something flutter in her chest—hope, maybe, or just the desperate desire to believe that her life wasn't entirely over. "What kind of position are you talking about?"

"I can't make any promises. It's not solely up to me. I need to discuss it with my family—figure out where you'd fit best in our expansion program. There'd be an application process, interviews, and if hired, the job wouldn't start right away. But..." He reached out and covered her hand with his. "You're talented and smart and capable. One bad day doesn't erase that."

The touch of his hand sent warmth shooting up her arm, and suddenly she was very aware that they were sitting on a bed together, that he'd spent the night taking care of her, that the morning light was making his dark eyes look almost golden.

"Why are you doing this?" she asked softly.

"Because I believe you'd be an asset to our vineyard."

"Is that the only reason?"

The question hung between them, loaded with possibility. Devon's thumb traced across her knuckles.

"No," he said quietly. "It's not. I haven't been able to stop thinking about you. I wanted to kiss you last night, but it wouldn't have been right. Not to mention you wouldn't have even remembered it considering how drunk you were."

The admission shifted something fundamental in the space between them. The careful distance he'd maintained, the professional tone, the protective barriers—all of it crumbled as they looked at each other in the soft morning light.

He leaned closer, his free hand coming up to cup her cheek. "You're a beautiful woman. The last time, we established that I've had a crush on you for years. I've followed your career because... You interest me."

"Not to sound cliché, but you had me at beautiful."

He kissed her then, soft and careful at first, then deeper when she melted into him. Her hands fisted in his wrinkled shirt, pulling him closer, and he gathered her against him like she was a bottle of wine from the Titanic, and he was afraid to spoil the vintage.

They fell back onto the rumpled sheets together, and this time there was no alcohol clouding her judgment, no desperation driving her actions. Just Devon's hands gentle on her skin, his mouth trailing heat along her throat, and the overwhelming rightness of being exactly where she was supposed to be.

One

THREE MONTHS LATER

The fire crackled softly in the stone pit, casting dancing shadows across the faces gathered around it. Devon's entire family had assembled, as they often did, for a night of good wine and conversation. However, tonight, the air hung heavy with unspoken grief, the darkness alive with hushed voices and shared sorrow. But Devon couldn't focus on the latter. He swirled the cabernet in his glass, watching the liquid catch the firelight, his attention drifting to the gravel driveway beyond the circle of warmth. Any minute now, Emery would pull through those gates, and this careful balance he'd been maintaining for the last few months would shift into something entirely new.

He didn't know what that looked like, or how he'd manage it. This was uncharted territory. She'd made it clear the moment his family got serious about hiring her that they couldn't ever be anything other than friends. He'd done his best to accept that.

Only, it wasn't working out so well. Having feelings of

love wasn't something that he understood—that was Bryson's department.

"I can't believe David Callaway is dead," Walter, his father, said, breaking the comfortable silence that had settled over the group. "His wife called me a few hours ago. Based on the medical scare he had last year, they think he had a heart attack. The medical examiner will be able to confirm that in a few days."

"I sent over a few pans of lasagna and some muffins," Brea, his mother, said, reaching for his father's hand. "He was only what, sixty? That's far too young."

"Sixty-one," his father confirmed. "I didn't always see eye to eye with David, but he was a good man. Built Callaway Wines back up after his dad's..." his father glanced up with that twitch in his eye that he always got when he was about to say something that didn't settle well in his gut. "...troubles."

Devon not only caught the uncomfortable expression, but the careful way his father phrased it. Jasper Callaway's criminal activities were old history. Still, in a small town like Stone Bridge, some stories never quite died—especially since Gabe Maxwell was related to someone associated with the illicit activities. But for the Boones, it was water under the bridge.

"I wonder if any of the rumors are true," Ashley, one of Devon's little sisters, said, bringing up another potential shadow hanging over Callaway Wines.

"Now is not the time for idle gossip." His mother lowered her chin. Her disapproving gaze still had the ability to make all her children recoil and rethink their actions.

"I'm sure I'm the only one wondering if David Callaway had an illegitimate child who's going to appear out of nowhere and stake a claim on his legacy." Ashley sank into her chair, lifted her glass, and took a big sip, ignoring the glares from their parents.

Devon remembered the first time he'd heard that rumor. Winston had gotten into a fist fight with some idiot in the center of town. He'd been all of fourteen, and Devon had to admit, if he'd been in Winston's shoes, he would've punched that kid, too.

The rumor circulated every once in a while, and Devon barely paid attention to it. He didn't care. It didn't matter. At least not the way people in this town gossiped about it.

"First, it's not our business," his father said. "Second, the Callaways are grieving. The last thing they need is for this town to whisper about something like that during a time like this."

"I feel bad for Winston and Callie," Riley, Bryson's girlfriend, said softly. "Losing a parent is devastating." She raised her hand and wiped away a tear that had fallen to her cheek.

"It's never easy." His father set aside his wine glass and rubbed a hand over his mouth. "In time, you learn to go on. Live your life. But the loss is always there."

"I might not like Winston, but I called him as soon as I heard the news. He sounded pretty shaken up by it." Bryson shifted. "He's going to have his hands full taking over the winery—especially the winemaking process, and he knows that. David was very hands-on and was an excellent vintner."

"He was incredibly controlling," his father mused.

"However, David and his children have always had different philosophies about the business."

"So have we," Devon added.

"Not in the same way." Bryson lifted his glass. "You and I might fight like we're still a couple of kids in preschool, and our sisters are insanely opinionated, but we know when to check our egos. Dad has taught us all well."

"Thanks for the compliment." His father's eyes beamed, and his smile was wide. But there was a sense of loss in the way his father spoke—slow and deliberate.

Three months ago, it had been Riley's father—a lifelong friend to Walter and all of the Boones, who'd died. David might not have been their father's closest ally. In fact, he was their biggest competitor. But David was still a decent man. Kind. Fair. And always fun to be around.

"I must say that I've never felt as though I've had to hover over you kids when it comes to this business." His father took a slow sip of his pinot—a family favorite.

"You've also never told us we had to be a part of it," Hasley, his other sister, said. "That makes a difference."

"David never forced Winston or Callie," Devon's mom said. "But there was some pressure, because of the... well... past."

"You don't have to dance around the topic of my grandfather and how he was tied to Jasper Callaway and what either one of them did," Gabe said. "What happened is a part of the history of this town. Even with time and space, it's still going to come up on occasion. Heck, some wine tours talk about the murder and my grandfather when they drive by the location."

His mother reached out and rested a hand over Gabe's. "We're just trying to be respectful."

"You always are." Gabe smiled.

"Dad, you think Winston and Callie will be able to carry on the same level of commitment to the family winery as his dad did?" Ashley asked.

"Hard to say," Walter replied. "Winston's got the education—went to UC Davis, same as Bryson and Gabe. But he's never shown the same passion for winemaking that his father did. Never spent the time honing that craft. More interested in the business side. And he's made some solid decisions. However, he often rushes into things and occasionally puts his foot in his mouth."

"Not to mention he's arrogant," Hasley added quietly. "And slightly chauvinistic."

"I'm with Hasley on this one." Ashley waved her hand wildly in the air, as if she were trying to swat an annoying fly. "I ran into him on my birthday last year, and he had the audacity to not only hit on me—as if I'd ever be interested —but he went on to say that any woman who was with him would never have to work again. That he didn't understand why I didn't focus on charities over the vineyard." She raised her drink. "Mind you, Winston had been drinking that night, and I doubt he'd admit to the conversation— especially the part about hitting on me, considering he used the line, *hey, your brother, my sister, so, why not us.*" Ashley shivered. "It was gross."

"I still can't believe you dated Callie." Bryson chuckled.

"Yeah, well, you married—"

"Can we not have this childish argument again?" his father interrupted. He held his glass up, swirling it, staring at the red liquid as the orange and yellow flames amplified the wine's rich tone.

"Honey, what has your brow wrinkled?" Devon's mom rested her hand on his dad's thigh.

"David and I had our fair share of arguments over the years," his dad said softly. "I didn't—I don't—agree with his methods, and he had opinions about mine. But even I can admit Callaway Wines are a decent product. I worry about what will happen to future harvests. Without a good vintner, a wine will end up wrapped in a brown paper bag and consumed for effect—not taste."

Devon observed his father's expression. There was history between the families—complicated history. They all knew the connection. Understood it—but it was one of those things that was rarely discussed and wouldn't be with Gabe present.

"There are many good wine makers in the area," Bryson said. "I can name two off the top of my head who've been working as assistants and would love the chance as head vintner, especially when they won't get the opportunity in their current roles for decades to come." He shifted his gaze toward Gabe. "I just hope you won't be one of them."

"You're talented, but we'd be lost without you as our operations manager," Devon said.

"Thanks for the vote of confidence." Gabe took his wine glass and finished off the last drop. "At one time, I might have had my sights set on being a head winemaker, but that notion left a few months into working here. I have no intention of going anywhere."

A long silence filled the air. The only noise was the crackle-pop of the flames which pointed like fingers toward the sky. Devon checked his watch. With every second that passed, his pulse increased. Devon held his glass by the stem, swirling the red liquid.

"You're going to wear a hole in that glass if you keep staring at it," Ashley observed, clearly ready to change the subject from their deceased neighbor.

"I'm appreciating the complexity of the blend," Devon replied smoothly, though he caught Hasley's knowing smirk from across the fire.

"The complexity of the blend, or the complexity of your feelings about Emery?" Hasley leaned forward with the kind of grin that suggested she was enjoying this far too much.

"Leave your brother alone," his mother said, but her tone suggested she was just as curious as her daughters. She sat curled against his father's side on the wide outdoor sofa, her hair catching the firelight and her green eyes bright with maternal interest. "Though, I do think it's wonderful that Emery is finally joining our team. Such a bright girl, and so accomplished."

Gabe stood. "I'm sorry. I need to go."

"Why?" Devon's father asked.

Gabe ran a hand over his mouth. His dark eyes still reflected the weight of Gabe's personal loss. "I promised Olivia I wouldn't be too late."

"Please let her know if there's anything at all she needs, we're here for her," Devon's mother said.

"She appreciated the flowers and food," Gabe said. "We'd barely even gotten used to the idea when she miscarried. The doctor said we'll be able to try again soon. It's just that she struggles late at night."

"We understand, and we don't want you to keep her waiting," Devon said. "However, I was hoping you'd be here when Emery rolled in, which should be any minute. I know you've had some concerns about her joining the team. You're a big part of why this winery's daily operations functions so seamlessly, and you'll be working closely with her."

"You've always encouraged me to express my opinions freely. I have no reservations about her qualifications, but with her current reputation, there hasn't been enough time between the scandal and the present day. I just want what's best for Stone Bridge Winery."

Bryson sighed from his position leaning against Riley's chair. "I don't disagree with you, but Emery has a lot to bring to the table."

Riley reached up to squeeze Bryson's hand, where it rested on her shoulder. Even after three months back in Stone Bridge, she still carried herself with the easy confidence of someone who'd seen the world. However, Devon could see how she'd softened around the edges since returning home. "I've come up with an entire media package to help Emery with her image. I'm happy to sit down with you and go over it, if it will help ease your mind. And from what I remember of Emery from high school was that she was always composed, always smart, and always figured out a way to come out on top."

"Exactly," Walter agreed, his deep voice carrying the authority of someone who'd built a successful business from nothing but his father's passion and a dream. "Her expertise in provenance and authentication is exactly what we need as we expand into premium markets. The scandal at Pemberton's? I heard her side, and I just don't understand why Harold wouldn't at least investigate the situation further. Or have a chat with her before publicly calling her a liar and then allowing that crap to be posted on social media."

"It's not about whether she's innocent or guilty. But this is about public perception," Gabe said. "People are still viewing that horrid scene. So, sure, I'd love to see what you have in mind. Maybe I can come up with some ideas, too. I do have a little experience in small-town gossip."

"That you do." His father leaned forward, resting his elbows on his knees. "Your perspective on this would be appreciated. Riley, you should email him your ideas."

"I can do that tonight." Riley smiled her sweet, genuine smile that lit up any room. She was so damn good for Bryson—for the entire family.

"I'm happy to take a look." Gabe ran his fingers through his hair. "You gave me a chance in Napa Valley when most probably wouldn't have, based on my name. I'm the grandson of a murderer. Jasper Callaway's muscle. I didn't do anything wrong. Nor did my parents. But who I am isn't always seen over the gossip this town churns. What's going to be hard with Emery is that she's at the center of this—not an ancestor. And her transgression was caught on video for the entire world to see, judge, and convict."

"Since when do we make decisions based on what other people think?" Devon asked, finally looking up from his wine. "We've always done what we believed was right, not what was safe."

Ashley shifted on her bench. "I'll admit I had reservations, initially. But after talking with Emery during the interviews, I think she'll be an asset. Besides her expertise in authentication, I was impressed and surprised at how well she knows the premium market. She'll be an asset when we launch."

"And she's not afraid to admit when she doesn't know something," Hasley added. "That kind of honesty is refreshing in this industry."

"That's exactly what I plan on playing into," Riley said.

"That should help." Gabe rubbed his jaw. "But if people are going to forgive and ignore the video, they're going to need to know the woman behind the mistake. They're going to need to know the things that make her tick, just like this town needed with me. Still does."

"That makes sense." Walter clasped his fingers together. "When we hired you, we did a full page spread on who you were and why we came knocking on your door."

"It worked, and it might work again with Emery," Gabe said, glancing over his shoulder, as if looking for something or someone.

Devon had known Gabe a long time and while he was sure that Gabe needed to get home, he also knew that Gabe was itching to leave before Emery showed up.

"I like this approach." Devon wanted Emery at Stone Bridge Winery, but he had concerns about the media circus and the gossip that had built this town.

"On that note, I'd best get home. Thanks for a lovely evening." Gabe waved as he strolled toward the driveway.

"I've always appreciated his honesty." Devon's father leaned back, lifted his glass, and sipped.

"He's a good boy." Devon's mother's smile turned sly.

"I'm glad he can pivot so quickly. Emery is such a lovely young woman. Don't you think she's lovely, Devon? And pretty, too."

"Mother," Devon warned. "She's here to work. Not be set up with me, or anyone else for that matter—and we don't need to give Bryson something else to complain about."

Bryson raised both hands. "Me? Why are we picking on me? I didn't say anything."

"Maybe not, but we all know what you were thinking." Devon bent over and tossed a wad of grass at his little brother. "A couple of mistakes in my youth, and this one never lets me live them down."

"Well, I'm simply observing that she's an attractive young woman with excellent qualifications. If she happens to make my eldest son smile more than he has in years, well, that's just a bonus." His mother shrugged.

Riley laughed. "Anyone who can make Devon blush deserves a place at this table."

"I'm not blushing." Devon shot Riley a stare. Not a hostile one. More of a pleading one to let it go.

"You absolutely are," Hasley said. "Your ears are practically glowing."

"This is giving me fodder to bust his ass for days to come." Bryson shook his head, chuckling.

Devon was saved from further torture by the sound of tires on gravel. A silver Honda Civic appeared in the driveway, headlights sweeping across the meticulously landscaped front yard before coming to a stop near the house.

"That would be our new team member," Walter said,

rising from the outdoor sofa with the easy strength of a man who'd spent his life working with his hands.

Devon's pulse quickened as the car door opened, and Emery stepped out. She was dressed professionally but not overly formal—dark jeans, a cream-colored blouse, and a blazer that probably cost more than she could afford right now. Her dark hair was pulled back in a low ponytail, and even from across the yard, he could see the careful composure she wore like armor.

"She looks nervous," Devon's mother observed.

"Wouldn't you be?" Riley asked. "Coming into all of this. Back to Stone Bridge after only three months. I remember that sensation well, and it wasn't fun."

"Ah, but look what you gained." Devon's mom smiled so wide, it was brighter than the flames. "You and Bryson—back together—as it should be."

Emery gathered a small suitcase and what looked like a laptop bag from her backseat, then turned toward the house. The firelight caught her face as she approached, and Devon saw the moment she spotted the group gathered around the fire pit. Her step faltered almost imperceptibly before she straightened her shoulders and continued forward.

"Emery," his mom called out, rising to meet her with the warmth that had made every friend the Boone siblings had ever brought home feel like family. "Welcome. I hope the drive from Arizona wasn't too bad."

"It was long but not horrible. My parents say hello. It's been a long time since they've been in Stone Bridge, but they've always loved your wine."

"So glad to hear that." His mom smiled. "The guesthouse is all set up for you, but if there's anything you need, please don't hesitate to ask."

"Thank you, Mrs. Boone. I'm sure it will be lovely. I can't tell you how much I appreciate this opportunity." Emery's voice was steady, professional, but Devon caught the slight breathiness that suggested she was more nervous than she was letting on. He stood as she approached the fire, and when their eyes met across the flames, he felt the same jolt of electricity that had been arcing between them for months.

"Please, it's Brea," his mother said.

"You remember my daughters, Ashley and Hasley," Walter said, making introductions. "And, of course, you know Bryson and Riley."

"Riley, it's so good to see you again." Emery's smile became more genuine as she greeted the other woman.

"We should let you get settled," Ashley said, standing and brushing off her jeans. "Tomorrow's going to be a full day of orientation and paperwork."

"All the exciting stuff," Hasley added with a grin. "Don't let Devon overwhelm you with spreadsheets on your first day."

"I make beautiful spreadsheets," Devon protested.

"I'm sure they're works of art," Emery said, and he caught the hint of humor in her voice that had been missing during her interviews but he knew was part of who she was from the time they'd spent together in private.

Bryson pushed off from Riley's chair and offered his hand to help her up. "We should head out, too. I keep trying to convince this one to move in with me, but she's stubborn."

"I'm not stubborn, I'm cautious," Riley replied, accepting his hand but rolling her eyes. "We're not there yet."

"When will we be there? I'm thinking of making a timeline, maybe some charts..." Bryson glanced toward the sky.

"Charts will definitely change my mind," Riley said, laughing as she swatted his arm. "Come on, walk me home before you start planning our entire future."

"Oh, he's got a plan," Devon said with a devilish smile. "One that I'm sure doesn't include coming home tonight."

"Not sure he's slept in his own bed all week." His mother laughed. "I really wish that the two of you would sometimes stay here."

"I believe it's those comments that keep my girlfriend from wanting to move in with me," Bryson said.

"Or maybe it's because you haven't popped the question." Devon's father swirled his wine. "You really should make an honest—"

"Enough of that." Bryson waved his hand over his head.

They said their goodnights, disappearing toward the road, heading into town, their voices fading as they walked. Ashley and Hasley followed suit, offering quick hugs to Emery and promises to get to know each other better tomorrow.

"We'll leave you to get settled," Walter said. "We're thrilled to have you as part of the family business. I think you're going to love it here."

"Thank you, Mr. Boone. I'm looking forward to getting started."

Devon's mom enveloped Emery in one of her trademark hugs—the kind that had been known to crack ribs and had definitely cracked emotional barriers. "None of this Mr. and Mrs. business. We're Walter and Brea, and you're family, now."

Devon watched Emery's careful composure slip just slightly. The vulnerability lasted only a moment before she pulled herself together, but it was enough to remind him why he'd been so determined to give her this chance.

"Thank you," Emery said softly. "That means more than you know."

His parents disappeared into the house, leaving Devon and Emery alone by the dying fire. The silence stretched between them, filled with three months of phone calls, carefully neutral emails about job details, and the weight of everything they weren't saying.

"So," Emery said finally, adjusting the strap of her laptop bag. "The guesthouse?"

"Right. Yes." Devon shook himself out of his reverie and gestured toward a path that wound around the side of the main house. "It's just through here."

They walked in silence, their footsteps crunching softly on the gravel path as he pulled her suitcase across the stones. Solar lights illuminated the way, casting a warm glow over the meticulously maintained landscaping his mother spent hours perfecting. The guesthouse sat about fifty yards from the main house, nestled among oak trees and connected by a stone walkway that his father had laid himself twenty years ago.

"This is beautiful," Emery said as they approached the small but elegant building. "Your parents really didn't have to—"

"They wanted to. Besides, it makes practical sense.

You'll be working side by side with all of us, and this keeps you close enough to be part of things but far enough away to have privacy."

Devon unlocked the front door and flicked on the lights, revealing the space his mother had spent the last month preparing. The main room combined a living area and kitchen in an open-concept design, with exposed beams, a stone fireplace, and French doors leading to a private patio. His mother had outdone herself with the decorating—soft blues and greens that echoed the vineyard beyond, comfortable furniture that invited relaxation, and fresh flowers on the dining table.

"Bedroom and bathroom are through there," Devon said, pointing to a hallway. "There's a small office space off the bedroom if you need somewhere quiet to work. Internet is fast, kitchen is fully stocked, and Mom left you a bottle of our best pinot noir as a welcome gift."

Emery set down her bags and turned in a slow circle, taking it all in. "This is incredible. I was expecting something more like a studio apartment, not a house that's nicer than anywhere I've ever lived."

"My parents don't do anything halfway."

"Apparently not." She moved to the French doors and peered out at the patio, where string lights created a canopy of stars above the outdoor furniture. "I don't know how I'll ever repay this kindness."

"Just be your brilliant self."

That earned him a smile—a big one too. "Sometimes you can be sweet."

The moment felt charged, reminiscent of their night together three months ago. Devon found himself stepping closer, drawn by the way the soft lighting caught the gold flecks in her brown eyes, by the subtle scent of her perfume, by the memory of how she'd felt in his arms.

"Devon." Emery's voice was quiet but firm, and he saw her walls go back up in real time. "We should probably talk about expectations."

"Expectations?"

"Boundaries." She moved away from the doors, putting the kitchen island between them. "This job means everything to me. It's my chance to rebuild my career and reputation. I spent the last three months at my parents' house examining my life. My career. My plan moving forward. I can't afford to complicate things, especially in this town."

Devon felt something cold settle in his chest. "And being with me would complicate things?"

"Being with anyone would do that. But especially being with my boss. With someone whose family I'll be working with every day." She wrapped her arms around herself, a gesture he recognized as protective. "I know what we agreed to a month ago when I accepted the position, but I wanted to make sure we're still on the same page."

They'd had this conversation before, over the phone, when she'd finally agreed to take the job. She'd been clear then about needing to keep things professional, and he'd agreed because he'd wanted her to feel safe taking the risk. But hearing it again now, in person, with her standing in the house his parents had prepared for her, like she was already part of the family... and the domesticity of it—her surrounded by his parents' warmth—made every vow he'd made about keeping things professional feel impossible. They couldn't let it happen again. He knew that. But God, seeing her like this made him want to forget every reason why.

"Right," he said, keeping his voice neutral.

"It's not that I don't—" She stopped herself, shaking her head. "This is just too important to mess up."

"I understand."

"Do you? Because the way you were looking at me just now..."

"How was I looking at you?"

Emery's cheeks flushed pink. "Like you were remembering things we agreed not to remember."

The way she looked at him when she said it—honest, unflinching—nearly broke him. Because she was right—he had been remembering. The taste of her mouth, the sound of her laugh when he'd made her forget her troubles, the way she'd fit against him like she'd been made for his arms.

"Maybe I was," he admitted. "But you're right. The job has to come first."

"Thank you."

Devon nodded, though understanding and liking it were two very different things. "I should let you get settled. Tomorrow's going to be busy—orientation, meeting with other key players, getting you set up with everything you'll need."

"I'm looking forward to it."

He moved toward the door, then paused with his hand on the handle. "Emery?"

"Yeah?"

"For what it's worth, I think you're going to be amazing at this. And whatever happened with Pemberton... it doesn't define you."

She was quiet for a moment. "Thank you. For believing in me."

"Everyone deserves a second chance."

"Do they? Because sometimes I wonder if I'm just running from one disaster to the next."

The vulnerability in her voice made him want to cross the room and pull her into his arms, professional boundaries be damned. Instead, he stayed where he was and offered her the only thing he could.

"You're not running," he said quietly. "You're starting over. There's a difference."

Emery's smile was small but real. "I hope you're right."

"I'm always right. Ask anyone in my family—they'll tell you how insufferably correct I am about everything."

That earned him a laugh, and the sound eased some of the tension that had been building between them.

"Goodnight, Devon."

"Goodnight, Emery. Welcome home."

He stepped out into the cool evening air and pulled the door closed behind him then stood for a moment listening to the sounds of her moving around inside. Professional boundaries. He could set professional boundaries.

He just wasn't sure he wanted to.

Two

The morning air carried the crisp bite of early autumn and the rich, earthy scent of ripening grapes. Emery pulled her cardigan tighter as she walked the stone path from the guesthouse to the main residence, her heels clicking softly against the flagstones.

The Boone family home—no, mansion—rose before her like something from a wine country magazine—a beautifully remodeled farmhouse that had been transformed into modern elegance. The original bones of the structure remained, but sleek lines and expansive windows had now been seamlessly integrated with traditional terra-cotta roof tiles that glowed amber in the morning sun. Ivy cascaded down white-washed walls in carefully cultivated patches, and floor-to-ceiling windows reflected the golden light like sheets of burnished copper, offering glimpses into rooms that felt both grand and welcoming.

The architectural marriage shouldn't have worked—farmhouse practicality meets modern sophistication—but somehow it created something unique. The wide front porch with its original stone foundation now supported elegant arches, and modern steel-framed doors replaced what had probably once been simple wood, creating an entrance that invited you in while making it clear this was no ordinary family home.

She'd barely slept, her mind cycling between excitement about her first official day and anxiety about proving herself worthy of the faith the Boones were placing in her. The guesthouse had been too quiet, too comfortable, too much like the life she'd always imagined having but had never quite achieved. And then there was the matter of Devon— the way he'd looked at her last night, the tension that had thrummed between them despite her carefully constructed boundaries.

Professional, she reminded herself. She was here to rebuild her career. Not complicate it with feelings she couldn't afford to have.

The front door opened before she could knock, revealing Ashley in workout gear with her dark hair pulled back in a high ponytail. "Morning, Emery. You're a little early."

"I wanted to make a good impression on my first day."

"Smart thinking. Though honestly, after the way Dad was singing your praises last night, I think you could show up in pajamas, and he'd still be thrilled." Ashley grabbed her keys from a table near the door. "I'm heading into town for a yoga class, but Mom and Riley are in the kitchen if you want coffee before your meeting. Most mornings, Elsa is here to cook breakfast. Since you're living on the property, you'll be invited when she does." Ashley leaned a little closer. "A small piece of advice. This family is overwhelming as hell. And you're gonna want to pass on that gathering. But for the first couple of weeks, don't. It will upset Elsa and offend my mother. However, after that, you can start cherry picking which mornings to bail."

Emery blinked. Her pulse raced. Growing up, the Boone children had strolled through the streets of Stone Bridge as if they were going places. Emery had been one of those kids who hadn't fit into any group. She hadn't been popular. She'd tried a couple of sports but wasn't any good. There were only three things that interested Emery. Art, history, and chemistry and it had made her a bit of an odd duck.

Leaving Stone Bridge had been an easy choice. College had been where Emery found her people—and herself. It was also where she'd fallen in love with wine, which was odd since she'd grown up in Napa. But living there, in some ways, had made her immune to what had been right in front of her.

An opportunity to do something distinctive. Something different. Something that combined a rich story with a dusty bottle, creating a unique piece of history that could be held onto for generations... or shared with those who appreciated and valued the tale.

Hasley appeared behind her sister, also dressed for departure with a purse slung over her shoulder. "Is my sister telling you all the tricks?"

"Just the breakfast one," Ashley said.

"Here's another one for you." Hasley adjusted her bag. "Our mother is a lovely woman. Kind, caring, and while I wouldn't say she meddles... she can be a little..." Hasley looked toward the ceiling and tapped her temple. "... Extra. She might ask a lot of questions. She might—"

"What my sister is trying to say is that because you're single and so is Devon, and she already believes something might have happened, she's gonna play matchmaker."

That was the last thing Emery needed.

"But it won't be as bad as it is with us girls. It's never as bad," Ashley said.

"No truer words." Hasley looped her arm around her sister. "And fair warning— our mom made her famous cinnamon rolls this morning. She only breaks those out for special occasions."

"Special occasions?" Emery asked.

"New family members, holidays, and whenever she's trying to butter someone up—or fix them up," Ashley explained with a roll of her eyes. "In your case, I think it's a combination of the first and last."

Emery groaned. *Professional boundaries*, she reminded herself. It's not like that was impossible. She and Devon had never been a couple. They only slept together a couple of times. Sexted on occasion. Flirted like crazy. But it all stopped now.

The sisters headed out, leaving Emery to follow the sound of voices toward the back of the house.

Family portraits lined the long corridor. She walked slowly, examining each one. There were images of Walter Boone as a young man, beginning the long process of turning his father's hobby into a thriving business.

More of the four Boone children and their various activities. Bryson and Devon playing football. The girls in the cheerleading outfits. Family portraits. Candid shots.

Even framed images of Riley's siblings and their children lined the walls.

The rich history that filled the space made Emery's chest tighten.

She continued toward the kitchen, which was enormous—all warm wood, granite countertops, and copper pots hanging from a wrought-iron rack. French doors stood open to a patio where herbs grew in terra cotta planters, and the morning sun streamed through windows that offered a perfect view of the vineyard beyond.

Riley sat at a massive island that could easily seat twelve, cradling a mug of coffee between her hands. She looked more relaxed than she had the night before, dressed in jeans and a soft sweater, her dark hair loose around her shoulders. Brea stood at the stove, transferring golden cinnamon rolls from a baking sheet to a platter.

"I thought I heard you come in." Brea turned with the warmth of a woman who'd been mothering people for decades. "I hope you slept well, sweetheart. The guesthouse can be a bit quiet if you're not used to country sounds."

"I slept wonderfully, thank you. And this kitchen is incredible—it's like something from a cooking show."

"Walter designed it for me as an anniversary gift twenty years ago. He said if I was going to regularly feed half of Stone Bridge, I needed proper facilities." Brea set the platter on the table and poured Emery a cup of coffee from a pot that looked like it could caffeinate a small army. "Now sit, eat something. You'll need fuel for whatever my boys have planned for you today."

Emery settled into the chair across from Riley,

accepting the coffee gratefully. "Where are Devon and Bryson?"

"Walking the vines," Riley said. "It's their morning ritual. They go out early to check on things, argue about irrigation schedules, and generally solve the world's problems before the rest of us are even awake."

"Don't let them fool you," Brea added, settling into a chair with her own mug. "Half the time they're out there gossiping like old ladies. Yesterday, I caught them having a heated debate about whether the new sommelier at Meadowbrook knows what he's talking about."

"And the verdict?" Emery asked.

"Bryson thinks he's pretentious. Devon thinks he's compensating for inexperience with big words." Riley's smile was genuine. "They're both probably right."

Brea glanced at her watch and stood. "I'm sorry, but I have to run. I had no idea how late it was, and I have an appointment with a fundraising committee in twenty minutes. Emery, help yourself to anything you need. Riley, don't let the boys intimidate her with too much on her first day." Brea bustled out, leaving Emery and Riley alone in the sun-drenched kitchen. The silence that followed was comfortable rather than awkward, filled with the domestic sounds of a settling house and distant birdsong.

"I wanted to chat with you about the interview I've set up with a local reporter," Riley said.

Emery's previous careers had forced her to learn to be comfortable in the spotlight. However, those situations never had anything to do with her personally. "Are you sure that's a good idea?"

"I do." Riley leaned back and held Emery's gaze. "We

know people enjoy gossiping, and they're going to do it whether we like it or not. Going on the offense is better than being on the defense, trust me on this. It gives us a chance to control the narrative from the get-go."

"I suppose that makes sense." Emery palmed her mug, staring into the dark liquid. During both her careers, she'd done many interviews. They'd never intimidated her before. But this one utterly terrified her.

"This must be strange for you." Riley shifted on her stool, leaned forward, and rested her clasped hands on the counter. "Coming back to Stone Bridge after everything."

"Being anywhere in wine country would be difficult." Emery took a bite of the cinnamon roll and nearly groaned with pleasure. "God, these are incredible. Your future mother-in-law is trying to fatten me up."

"I'm not engaged yet. I'm sure we'll be taking that trip sooner rather than later. But for now, I just want to enjoy what Bryson and I have. It's been a long road getting here." Riley's expression grew thoughtful. "I know what it's like, starting over in a place that holds so many memories. It can be overwhelming."

"It's not the childhood memories this place holds that's making my return difficult. When I left after high school and my parents moved away, I never had any intention of returning. I wanted to live in a big city. Something with crowds of people. Culture. Art. I grew tired of that real quick, and the job I took with Harold was supposed to be my ticket to something else. I loved it—even if my mentor turned out to be a dick."

A flash of her father sitting at the kitchen table, her

mother next to him, holding his hand, while he tried to explain what had happened.

The insurance fraud. The charges. The loss of his job.

The father she'd known—loved and idolized—had possibly committed a crime. One that could send him to a federal prison.

None of it made sense.

"I don't really know Harold—only what Bryson and his family have told me. And while Harold has always had a solid reputation, they had their reservations about the way he's handled a few things over the years."

"I wish I had seen it all sooner." Emery sighed. "But it doesn't matter. I'm the one who went down for it." Emery wanted to put the whole thing behind her—pretend it had never happened, which was why this interview settled in her chest like a bad cold. "Thank you for not jumping right to the conclusion that I did what I was accused of."

"Almost thirteen years ago, I made decisions based on half-truths. It cost me Bryson." Riley's fingers tightened around her mug. "I'm sorry about everything you went through with the scandal. I can't imagine how devastating that must have been."

"Thank you. And I'm sorry about your father and the pending trial with your mom."

A shadow crossed Riley's face. She glanced at her hands, fiddling with her thumb. "It's been hard. The whole family is still reeling."

Emery had watched from a distance and had heard whispers about the Callahan family drama—murder, fraud, and embezzlement that had landed Riley's mother right in the middle of it all. "How are your siblings handling it?"

"Better than expected, actually. Grant's struggling the most—he's always been the one who tried to hold the family together, so he's taking it personally—especially because he still feels responsible for my father's death. No one blames him, but he can't help it. He still tortures himself, and I don't think he'll be able to let it go until my mother is firmly behind bars."

"It's got to be awkward to run into her."

"That's putting it mildly," Riley said. "Fortunately, that doesn't happen often since she doesn't leave home that much. Not out of guilt, but because she doesn't like it when people whisper behind her back. She's tried to spin this, but no one in this town is giving her the time of day."

"Not that I'm comparing, but people pointed and stared before I left three months ago. I'm afraid that might not have changed."

"I'm here to fix perceptions, and what happened wasn't anywhere near as bad as what my mother did."

"I'm sorry. I didn't mean to imply that it was." Christ. What a rotten thing to say.

"It's all good. I totally understand," Riley said. "While the whole thing sucks, it did bring me and my siblings together. Erin and I are closer than we've been in years, and the kids are adjusting. It's strange how a crisis can unite people even as it tears other things apart."

"Are you glad to be back?"

Riley's smile was soft, private. But the glimmer in her eyes told the entire story. "I'm glad to be home. I didn't think I'd ever be able to say that, but here we are." She gestured toward the window where the vineyard stretched into the hills. "And I'm especially glad to have Bryson back.

In high school, everyone always said we were perfect for each other, and it turns out everyone was right."

"I remember you two together. You were the couple everyone else wanted to be."

"Until we weren't." Riley's laugh held old pain. "We were so young, so stubborn. We both made mistakes."

"Speaking of mistakes, I nearly choked on my coffee when I heard Bryson had married Monica Gilford."

Riley rolled her eyes so hard Emery was surprised she didn't strain something. "Monica. The rebound marriage that lasted exactly eighteen months and should've lasted about eighteen minutes."

"That bad?"

"She married him because she wanted to be a Boone, not because she wanted to be married to Bryson. And she spent most of their marriage trying to turn him into someone he wasn't." Riley pushed her mug aside. "Thank God they never had kids."

"I heard she's dating Winston Callaway now."

"She is, and they're welcome to each other. Winston's got enough ego to match hers, plus he's got money, which is really all Monica's ever cared about." Riley paused. "I have to admit, it's nice having her focused on someone else. She spent years trying to get her claws back into Bryson every time she was between relationships."

"And now she's Winston's problem."

"Exactly. Let him deal with her social climbing and her passive-aggressive comments about his wine choices."

The back door opened with a bang, followed by the sound of male laughter and good-natured arguing.

"—telling you, if we irrigate Block Seven any more,

we're going to drown the roots," Bryson's voice carried into the kitchen.

"And I'm telling you that Block Seven has different drainage than Block Six. We can't treat them the same way." Devon's reply was patient but firm, the tone of someone who'd had this argument before.

The brothers appeared in the kitchen doorway, both mud-splattered and windblown from their morning walk. Bryson headed straight for Riley, dropping a kiss on the top of her head before settling into the chair beside her. "Morning, beautiful. Did my mother feed our new employee yet?"

"She tried to feed her to death with cinnamon rolls," Riley said, leaning into his side. "I barely saved her from a sugar coma."

Devon caught Emery's gaze and smiled, and despite her best efforts, she felt that familiar flutter in her chest. "Ready for your first official day?"

"Ready as I'll ever be." She stood and carried her empty mug to the sink, hyperaware of his presence behind her. "Thank you for the breakfast, Riley. And for the company."

"Anytime. It's nice having another woman around who's not related to these two." Riley jerked her thumb between the two men.

Bryson mock gasped. "I'm wounded. Deeply wounded by your lack of loyalty."

"You'll survive," Riley said dryly. "Your ego's too big to be permanently damaged."

"My ego is perfectly sized, thank you very much." Bryson reached across the counter and picked off a piece of one of the tasty treats.

"If by perfectly sized you mean enormous, then yes." Riley cocked a brow.

Devon laughed. "She's got you there, brother."

"Et tu, Devon?" Bryson placed a hand over his heart in theatrical betrayal. "My own blood, turning against me."

"I'm not turning against you. I'm just acknowledging reality." Devon leaned against the counter.

Emery watched the easy banter between them, the way Riley fit seamlessly into their dynamic, the obvious affection that underscored even their teasing. This was what family looked like—not the careful politeness that had developed between her and her parents, even her sister, since her dad's professional nightmare changed the family dynamics.

"Speaking of reality," Devon said, glancing at his watch. "We should head to Dad's office. He's probably been awake since five, making notes about expansion plans—as if premium wines haven't been in the making for a few years now."

"Perhaps, but jumping into selling our vintage bottles is something entirely new," Bryson muttered. "And when Dad gets excited about a new project, he goes into full strategic planning mode."

"Is that bad?" Emery asked.

"Let's just say you might want to bring a notepad," Riley advised. "And maybe some caffeine. Walter Boone, with a business plan, is a force of nature. And for the last two months, all he can talk about is the idea of creating wines that can be considered vintage and collector items."

"Nothing like piling on the pressure," Emery mumbled.

"You think that's pressure?" Devon asked. "Bryson and

I are the ones who have to create wines worthy of not only our premium lines, but ones to set aside for these rare auction items." He motioned toward another hallway that led deeper into the house. "Come on, let's go see what empire-building scheme he's cooked up overnight."

As they left the kitchen, Emery caught Riley's encouraging smile and felt some of her nervousness ease. Whatever came next, at least she wasn't facing it alone.

"By the way," Bryson said as they walked down a hallway lined with more family photos and wine awards. "I owe you an apology."

Emery looked at him in surprise. "For what?"

"For being resistant to hiring you. It wasn't personal—I'm just protective of what we've built here. But Devon was right to push for you, and I'm sorry if my hesitation during the interview process made you feel unwelcome."

The admission was unexpected and clearly cost him something to make. Emery felt a rush of gratitude for his honesty.

"Thank you for saying that. And for the record, I understand the hesitation. If I were in your position, I'd probably have the same concerns."

"The difference is, your baby sisters wouldn't have been so harsh with their opinions regarding you and your reservations," Devon said with a grin.

"Ashley and Hasley ganging up on you is a fate I wouldn't wish on anyone," Bryson agreed. "They're ruthless when they think they're right."

"They're usually right," Devon pointed out.

"Which makes them even more dangerous—and annoying." Bryson chuckled.

They stopped outside a heavy wooden door marked with a brass nameplate reading: "Walter Boone, Proprietor." Devon knocked once before opening it, revealing an office that was both impressive and welcoming. Floor-to-ceiling bookshelves lined two walls, filled with volumes on viticulture, business, and what looked like several decades' worth of wine industry publications. A large desk dominated the space, but Walter rose from a comfortable seating area by the windows where he'd apparently been reviewing documents.

"There you are," he said, standing to greet them. "I hope you found everything you needed in the guesthouse, Emery."

"It's perfect, thank you. I can't tell you how much I appreciate your hospitality."

"Nonsense. You're family now." Walter's smile was warm and genuine. "Now, shall we talk about how we're going to take Stone Bridge Winery to the next level?"

Emery settled into one of the leather chairs arranged around a coffee table, notebook in hand and professional mask firmly in place. This was her chance to prove herself, to show that Devon's faith in her wasn't misplaced.

She just hoped she was ready for whatever Walter had in mind.

The morning sun had climbed higher by the time they left Walter's office, burning off the last wisps of fog that clung to the valley floor. Emery felt energized despite the information overload from their two-hour planning session.

Walter's vision for Stone Bridge's expansion into premium collectors' markets was ambitious and exciting—exactly the kind of challenge that made her pulse quicken with professional anticipation.

"So," Devon said as they descended the stone steps from the main house. "Honest assessment. How do you think that went?"

"Your father is either a visionary or completely insane."

"Those aren't mutually exclusive in the wine business."

Emery laughed, adjusting her blazer against the warming air. "I think it went well. The authentication and provenance documentation program he outlined could really set Stone Bridge apart in the premium market. Building those relationships with high-end collectors and auction houses..." She paused, remembering her own painful exit from that world. "Well, it's exactly the kind of work I used to love doing."

"Used to?"

"Before Harold made me toxic in those circles." The bitterness crept into her voice despite her best efforts to sound professional. "I worry that my name will make this harder for Stone Bridge Wines—especially with this interview Riley's set up."

Devon stopped walking and turned to face her. "You're not toxic. A bad thing happened, and unfortunately, it went viral on social media. But Riley's plan to introduce you as a member of our team is brilliant."

"Try telling that to the collectors who won't return my calls." She held up her hand when he opened his mouth in protest. "Before your family offered me this job, I tried to find work. I couldn't get a single interview."

"We have established relationships, and you're working for us. We'd like to believe that means something. And we'll find the right buyers." His conviction was so absolute it almost made her believe it. "That's part of why we hired you—not just for your experience or existing connections, but for your expertise and innovative ideas. This isn't going to happen overnight. It's going to take time to get this program off the ground."

That was if her scandal didn't destroy everything they wanted to achieve. She really needed to push those kinds of thoughts from her mind. They weren't constructive. She drew in a deep breath, forcing her attention to the vineyard around them.

They continued down a gravel path that wound between meticulously maintained flower beds toward the heart of the vineyard. The property stretched out before them in geometric precision—row upon row of vines creating perfect lines that seemed to stretch to the horizon. The leaves had begun their autumn transformation, shifting from deep green to gold and crimson, creating a patchwork of color that took Emery's breath away.

"This is incredible," she said, stopping to take in the view. "How many acres?"

"One hundred and twenty. However, we only have about seventy-five under vine right now. The rest is environmental balance, along with some olive trees. We've done well in the olive oil business, though it's a very small portion of our overall income." Devon pointed toward the hills that rose beyond the vineyard. "Those hillside blocks get the best sun exposure, so that's where we grow our cabernet, syrah, and pinot. The valley floor is better for our whites—chardonnay, sauvignon blanc, a little viognier."

They walked between the rows, and Emery marveled at the meticulous care evident in every detail. The vines were perfectly spaced, the soil tilled to optimal consistency, and the trellising system was so precisely aligned it looked like agricultural art.

"Your family really doesn't do anything halfway, do they?"

"Dad used to say that good enough isn't good enough when you're working with something that takes decades to perfect." Devon reached out to touch a cluster of grapes hanging heavy on the vine. "Every decision we make this year affects not just this harvest, but the next five, ten, twenty years of harvests."

"That's a lot of pressure."

"It's also a lot of privilege. How many people get to build something that outlasts them?" He plucked a grape from the cluster and held it out to her. "Try this."

Emery accepted the grape, their fingers brushing as she took it from his palm. The contact sent electricity shooting up her arm. From the way his eyes darkened, he'd felt it too.

"It's perfect," she said after tasting it, though she was no longer thinking entirely about the grape.

"Due to weather and other conditions, harvest is incredibly late this year." Devon's voice had gone slightly husky. "You'll love it—the energy, the urgency, everyone working together toward the same goal."

They were standing close now, close enough that she could see the gold flecks in his brown eyes, could smell his cologne mixed with the clean scent of sunshine and growing things. The attraction that had been simmering between them for months suddenly felt impossible to ignore.

His kiss was soft, tentative, giving her every opportunity to pull away. Instead, she found herself melting into him, her hands fisting in his shirt as he deepened the kiss. He tasted like coffee and possibilities, and for a moment, she forgot every reason this was a terrible idea.

Then reality crashed back in.

"We can't do this." She pushed against his chest, stepping backward until she hit the wire trellis behind her.

He ran a hand through his hair, looking as shaken as she felt. "That was completely inappropriate—at work."

"It was."

"This is harder than I thought it would be." The admission hung between them, raw and honest. "I know you want to keep things professional, and I'll respect that. I want you to feel safe and comfortable in your role here, and me doing stuff like that doesn't help. It's just that there's this thing between us."

"There is no us. There can't be." Emery's pulse spiked, and something else she refused to name was warring inside her. "What happened between us was because I was in a vulnerable situation. I was drunk and devastated, and you were being kind. That's not anything other than convenience."

"That might explain the night Harold fired you. But what about the time before that?"

"Not the point and you know it."

"I do, and I'm sorry. I shouldn't have said that. I'm zero for two right now."

She forced herself to hold his gaze, even though every instinct begged her to look away, because she wasn't sure she could hide how she was really feeling. Her face always gave her away. "I think you're a good man, and I appreciate everything you've done for me. I just can't risk what I'm trying to rebuild here."

Devon was quiet for a long moment, studying her face like he was trying to read something written there in a language he didn't quite understand. "All right," he said finally. "I can live with that. I want you to be successful here. I mean that."

"Thank you. That means a lot."

He turned, pressed his hand on the small of her back, and continued down the path. Her heart hammered, and her solidly constructed walls felt distinctly unstable. No matter how much she told herself and Devon that she wanted things to remain strictly professional, it was impossible not to notice that Devon was all man, and she wanted him outside of the workplace.

They walked in charged silence through several more vineyard blocks, Devon pointing out different varieties and growing techniques with the detachment she'd requested. But underneath the surface courtesy, the tension hummed between them like a live wire.

The production building rose ahead of them—a long, low structure that had clearly been designed to blend seamlessly with the landscape. Large windows offered glimpses of stainless-steel tanks and oak barrels within.

"This is the heart of the operation," Devon said as they approached the main entrance. "Crush, fermentation, aging, bottling—everything happens here during harvest season. Bryson and I share an office here. But, I do most of my work from my office in the main house, or from the tasting room, or the road. Both Bryson and I oversee everything, but he prefers winemaking, and I prefer the business aspects. Minus our teenage banter, as our mother calls it, we're a perfect partnership."

Inside, the building was a study in controlled chaos. Workers moved between towering fermentation tanks, checking readings and adjusting equipment with the focused intensity of people preparing for battle. The air smelled of grapes with undertones of yeast and the faint sweetness of alcohol.

"During harvest, this place runs twenty-four hours a day," Devon explained as they walked past a row of steel barrels. "We'll have crews working in shifts, tons of fruit coming in every hour, decisions being made about everything from fermentation temperature to blending ratios."

"And you manage all of this?"

"Like I said before, Bryson handles the winemaking decisions—he's got the palate and the instincts for that. I handle logistics, scheduling, and making sure we have the right people and equipment where we need them when we need them. My sisters handle the books, payroll, and marketing. Riley handles social media and helps manage both the tasting room in town and the on-site one, with her sister, Erin. And Dad, well, he's the heart. While he leaves most of the daily stuff to us kids, he does still own this place, and he can overrule if he wants."

They stopped outside a glass-walled office that overlooked the production floor. Through the windows, Emery could see a man in his early thirties sitting at a desk covered with charts and computer printouts. He had sandy brown hair and the kind of weathered hands that spoke of years working with both soil and machinery.

"That's Gabe Maxwell, our Operations Manager," Devon said.

"I've met Gabe a couple of times."

"He's a good man. Been with us eight years now. Basically keeps this whole place running." Devon knocked on the office door and opened it without waiting for a response. "Gabe, I believe you know Emery."

Gabe looked up from his papers and stood to greet them, his face lighting up with genuine warmth. "It's good to see you again, Ms. Tate. Devon's been singing your praises for weeks. Welcome to the Stone Bridge family."

"Please, call me Emery. And thank you—I'm excited to be here."

"Well, you've certainly picked an interesting time to join us. We're at the tail end of a late harvest, so things are intense right now." Gabe's handshake was firm and calloused, his smile reaching his eyes.

Devon glanced at his watch. "I have a phone call I need to make, so I'm going to leave you two to get acquainted. Gabe knows this operation better than anyone—he's the guy who makes sure we actually have wine to sell when all our grand plans are said and done."

"Devon's being modest," Gabe said with a chuckle. "He's the one who keeps us all organized. But I'm happy to talk Emery through the technical side of things."

"Thanks," Emery said. "Where should I find you when we're done?"

"If I'm not back before you're done, I'll be in mine and

Bryson's office down the hall—Gabe's got a lot to discuss with you, and he actually enjoys talking about fermentation schedules and barrel rotation."

"Guilty as charged," Gabe admitted as Devon left. "Coffee? I've got a decent machine in here, and you're going to need caffeine if I start talking about malolactic fermentation as it's implemented in organic wineries."

"Coffee would be great, thanks."

He poured two cups from a machine that looked like it had seen better days but produced surprisingly good coffee. "So, business development focused on premium collectors. Walter filled me in on the broad strokes. Authentication and provenance documentation, building relationships with high-end auction houses—it's ambitious work."

"It is. And honestly, a little intimidating after..." She gestured vaguely, not wanting to rehash her professional downfall.

"Yeah, sorry. I did have a front row seat to what happened." Gabe's expression darkened. "Harold can be quick to judgment."

"Do you know him well?"

"Our paths have crossed a few times at industry events, and he's not my biggest fan either, so we have something in common." Gabe settled back into his chair.

Emery swallowed. "Mind if I ask why?"

"Well, that's a dark and dangerous story that I'd rather not get into on your first day. But if you Google my last name, Maxwell and Callaway Wines, you'll get a few articles, and Harold likes to remind me of the history," Gabe said.

Something familiar tickled her brain—as if she should know this history.

"You're in good hands here. The Boones are solid people—they don't throw anyone under the bus, ever. Walter especially has this thing about second chances and loyalty. Once you're family, you're family." Gabe took a sip of his coffee. "Speaking of which, what are you thinking in terms of specific initiatives when it comes to the new premium wines line? Walter shot me a memo about a half hour ago. I was only able to skim it, but it looked impressive." He spoke so fast it made her head spin, and something told her that was the point—getting her off the subject of why Harold didn't like him.

Which made her even more curious.

They spent the next hour discussing her preliminary plans. Gabe listened intently, asking thoughtful questions and offering insights that showed both his deep knowledge of the operation and genuine enthusiasm for her ideas.

"He also highlighted the authentication process—the family has some incredible older vintages in their private cellar that would be perfect for that kind of program," he said, pulling out a thick binder. "Some bottles date back to when the grandfather first started making wine. Maybe thirty bottles total, but with proper authentication and marketing, they'd be incredibly valuable to serious collectors, but I'm sure Walter already told you about them."

"Actually, he said I should talk to you about what might be a good fit. So, yes and no," she said. "Could I see them sometime? I'd love to assess their condition, research their provenance."

Gabe placed his hand over his chest. "Walter has always

been so good to me. However, those wines are stored in the family's cellar. Devon can show you, but I do have a log of them." Gabe flipped through pages of meticulous inventory records. "Anything that was produced commercially is stored in this building. Fair warning—I'm a bit obsessive about record-keeping. Everything's documented, cross-referenced, temperature and humidity logged daily."

"That's not obsessive, that's perfect. Collectors pay premium prices for that kind of documentation."

"I do it because one slip up, and we've got an entire bad run." Gabe had a boyish grin. "You know, it's refreshing to work with someone who understands the premium market. Most of our focus has been on volume sales—restaurants, distributors, wine clubs. This collector-focused approach could really be a game changer for us."

"That's exactly what Walter wants. Build Stone Bridge's reputation as a source for investment-quality wines."

"Smart strategy. And honestly, long overdue. We've got the quality, we've got the terroir, we just haven't been positioning ourselves properly in those high-end markets." Gabe closed the binder and leaned forward. "I want to see this authentication program succeed. Whatever you need—access to records, introductions to staff, someone to bounce ideas off—I'm your guy."

"And my past, what happened with Harold, doesn't bother you?"

"Bother? No. Concern? I can admit to having some reservations. Not about your talent. Or your qualifications. Just about the optics."

"Yeah, those are a bit problematic now, aren't they?"

"Riley has a plan."

"She has me doing an interview with the local paper early next week. She believes we need to control the narrative."

"She's a smart one," Gabe said. "The Boones... they're good people. They gave me a chance when I was just some kid with a degree and big dreams, and they've supported me ever since." His expression grew thoughtful. "Walter especially."

There was something in his voice—deep respect mixed with genuine affection—that told Emery this wasn't just professional loyalty.

"It shows. How the place runs, how people talk about the family. It's not just a business, is it?"

"No, it really isn't. It's a legacy. Something built to last." Gabe glanced out his office window at the production floor, where workers were checking equipment with the focused intensity of people preparing for something important. "That's what harvest is really about—not just making wine but continuing something that started long before us and will hopefully continue long after we're gone."

"Your degree was as a vintner, right?"

Gabe nodded. "I work closely with Bryson, making sure we've got the right blend. I've learned a lot from him."

"Have you ever thought about looking for a head wine-maker position?"

Gabe shrugged. "Not really. I don't need the accolades. I like what I do here. I get to oversee all aspects of production. My hands are dirty from planting to bottling to distribution. It's a thrilling position. In my opinion, there's no better winery in all of Napa Valley."

"That's quite the compliment."

As if summoned by their conversation, Devon appeared in the office doorway. "Ready to head back? Dad wants to go over the quarterly reports before lunch."

"Actually, before heading out," Gabe said, his expression growing more serious. "I meant to ask this last night. Are we planning to send something to the Callaways as a group? I'd like to contribute if we are."

Devon looked surprised. "Mom's organizing a food delivery schedule. Dad wanted to send a nice arrangement. And we're going to take up a collection to donate to his favorite charity."

"I didn't know David well. Actually, tried to avoid him and his family. But he was always kind to me at industry events, and when Olivia miscarried, he and his wife sent a nice arrangement." Gabe paused, glancing between Devon and Emery. "If possible, I'd also like to attend calling hours," Gabe continued. "I know it might be awkward given... my last name, but David was a decent man. I'd like to pay my respects."

"I'm sorry. I don't mean to pry, but can I ask what your name has to do with you going to a funeral?" Emery asked, that gnawing sensation that she should know more ate at her.

Gabe shifted uncomfortably. "My grandfather worked for Jasper Callaway," Gabe explained. "Back when Jasper was running his... less legitimate operations alongside the winery. When everything came crashing down and Jasper went to prison, so did my grandfather, and my family lost everything. My parents moved away from Stone Bridge before I was even born."

"Oh, I hadn't made the connection," Emery said softly. "I've heard the story over the years."

"There are a few people who never put it together, but it's also something I don't advertise." Gabe's smile was rueful. "David always treated me with respect and never made me feel like I had to answer for my grandfather's choices. That meant something."

"Once we hear what the arrangements are, we'll find out who from the staff wants to attend and try to accommodate everyone. I think it would be appropriate for you to go, Gabe," Devon said. "And for the record, your grandfather's mistakes aren't yours to carry."

Gabe smiled. "That's very generous of you to say."

"It's not generous, it's the truth." Devon checked his watch. "But we really should head back before Dad sends out a search party."

Emery stood and extended her hand to Gabe. "Thank you for taking the time to walk me through everything. And for being so open about your background. It can't have been easy growing up with that kind of shadow."

"It wasn't," Gabe admitted, shaking her hand. "But just like you, the Boones gave me a second chance. Welcome to the family," he added with a genuine smile. "I think we're going to do some amazing work together."

As they left his office and headed back toward the main house, Emery found herself thinking about second chances and the weight of family history. She understood better than most what it felt like to carry someone else's mistakes, to have your own reputation tainted by association.

Gabe was right. This was a gift. And she was needed to make sure she deserved it.

Three

The reserve cellar was Devon's favorite place on the entire property—a cool, stone-walled sanctuary beneath the main house where their most precious bottles lay sleeping in perfect darkness. The air smelled of oak and time, with the faint sweetness of wine that had been aging gracefully for decades. LED strips provided just enough light to navigate between the custom-built racks without disturbing the sediment in bottles that were older than he was.

"So," Bryson said, pulling a dust-covered bottle from a rack. "How do you think our new Business Development Manager is fitting in?"

Devon looked up from his notebook, where he'd been cataloging potential auction pieces. "She's been here exactly one day, bro. Give the woman a chance to unpack her suitcase before you start grading her performance."

"I'm not grading her anything." Bryson held up the bottle to examine the label in the dim light. "I'm asking my brother how he thinks she's adjusting. There's a difference."

"God, I hate it when you add that, *there's a difference,* qualifier. She's fine. Professional. Enthusiastic about the authentication program and premium wine lines." Devon made another note in his book, trying to keep his voice neutral. He loved his little brother, and for most of their lives, they'd been the best of friends. But Bryson could often be… prickly. "Gabe seems to like her."

"Gabe likes everyone, and he's super nice, too. It's his fatal flaw." Bryson set the bottle carefully on the table.

"Partly because he's always worried someone's going to remember and remind him what his grandfather did. Murder is a big cloud to have over you," Devon said.

"I'm aware." Bryson rubbed the back of his neck. "Riley and Erin are handling their mother's pending trial much better than Grant. But he blames himself, as if he did the murdering, not his mother."

"Wouldn't you feel the same way in his shoes?"

"Maybe. I don't know. He might have handed his father that cup of coffee, but he had no idea his mom laced it with poison," Bryson said. "I'm tempted to ask Gabe to have a chat with Grant."

"Might not be a bad idea. And I think Gabe and Emery have already bonded over shared trauma."

"Your girlfriend—"

"She's *not* my girlfriend." Devon glared at his brother.

"And yet, here we are, going through our collection, looking at potential bottles we might be willing to part with… because Emery thought it would be a good place to start. Which I'm totally on board with, just not at nine o'clock at night when I could be at Riley's place, doing something else."

"It wasn't just her idea," Devon said, his voice sharpening. "Gabe's been suggesting we auction some of these off for the last couple of years. Dad was on board the moment she explained the authentication process."

Bryson raised his hands in mock surrender. "Hey, no need to get so defensive. I was just mocking the time, not the idea. Building provenance documentation for bottles with this kind of history could set us apart from every other winery our size trying to break into the collector market." He pulled another bottle from the rack. "But you can't stop looking at her. And don't try to tell me there isn't something there. Sometimes, I know you better than I know myself, and I saw the way you watched her when she worked for Pemberton, and now here, when you think no one's paying attention..."

Devon set his notebook down with more force than necessary. The sound echoed off the stone walls, followed by a silence that stretched between them like a held breath. This was his brother. His best friend. His future business partner. They might fight like cats and dogs over business decisions and other life choices, but they didn't keep secrets from each other. Not the important ones, anyway.

"Fine," he said, running a hand through his hair. "Yes, I'm attracted to her. More than attracted, if you want the truth. But we're keeping things strictly professional because that's what she wants and what she needs right now."

"What about you?"

"In this case, what I want doesn't matter."

"Wow." Bryson whistled. "Don't go throwing that pad of paper at me, but since when do you put a woman's need in front of your own?"

"Why do you have to be such a dick?"

"I'm sorry. I didn't mean it the way that came out." Bryson's expression softened. "All I meant was that you've never really had a lasting relationship. Sure, there was Gretchen, but we all knew she wasn't going to last."

"And why is that?"

"You didn't love her."

Devon chuckled. "At least I didn't marry her."

"This family does love to remind me of Monica," Bryson mumbled. "Dumbest thing I've ever done."

"No. That was letting Riley go in the first place." Devon waved his hand. "Now, all you have to do is convince her to marry you."

"I thought we'd live together first," Bryson said.

"That, I don't understand."

Bryson sighed. "She's the one who wanted to take things slow. Get through the trial. Date. Do all the things we missed out on. Living together would have been one of those things."

"Jesus, for being the smart brother, you're really fucking stupid." For theatrical purposes, Devon smacked his palm against his forehead. "Did you ever think that Riley might want the romance, the ring, the proposal, and the wedding? Not the shit in between?"

"She doesn't play games."

"I didn't say that's what she was doing," Devon said. "However, I'd bet if you popped the question, her answer would surprise you."

"This coming from a man who's never been in love. Has no interest in getting married or having kids." Bryson set another bottle aside and leaned against the wall. "And who's a master at changing the subject."

Devon smiled. "I'm rather good at the last one. But for the record, I might not have truly loved anyone, but I'm rethinking the family concept."

"Are you serious?" Bryson's eyes grew wide. "Because of Emery?"

"Not only because of her. I'd say some has to do with age and maturity. But if Mom heard me say that, she'd die of a fit of laughter."

"Yeah, she thinks we're still fourteen." Bryson chuckled. "And Riley says that sometimes when we're together, we act like grown men in diapers."

"She's not wrong."

"No jokes. No judgment. Just brothers." Bryson gave Devon that look that reminded him of their father. Furrowed brow. Tense lips. The look that said, *you can trust me, but wait five minutes, and I'll find ways to poke fun.* It was the Boone way. It drove Devon crazy. "You really care about Emery, don't you?"

"I haven't been able to get her out of my brain for months. I'd be lying if I didn't say I want more than a working relationship. More than friendship. It's not fair that her career got destroyed by some asshole's greed, and now she has to choose between rebuilding her reputation and..." He gestured helplessly at nothing. "This is why I don't usually talk to you about women."

"Because I make too much sense?"

"Because I'm always waiting for the punchline."

"No ball busting. Promise," Bryson said. "You were

there for me when Monica nearly destroyed me. I know what it's like to want something you can't have, to watch the person you care about struggle with impossible choices."

There was weight in his words that spoke to his own complicated history with Riley and the years they'd spent apart because timing had been wrong in so many ways.

"Give her time," Bryson continued. "Let her get a solid understanding of our business—how we work. Let her rebuild her reputation and prove to herself that she can succeed here. Then make your move."

Devon stared at his brother. "I'm not used to this side of you. Must be the Riley factor."

"Having her back in my life has changed me. It's also reminded me that timing matters. We're asking Emery to take huge professional risks, and she needs our help to rebuild her career. We need to let that breathe."

"So, what are you saying? Wait six months? A year? Until she doesn't need the job anymore and can tell us all to go to hell if she wants?"

"I'm saying wait until she's confident in her place here. Until she knows she's valued for her work, not just because she's sleeping with the boss." Bryson pulled another bottle from the rack, examining the vintage date. "Trust me on this—nothing kills a relationship faster than one person feeling like they can't succeed without the other person's protection."

Devon considered this, remembering the careful distance Emery had maintained during their tour, the way she'd pulled back when he'd kissed her in the vineyard. She'd been clear about her boundaries, about what she needed to feel safe in order to take this risk.

"When did you get so wise about relationships?" he asked.

"When I spent twelve years regretting every stupid thing I did wrong the first time around." Bryson set the bottle on the table next to the others. "Riley and I could have had something amazing if we'd been smarter about timing, about priorities—which is why I'm not rushing this proposal. It has to be perfect. Don't make the same mistakes I did."

"Wait a second." Devon stood and closed the gap. "Are you planning to ask Riley to marry you?"

"I might be." Bryson poked his brother in the chest. "But if you ruin this for me, I'll kick your ass."

Devon raised his hands and backed up with a smile on his face. "I just want to be there to watch you stumble over your non-existent romantic words."

"Ye of little faith." Bryson didn't look up, but he did smile.

That was telling.

They worked in silence for a while, pulling bottles and checking dates, building a list of potential auction pieces that would showcase Stone Bridge's history without depleting their most irreplaceable stock. The ritual was soothing—brother working alongside brother, continuing a tradition that stretched back generations.

"You know what the strangest part is?" Devon said eventually. "Three months ago, if someone had told me I'd be helping a woman with a scandal-plagued background launch her career comeback using our family's wine collection, I'd have thought they were insane."

"And now?"

"Now, I think it might be the smartest business decision we've ever made. And the most terrifying personal one."

Bryson clapped him on the shoulder. "The best decisions usually are both. Just remember—she's not going anywhere. The job is real, Dad believes in the program, and she's too stubborn to let Harold Pemberton's betrayal define her career forever."

"How can you be so sure?"

"Because I've seen the way she looks at wines, like she's seeing liquid history. And I've seen the way she talks about authentication, like it's not just a job but a calling." Bryson grinned. "Plus, she turned down staying in your garage apartment and insisted on professional boundaries. That's not the behavior of someone planning to cut and run."

Devon's shoulders dropped slightly as some of the tension he'd been carrying, eased. His brother had a point —Emery was here for the long haul, building something that mattered. The timing would work itself out eventually.

"So," Devon said, picking up his notebook again. "Think we've got enough bottles for a decent auction preview?"

"I think we've got enough to make every collector on the West Coast very interested in what else we might have hidden down here." Bryson surveyed their selection with satisfaction. "Your girlfriend—sorry, your future girlfriend —is going to have her work cut out for her documenting the provenance on all of these."

"She's going to love it," Devon said, and realized he was smiling despite himself. "She gets this look when she talks about research, like she's about to uncover buried treasure."

"There's that lovesick expression again."

"Shut up and help me carry these upstairs. We've got a reputation to rebuild and a romance to put on hold."

"Now you're thinking like a Boone," Bryson said, gathering bottles with the careful reverence they deserved. "Business first, feelings second, family always."

As they climbed the stone steps back to the main house, arms full of liquid history, Devon felt cautiously optimistic about the future. Emery would have her chance to prove herself, the authentication program would succeed, and eventually—when the timing was right—maybe they'd have their chance, too.

He just hoped he could wait that long without going completely insane.

The kitchen had taken on the warm glow of the moon, lit by pendant lights hanging over the massive island where they'd gathered after dinner. Emery nursed a glass of Stone Bridge's 2018 pinot noir, feeling more relaxed than she had since arriving.

"Devon told me you've been all over the globe," Emery said to Riley. "A real adventurer. Hiking, skiing, and white-water rafting. Being a tour guide and basically going wherever the wind took you."

"That's one way of putting it." Riley raised her glass. "I will admit, I had a lot of fun for a few years in the middle. Near the end, it got lonely. And the beginning? Well, let's just say I learned a lot of things the hard way and banged up my body."

"You survived." Brea smiled. "And you came home—to

Bryson—where you belong. Now you just need to move into this house." She waggled her perfectly manicured finger in the direction of Riley.

"You're worse than Bryson," Riley said.

"I wouldn't be surprised if he paid his mother to say that." Walter leaned away from Brea, but it didn't stop her from playfully smacking his biceps.

"Well, I never," Brea said with a smile.

Gabe chuckled.

"Learning to be a tour guide in all those activities had to have been hard," Emery said.

"Once I got the hang of it, not so much. But early on, I made some really dumb mistakes."

"TikTok worthy ones?" Emery asked, hoping everyone would appreciate her poking fun at herself.

"Oh, a few." Riley nodded, offering a soft smile. "I lied once about knowing all the ins and outs of tree jump ziplining. I called myself an expert. I figured it couldn't be that hard. However, I didn't know the language, which was a problem during the training. Not to mention, they were super short-handed, so I was paired with another guide on day two, who didn't speak a lick of English. We were like frick and frack out there."

Emery leaned forward, resting her elbows on the island, riveted by Riley's storytelling abilities. "What happened?"

"There I was," Riley said, gesturing with her wine glass. "Hanging upside down from a zipline in the Costa Rican rainforest, and the other guide starts yelling at me in Spanish. Apparently, I was supposed to use the brake to slow me down as I approached the next tree long before I even thought about it. You know, because I was too busy enjoying the view... upside down."

"Please tell me you didn't crash into a tree," Brea said, covering her eyes in mock horror.

"Worse. I crashed into one of our guests. A very large, irate German man who was not amused by my lack of ziplining skills." Riley grinned.

The sound of footsteps echoed as the door to the private cellar opened, and Bryson and Devon appeared carrying two small cases of wine.

"What are we discussing?" Devon asked.

"The fact that Riley's not the most athletic, but she managed to make a career out of it," Walter said in a teasing tone.

"She's pretty good at scaling walls." Bryson leaned against the counter and winked at his girlfriend. "Used to sneak into my bedroom at night when we were kids. I used to lecture her about how she could break her neck if she ever fell."

"Says the man who once tried to surf during a lightning storm," Riley shot back.

Walter chuckled from his position at the head of the island. "Your mother made me ground you for that stunt. Do you remember, Brea?"

"I remember wanting to ground him permanently," Brea replied dryly. "And I also remember a certain someone encouraging that behavior."

"I was building character," Walter protested.

"You were building gray hairs," Brea corrected, but her smile was fond.

Emery swallowed. She loved her parents. And her sister.

They were terrific people. Kind. Considerate. Loving, even. But the world flipped when her father had done... well, that insurance fraud had been a nightmare, and her family paid a huge price—two years later, and they were still paying for it.

Gabe laughed, swirling his wine. "I'm beginning to understand how this family built such a successful business. You're all completely insane."

"Sanity is overrated," Devon said, leaning against the sink. "Risk-taking is what separates the successful from the safe."

"Speaking of risk-taking," Bryson said. "Wait until you see what we found in the reserve cellar. I've been down there a million times, but I can't say I've ever studied some of those bottles."

"Let's take a look." Walter rose and pulled out the first one, giving a low whistle. "Early on, my dad and I would pluck a bottle here and there and stick them down in the reserve cellar. Our intention was always to drink them during celebrations. Sometimes we did." He waved the bottle. "This one was from our wedding, Brea."

"We can't auction that," Emery said.

"There are two more with that label down there, and I know there's more in the main cellar." Devon moved closer, leaning over the island. "All we need to do is make sure we have two of everything.'

"An heir and spare." Bryson chuckled.

"Don't let your sisters hear you say that." Brea arched a brow.

Each bottle they revealed made Emery's breath catch. Even in the kitchen lighting, she could see the age in the labels, the careful way sediment had settled in the glass, the patina of time that marked truly exceptional vintages.

"My God," she whispered, leaning forward to examine one particular bottle. "Is this from your grandfather's original plantings?"

"That one is," Walter said with evident pride. "Third harvest. Might have only made one hundred bottles."

Gabe tapped his knuckles on the counter. "I wish I had my binder. There are some old records in there that your grandfather kept."

"There were a few more down there with that label," Devon explained, pulling out his notebook. "We thought it might be a good starting point for the authentication program—pieces with real history and provenance we can document completely."

Emery lifted the bottle with reverent hands, studying the label's condition and the wine's color through the dark glass. "This is incredible. With proper documentation and marketing, bottles like this could establish Stone Bridge as a serious player in the collector market."

"That's the idea," Walter said. "I'll need you to be thorough with the research. Collectors at that level don't just buy wine—they buy stories, history, proof of authenticity."

"I can do thorough," Emery assured him, already mentally cataloging the research she'd need to conduct. "But I'll need access to your records—harvest notes, production details, storage conditions over the years."

"Everything's documented in my home office, and Gabe has records as well. I have meetings with distributors tomorrow, so you're welcome to use the space. Just don't reorganize my filing system—Brea tried that once, and I couldn't find anything for weeks."

"I heard that," Brea called out, refilling wine glasses. "And it was an improvement."

"It was alphabetical," Walter complained. "Wine records should be organized by vintage year, not grape variety."

"Here we go," Bryson muttered to Riley. "The Great Filing System Debate of 2019."

The easy banter was interrupted by a sharp knock at the back door. The sound cut through their laughter like a blade, and Emery noticed the family's relaxed postures shifted immediately to a more guarded stance.

"I'll get it," Devon said, but Walter was already moving toward the door.

"Winston," Walter said as he opened it, his voice carefully neutral. "Monica. This is unexpected."

Riley audibly groaned, and Bryson looped a protective arm around her shoulders.

Emery's pulse increased. When she'd taken the position at Terroir and Gavel Auction House two towns over from Stone Bridge, her encounters with David Callaway had always been professional, and she'd found him to be kind and considerate. His son and daughter, Winston and Callie, had been a little bit cooler, but they treated her with respect, even if they had reservations about someone who'd worked in a museum having her position in the wine industry. However, as time passed, both Winston and Callie became nothing short of insulting by refusing to work with her when looking for premium wines and collector bottles.

"Sorry to stop by so late—unannounced." Winston Callaway stepped into the kitchen with the kind of presence that demanded attention—tall, impeccably dressed despite the late hour, with the sort of polished confidence that came from old money and older grudges. Behind him, Monica looked like she'd stepped from the pages of a society magazine, her hair perfectly styled and her designer dress probably worth more than most people's monthly salary.

Emery glanced down at her twenty-dollar sweater and faded slacks and sighed. Her career at the museum had barely taken off when she'd decided to switch jobs. She'd taken two years out of her life to train for her position with Harold. It required education, certification, and an unpaid apprenticeship. The process had drained her financially.

"It's not a problem," Brea said. "We're all so sorry about your dad."

"I wanted to thank you personally for the food and flowers. The gesture meant a great deal to my mother during this difficult time," Winston said, his voice carrying the cadence of practiced sympathy.

"Of course," Brea said, her natural warmth evident despite the apparent tension. "I can't imagine what she's going through."

Winston's gaze swept the kitchen, taking in the bottles on the counter and the family gathered around the island. When his eyes landed on Emery, something flickered across his face—recognition quickly masked by politeness, but not quite fast enough. His jaw tensed almost imperceptibly before smoothing into an expression of concern.

"I see you have company," Winston said, his smile not quite reaching his eyes as he looked at Emery. "Ms. Tate, from Pemberton's Auction House." He paused, tilting his head as if searching his memory. "I heard...saw... well, I'm sorry about what happened. That must have been difficult."

The false sympathy in his voice made Emery want to duck under the counter and hide. There was something calculated in the way he watched her, as if he were studying her reaction rather than actually expressing concern.

"Thank you," she managed, forcing herself to meet his gaze.

"Are you back visiting?" Winston let the question hang, his tone casual but his attention laser-focused on her answer. Monica shifted beside him, her eyes darting between Winston and Emery with barely concealed interest.

"Emery's joined our team," Devon said, stepping slightly closer to her in a protective gesture that didn't go unnoticed.

"Has she?" Winston's expression remained pleasant, but Emery caught the brief tightening around his eyes, the way his hand curled into a fist at his side before he relaxed it. "How... fortunate. For both of you, I suppose." He glanced at the bottles on the counter. "Starting a new authentication program if the rumors are true?"

There was an edge to his words that made the statement feel less like congratulations and more like an assessment of a problem he'd need to solve.

"Our expansion plans are ambitious," Walter said carefully. "But we're confident in our team."

"I'm sure you are." Winston's smile remained fixed. "I have to say, it's quite bold to enter the premium market given the current... climate." His gaze flickered to Emery again. "Competition is fierce in that space."

"We're not concerned about competition," Bryson said, his voice carrying an edge.

"No, I suppose you wouldn't be. The Boones have always been... optimistic." Winston said, shifting his gaze to Walter. "I came by also to ask a favor. We were hoping Bryson and Devon might consider serving as pallbearers at my father's funeral. I know there was business rivalry between our families, but my mother specifically requested it. She said it would have meant something to Dad."

The request hung in the air, heavy with unspoken history. Emery watched the brothers exchange glances, seeing the internal debate play out in their expressions.

"Of course," Bryson said finally. "We'd be honored."

"Thank you." For a brief moment, Winston's smile seemed genuine, but his eyes remained cold when they slid back to Emery. "That means more than you know. The funeral is Saturday at two. St. Mary's."

Monica, who'd been silently surveying the kitchen like a predator assessing territory, finally spoke. "I have to say, I'm surprised to see Emery here," she said as if Emery wasn't even in the room. "Considering the scandal and all. I would think this family has been through enough without bringing that kind of reputation into the home."

The temperature in the room plummeted. Emery felt her face flush with mortification and anger, but before she could respond, Brea stepped forward with the kind of maternal fury that could level mountains.

"That's rich coming from you," Brea said, her voice deadly calm. "Considering your role in helping Elizabeth Callahan embezzle money from the town's charity fund. Glass houses and stones, dear."

Monica's perfect composure cracked. "That was never proven—"

"Because you made a deal with the prosecutor to testify against Elizabeth in exchange for immunity," Riley added quietly, her voice steady but her eyes blazing. "My family lost everything, and you walked away without consequences."

"That's enough," Winston said sharply. However, his attention remained fixed on the confrontation with an almost clinical interest, as if he were taking mental notes. He placed a restraining hand on Monica's arm. "I apologize for my companion's inappropriate comments." But then he turned to Walter, his expression shifting to something more complex. "I'm curious—did you actually hire Ms. Tate? In a professional capacity?"

Walter's jaw tightened. "Our staffing decisions aren't your business."

"No, of course not. I'm simply... surprised." Winston's gaze returned to Emery. "Given the circumstances, it's quite the risk you're taking. For everyone involved." The words carried implications that made Emery want to go hide in a museum. "I hope for the sake of your winery—and Ms. Tate—that it works out. The premium wine market can be... unforgiving of mistakes."

"We don't make mistakes," Devon said, his voice tight with controlled anger.

"Don't you?" Winston's smile was cold. "Well. I suppose we'll see." He turned toward the door. "We should go, Monica. Mother and Callie are waiting."

"Yes, we should." Monica smiled and waved politely.

Winston paused at the threshold, looking back at the

family gathered protectively around Emery. "Thank you again for agreeing to serve as pallbearers. I'll make sure all the details are forwarded to you."

After they left, the kitchen remained silent for a long moment. Gabe pulled out his cell, tapped at the screen, cleared his throat, and stood. "I need to head home, but before I do, there's something I need to tell everyone," he said quietly.

"Sounds serious." Walter reached for his wine and sipped.

"I don't know about that. But it *is* weird." Gabe pushed his chair in. "I was given notice about the reading of David's will. Turns out, I'm in it. Something about an item David had in his possession that belonged to my grandfather." He ran his fingers through his hair. "I have no idea what that could be. I called my folks and asked them. They said it could be any number of things, but they couldn't take a stab at a guess. But the bizarre thing for me is I never even met my granddad." He pulled out his phone and glanced at the screen. "Well, it's getting late, and tomorrow's going to be busy."

"Does it bother you that he didn't even acknowledge you, but he did everyone else in this room?" Walter asked. "Is that why you're leaving so abruptly?"

"I'm used to it. Winston only spoke to me when his father was around." Gabe inched toward the door and waved his cell. "Olivia texted, and she needs me to pick up a few things on the way home. Physically, she's fine. Emotionally, she's still struggling. I just really need to get home."

Brea raced to Gabe's side, resting a hand on his forearm. "I'll stop by and visit her tomorrow. I had a miscarriage between Devon and Bryson. The situations are vastly different. I already had a child who demanded my attention. If it hadn't been for Devon, I'm sure I would've fallen apart."

"Olivia always enjoys your company." Gabe kissed Brea's cheek. "She's getting better with each day, and she doesn't want to let this loss control her entire life. It's just having two miscarriages so close together..." He closed his eyes for a brief moment. "Well, she's worried we won't be able to have kids."

Emery flattened her hand against the counter. This wasn't her business. It wasn't her place to open her mouth and offer an opinion. But she was going to do it anyway. "Not many people know this about me, and it's not because it's some big secret. It's just because my parents and I believe a family is a family, no matter how it's made." Everyone stared at her, and her heart thumped in her chest like a wild rabbit. She swallowed. "My sister and I are both adopted. My mom couldn't have children. She'd known that since she was a teenager, so adoption was always the solution for them. They never lied to us about it. We just never felt the need to advertise it."

"I appreciate you sharing that." Gabe smiled. "I'd love for the two of you to meet sometime."

"I'd enjoy that," Emery said.

After Gabe left, the family stayed still and quiet for a long moment.

"He took that miscarriage as bad as Olivia did," Brea broke the silence. "He's holding it together. Being strong for his wife. But that's a man built for a family, and I can see how hurt he is." Brea rested her head against Walter's shoulder. "I saw that same hurt in your eyes once."

"Some of that pain isn't for the loss of the promise of life." Walter kissed the top of Brea's head. "It's about being powerless to help the person you love more than anything. It's the one loss that you really can't share in. Even though I was excited to have another child, it was only an idea. I couldn't see or feel it like you."

Emery wiped a tear that had rolled down her cheek.

"I don't know what was worse. Seeing Gabe so distraught, or Monica's rudeness," Walter said, his voice heavy with regret. "She has no class, and Winston... well, he can be somewhat entitled at times."

Emery managed a smile that felt more genuine than she'd expected. "Thank you. All of you. For defending me." She stood, suddenly exhausted by the emotional roller coaster of the evening. "But I think I need some air. It's been a long day."

"Emery," Brea started, but Emery was already moving toward the door.

"I'm fine, really. Just tired. Thank you for dinner, for the wine, for... everything."

She slipped out the back door before anyone could protest, breathing deeply of the cool night air. The guesthouse beckoned like a sanctuary, but she'd barely made it halfway down the path when she heard footsteps behind her.

"Hey, wait up."

She turned to find Devon jogging after her, his expression concerned in the dim lighting from the solar path markers.

"I wanted to thank you for what you shared with Gabe," he said. "He hasn't been himself lately."

"I can't imagine what he and his wife are going through," she said automatically, then sighed.

"They really want kids, so this hasn't been easy." He stopped about two feet away and stuffed his hands in his pockets. "But I also wanted to make sure you were okay. Both Winston and Monica were out of line."

"Maybe, but that's the kind of thing we're going to face because of my public shaming, and I'm starting to wonder if taking this job was a mistake."

"It wasn't."

"The scandal is too raw, too fresh. People are going to question your judgment in hiring me, and that could hurt the winery's reputation."

He stepped closer, and she could see the intensity in his dark eyes. "Monica Gilford is a bitter woman who destroyed lives for money, and Winston Callaway has never liked us. Their opinions don't matter."

"But other people's might."

"Then we'll prove them wrong. All of them." His conviction was absolute, unshakeable. "Emery, you're brilliant at what you do. One asshole's betrayal doesn't change that, and neither does the gossip of small-minded people who have nothing better to do than tear others down."

She wanted to believe him, wanted to let his certainty anchor her against the waves of her own doubts. "It's going to take time."

"Then we'll take time. However much you need." He paused, seeming to choose his words carefully. "But please don't let tonight make you doubt your place here. You belong at Stone Bridge."

The sincerity in his voice made her chest tight with emotions she couldn't afford to examine too closely. "I'll try to be patient."

"That's all anyone can ask."

They walked the rest of the way to the guesthouse, stopping at her front door under the soft glow of the porch light. For a moment, they stood looking at each other, the air between them charged with possibilities neither of them could act on.

"Thank you," she said finally. "For coming after me. For caring whether I'm okay."

"Always," he said simply, and the single word carried more weight than a longer declaration might have.

"Goodnight, Devon."

"Goodnight, Emery."

She watched him walk back toward the main house before letting herself inside, leaning against the closed door as she tried to process everything that had happened. Monica's venom, Winston's calculating stare, the family's fierce defense of her, Devon's unwavering support—it was too much to unpack in one evening.

But as she poured herself a glass of water and prepared for bed, one thought kept surfacing above all the others: for the first time in months, she wasn't facing her battles alone. Whatever came next, the Boones had made it clear she was part of their family now.

She just hoped she was strong enough to live up to their faith in her.

Four

The Stone Bridge Tasting Room occupied a converted Victorian on Main Street. Its wraparound porch was dotted with bistro tables where tourists lingered over flights of wine and cheese plates. Inside, the walls displayed awards and family photos dating back to the vineyard's founding. A gleaming mahogany bar dominated the space, lined with bottles that caught the afternoon sunlight streaming through tall windows.

Emery followed Riley through the side entrance, noting how the space managed to feel both elegant and welcoming—no small feat in a town built on pretension.

"This is our bread and butter," Riley explained, gesturing around the room. "Tourists, locals, weekend wine enthusiasts. We do flights, by-the-glass service, and bottle sales. During peak season, we're slammed from open to close."

A woman about Emery's age looked up from behind the bar. Her auburn hair was pulled back in a practical ponytail, and her smile was warm and genuine despite the weariness around her eyes. Erin Callahan had the same delicate features as her sister, but where Riley carried herself with the confidence of someone who'd survived and thrived, Erin bore the invisible marks of recent emotional battles.

"Emery." Erin came around the bar to greet her. "It's so good to see you again. Riley told me you'd joined the team."

"It's good to see you, too. You look well." And she did—tired, perhaps, but there was a strength in her bearing that hadn't been there during those awful days after her father's death when Emery had still been living in Stone Bridge.

"I'm getting there." Erin's smile held a hint of hard-won peace. "One day at a time, as they say. But this job has been a lifesaver. Literally. Working here gives me purpose, income, and the best co-workers." She squeezed Riley's hand.

"We make a good team," Riley agreed. "Erin does most of the heavy lifting. She's got the best palate in the family—can describe tasting notes like my father, and Bryson is just giddy over it."

"Riley's being modest. She's the one who turned our social media from sleepy to spectacular." Erin moved back behind the bar and pulled out three glasses. "But enough about work. Let's have a proper welcome toast."

She poured a chardonnay that gleamed golden in the afternoon light, passing glasses across the bar. "To new beginnings. For all of us."

They clinked glasses, and Emery felt some of the tension she'd been carrying ease. The wine was crisp and bright with notes of apple and a hint of vanilla oak.

"This is beautiful," Emery said.

"Our 2021 vintage. One of Bryson's best." Erin leaned against the bar. "So, Riley says you're interviewing with the local reporter next week?"

"Unfortunately." Emery set down her glass. "I'm terrified."

"Don't be." Riley pulled out her tablet. "I've been working on talking points and a full media strategy. The key is to control the narrative before it controls you."

They spent the next hour going over Riley's plan—how to address the Pemberton scandal directly without being defensive, how to highlight her qualifications and the authentication program's potential, how to position her return to Stone Bridge as intentional rather than desperate.

"The interviewer, Sarah Martinez, is fair but thorough," Riley explained. "She'll ask hard questions, but if you're honest and confident, she'll give you a fair shake."

"What if she brings up Harold's accusations specifically?"

"You acknowledge them, explain your side briefly, and pivot to the future." Riley tapped her screen. "Something like: 'What happened at Pemberton's was devastating, but it also taught me valuable lessons about due diligence and documentation. Those lessons are exactly what make me uniquely qualified to guide Stone Bridge Winery into the premium markets.'"

"Turning a negative into a positive," Erin said approvingly. "I like it."

The bell above the door chimed, and Grant Callahan walked in carrying a case of wine under each arm. He looked better than the last time Emery had seen him—the dark circles under his eyes had faded, and there was more color in his face—but the weight of recent events still showed in the set of his shoulders.

"Ladies," he greeted them, setting the cases on the bar. "Special order for the Hendersons. They're hosting some anniversary party tomorrow."

"Thanks for giving us a hand with this. I'll get them packaged up," Erin said, already moving toward the storage room.

Grant turned to Emery, extending his hand. "Good to see you again. Heard you'd joined the Boone operation."

"News travels fast."

"Small town." His smile was wry. "Though, I imagine David Callaway's will reading today has the whole valley buzzing."

Riley looked up sharply. "How did you hear about that?"

"Bryson texted me about an hour ago. Said Gabe told him some interesting things came up." Grant accepted the glass of wine Erin poured for him when she returned. "Something about a third heir?"

Riley set down her tablet. "Gabe said what now?"

"According to Bryson, David's will specifically states that he had another child before his marriage and that this person should be found within three months and given their share of the inheritance." Grant's expression was thoughtful. "Bryson said Gabe was shaken by the fact that David left him his grandfather's gun collection, which was extensive. I guess Gabe wants nothing to do with that. Even though the gun that was used to murder EJ Callaway, Jasper's brother, was found and should still be locked up somewhere in evidence, that whole collection is tainted for

Gabe. But what really rattled Gabe was the notion that his mom once dated David."

The room went still.

"Gabe couldn't possibly be a third heir, could he?" Riley asked carefully. "His parents moved before he was born."

"Interestingly enough, Gabe wasn't supposed to be in the room for that part—they asked him to leave after presenting him with his grandfather's guns—but he heard enough and yeah, his folks moved about a year before he was born, so no, the timing isn't right, but his folks did return a few times and the whole thing is just freaking him out. It's bringing up too much history for the man, which I understand." Grant took a sip of wine. "I ran into Mom early today, and all it took was a glance, and I'm down that rabbit hole."

"She could go back to jail if she has any contact with any of us." Erin set down her glass and tightened her ponytail.

"She didn't speak to me," Grant said. "She just paused, stared, and then scurried off into the salon. But not my point. Gabe carries the burden of what his granddad did. Something that I worry about for my kids. For Erin's kids." He reached across the table and grabbed Erin's hand. "It's a lot of weight to have on your shoulders."

"It is," Riley agreed. "But we're not going to let those kids, or each other, do any of this alone."

Emery lifted her wine and stared into the rich, buttery liquid. An insurance scam had ruined her father's reputation. He never denied the accusation. At least, not loudly.

All he'd said was that there were things yet to be revealed, and that in time, she'd understand.

But for the last two years, she'd dealt with the shame of what happened. She carried her father's guilt. So had her sister.

Only, now she had her own cross to bear, and when she'd been fired, her parents welcomed her home. No questions asked. No demands of apologies for the way she'd distanced herself from her dad. The way she still struggled with his quiet resolve that things would... work themselves out.

Both her parents emphatically believed her when she told them she hadn't done what she'd been accused of. It left her wondering about her father and his words and what they'd really meant.

Grant leaned back. "I kind of wish I'd been a fly on that office wall when Winston and Callie learned they have another sibling. I can't imagine those two being curious to know who this person is. I bet they only want to safeguard their inheritance."

"I imagine they want to protect it from people coming after them pretending to be a long-lost sibling," Erin said.

"That's easily proved these days with DNA testing," Riley said.

The door chimed again. Sandy Kane walked in with her husband, Mason, both dressed casually—her day off from being Stone Bridge's Chief of Police evident in her jeans and Stanford sweatshirt.

"Happy hour crew," Sandy called out cheerfully, then spotted Emery. "I heard you were back in town. How are you settling in?"

"Still getting my bearings," Emery admitted. Sandy had been two years behind her in high school, and they'd run in different circles—Sandy with the athletes, Emery with the academic crowd. They hadn't been friends, but Sandy had always been kind and full of sunshine.

"Well, if you need anything, you know where to find me. Hopefully not in an official capacity." Sandy laughed, sliding onto a barstool. "What are we drinking?"

Erin poured two glasses of their pinot noir for Sandy and Mason. "Grant was just telling us about David Callaway's will reading."

"Oh?" Sandy's professional interest flickered across her face. "I imagine that was emotional."

"Apparently, there was a provision about a third heir," Riley said.

Sandy's eyebrows rose. "The old rumors were true, then?"

"Seems like it." Grant leaned against the bar. "You remember when we were kids? Everyone used to whisper about it."

"I remember," Sandy said. "There was this period— what, when we were in middle school?—where it was all anyone talked about. Some kid supposedly had David's eyes or mannerisms or whatever."

"But then it died down," Erin added. "I always figured it was just gossip."

"Me too," Grant said. "But apparently, the will is pretty specific. This person exists and should inherit. So, there must be substance to it."

"Do Winston and Callie know who it is?" Erin asked.

"No idea. Bryson said Gabe only caught fragments of

the conversation before he left." Grant shrugged. "But knowing Winston, if there's a way to contest it, he'll find it."

The door chimed again, and Emery's blood ran cold.

Harold Pemberton walked in with a woman Emery recognized immediately—Vanessa Wright, mid-thirties, blonde, dressed in the same kind of professional attire Emery used to wear. Vanessa had been Harold's assistant for years, always hovering in the background during authentications. They were deep in conversation, Harold gesturing animatedly, until he looked up and spotted Emery at the bar.

His expression shifted from surprise to something harder, more calculating.

"Well," Harold said, his voice carrying across the room. "I heard through the grapevine that you'd landed on your feet. I have to say, I'm surprised the Boones would take such a risk."

Emery felt everyone's eyes on her. Sandy had straightened on her barstool, her cop instincts clearly engaged. Riley had gone very still beside her. Even Grant's expression, as he stared at the other man, had turned cold, which Emery appreciated.

Vanessa had the decency to look uncomfortable, her gaze dropping to the floor.

"Harold." Emery forced herself to sound calm despite her racing heart. "I didn't expect to see you here."

"Client meeting in the area. Thought we'd stop for a taste." He gestured to Vanessa. "You remember Vanessa, of course. She took over your position after your... departure. Turns out loyalty and attention to detail are valuable traits."

The implication was clear.

"Hello, Vanessa," Emery said quietly. "Congratulations on the promotion."

Vanessa finally looked up, her expression pained. "I—"

"As I explained to the assembled buyers at the auction," Harold continued smoothly, cutting off Vanessa. "I had to let you go for forging authentication documents—with evidence bearing your signature."

"Evidence that was planted," Emery said, the words escaping before she could stop them.

"Planted?" Harold's laugh was cold. "That's quite creative. Though, I suppose when you've destroyed your own career, you need someone to blame."

"You set me up. I don't know why, but it's the only explanation."

Harold's expression flickered—a flash of hardened outrage. "That's absurd. And defamatory." His voice carried an edge. "I run a legitimate business. Have for twenty years. My reputation is built on integrity and accuracy. The idea that I would fabricate evidence against an employee is not only insulting but also actionable."

"Get out," Riley said quietly.

Harold turned to her, eyebrows raised. "Excuse me?"

"You heard her," Grant said, standing. "This is a private business, and you're not welcome here."

"We're paying customers—"

"Not anymore." Erin moved to the door and held it open. "Please leave."

Sandy rose from her barstool, her casual demeanor evaporating into pure cop. "I think you should listen to them. Before this becomes an official matter."

Vanessa was already backing toward the door, clearly uncomfortable. "We should go."

But Emery's control had finally snapped. All the humiliation, the months of rebuilding, the constant doubt—it came flooding out in a rush of anger she couldn't contain.

"Someone paid you," she said, her voice shaking. "Your operation has been legitimized for decades. You had no reason to come after me unless someone made it worth your while. What happened that day—the public firing, the social media posts, the speed with which you turned the entire industry against me—that wasn't about protecting your business. That was personal. That was orchestrated."

"You're grasping at straws." Harold straightened to his full height, his voice cutting through the space between them. "Trying to create conspiracy theories to explain your own mistakes."

"What mistakes? I never forged those documents. My work was always thorough, always accurate. You know that. For two years, I authenticated hundreds of bottles without a single complaint." Emery stepped closer. "And then suddenly, within the span of a week, you 'discover' forged certificates with my signature? Documents I never created for wines I never authenticated?"

"You're delusional."

"Am I? Or am I too close to the truth?" Emery's voice rose. "Who paid you? Who wanted me destroyed badly enough to compromise your precious reputation?"

"Emery—" Riley touched her arm, a warning.

But Emery couldn't stop. "You humiliated me in front of an entire auction house. Posted it on social media. Made me unemployable. A man with your reputation didn't need to do all that just to fire an employee. You were making a statement. Making sure everyone in the industry knew I was finished."

Vanessa had gone pale, her eyes darting between Harold and Emery. "We should—"

"Enough," Harold said coldly. "You forged authentication documents. I have the evidence. End of story."

"Evidence that someone paid you to create."

"That's slander." Harold's face flushed with anger—or was it fear? "And if you continue making these baseless accusations, you'll find yourself facing legal consequences."

"Truth is a defense against slander," Sandy said from her position by the bar, her cop voice fully engaged now.

Harold's gaze snapped to her. "Are you threatening me, Chief?"

"I'm stating a legal fact. If what Emery says is true, it's not slander."

"It's not true. It's the desperate fantasy of someone who can't accept responsibility for her own actions." Harold turned toward the door. "I suppose desperation makes people believe all sorts of things." He glanced at Riley. "Your family would know something about that, wouldn't they? With your mother's trial coming up, and all."

Grant moved forward, but Sandy held up a hand. "It's best if you leave. Now."

"With pleasure. This establishment clearly has questionable judgment in its staffing choices." Harold pushed past Erin toward the exit but paused to look back at Emery. "A word of advice? Stop making wild accusations you can't prove. My lawyers will be very interested to hear about your conspiracy theories if you keep spreading them around the valley."

As they reached the door, Vanessa looked back at Emery, her expression tortured. "I'm sorry," she mouthed silently before Harold grabbed her arm and pulled her outside.

After they left, the silence in the tasting room was deafening. Emery realized her hands were shaking, her breath coming in short gasps. She'd completely lost control, said things she shouldn't have said, made accusations she couldn't prove.

"I'm sorry," she whispered. "I shouldn't have—"

"Don't apologize," Riley said firmly. "That man is guilty of something."

"But I just made everything worse." Emery sank onto a barstool, tears prickling her eyes. "That interview was supposed to be my chance to control the narrative, and I just gave him ammunition to make me look unstable and vindictive. Now he's threatening to sue me for slander."

Sandy came around the bar, her expression thoughtful. "Actually, that was very interesting."

"Interesting how?" Grant asked.

"The way he reacted. For someone who claims he did nothing wrong, he was awfully defensive. And threatening legal action that quickly?" Sandy pulled out her phone. "That's not the behavior of an innocent man. That's someone trying to shut you up before you dig any deeper."

"You believe me?" Emery looked up, hardly daring to hope.

"I believe something's not right. And I believe Harold Pemberton's reaction was completely disproportionate to your accusations—unless those accusations hit close to home." Sandy tapped a few times on her cell screen before tucking her phone in her back pocket. "And did you see Vanessa's face? That woman knows something. I'm off duty, but I have some friends in fraud investigation who might be interested in hearing about this. Can't promise anything, but if someone did pay Harold off, there'll be a paper trail somewhere."

"I'm texting Bryson and Devon. They should know what just happened," Grant said.

"Don't," Emery said quickly. "Please. I've already caused enough trouble."

"This isn't trouble," Erin said gently. "This is defending yourself."

Riley pulled Emery into a hug. "You're family now. And family protects each other. Even when—*especially* when—we lose our tempers with people who deserve it."

Emery felt something break loose in her chest—relief, gratitude, the overwhelming sensation of not being alone anymore. For three months, she'd carried the weight of Harold's betrayal by herself. Now, surrounded by people who believed her, who were willing to fight for her, she finally felt like she might survive this after all.

She just hoped her outburst wouldn't destroy every-thing the Boones were trying to build.

The Rusted Rail looked different at happy hour than it had three months ago when Devon had found Emery there, drowning her sorrows. Now, the space was packed with after-work locals, the noise level rising with each round of drinks, and the jukebox playing classic rock just loud enough to cover conversations people didn't want overheard.

Devon spotted Gabe in the back corner booth, nursing a bourbon. Bryson slid in across from him while Devon took the seat next to Gabe, leaving room for Mason, who'd texted he was running five minutes late—Mason was always running late. He was either running errands for Sandy or giving his kids one more hug and kiss.

"Thanks for coming," Gabe said, his voice rough around the edges. "I know it's last-minute."

"You sounded like you needed to talk," Bryson said. "What's going on?"

Gabe stared into his empty glass. "The will reading was... intense."

"Grant mentioned you were left...," Devon said carefully. "...your grandfather's gun collection?"

"Fifteen guns. All meticulously maintained, all with paperwork documenting their history." Gabe's laugh was bitter. "David kept them all these years. Said in the will that he didn't know if I'd want them given what my grandfather did, but he thought I should be the one to decide their fate."

The bartender appeared with three more bourbons, and Devon waited until she left before responding. "That's a hell of a thing to inherit."

"I don't want them," Gabe said flatly. "But I'm terrified of what happens if I get rid of them. What if a collector buys them and turns them into a macabre trophy? 'The guns that belonged to Jasper Callaway's enforcer.' What if they end up on the black market? What if selling them profits someone who romanticizes what my grandfather did?"

"You could destroy them," Bryson suggested.

"Could I?" Gabe looked up, his eyes red-rimmed. "These are historical artifacts, whether I like it or not. My grandfather murdered a man, but that doesn't erase the fact that these guns are part of this valley's history. Dark history, but history nonetheless."

Mason arrived, sliding into the booth. "What'd I miss?"

"Gabe's wrestling with some difficult choices," Devon said, then gave Mason a quick summary.

"That's rough, man." Mason had moved to Stone Bridge nearly ten years ago after meeting Sandy on a golf trip, and while he'd learned the town's history, he didn't carry the same weight of it that the locals did. "For what it's worth, I think there's honor in not profiting from it. Maybe donate them to a museum? Let them be educational rather than glorified? I bet Emery could help with that."

"Maybe." Gabe didn't sound convinced. He pulled out his wallet, fumbling with it before extracting a worn photograph. "But that's not the only thing that's been messing with my head."

He set the photo on the table. Devon leaned closer, studying the image. A young woman—had to be Gabe's mother based on the resemblance—stood wrapped in the arms of a man Devon recognized even in his twenties. David Callaway.

"I found this when I was helping my parents clean out their attic a few years ago," Gabe said quietly. "Stuck in a box of my mom's old things. I don't know why I took it.

Don't know why I've kept it hidden in my wallet all this time."

"I guess I knew your mom dated David," Bryson said before taking a sip of his bourbon.

"She never hid that fact. It was before she met my dad, obviously. But she never liked to talk about it, and I've never asked." Gabe traced the edge of the photo with his finger. "But look at them. The way he's holding her. The way she's leaning into him. That's not casual. That's…"

"Puppy love," Mason finished, waving his hand over the image. "It means nothing. You should see the photographs I have of my ex. You'd swear I was in love with the crazy woman."

"The one that's in prison?" Bryson asked.

"The same one." Mason leaned back as the waitress slipped another bourbon onto the table.

"It's just weird looking at it." Gabe's voice cracked slightly. "And I can't stop thinking—what if I'm the third child?"

The words hung in the air, heavy with implication. Devon exchanged glances with Bryson across the table.

"Have you asked your parents?" Devon asked.

"How do I ask them that? 'Hey, Mom and Dad, am I actually David Callaway's son?'" Gabe laughed, but there was no humor in it. "My parents have been married for thirty-five years. They're happy. They've built a good life. If my mom had a relationship with David before she married my dad, that's her business. But if I'm his son…"

"It would explain why David left you something in his will," Mason said.

"Or it could just be that David was a decent man who

wanted to return something that belonged to my family," Gabe countered. "A gesture of closure or respect or whatever."

"When was this picture taken?" Bryson asked, pulling it closer to examine.

"I don't know. There's no date on the back. My mom's not wearing any identifying jewelry, and there's no background to help place it. Her hairstyle and color have been the same since she was in her early twenties. I'm assuming it was before they moved away, which was before I was conceived, but years after the incident." Gabe took a long drink. "I've stared at this thing for hours trying to figure it out."

"You could get it dated," Devon suggested. "Photo experts can sometimes narrow down timelines based on the film type and processing methods."

"And then what? Confirm that it was taken right around the time I was conceived?" Gabe shook his head. "That doesn't prove anything. Just makes the questions louder."

Devon watched his friend struggle, seeing the weight of uncertainty pressing down on him. "Do you want it to be true?"

Gabe opened his mouth, closed it, then took another drink before answering. "I don't know. David was a good man. Better than my grandfather, certainly. But my dad—the man who raised me—he's the best father I could have asked for. Finding out he's not my biological father..." He paused. "That would break something. Even if he knew all along, even if my parents had some arrangement, it would change everything."

"Not necessarily," Mason said. "Biology doesn't define family. Sandy's got a half-brother she didn't meet until she was twenty. Didn't change how she felt about the siblings she grew up with."

"It's different when you're the one potentially discovering you're not who you thought you were." Gabe stared at the photo. "I've built my entire identity on being Gabriel Maxwell, son of Robert and Anne Maxwell. What happens if I'm actually Gabriel Callaway?"

"You're still you," Bryson said firmly. "DNA doesn't change who you've become, the choices you've made, the man you are."

"Doesn't it, though? What if being David's son explains things about me? The way I am with wine, my connection to the land, the fact that working with vines has always felt like coming home." Gabe's voice grew more agitated. "What if I've been living someone else's life this whole time?"

"Stop," Devon said, his voice cutting through Gabe's spiral. "You're catastrophizing. You don't even know if this is real."

"The will mentioned a third child. The timing works. My mom clearly had a relationship with David that meant something." Gabe gestured helplessly at the photo. "How can I ignore that?"

"You can't," Mason said. "But you also can't let it consume you before you have any facts."

"According to the will, Winston and Callie have three months to find whoever it is," Gabe said. "What if they come looking at me? What if they've already figured it out?"

Devon hadn't considered that angle. "Would they tell you if they had?"

"I don't know. Winston barely acknowledges my existence most of the time. Finding out I might be his half-brother?" Gabe laughed bitterly. "That would probably make him hate me even more."

"Or it might not be you at all," Bryson pointed out. "You're spiraling based on a photograph and circumstantial timing. Your parents could have a perfectly innocent explanation."

"Then why did my mom keep the photo? Why hide it away in a box in the attic?" Gabe's hands were shaking now. "People don't hold onto pictures like this unless they mean something."

Devon reached over and gripped Gabe's shoulder. "Listen to me. Whatever the truth is, it doesn't change the fact that you're our brother. Not by blood, maybe, but by choice. You've been part of the Stone Bridge family for eight years. That doesn't go away."

"Devon's right," Bryson added. "Whatever you find out, whatever happens with this inheritance situation, you're not alone in it."

Gabe's eyes were wet. "I don't even know if I want to know the truth. Some questions are better left unasked, right?"

"That depends," Mason said. "Can you live with not knowing? Because that photo in your wallet suggests you've been carrying this question for years already."

"I thought I could ignore it. Convince myself it didn't matter." Gabe carefully returned the photo to his wallet. "But then David died and left me those guns and mentioned a third child in his will, and suddenly I can't stop thinking about it."

"Have you talked to Olivia about any of this?" Devon asked.

"How can I? She's still devastated about the miscarriage. She's been trying to pull herself out of it and she's been doing better. The last thing she needs is me having an identity crisis on top of everything else." Gabe rubbed his face. "She thinks I'm upset about the guns. Which I am, but not for the reasons she believes."

"You need to tell her," Bryson said gently. "Keeping this from her isn't protecting her. It's isolating both of you. And maybe call your folks. They're good people."

"I know. I just..." Gabe's voice broke. "What if I'm not who she married? What if finding out I'm David Callaway's son changes everything?"

"It won't change the fact that she loves you," Devon said.

"You don't know that."

"I do. Because love isn't about DNA or family trees or any of that. It's about who you are, the life you've built together, the person you choose to be every day." Devon squeezed Gabe's shoulder again. "You're a good man. That doesn't change regardless of who your biological father is. You should talk to Emery. Being adopted has never defined her family."

They sat in silence for a moment, the noise of the bar washing over them. Finally, Gabe spoke again. "I keep thinking about what David wrote in the will. About wanting this third child to be found and given their inheritance. What if that's me? What if he knew all along and this was his way of trying to make it right?"

"Or what if it's not you," Mason said. "What if David

had another relationship entirely, another child you don't know about?"

"Then why leave me the guns? Why that specific gesture?" Gabe sighed.

"Because your grandfather worked for his father," Bryson said. "Because David was a decent man who probably felt guilty about what happened to your family when everything collapsed. The guns could be exactly what they seem—a gesture of closure, nothing more."

"But what if they're not?" Gabe looked around the table, his expression desperate. "What if I'm supposed to figure this out and I'm too scared to ask the questions that need asking?"

Devon didn't have an answer for that. None of them did.

"All I know," Devon said, "is that you don't have to figure it out alone. Whatever you decide—whether to investigate this or let it lie, whether to keep the guns or get rid of them, whether to ask your parents or not—we're here. The whole family. You understand that, right?"

Gabe nodded, though tears were streaming down his face now. "I'm sorry. I shouldn't be falling apart like this."

"You're human," Mason said. "And you've been hit with a lot all at once. Give yourself permission to feel."

"I don't even know what I'm feeling," Gabe admitted. "Scared? Curious? Angry? All of it at once?"

"That sounds about right for this situation," Bryson said.

They ordered another round, the conversation shifting to lighter topics as Gabe slowly pulled himself together. But Devon couldn't stop thinking about that photograph, about the way young David Callaway had held Gabe's mother, about the timing and the will and the guns.

If Gabe were David's son, it would explain so much. But it would also complicate everything—for Gabe, for Winston and Callie, for the entire valley.

And somewhere in the back of Devon's mind, a small voice wondered, if Gabe wasn't the third child, then who was?

Five

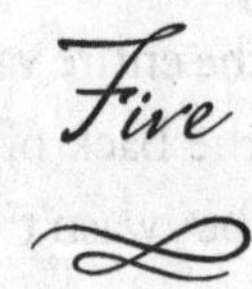

The morning fog was just beginning to lift from the vineyard when Devon and Bryson made their way back toward the main house, boots squishing in the wet grass. They'd spent the better part of an hour walking the blocks, checking sugar levels, and discussing harvest timing—the kind of routine that grounded Devon in the rhythm of the seasons and the predictability of the vines.

"So, how are the proposal plans coming?" Devon asked.

"What proposal?" Bryson kept his gaze focused on the ground, his one hand stuffed in his pocket, his other gripping his coffee mug.

"The marriage one, you idiot."

Bryson groaned. "I've watched a million proposals online to get ideas, and all they do is remind me that Riley's been everywhere. Done everything. And there's no way I'll be able to impress her. I'm just going to make an ass out of myself."

Devon looped an arm over his little brother's shoulder, who happened to have two inches on him. "Man, watching you grovel at her feet, begging her to move in with you, is making an ass out of yourself. I don't think you can make it worse."

"You're a jerk." Bryson flung Devon's arm off and gave him a good shove.

"Nothing new there." Devon chuckled. "Have you asked our sisters?"

"Good Lord, no." Bryson shook his head. "Ashley will suggest a romantic candlelit dinner with roses at some fancy restaurant. That's not my Riley. And Hasley, she'll offer some grand gesture that includes skydiving—because she once saw someone else do it. Like I'm gonna jump out of a perfectly good airplane."

"But Riley would."

Bryson snorted. "She already has."

"So, why don't you just go buy a ring and ask her under that tree where you carved your names?" Devon pointed toward the old oak visible from the path.

"I've thought of that." Bryson nodded. "You don't think it's too... boring?"

"You two have done everything but have sex under that damn tree. Your first kiss. You asked her to prom. Hell, I even think you broke up once under that thing. It's perfect."

"You might be right."

"I know I am," Devon said.

"Devon. Bryson." Walter's voice boomed from the porch, carrying an urgency that made both brothers stop dead in their tracks. "I need you in the den. Now." He turned, the door slamming shut behind him.

"What do you think that's all about?" Devon asked.

"No idea, but the last time he summoned anyone like that was when my ex-wife decided she thought it would be fun to rearrange the living room."

"Bro, she didn't rearrange it. She bought new furniture and was trying to donate Grandma's antique desk." Devon smacked his forehead. "What did you see in her?"

"I couldn't tell you. It was temporary insanity."

Devon kicked off his boots and washed his hands at the kitchen sink. His brother followed suit.

They found their father pacing behind the old desk their mom had put in the den near the leather sofa while Riley sat in one of the matching chairs, tablet in hand, and a scowl that could have curdled milk darkening her features.

"What's wrong?" Devon asked, but the knot forming in his stomach suggested he already knew it had something to do with Emery.

The last forty-eight hours had been relatively calm. But still, she'd been keeping her distance since Winston had shown up, and Devon figured she was planning her escape.

Riley turned the tablet toward them without a word. The headline hit Devon like a physical blow: *"Scandal-Plagued Wine Expert Finds Refuge at Stone Bridge Winery —But at What Cost?"*

"Jesus," Bryson breathed, leaning over Devon's shoulder to read.

The article was thorough in the way that only malicious journalism could be. It recapped Emery's career, the Pemberton authentication scandal, and her subsequent blacklisting from major auction houses. But it didn't stop there. Devon's jaw clenched as he read about Emery's father —a former insurance investigator who'd been forced to quietly resign after accusations of accepting bribes to overlook fraudulent claims. The charges had never been proven, but the implication was clear: questionable ethics ran in the family.

"This is character assassination," Devon said, his voice tight with anger.

"Keep reading," Riley said grimly.

The worst part came in the middle section. Two photographs, grainy but unmistakably clear, showed Devon helping an obviously intoxicated Emery from Rusted Rail to her Airbnb. The second photo, time-stamped the following morning, showed him leaving the same building, his clothes wrinkled and his hair disheveled.

"The relationship between Ms. Tate and Devon Boone appears to predate her employment at Stone Bridge Winery by several months," the article speculated. *"Sources close to the situation suggest the job offer may have been motivated by personal rather than professional considerations, raising questions about nepotism and the vineyard's commitment to maintaining industry standards."*

But the final section was even worse. Someone had captured footage of yesterday's confrontation at the tasting room—shaky cell phone video that clearly showed Emery yelling at Harold, making accusations she couldn't prove, losing control in front of witnesses.

"Ms. Tate's behavior at the Stone Bridge Tasting Room yesterday afternoon raises additional concerns," the article continued. *"Witnesses report an 'unhinged' confrontation with her former employer, Harold Pemberton, in which she made wild accusations of conspiracy and sabotage. Video footage obtained shows Ms. Tate becoming increasingly*

agitated and irrational, despite staff's attempts to calm the situation. One witness, who asked not to be named, stated: 'She seemed unstable. If I were the Boones, I'd be concerned about who they've brought into their business.'"

"Motherfucker," Devon growled, tossing the tablet onto his father's desk.

"Language," his dad said automatically, but his heart wasn't in the reprimand. His expression was grave as he fixed Devon with a stare perfected over decades of fatherhood.

"No offense, but Devon took the word right out of my mouth," Bryson said. "Who the hell was filming that?"

"Could have been anyone in the tasting room," Riley said. "It's a public space. All it takes is one person with a phone."

"And the photos from three months ago?" Devon asked. "Those weren't random. Someone saved them, waited for exactly the right moment to use them."

Walter was quiet for a moment, his expression thoughtful. "I don't know anything about her father, but we did a background check."

"On her. Not her family," Bryson added.

"I've already called Harlan, my lawyer, and asked him to have his PI, Declan, look into the matter." His father held up his hand when Devon opened his mouth. "Whether her father is guilty or not makes no difference. My opinion of her won't change. Nor would it change her employment status."

"Then why do it?" Devon asked, though he knew the answer. He just wanted to hear it.

"Knowledge is power. And the more we know, the more

we can get ahead of this," his father said. "For us—and for her. But I also want Declan to look into who filmed the incident at our tasting room and who took those pictures. That feels like a personal attack."

"There's more," Riley said quietly. "The article also mentions my hiring three months ago. Says it's part of a 'pattern' of questionable nepotism practices."

"That's bullshit," Bryson said immediately. "You were hired for your qualifications."

"We both know that's not true since I didn't even have any social media accounts or training. But the issue here is in the optics..." Riley gestured at the tablet. "Two women with connections to the Boone brothers hired within months of each other? The article makes it look like Stone Bridge is some kind of dating service."

Walter turned to Devon, his voice measured but firm. "I need to ask you something directly, and I need a straight answer. Were you sleeping with Emery before we hired her? And are you sleeping with her now?"

"Dad—" Bryson started, but Walter held up a hand again.

"This isn't about judgment. I need to know what we're dealing with."

Devon felt heat creep up his neck, but he held his father's gaze steadily. "We've been... together."

The silence in the room was deafening.

"How long?" Walter asked.

"We're not together. We saw each other once before she was fired. That night, and again more recently." Devon's voice was firm despite the embarrassment. "But when she accepted the job offer about a month ago, we both agreed to keep things strictly professional. Since she started working here, we haven't been together. Not once."

"But the relationship did exist before her employment," Walter said.

"It did," Devon admitted. "But I didn't ask you to create a position for her because we were sleeping together. I recognized her talent at that auction three months ago. The personal stuff... that complicated things, but it didn't create the job opportunity. The job was real regardless of what was or wasn't happening between us."

Bryson stepped forward. "And for the record, Devon's been pretty miserable keeping his distance. If this was just about convenience or nepotism, he wouldn't be trying so hard to maintain boundaries."

"I'm not questioning your brother's character," Walter said, but his tone suggested he wasn't entirely pleased with the situation. "But this doesn't look good, Devon. Not for you, not for the winery, and especially not for Emery. Between the photos, her father's background, and this video of her losing control at the tasting room, the article paints a picture of someone unstable and opportunistic who's using a personal relationship to rebuild her career."

"She's not," Devon said firmly.

"I believe you. But the rest of the wine industry isn't going to know that." Walter sank into his desk chair. "What concerns me most is the timing and coordination of all this. First, someone plants that story about her hiring right after she starts. Now this—photos from months ago, video from yesterday, details about her father's background. This isn't random gossip. Someone is systematically attacking her."

Devon felt his stomach drop. His father was right. This was too organized, too deliberate.

"But why?" Riley asked. "What does anyone gain from destroying Emery's reputation?"

No one had an answer.

"Regardless of who's behind it," Walter said, "we need to address it. And I think we need professional help." He looked at Riley. "That's why I asked Declan to examine all the angles, and he's going to need to speak with Emery."

"You really think someone's orchestrating all of this?" Bryson asked.

"I think the timing is too convenient to be a coincidence," Walter said. "Emery's been in Stone Bridge for three days. In that time, we've had a damaging article, a public confrontation that was conveniently recorded, and details about her personal life that someone had to dig for. That's not bad luck. That's targeted."

Devon's mind raced. His father was right—this was an attack. But who would go to such lengths? And why?

"What do we do about the article?" he asked.

Riley leaned forward. "We stick with the interview plan, but we address everything head-on. The photos, her father, and the confrontation with Harold. We don't hide from any of it."

"That's risky," Devon said. "The tasting room video makes her look like she's spinning out of control."

"It also makes Harold look defensive," Riley countered. "Sandy was there. She saw the whole thing. Grant and Erin, too. If we can get them on record saying Harold's reaction was suspicious, that he threatened legal action to shut Emery up—that changes the narrative from 'unstable woman making wild accusations' to 'whistleblower being silenced by a powerful man with something to hide.'"

"That's clever," Bryson admitted.

"The photos are still a problem," Walter said. "The timing. The article makes it look like Devon hired someone he was sleeping with."

"Then we own it," Riley said. "We acknowledge Devon helped her that night because she was in distress. We explain that the conversation led to recognizing her qualifications. We turn it from nepotism into networking—which is how most people find jobs anyway. And we're honest about the fact that they saw each other casually for a few months but ended things when the professional relationship began."

"And her father?" Devon asked.

"Again, it's a reality we need to acknowledge, but we need some facts. Ultimately, Emery isn't responsible for her father's mistakes—just like we've always said Gabe isn't responsible for his grandfather's." Riley's expression was determined. "The key is controlling the narrative before it controls us."

Walter was quiet for a long moment, staring out the window at the vineyard beyond. "It could work. But it all depends on Emery. She has to be willing to open up about all of it—her father, that night with Devon, their relationship, the confrontation with Harold. If she's not comfortable doing that, we need to respect her decision."

"Agreed," Devon said. "I need to talk to her first. This is her story to tell or not tell."

"Where is she now?" Bryson asked.

"In my office, working on authentication research,"

Walter replied. "She's been there since seven this morning, completely absorbed in the provenance documentation."

"Someone should warn her before she sees this online," Riley said gently.

Devon was already moving toward the door. "I'll talk to her. Figure out how she wants to handle this."

"Devon," Walter called after him. "Whatever she decides, we support her. United front. No wavering."

"Always."

"And son?" Walter's voice stopped him at the threshold. "I'm going to have Declan start digging today. Whoever's doing this—we're going to find out who and why. Nobody attacks our family without consequences."

Devon nodded, grateful for his father's protective instincts even as dread settled in his stomach. The article didn't just attack Emery's reputation—it systematically dismantled every defense she might have. Someone had orchestrated this perfectly. Every piece of ammunition carefully collected and deployed at precisely the right moment.

But who? And why target Emery specifically?

He pushed aside the questions as he made his way down the hallway. Right now, all that mattered was making sure Emery knew she wasn't facing this alone.

He knocked softly before opening his father's office door.

Emery sat at the desk, surrounded by open ledgers and vintage photographs, completely absorbed in her work. She looked up as he entered, her smile fading as she registered his expression.

"What's wrong?" she asked immediately.

Devon closed the door behind him and leaned against

it, trying to figure out how to deliver news that would break her heart.

"We need to talk," he said quietly. "There's been an article. About you. About what happened at the tasting room."

The color drained from her face. "How bad?"

"Bad," he admitted. "But Emery—we're going to get through this. Together. I promise you that."

He just hoped it was a promise he could keep.

The production facility felt different on Friday afternoon—quieter, more contemplative, as if the building itself was holding its breath before the weekend. Emery sat across from Gabe in his glass-walled office, surrounded by ledgers documenting decades of Stone Bridge's history. She'd been cross-referencing storage conditions with vintage years, building the kind of provenance documentation that serious collectors demanded.

"You've got good instincts for this," Gabe observed, watching her make notes in the margins of a harvest report from 1998. "Most people would just record the data. You're telling the story."

Emery looked up, surprised by the compliment. "That's what provenance is, really. Not just facts and figures, but the narrative of how something came to be. Why it matters."

"Is that what drew you to this work originally? The storytelling?"

The question was casual, but something in Gabe's tone suggested genuine curiosity. Emery set down her pen, considering how much to reveal.

"My parents used to take my sister and me to museums every weekend when we were kids," she said finally. "Not the big flashy exhibits—the archives. The storage rooms where they kept things not currently on display." She smiled at the memories filling her brain. How she'd hold her sister's hand and skip through the massive hallway, listening to the heels of her patent leather shoes echo against the walls, while her father would smile that massive grin and remind them that history and art were bound together like the stars and the moon. "My mom would point to some dusty artifact, and then my dad would ask us to imagine its story. Who made it? Who owned it? How did it survive?"

"Your parents sound wonderful."

"They are." The words came out fierce, protective, as if the last two years hadn't put a rift in their relationship. "They chose us. My sister and me. When they looked at the two of us, they said it was love at first sight. They built our family from intention, not accident. But adoption isn't always easy, and there were some bumps in the road."

Gabe went very still, his coffee mug halfway to his mouth. "That's... Quite the story."

"It was. My mom talks about it sometimes—the bureaucracy, the home visits, the constant evaluations. But she says choosing us was the easiest decision she ever made. Everything else was just paperwork." Emery felt her throat tighten. "She always told us that biology doesn't make a family. Showing up every day does. Loving someone even when it's hard does."

"Your mom sounds like a wise woman."

"She is. Which makes the article about my father so much worse." Emery hadn't meant to say it, but the words tumbled out anyway. "Because if he did what they say he did—if he really accepted bribes, which he denies, but things are so oddly quiet about it all—then what does that say about the man who taught me about integrity?"

Gabe's expression shifted, something complicated passing across his features. His hand trembled slightly as he set down his mug, and for a moment, he looked like he wanted to say something—something important—but he sighed instead. "You don't know that he did anything wrong," Gabe said. "Especially since he's telling you he didn't."

"He denies it, but he's also telling me not to go defending him or making waves. To let the wheels of justice work, whatever the heck that means." Emery's chest tightened, as it did every time she allowed herself to think about her dad and the situation. "And that's the worst part. Not knowing. Not being able to ask more questions because he won't talk about it until it's all cleared up."

Gabe was quiet for a long moment, his gaze distant. "Sometimes, parents keep secrets to protect us. Even when the protection hurts more than the truth would."

There was weight in those words, layers of meaning Emery couldn't quite decipher. She watched Gabe struggle with something internal, saw his jaw clench and release.

"Gabe? Are you okay?"

"Yeah." He shook his head as if clearing cobwebs. "Sorry. Your story just... it resonated."

"Because of your grandfather?"

"Partly." Gabe stood abruptly and moved to the window overlooking the production floor. "My father spent his entire life trying to be the opposite of his dad. Honest, ethical, almost painfully rule-following. But he never talked about what it was like—watching his own father get arrested, seeing his mother ostracized. He kept all that pain locked away, trying to protect me from it."

"Did it work?"

"No. Because secrets don't protect—they just fester." Gabe turned back to face her. "When I was ten, some kid at school called my grandfather a murderer. I had no idea what he was talking about. Had to learn my family's history from gossip and old newspaper articles."

"God, Gabe. I'm so sorry."

"The point is, I understand what it's like to love someone and simultaneously wonder if you ever really knew them." His voice was gentle but firm. "But whatever your father did or didn't do—that's his burden, not yours. Just like my grandfather's crimes aren't mine to carry."

Emery felt something crack open in her chest. "How do you stand it? Coming back here, where everyone knows?"

"Because the people who matter see past the history to who I actually am." Gabe returned to his chair, his expression earnest. "And because I decided that I get to write my own story, not live in the shadow of someone else's mistakes, even though some days that's harder than the ground during a drought."

She leaned back, resting her hands in her lap. "Devon told me there was a third heir named in the Callaway will."

Gabe coughed, pounding the center of his chest. "That's a strange segue."

She chuckled. "Yeah. Maybe a little. But I was just thinking about how no matter what happens with my dad, it doesn't change who I am. Or the fact that I know he loves me with all his heart. Sometimes, I think knowing I was adopted my entire life made me feel more loved because my parents went out of their way to find me. They specifically chose me over lots of other cute babies."

"That's a beautiful way of looking at forming a family." Gabe leaned forward. "I might ask you to tell Olivia that when she's ready. I'm not sure she could handle another miscarriage."

"I'm happy to share my story with your wife," Emery said. "But as a woman, I can also understand wanting to carry your own child. So, take it from me, if she wants to try again, that might be something you need to support her in."

"I want kids just as much as she does. I just can't stand to see her in so much pain."

"She needs to get through it, and you seem to be doing all the right things." She reached out and took his hand.

He squeezed and then pulled away. "I have to ask, why did you bring up the third heir?"

"I had a friend who didn't learn she was adopted until middle school. It messed with her identity," Emery said. "I didn't know David well, but it seems cruel to not only toss that out there in a will but put a time frame on how long his family has to find the child. Which brings up the question, would Winston and Callie even do that?"

Gabe's eyebrows rose. "That's an interesting observation, and I suppose it's possible they wouldn't, but their mom, she's a different person altogether. I suspect she'd honor David's wishes."

Emery picked up her pencil and tapped it against the desk. Her mind splintered off into a million different directions, but one had her heart racing. She wasn't sure if she should bring it up. However, as much as she wanted to bury her head in the sand over what had been happening to her, she was grateful she knew what people were saying behind her back. "I probably should leave this alone, but I feel like someone would say something."

"About what?"

"David left you something in his will, and this town loves a good piece of gossip." Emery felt herself flushing. "I'm sorry, this is none of my business."

"It's okay." Gabe's smile was rueful. "I did hear a couple of people in the coffee shop speculating about what David might have left me and then moved right into the who-third-heir thing. This town was built on gossip."

"I'm sorry."

"If I had heard it yesterday, I probably would've taken a personal day today. But I had a long conversation with Devon, Bryson, and Mason last night. Whatever David's reasons for leaving me my grandfather's guns, it doesn't change my life. I have a career I love, a wife I adore. I don't need or want any piece of the Callaway legacy—not that its mine to claim, because that's absurd."

"But what if you did have a claim to it?"

"Honestly, I'd probably want it less." Gabe's conviction was absolute. "Winston and Callie are David's children. That's their inheritance, their legacy to build or squander. I have no interest in complicating that. Just like you felt loved and cherished your entire childhood, so did I."

The finality in his voice settled something in Emery's mind. Whatever secrets the Callaway family held, Gabe wanted no part of them.

"Speaking of the guns," Emery said, shifting to safer ground. "Have you decided what to do with them?"

Gabe's expression darkened. "That's been keeping me up at night. I don't want them, but I'm terrified they'll end up in the wrong hands, and I don't want anyone, myself included, profiting off what my granddad did."

"What about donating them to a museum? The local historical society?"

"Devon mentioned that I should talk to you about that," Gabe said.

"They're historical artifacts—uncomfortable ones, but history, nonetheless. If you donate them with full context, not glorifying what happened but documenting it honestly, they become educational rather than collectibles." Emery leaned forward. "I could help you with that. I still have museum contacts who understand how to present difficult history responsibly."

"I'd appreciate that. I don't know anything about history, and I've never set foot inside a museum. Olivia says, outside of wine, I'm the most uncultured person she knows."

Emery laughed softly. "I doubt that."

"No, really, it's true. I look at a fine piece of art, and I think Willa could do better." Gabe smiled. "Olivia would love to have those guns out of the house. Not only is she not a fan of firearms, but she also doesn't like what my grandfather's legacy does to me sometimes."

"It doesn't have to be all bad. I understand your grandfather was a criminal. He did terrible things. But that doesn't mean those guns should disappear, nor should they be romanticized." She met his gaze steadily. "Documenting that history honestly—making it a cautionary tale rather than a trophy—that seems like the most responsible option."

Gabe stared at her for a long moment, something like relief washing over his features. "I'd appreciate that more than you know. The idea of those guns ending up at auction turned into some morbid collector's item..." He shuddered. "That's been my nightmare."

"Then let's make sure it doesn't happen. I'll make a call for you."

"Thank you. Truly."

For the next ten minutes, they both returned to their work, but Gabe was still fidgeting. "Can I ask you something? About the articles?"

Emery felt her stomach tighten. "What about them?"

"Your not planning on using them as a reason to leave, are you?"

The directness of the question caught her off guard. "What makes you think that?"

"Because I've been exactly where you are right now. Convinced that everyone sees you as your worst mistake, that no amount of good work will ever be enough to overcome the whispers." Gabe rested both hands on his desk. "And I'm back in that thick of things with the reading of

David's will, only I won't let it make me pack my bags and buy a plane ticket this time."

"You left?"

"Nope. Never got out of the driveway."

"What stopped you?"

"Walter asked me one question. 'Are you leaving because you want to, or because you're scared?'" Gabe smiled a big, toothy grin that reached his ears. "I couldn't answer him honestly, which told me everything I needed to know."

Tears burned at the corner of Emery's eyes. "I *am* scared. Terrified, actually. That no matter what I do here, I'll always be the woman from the scandal."

"Maybe you will be, for some people, because for Winston and Callie, I'll always be the grandson of the man who murdered their great uncle. But for the people who matter—the Boones, the staff here, the collectors who actually care about provenance and expertise—you'll be Emery Tate, brilliant authenticator and historian." Gabe's voice was firm. "The question is whether you're going to let other people's limited vision determine your future."

"You make it sound simple."

"It's not simple. It's actually incredibly hard." Gabe stood, gathering the scattered ledgers. "But I'll tell you what Walter told me. The people worth keeping in your life are the ones who see past the scandal to the person underneath. And the Boones are exactly those kinds of people."

Before Emery could respond, footsteps echoed in the hallway, and Devon appeared in the doorway, his dark hair windblown and his work shirt rolled up at the sleeves. He looked between them, clearly sensing the emotional weight of the conversation.

"Sorry to interrupt," he said. "But it's past five. Thought we could head back to the house together?"

Gabe glanced at his watch and whistled. "I need to get going. I'm serious about the museum thing—let's set up a time next week."

"Absolutely."

After Gabe left, Devon and Emery walked the gravel path back toward the main house. The evening had that particular quality of late autumn light—golden and melancholy, beautiful in its impermanence. The vineyard stretched out on either side of them, rows of vines heavy with the season's last fruit, leaves beginning their slow transformation into harvest colors.

"That looked intense in there," Devon said finally. "You okay?"

"More than okay, actually. Gabe..." Emery searched for the right words. "He understands what it's like to build an identity in the shadow of someone else's mistakes."

"The Maxwell family history."

"Yes. But also, just the weight of not knowing who you are sometimes." Emery stopped walking, turning to face the vineyard. The setting sun painted everything in shades of amber and gold, transforming the ordinary into something transcendent. "He asked me about being adopted. About what makes a family. It brought up a lot."

"About your dad?"

"It's hard not to be able to reconcile the man who raised me with someone who might have been unethical."

Devon moved closer, his presence warm and solid beside her. "Have you considered just asking him directly?"

"He won't discuss it. Says he can't while things are still being investigated." She turned to face him. "How do you live with not knowing? With uncertainty about the people you love most?"

"I don't think you ever stop wondering. But maybe that's not the point." Devon held her gaze, intently. It wasn't judgmental. Wasn't even scrutinizing. He just looked at her like he cared. "Maybe the point is deciding who you're going to be regardless of what they did or didn't do."

Emery j in her chest—a loosening of the knot of anxiety that had been her constant companion. "Gabe said something similar."

"He's a smart man."

"He's also convinced I'm planning to run."

Devon's expression grew serious. "Are you?"

The question hung between them, weighted with implications that went far beyond professional concerns.

"I don't know," Emery admitted. "Part of me wants to disappear, start over where no one knows about any of this. I hear Central New York's wine country can be beautiful in its own way, nestled in all those Finger Lakes. But another part of me is tired of running. Tired of letting other people's cruelty determine where I go."

"I don't want you to leave." Devon's voice was quiet but intense. "Not just because you're brilliant at your job. But because I think you're exactly where you're supposed to be."

They had reached the edge of the vineyard, still hidden from view of the main house by towering oak trees. The privacy felt intimate, charged with all the things they'd been carefully not saying.

He stepped closer, his hand coming up to cup her face with a gentleness that made her breath catch. "I know all the reasons this is complicated. But I'm done pretending I don't care." He kissed her then—soft, careful, giving her every opportunity to pull away. Instead, she melted into him, her hands fisting in his shirt as he deepened the kiss. This wasn't the desperate passion of three months ago, or the rush of tangled limbs that couldn't wait for release. This was something more profound, more intentional, more terrifying in its implications.

"Uncle Devon and the new lady are kissing."

They sprang apart as a small figure burst through the trees—a little girl with auburn hair and bright, delighted eyes.

"Willa!" Devon called after her as she raced toward the house, her voice carrying clearly.

"Uncle Devon and the new lady are kissing."

Emery felt her face burn. "Oh God."

"It's fine," Devon said, though he looked frustrated. "That's Erin's youngest. She's eight and tells everyone everything."

"So, by dinner—"

"Everyone will know." Devon's expression was remorseful but not apologetic. "I'm sorry about the timing, but I'm not sorry I kissed you."

Emery stared at him, mind racing through implications. But underneath the panic, something else stirred. Relief, maybe. Or hope.

"We should go," she said finally. "Your mother's making pot roast, and apparently we have explaining to do."

Devon's laugh was warm. "Welcome to the Boone family. Privacy is a rare commodity."

As they walked toward the house, Emery couldn't decide if she was mortified or relieved. Either way, there was no going back now.

But for the first time since that article was published, she thought maybe she was ready to stay and find out what came next.

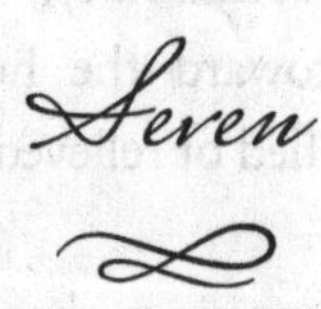

Seven

St. Mary's Catholic Church sat at the heart of Stone Bridge like a granite sentinel, its bell tower visible from nearly every corner of town. Devon had attended countless services here over the years—christenings, weddings, his grandfather's funeral—but today felt different. Heavier. The parking lot overflowed with vehicles—a testament to David Callaway's standing in the community—and the afternoon sun beat down with an intensity that made his black suit feel like a form of punishment.

"Christ, it's hot," Bryson muttered, tugging at his collar as they crossed the asphalt. "You'd think October would have the decency to cool down."

"Weather doesn't care about our comfort." Devon scanned the crowd gathering on the church steps. Half the valley had turned out—vintners, restaurant owners, shop proprietors. Even competitors who'd publicly sparred with David over the years had shown up to pay respects.

That was the thing about small towns. Death temporarily suspended rivalries.

"There's Winston," Bryson said, nodding toward the front where Winston Callaway stood greeting arrivals with the practiced grace of someone who'd been groomed for public appearances since childhood. Tall, impeccably dressed despite the heat, he wore grief like a well-tailored garment—present but controlled.

Beside him, Callie looked like she'd stepped from the pages of a fashion magazine. Her black dress probably cost more than most people's monthly mortgage, and her designer sunglasses hid whatever emotions she might be feeling. Monica clung to Winston's other side, her freshly colored blonde hair gleaming in the sunlight. Her expression was appropriately solemn.

"The grieving family and their pet viper," Bryson said.

Devon elbowed him. "Be respectful. Whatever else they are, they just lost their father."

"I know. Doesn't mean I have to like Monica."

They joined the receiving line, moving slowly toward the family. Devon caught sight of Gabe and Olivia near the church entrance. Gabe wore a dark suit that looked uncomfortable on his normally casual frame. Olivia stood beside him in a simple black dress, her hand resting protectively on her stomach despite the recent miscarriage. She was petite, barely reaching Gabe's shoulder, with dark hair pulled back in a bun that emphasized the delicate bone structure of her face. Even from a distance, Devon could see the grief etched in her features—not for David, but for the loss she'd recently endured.

"Boone brothers," Winston said, as they reached him, extending his hand first to Bryson, then to Devon. His grip was firm, professional, utterly devoid of warmth. "Thank you for serving as pallbearers. It means a lot to all of us, but specifically our mother."

"Our honor," Devon said, meaning it. Whatever complicated business existed between their families, David had been a decent man, and their mother a sweet woman.

"How's your mom holding up?" Bryson asked.

"As well as can be expected. The suddenness of it has been difficult." Winston's polished veneer cracked slightly. "One minute, we're discussing harvest projections, the next..."

He trailed off, and for a moment Devon glimpsed genuine pain beneath the careful composure.

"If there's anything we can do," Devon offered.

"Actually, there is." Winston's expression shifted, hardened almost imperceptibly. "I'd appreciate it if we could have a word after the service. About business matters."

Before Devon could respond, Callie stepped forward. Up close, her perfume was overwhelming—expensive and cloying, like flowers left too long in a closed room.

"Devon." Her smile didn't reach her eyes. "I heard you've been busy lately. Hiring new staff. Making... interesting choices."

The emphasis on "interesting" carried the kind of weight that implied something Devon didn't appreciate and demanded a response, even if it meant another elbow to the ribs by his little brother.

"We hired an exceptional authenticator," Devon said carefully. "Someone with credentials that speak for themselves."

"Do they?" Callie's sunglasses prevented him from reading her expression fully, but her voice dripped with false sweetness. "Because from what I've read, her credentials include public humiliation and questionable ethics. But I suppose that's Stone Bridge's problem now, not ours."

Bryson tensed beside him, but Devon kept his expression neutral. "Emery's brilliant at her job. The scandal at Terroir and Gavel was Harold's doing, not hers."

"If you say so." Callie dared to shrug. "But I have to wonder about the wisdom of mixing business with pleasure. Doesn't that usually end badly?"

"Callie," Winston said sharply. "This isn't the time."

She shrugged, already turning to greet the next mourners. Monica leaned closer to Winston, whispering something that made his jaw tighten.

"That was pleasant," Bryson muttered as they moved toward the church entrance.

"I want to believe she's hurting, and that's the only reason she tossed that in my face." Devon's stomach churned. "But she was too smug about it."

Bryson paused at the door. "The question is why she cares enough to bring it up at her father's funeral."

If this had been three months ago, Devon would've known the answer—jealousy. But this didn't feel like a woman scorned.

Inside, the church's air conditioning provided blessed relief. Stained glass windows cast colored light across polished pews, creating patterns that shifted as clouds moved overhead. The smell of lilies and incense hung heavy, mixing with the subtle scent of old wood and candle wax.

"Devon. Bryson." Riley appeared from a side pew, looking elegant in a simple black dress. Beside her, Erin offered a subdued wave. Both women had their hair pulled back, their faces reflecting the particular gravity of a funeral for someone who'd been a fixture in their lives despite complicated family dynamics.

"How's it looking out there?" Riley asked quietly.

"Tense," Devon said. "Callie decided to take a shot at Emery."

Riley's eyes twitched, like they always did when anyone said something that offended her. "At her father's funeral? Seriously?"

"Winston shut her down, but the damage was done." Devon scanned the filling church. "I take it you couldn't talk Emery into coming?"

"Nope," Riley whispered. "Said it didn't feel appropriate given everything happening."

"Smart woman," Erin added. "This crowd would've eaten her alive."

Disappointment settled in Devon's chest. He understood Emery's reasoning, but part of him had hoped she'd show up anyway. Prove she wasn't going to hide.

"There's Mom, Dad, Ashley, and Hasley," Bryson said, nodding toward the front where Walter and Brea Boone had eased into a pew on the left side. Brea wore an elegant black suit, her graying hair swept up in a French twist, while Walter looked distinguished in his dark suit, his expression grave.

The girls made their way forward, taking a seat in the pew behind their parents while Devon and Bryson hung at the back of the church.

Mason appeared moments later with the quiet competence of someone who'd learned to navigate small-town social dynamics despite being an outsider. "Sandy's working," he explained in a low voice. "Someone had to be on duty during the funeral. Half the valley is here."

The organ began playing, and the congregation rose. Devon and Bryson joined the other pallbearers—Winston's golf buddy, two cousins Devon vaguely recognized, and Mason. The casket was surprisingly heavy, the weight of it a physical reminder of mortality's finality.

They settled it at the front of the church, and Father Michael began the service.

Devon's mind wandered during the readings and prayers. He found himself cataloging who'd shown up—which competitors, which business associates, which town dignitaries. David Callaway had been well-respected, if not universally loved, in spite of his father's criminal activity. The turnout reflected that complicated legacy.

It wasn't until communion that things got interesting.

Devon watched Gabe and Olivia move toward the altar, Olivia's hand firmly clasped in Gabe's. She moved carefully, as if afraid her body might betray her again. When they returned to their pew, Winston's gaze followed them with an intensity that seemed out of place.

"Did you see that?" Bryson whispered.

"Winston staring at Gabe? Yeah."

"Winston doesn't generally even acknowledge Gabe with a sideways glance. It's almost like he's invisible."

"That will changed everything." Unease prickled at the back of Devon's neck.

The service concluded, and the congregation filed out for the burial. The cemetery lay adjacent to the church, shaded by oak trees that had stood for generations. Grave-stones marked the valley's history—pioneers who'd first planted vines, families who'd built the wine industry, children who'd never had the chance to grow old.

They lowered David Callaway into the ground that had held Callaways for a hundred and fifty years.

After the final prayers, the gathering fractured into small groups. Some headed to their cars, others lingered to offer condolences. Devon noticed Monica break away from Winston, her expression predatory as she approached their family cluster.

"Well, well," she said, her voice carrying just enough to draw attention. "The Boone family, out in force. How touching."

"Monica." Brea's voice was ice. "This isn't the time."

"Isn't it? I was just wondering where Devon's girlfriend is. Too ashamed to show her face after that article?" Monica's smile had that same venomous twist it had the day she showed up on Bryson's arm as if she'd won the damn freaking lottery. "Or is she off having another public meltdown? I heard she made quite the scene at your tasting room."

Devon felt Bryson tense beside him, but it was his dad who stepped forward.

"This is David's funeral, not an opportunity for you to indulge your vindictive nature," his father said softly, but in a firm and fierce tone.

Monica's smile faltered. "I was just making conversation."

"You were being deliberately cruel. There's a difference." His dad's expression could have carved stone. "Now, if you'll excuse us." He turned his back on her, a dismissal more cutting than words. Monica's face flushed red before she stalked off toward Winston.

"That woman is poison," Brea said.

"Always has been," Riley agreed.

"Besides wishing I had never married her, I wish it hadn't cost us a few million to force her to give up the Boone name." Bryson rubbed the back of his neck.

"Worth every penny," Brea said.

Movement caught Devon's eye. Across the cemetery, Winston had cornered Gabe near a cluster of oak trees. The distance prevented Devon from hearing their conversation, but the body language was clear—Winston leaning in, aggressive, while Gabe stood his ground, his expression stony.

"What the hell?" Bryson glanced between the exchanged and Devon.

"Winston never talks to Gabe," Mason observed. "Like, ever. What changed?"

Devon watched the conversation escalate. Winston's face reddened, his gestures becoming more animated. Gabe remained calm, but Devon could see tension in every line of his body. Olivia hovered nearby, her expression anxious.

"Should we intervene?" Bryson asked.

"Not yet." Devon kept watching. "But be ready."

Whatever Winston said next made Gabe's fists curl. For a moment, Devon thought his friend might actually throw a punch at a funeral. Instead, Gabe leaned in close, said something sharp and short, and walked away. Olivia followed, casting a worried glance back at Winston.

Winston stood alone among the gravestones, his expression unreadable from this distance.

"That was intense," Mason said.

"Something's happening." Devon felt certainty settle in his gut. "Something more than grief."

"You think it's about the will?" Bryson asked.

Before anyone could answer, Callie appeared at Winston's side. They engaged in a heated conversation, Callie gesturing emphatically while Winston's expression grew darker.

"This family is imploding," Riley observed quietly. "And we're getting a front-row seat."

Sandy Kane appeared from the direction of the parking lot, still in her police uniform. She scanned the crowd with professional efficiency before spotting their group.

"Everything alright?" she asked, joining them. "I saw some tension from the road."

"Just the Callaways being the Callaways," Mason said, dropping a kiss on his wife's cheek.

"Actually," Devon said, "did you see that conversation between Winston and Gabe?"

"Hard to miss. Winston looked ready to start a fight." Sandy's cop instincts were clearly engaged. "You know what that was about?"

"No idea. But given Winston's never given Gabe the time of day before..." Devon trailed off.

"It's worth noting," Sandy finished. "I'll keep an eye on things."

The crowd began dispersing in earnest now, families heading to their cars, conversations wrapping up. Devon saw Gabe and Olivia hurrying toward their vehicle, Gabe's arm protectively around his wife's shoulders.

"We should talk to him," Bryson said.

"Not here. Not now." Devon watched Winston and Callie still locked in a heated discussion. "But soon. Something's happening, and I want to know what."

"Could be about the third heir," Mason suggested. "Maybe Winston thinks it's Gabe?"

"Gabe doesn't want anything to do with the Callaway legacy," Devon said. "He made that clear."

"Doesn't mean Winston would believe him."

Fair point.

"Boys," Walter called. "We should head out. Your mother wants to get home before the vultures start circling for the reception."

"We're not going to the Callaway house?" Bryson asked.

"Absolutely not." Brea's tone brooked no argument. "I will not spend an afternoon watching Monica preen and Callie play the victim while they plot God knows what. We've paid our respects. That's sufficient."

They made their way to the parking lot, the afternoon heat hitting like a physical force after the cemetery's shade. Devon loosened his tie, already sweating through his shirt.

"Devon." Winston's voice carried across the lot. "That word? Now would be good."

Devon exchanged glances with Bryson, who shrugged. "Want me to come?"

"Please."

They approached Winston, who'd shed his jacket and rolled up his sleeves. Sweat beaded on his forehead, and his carefully maintained composure had frayed at the edges.

"What can we do for you?" Devon asked.

Winston glanced around, ensuring privacy before speaking. "I understand you've hired Emery."

"We have."

"Interesting choice." Winston's tone was neutral, but Devon heard judgment underneath. "Given her history."

"Her qualifications speak for themselves."

"Do they? Or did other factors influence your decision?" Winston's gaze was sharp, assessing.

"Her hiring was based purely on merit," Bryson said, his voice tight. "What's this about?"

"I'm curious about Stone Bridge's expansion plans. The premium market, authentication services, collector outreach—that's new territory for you." Winston's expression remained carefully blank. "Territory that could overlap significantly with Callaway interests."

"There's room for multiple players in the premium space," Devon said carefully. "We're not trying to edge you out." But what bothered him more was the idea that Winston was fishing for information—something that Devon and his family wasn't willing to discuss with the competition.

"Aren't you?" Winston's mask cracked slightly. "My father spent years building relationships in that market. Now Stone Bridge is positioning itself as a major player, hiring someone with—questionable ethics aside—exactly the expertise needed to compete directly with us."

"Competition is healthy," Bryson pointed out.

"Competition is one thing. Predatory business practices are another." Winston's voice dropped. "I'm aware that Emery has contacts in auction houses and collector circles that took my father decades to cultivate. If she's using those relationships to benefit Stone Bridge at Callaway's expense..."

"She's doing nothing of the sort," Devon said, anger flaring. Winston had always been a bit of an asshole, but this was a new low, even for him. "And I resent the implication."

"That's funny. Because from where I stand, this looks like opportunism disguised as compassion." Winston stepped closer. "You swoop in when she's vulnerable, offer her a job, and suddenly have access to every connection and piece of insider knowledge she gathered working for Harold Pemberton."

"That's not what happened."

"Then explain why someone so careful about business as you are would hire someone radioactive in the industry."

"Her ethics are impeccable," Bryson said, his voice carrying that deep tone he only used when someone had pushed him too far.

"Perhaps. Or perhaps you're too close to see clearly." Winston's gaze locked on Devon. "I hear you two have a personal relationship. That you've had one for months. Makes me wonder if your judgment is clouded by factors that have nothing to do with business."

Devon felt heat creep up his neck. "My personal life is none of your concern."

"It is when it affects business relationships in this valley. When it potentially damages Callaway interests." Winston straightened his tie, composure sliding back into place. "Consider this a courtesy warning. If Stone Bridge's expansion comes at Callaway's expense—if we lose clients or relationships because of your new hire—there will be consequences."

"Is that a threat?"

"It's a statement of fact." Winston's smile was about as stone-cold as an ice cube. "We're competitors. Always have been. But we've maintained a certain professional respect. Don't let poor judgment destroy that." He walked away before either of them could respond.

"What the hell was that?" Bryson asked.

"A shot across the bow." Devon watched Winston rejoin Callie and Monica. "He's worried about Emery. About what she brings to the table."

"Good. Let him worry." Bryson's expression had that hard edge their father had—untrusting, unwavering, and if someone took a shot at family, Bryson would crush them like bad fruit. "But I don't like the implications. That sounded like he's planning something."

Devon didn't respond, but unease coiled in his gut. Winston's warning had been specific, calculated. This wasn't grief talking or an emotional reaction to his father's death.

This was strategy.

And Devon had a sinking feeling they were only seeing the opening moves.

Emery settled deeper into the bed in the guesthouse, her phone screen casting a soft glow in the darkened room. Outside, the vineyard sprawled in shadowy rows beneath a sliver of moon, and the only sounds were the whisper of wind through leaves and the distant hoot of an owl.

Her phone buzzed with another text from Devon.

Devon: *You should be sleeping. Early morning tomorrow.*

Emery: *Says the man who's also awake texting me.*

Devon: *Fair point. But I have an excuse. I'm reviewing harvest schedules.*

Emery: *And I'm reviewing provenance documentation. We're both workaholics.*

Devon: *Okay, but you're obsessed.*

She smiled despite herself. He wasn't wrong. She'd spent the last four hours cross-referencing storage conditions with vintage years, building the kind of meticulous documentation that would make collectors salivate.

Emery: *Fine. I'm turning off the light now. Happy?*

Devon: *Delighted. Sleep well.*

Emery: *Goodnight.*

She set the phone on the nightstand and reached for the lamp, plunging the room into darkness. The sudden absence of light made the shadows deeper, the silence more pronounced. She pulled the throw blanket over herself, closed her eyes, and let exhaustion pull her under.

She had no idea how long she'd been asleep when a sound woke her—sharp, distinct, entirely out of place.

Metal scraping against metal. The unmistakable click of a lock disengaging.

Emery's eyes snapped open, her heart immediately racing. She lay frozen on the bed, straining to hear over the rush of blood in her ears. The darkness pressed in, familiar furniture shapes rendered menacing by adrenaline and fear.

Another sound. Softer this time. Footsteps? Or just the house settling?

She reached for her phone with trembling fingers, the screen's brightness making her squint—2:47 AM.

Swinging her legs over the side of the mattress, she found her slippers and tiptoed toward the slightly opened door.

Movement. Definite movement near the French doors that led to the patio.

Terror flooded her system, sharp and chemical. Someone was inside the guest-house.

With trembling fingers, she tapped the screen on her cell as she raced toward the bathroom, quietly closing the door behind her.

"9-1-1, what's your emergency?"

"Someone's in my house." Her whisper came out strangled, barely audible. "Stone Bridge Winery, the guesthouse. Please, someone's here."

"Are you in a safe location, ma'am?"

"I'm in the bathroom off the bedroom. I saw movement in the living room."

The French doors rattled. Then silence.

"I think they're leaving." Emery glanced out the window but couldn't see anything. Every muscle tensed for flight. "I can't see anything from where I am."

"Officers are three minutes away. Stay on the line with me."

But Emery's mind was already moving, already pulling up Devon's number with shaking fingers.

"I'm texting the owners," she told the dispatcher.

Emery: *The guesthouse was broken into. I'm on the phone with the police. I don't know if they're still in the house.*

Devon: *Where are you?*

Emery: *Bathroom.*

Devon: *Don't move. Stay there until the police get there. I'm on my way. Won't take but five minutes to get there.*

Emery clutched the phone like a lifeline, the dispatcher's voice a steady anchor in her ear as sirens wailed in the distance, growing closer. She stepped from the bathroom, slowly opened the bedroom door, and peeked her head out.

Nothing.

Red and blue lights strobed through the windows as a patrol car pulled into the driveway. Sandy Kane emerged first, her uniform crisp despite the ungodly hour, followed by a younger deputy with sandy hair and a calm, assessing gaze.

"Emery." Sandy's voice was professional but warm. "Are you in there? Are you safe? You called about an intruder?"

"Ma'am," the dispatcher's voice came over the phone. "You can hang up now that the police chief is there."

"Thank you."

Devon's truck pulled into the driveway. He leapt from the driver's seat, pushed past Sandy, nearly knocking her over, and burst through the front door, wearing sweatpants and a t-shirt, his hair disheveled, his expression fierce. He scanned the dimly lit room before his eyes found hers. "You're okay?" He crossed to her in three strides. "You're not hurt?"

"I'm fine. Scared, but fine." She stood on shaking legs. "They ran when I woke up. I heard the doors, heard movement."

Sandy cleared her throat. "Now that we've established that Devon here hasn't changed since high school, mind if I do my job?"

"Sorry, Sandy." Devon turned, keeping his arm around Emery. "What are you doing out on patrol at this hour? It's like you're a rookie all over again, pulling double shifts."

"I've got a rookie and one out on medical for another week. My team and I are all stepping up and working overtime," she said. "You know Deputy James Chen." Sandy gestured to the other officer. "We're going to check the perimeter, then I want to walk through everything with you. Devon, I take you're going to be glued to her for the time being?"

"Not leaving her side."

Sandy and Chen moved through the guesthouse with practiced efficiency, checking windows, testing locks, and examining the French doors. Chen crouched near the lock, pulling a small flashlight from his belt.

"No signs of forced entry," he said. "But the lock here is a standard residential model. Easy enough to pick if you know what you're doing."

"Is anything missing or disturbed?" Sandy rejoined them, her expression thoughtful.

"Not that I can tell," Emery said.

"Did you see the intruder?" Sandy asked, taking out a small notebook.

"I saw a shadow, and I heard them. Movement near the doors, then they left."

"Devon, do you have security cameras on the guesthouse?" Sandy pulled out her phone. "And if so, can you access the cameras from here?"

Bryson appeared in the doorway before Devon could answer, fully dressed and grim-faced. "Heard the sirens. What happened?"

Devon gave him a quick summary while Sandy waited patiently.

"Security footage," Bryson said immediately. "Let's pull it up at the main house. Bigger screen, easier to see details, and you can look at the entire property."

"Good idea," Sandy agreed. "Devon, you stay with Emery. Bryson, Chen, and I will review the footage."

After they left, silence engulfed the guesthouse like a weight. Emery sank back onto the couch. Her adrenaline crash left her shaky and cold. Devon grabbed the throw blanket and wrapped it around her shoulders.

"Someone was here," she said quietly. "I know what I heard."

"I believe you."

"Even if the cameras don't show anything?"

"Even then." Devon sat beside her, close enough that she could feel his warmth. "You're not the kind of person who imagines things."

"The article made me look unstable. Another incident like this—"

"This isn't like the article. This is someone breaking into your home." His voice was firm. "That's a crime, not a PR problem."

Tears stung her eyes.

He wrapped his arm around her body and tugged her close. "Sandy will figure this out. She's the best chief we've had in years."

She dropped her head to his shoulder and tried to suck in a deep breath, but her lungs wouldn't expand. Her muscles trembled. She couldn't remember a time in her life when she'd been this terrified.

"Hey. It's okay. I've got you."

"Someone was here. While I was sleeping." She glanced up at him. "What if I hadn't woken up? What if they wanted to..." she let the words trail off, but the thought didn't leave her brain. The idea that someone could've raped her, or worse, made her heart race faster.

"I'm not going to let anything happen to you." He pressed his lips against her temple and smoothed her hair.

She completely collapsed into his strong frame, giving way to all the emotions. Fear. Panic. Confusion. Anger. Tears came hot and fast.

Devon just held her tighter. He didn't say a word. She had no idea how long they sat there while she unraveled.

But shortly, Sandy returned with Bryson and Chen. Her face was tight. "We found something," she said, pulling up her phone to show a grainy video. "Front door camera, timestamp 2:38 AM."

The footage showed the front entrance to the guesthouse, lit by the porch light. For several seconds, nothing moved. Then—a shadow. Brief, indistinct, moving quickly across the frame from right to left.

"That's it?" Emery leaned closer. "You can't see anything."

"No clear view of the person, no identifying features," Chen confirmed. "But someone was definitely here."

"The angle's wrong to catch them approaching," Bryson explained. "Cameras positioned to show who's at the front door, not movement along the side of the building. But whoever this was, they knew to avoid the main camera coverage. And they knew where most of our cameras are located on the property. The only thing we got is someone jumping the fence on the west side near the access road."

Sandy held her notebook in her hands. "That suggests more than a familiarity with the layout. Someone who knows how the security system works and what would set off an alarm, which wasn't activated."

The implication hung in the air, heavy and unsettling.

"Nothing was taken," Sandy continued. "Nothing appears disturbed. Can you think of any reason someone would break in without stealing or vandalizing?"

Emery gestured helplessly at the provenance files scattered across the coffee table. "I've been working on authentication documentation. That could be valuable to someone who wants to sabotage the program."

"Or to the Boone's competitors," Sandy said thoughtfully. "Someone who wants to know what Stone Bridge is planning, but they'd have to know to look here. While this is a small town, and people are whispering about your role, it's not the first place I'd go looking for Stone Bridge Winery secrets."

"Industrial espionage?" Devon's tone was not only skeptical, it was laced with a touch of frustration. "While I get it happens, it's extremely rare in the valley."

"It's happened before. The premium wine market is worth millions. If someone wanted an edge, knowing your authentication processes, your target collectors, your expansion strategy—that's valuable information." Sandy closed her notebook.

"But breaking in to look at paperwork?" Emery pulled the blanket tighter around her body. "Why not just hack our email? Take photos with a telephoto lens? Breaking and entering seems like a good way to get caught. Especially in the middle of the night. And a little stupid when the majority of the important pieces are either locked up in the production building, which has people in twenty-four-seven right now, or the main house offices."

"Unless the point wasn't just gathering information," Chen said quietly. "Maybe the point was intimidation."

The word settled like ice in Emery's stomach.

"That's what I believe. That someone's targeting her," Devon said, his voice tight with anger. "The article, the video from the tasting room, now this."

"I'm certainly not going to rule that out," Sandy agreed. "Which brings me to my next question. Harold Pemberton —I've been looking into him like I said I would—back-ground check, financial records, business practices. Every-thing comes back clean. Almost suspiciously clean."

"What does that mean?" Emery asked.

"It means either he's genuinely innocent of any wrong-doing, or he's very good at covering his tracks." Sandy stuffed her pad into her pocket. "No red flags, no complaints, no financial irregularities. I can't find anything that suggests he's ever forged a vintage collection, and no trace of large sums of money that suggests a payoff."

"So we're nowhere," Emery said softly.

"Not nowhere. We know someone broke into this guesthouse tonight. We know someone submitted an anonymous tip to the reporter. We just don't know who or why." Sandy moved closer toward the door. "I'm going to file a report, increase patrol frequency through the vine-yard. And I'd recommend you don't stay alone for a bit. And maybe set up a different security system in this place."

"I'll have something installed by tomorrow afternoon," Devon said.

"We'll be in touch." Sandy turned, and she and her deputy strolled out of the guesthouse.

After the police left, Devon and Emery sat in silence. The weight of everything—the break-in, the ongoing attacks, the feeling of being hunted—pressed down like physical force.

"My father has a PI looking into things," Devon said finally.

Emery's head snapped up. "What?"

"Declan. He worked on Riley's mother's case. Dad hired him after that article. He's investigating Harold, the article, and anyone who might have motivation to come after you." Devon wouldn't meet her eyes.

"What aren't you telling me?"

"He's looking into your father as well," Devon said.

Fury ignited in Emery's chest, hot and sharp. "You're having me investigated? My family?"

"Not you. Never you." Devon turned to face her. "But the article brought up your father's situation. We need to know if there's truth to it, if someone could use it against you—against us."

"So you just decided to dig into my family's private business without asking me?"

"We're trying to protect you."

"By treating me like a suspect?" She stood, the blanket falling away. "By assuming my father's guilty of something?"

"That's not what this is—"

"Then what is it? Because from where I'm standing, it

looks like you don't trust me. Like you think there might be fire with all that smoke."

Devon rose, closing the distance between them. "I think someone is systematically destroying your life, and I want to know who and why. If that means investigating every angle, including uncomfortable ones about your father's past, then yes, that's what we're doing."

"Without telling me. Without giving me a chance to—"

"To what? To protect him? To hide evidence?" Devon's voice rose. "Someone broke into your house tonight. Someone is targeting you specifically. This isn't about hurting your feelings or doubting your integrity. This is about keeping you safe."

"By violating my privacy?"

"By finding answers before whoever's doing this escalates from break-ins to something worse."

The words hit like cold water. Emery felt her anger deflate, replaced by the same crushing fear that made her hide in a damn bathroom.

"What if the PI finds something?" Her voice came out small. "What if my father really did what they accused him of?"

"Then we deal with it. Together." Devon's expression softened. "But whatever he did or didn't do, that's not on you. You're not responsible for his choices."

"Everyone will think I am. They'll say it runs in the family, that questionable ethics are hereditary—they're already saying it." Tears threatened once again. "I've spent my entire life trying to prove I belong somewhere. That I'm good enough, smart enough, honest enough. And now—"

Devon pulled her into his arms, cutting off her words.

She resisted for a moment, then melted into him, her face pressed against his chest.

"You are good enough," he said fiercely. "You're brilliant and talented and ethical. Anyone who knows you knows that."

"But people don't know me. They know the scandal, the articles, the drama."

"Then we change that narrative—like Riley said. We prove them wrong." He pulled back enough to look at her face. "But we can't do that if we're hiding from the truth. If your father made mistakes, we face them head-on. If he's innocent, we prove it. Either way, you're not alone in this, and if you'd rather Declan not do this behind your dad's back, we can make that phone call."

Emery looked up at him, seeing determination and something deeper in his dark eyes. Something that made her heart stutter.

"I'm scared," she admitted.

"I know. Me too."

"Of what?"

"Of losing you. Of watching whoever's doing this drive you away." His hand came up to cup her face. "Of not being able to protect you."

The vulnerability in his voice undid her. This man who'd defended her, believed her, stood by her through everything—he was scared too.

"I'm not going anywhere," she said softly.

"Promise?"

"I promise."

He kissed her then, gentle and careful, as if she were something fragile that might break. Emery leaned into him, letting the warmth and solidity of his presence chase away the lingering fear.

When they finally pulled apart, Devon rested his forehead against hers.

"Pack a bag," he said. "You're staying at my place tonight."

Emery pulled back, shaking her head. "No."

"Emery—"

"I'm not letting whoever did this drive me out of my own space." Her voice was firm despite the lingering tremor. "That's exactly what they want—to make me feel unsafe, to make me run."

"I can't let you stay here. That's crazy, and my mom, she'd have my hide."

"Then you stay here." She met his gaze. "Stay with me. But I'm not leaving."

Devon studied her face, seeing the determination beneath the fear. "Okay, we'll stay here."

He kissed her forehead. "But I'm staying until this is solved. Not just tonight. That's not negotiable. Otherwise, you either have to move into the main house or down the street with me."

"I don't have the energy to fight you."

"Even if you did, you'd lose," he said. "Now, you should try to get some sleep. I'll take the sofa."

"I don't think I can." Emery stood there, staring at him, exhaustion warring with residual fear. "Every sound is going to make me jump."

Devon inched closer. "Then we'll stay up together. Or at least until you can't keep your eyes open anymore."

"We could watch a show." She leaned into him, drawing

comfort from his solid presence. "The bed is big enough for both of us, and I trust you to keep your hands to yourself."

"Now, that's a big ask."

He took her by the hand and led her into the bedroom, drawing back the covers and helping her in, before climbing between the sheets. He flicked on the television, keeping the volume low, as he searched for a movie. They lay in silence for a while, the guesthouse settling into quiet around them. Outside, the wind rustled through the vineyard rows, and somewhere in the distance a dog barked—normal sounds. Safe sounds.

"Devon?" Her voice was drowsy now, sleep finally pulling her under despite her earlier certainty that she couldn't rest.

"Yeah?"

"What if we never figure out who's doing this?"

"We will." His voice was firm, confident. "I promise you, we'll figure it out."

Emery let her eyes close, lulled by his heartbeat steady beneath her ear and the warmth of his arms around her. Tomorrow, she'd be scared again. Tomorrow, she'd have to face more questions, more uncertainty, more attacks on her reputation.

But tonight, she wasn't alone.

And maybe that was enough.

Eight

Sunrise crept through the bedroom curtains in shades of amber and rose, painting soft patterns across the twisted sheets. Devon blinked awake slowly, his body warm and relaxed, and realized Emery was still curled against him, her head tucked beneath his chin, her breath steady against his chest.

They'd fallen asleep sometime after four in the morning, exhaustion and the comfort of not being alone finally pulling them under. Now, she slept peacefully, her dark hair spilling across the pillow and his shoulder, one hand resting over his heart.

He didn't dare move. Didn't dare disturb this moment.

The panic of last night had faded, replaced by something softer, more dangerous. Devon looked down at her sleeping face—the delicate curve of her cheekbone, the slight furrow between her brows that suggested she dreamed of something troubling, the vulnerable set of her mouth—and felt something shift in his chest.

This was different.

Every relationship he'd ever had, had come with an expiration date. He'd known it going in, accepted it, sometimes welcomed it. Gretchen had wanted more attention than he could give during harvest season. The relationship he'd been in before that had fizzled out after six months of pleasant but unremarkable dates. Callie—God, what a disaster that had been both times—had wanted something he couldn't name and certainly couldn't provide.

But none of them had ever made him feel like this.

Like his heart might crack open just watching her sleep. Like the thought of her leaving Stone Bridge physically hurt. Like he wanted to wake up every morning and see her face first thing for the rest of his life.

The realization should have terrified him. For months, he'd been fighting this pull toward her, telling himself it was just attraction, just chemistry, just the wrong timing making everything more intense. He'd maintained those careful boundaries she'd requested, kept things professional despite every instinct screaming to pull her close.

But lying here with her in his arms, feeling her trust in the way she'd let herself fall asleep against him, he couldn't pretend anymore.

He was falling for her. Had been falling since that night three months ago when she'd looked at him with devastation in her eyes and asked him to stay. Maybe longer—maybe since that auction when he'd watched her passion for wine authentication light up her entire face.

And he was tired of fighting it.

His parents had this. They were the couple who still held hands at dinner after thirty-six years of marriage. Bryson had found it with Riley, that once-in-a-lifetime love that had survived a decade apart and come back stronger. Devon had watched them both and felt nothing but mild bewilderment at the intensity, the certainty, the absolute conviction that this person was it.

Now he understood.

Emery stirred against him, making a slight sound of protest as consciousness pulled her from sleep. Her hand flexed against his chest, fingers curling in his shirt, and then she went very still.

"Devon?" Her voice was rough with sleep, muffled against his shoulder.

"Right here."

She lifted her head slowly, blinking in the morning light filtering through the curtains. Her hair was a disaster, and she had the crease of the pillow imprinted on her cheek. She was absolutely beautiful.

"You've made a weird habit of spending the night," she said, stating the obvious with the kind of solemnity that suggested she was still half-dreaming.

"I don't think it's weird at all," he whispered. "Besides, I promised I would." Devon tucked a strand of hair behind her ear. "How'd you sleep?"

"Better than I should have after someone broke in." She didn't pull away from his touch. Instead, she seemed to lean into it slightly. "You?"

"Best sleep I've had in months."

That earned him a small smile. "Even after everything that happened?"

"Especially after everything that happened." His fingers traced the line of her jaw. "You're safe. That's all that matters."

Something shifted in her expression—surprise, maybe, or recognition of what he wasn't quite saying. Her green eyes searched his face, looking for something, and Devon let her look. Hoped she'd see whatever she needed to see.

"Devon," she whispered, and the way she said his name—like a question, like a prayer—made his breath catch.

He cupped her face, his thumb tracing the curve of her cheekbone. "I'm done pretending this is just professional interest. I'm done keeping my distance because it's the smart thing to do."

"What are you saying?"

"I'm saying I'm falling for you. Have been for months. And I'm tired of fighting it."

Her breath hitched. For a moment, she just stared at him, her expression unreadable. Then she leaned in and kissed him.

It was soft at first, tentative, as if testing the waters. But when Devon responded, pulling her closer, the kiss deepened into something more. She shifted in his arms, her hands sliding up to frame his face, and he forgot about boundaries and professionalism and all the very good reasons they should take this slow.

Her mouth was warm and sweet, and she made a slight sound in the back of her throat when he traced her bottom lip with his tongue. The sound went straight through him.

"Emery," he murmured against her mouth. "We should—"

"No more should or shouldn't." She pulled back just enough to meet his eyes. "Don't tell me we should slow down, or think about this, or be smart. If last night taught me anything, it's that life is too short not to be honest about certain things."

"What does that mean?"

"I want this. Want you." Her fingers threaded through his hair. "And I'm tired of all the reasons we shouldn't. I know it's a risk to both my career and this winery, and if you want to get out of this bed, I'd understand. I'm just telling you I don't want to play it safe anymore."

Devon searched her face, looking for doubt, for fear, for any sign this was the adrenaline and trauma of last night talking. But all he saw was certainty and desire and something that looked a lot like the feelings he'd just confessed.

"You're sure?"

"I've never been surer of anything."

That was all the permission he needed. Devon kissed her again, deeper this time, pouring months of suppressed longing into the contact. She responded with equal intensity, her body pressing against his, her hands exploring the planes of his chest through his shirt.

His hands found the curve of her waist, the warm skin just beneath the hem of her shirt, and she arched into his touch with a soft gasp that made his pulse spike.

"I've wanted this," she breathed against his mouth. "Wanted you. For so long."

Devon rolled, bringing her beneath him, caging her body with his as he kissed a path along her jaw, down the column of her throat. She arched beneath him, her hands gripping his shoulders, and laughed—actually laughed—a sound so light and free it made his chest ache.

"What's funny?"

"Nothing. Everything." Her fingers traced the muscles

of his back. "I just—this feels right. For the first time in months, something feels completely right."

Devon lifted his head to look at her, his heart hammering against his ribs. Long brown hair pooled around her head, framing her face as she gazed up at him. The intimacy of the moment—her there, looking at him like that—hit him hard. She was the most beautiful thing he'd ever seen.

"You're gorgeous," he whispered.

"That's my line."

His hands found the hem of her shirt, fingers hesitating at the fabric. "Tell me to stop if you need to."

"I'm not going to tell you to stop."

He pulled the shirt up and over her head, and she helped him, laughing again when her hair got caught in the neckline. The sound was intoxicating—joy mixed with desire, trust blended with want.

His lips brushed against her shoulder, following the path his fingers had traced. He tasted the salt of her skin, the sweet hint of vanilla. The scent of her was intoxicating, a heady blend of vanilla and something uniquely her— something that made him want to bury his face in her neck and just breathe her in.

Kissing her again, he explored her in layers of silky whis- pers and searing touches. Emery gasped at the heat of his mouth against her skin, her fingernails scraping lightly against the back of his neck. The sound turned his blood into a river of fire coursing through his veins. He committed the fervor of her breathless whimpers to memory, relishing the way her body arched towards him like a flower straining for sunlight.

He slid his fingers down her body, tracing a path along the ridges of her ribs, circling her hips. Her skin was warm, silky against his touch, and he could feel the gentle rise of her breathing beneath his hand. A soft sigh escaped her lips as his fingers traveled further south, tracing the elastic band of her panties. She rewarded him with a shudder, her hips bucking up to meet his touch.

This—being with her—it was like coming home. A thought that was both shocking and humbling at the same time.

"Devon," she breathed, lifting her head, dark eyes sparkling in the morning light. Her voice, so sultry and thick with lust. The echo of his name on her lips, the way she bit her lower lip, the exposed, tantalizing stretch of her neck—everything came together in a mesmerizing symphony of temptation.

His eyes traced every contour, every line, every mark. He followed the path of his touch and watched as his fingers skimmed over the material of her underwear. The play of her body beneath his touch demanded to be explored.

She was perfect. Each inch of her was a new revelation. Each soft gasp echoed his desire. He reveled in the way she moved, the way she held her breath when he touched her in a place she liked, the soft moans she didn't bother to stifle. Every reaction was an entry in her guidebook, directing his hands and mouth to the places that delighted her most.

Something shifted in his chest—more like cracked open. She was different. They were different—together.

Their eyes locked, and for a moment, she stilled, her

gaze holding his as if he were the roots and she was the ground holding him in place.

She was exquisite, a masterpiece of curves and hollows that called to him.

With a growl, he descended on her, his lips finding her bare breast, his tongue tracing the tightened nipple. She clung tighter to him, her fingers threading through his hair as he tasted her, savored her.

His clothing quickly became a barrier, an annoying impediment to the closeness they both craved. Her fingers tugged at the waistband of his sweatpants, echoing his own urgency. He helped her, kicking them and his underwear aside before joining her back on the bed.

Her hands roamed across his chest, over his abdomen, tracing every muscle that flexed beneath her touch. Her touch brought him to life, each caress as potent as a lightning strike, leaving tingling pulsating arcs across his skin.

When she finally grasped him, his skin was so sensitive, so hungry for her touch, the sensation shocked him. He groaned against her neck, his body jerking in response.

"Emery," he rasped against the shell of her ear, his voice hoarse with desire. Her name tumbled like a secret confession from his lips, filled with a reverence he hadn't known he was capable of.

With his heart pounding against his ribcage like a wild beast cornered, he was on the brink, a hundred demands crowding at the tip of his tongue—be gentle, be wild, be everything that he'd been aching for. But the words stuck in his throat as he lost himself in her touch, in the overpowering sensations that she drew from within him.

He shifted, bringing his weight onto one arm to free his

other hand. His fingers found her thigh, coaxing her to wrap it around his waist as he pressed himself against her. His body was a live wire, buzzing with pent-up tension, poised at the apex of pleasure and patience.

Her fingernails scraped down his chest, leaving trails of fire on his skin, bringing him back to the moment. He reached for her other thigh, guiding it to join its mate around his hips. The position brought their bodies even closer, their centers aligning in a way that elicited a gasp.

With a deep intake of breath, Devon nuzzled the crook of her neck, breathing in her scent. The sweet, intoxicating aroma was becoming as necessary as air.

Emery's grip on him tightened, her nails digging into his back in a delicious sting. The sensation was sharp, full of promise, leaving his senses humming with anticipation.

Threading her fingers in his hair, she tugged him down for another searing kiss. He reveled in the warmth of her lips against his, the feel of her body undulating beneath him, the sound of her soft moans mingling with his own. The kindling spark of desire flared into a full-blown firestorm, consuming him from the inside out.

He eased into her, holding his breath, trying to maintain control, but that seemed like it was no longer possible.

Her hands clung to his back, her nails digging into his flesh, anchoring them together. The bite of pain mixed with pleasure, sharp and sweet, and the intensity of it—her grip, her body, the way she moved with him—burned through every nerve ending until nothing existed but this, nothing existed but her.

When she finally crumbled beneath him, her climax washing over them both in a wave of intense, breathtaking pleasure, he held her tight. Her name spilled from his lips like a prayer even as her soft cries filled the room. Her body went limp beneath his, her chest heaving, her muscles still shivering with aftershocks.

He stroked her hair, reveling in the silkiness beneath his fingers. He kissed her forehead, the side of her neck, the corner of her mouth. He tasted salt and sweat on her skin, breathing her in like she was oxygen he'd been starving for his entire life. And just like that, he knew—he was wrecked. Ruined. Every other woman, every carefully constructed wall, every promise he'd made himself about staying free— gone. She'd branded herself on him, body and soul, and there was no coming back from this. His skin tingled where it touched against hers. He'd never felt so alive, so complete, so utterly consumed by another person. The depth of his feelings was overwhelming, and yet he wouldn't have it any other way.

Her eyes fluttered open after a moment, meeting his with a calmness he hadn't expected. Breathless, satisfied, a weak smile played across her lips. She looked at him with a newfound intimacy, an understanding that bound them closer together. Her hand found his, their fingers intertwining and squeezing gently.

"Wow," she said softly, her gaze still locked with his.

He echoed the word, a soft rumble from deep within his chest. Words were inadequate, but "wow" encompassed it, somehow.

He rolled to his side, keeping her close, pulling the covers over the bodies.

Emery's head rested on his chest, his fingers tracing lazy patterns on her bare shoulder. The room was fully light now, Sunday morning sounds filtering in from outside—birds singing, the distant rumble of a tractor, the peaceful rhythm of a vineyard at rest.

"Are we crazy?" Emery asked quietly.

"What do you mean?"

"I mean, this? Us?"

Devon's hand stilled on her shoulder, and his heart plummeted to his toes. "Second thoughts already?"

She lifted her head to look at him. "Not about how I feel, but about what others will think. About how it looks. About what people will gossip about and put in online articles." Her hand flattened against his chest. "And it's not just about how it will affect my career, but this vineyard."

"The rumor mill is already buzzing. Those pictures from three months ago are something we need to address." He met her gaze steadily. "We can't lie about this. If we do that, it'll come out, and that would be worse." He kissed her softly. "I don't think it's something we have to announce. Just answer truthfully when it's brought up. But if I'm being completely honest here, we've got nothing to hide or be ashamed about."

"This is a complicated story, and I don't like it being on display all because someone is targeting me for a reason I can't even fathom."

"We're going to figure this out. The PI my dad hired is excellent. And maybe this all has to do with the insurance thing your dad was involved in." Devon pulled her closer.

"I have thought about that." She rested her chin on his chest. "My father's told me for the last year that things will eventually become clear. I just need to be patient and let the system work. That I'll understand soon enough. It's hard because he's constantly telling me that he can't talk about it. But I don't know why someone would target me."

"That's what Declan is for," Devon said. "You're not alone in this. Whatever comes next, we face it together."

She was quiet for a long moment. "I'm scared."

"Of what?"

"Of losing this. Of someone taking it away before we even have a chance to figure out what it could be."

"No one's taking anything." The words came out rough, harder than he intended. Jaw locked, he caught himself leaning toward her before forcing himself to ease back against the pillow. *Breathe. Don't crowd her.* "We'll figure out who's behind the attacks, clear your name, build the authentication program, and prove everyone wrong. Together."

"You make it sound simple."

"It's not simple. It's probably going to be messy, complicated, and difficult. And my family is going to pick on us. Well me. And we do have to tell them that we are now a thing because of how this town likes to listen to the whispers in the vines." Devon tilted her chin up, so she had to meet his eyes. "But I'm not going anywhere. You've got me, for as long as you'll have me."

Emery's eyes filled with tears, even as she smiled. "Have you ever had a girlfriend for longer than a few months?"

"If I say no, is that going to be a problem?"

"It's one of the reasons I stayed clear for so long."

"Can't say I blame you for that." He chuckled. "But I've never felt about someone like I do you."

She kissed him, soft and sweet and full of promise. When she pulled back, the fear in her expression had eased, replaced by something that looked a lot like hope. "We should get up," she said reluctantly. "Your family has probably already noticed your truck parked in front of the guesthouse, and Bryson can't cover for you all day at work."

"Let them notice." Devon pulled her back down against him. "We've got time. It is Sunday, and while it's still harvest, it was a traumatic night."

She laughed, settling into his embrace. "Your mother is going to have a field day with this."

"Oh, absolutely. She's probably already planning the wedding."

"That's not funny."

"I'm kidding. " He grinned at her scandalized expression. "Mostly kidding. Though, knowing my mother, she's at least mentally redecorating the guesthouse for grandchildren and figuring out a way to talk you into talking me into moving into the main house."

"We literally just admitted we have feelings for each other. Can we maybe get through breakfast before your mother starts planning my entire future?"

"That's optimistic. My money's on her cornering you before coffee."

Emery groaned, burying her face in his chest. "This family is going to eat me alive."

"This family already loves you." Devon stroked her hair. "They have for weeks. This just makes it official."

She lifted her head, her expression turning serious. "What if we don't last? What if whoever's targeting me escalates? What if—"

"Hey." He cut her off with a gentle kiss. "We'll handle it. Together. One day at a time."

"One day at a time," she repeated, as if testing the words. Then she smiled. "I can do that."

Outside, the vineyard stretched under the morning sun, rows of vines heavy with the last of the harvest's fruit. Birds sang their morning songs. The world kept turning.

And inside the guesthouse bedroom, Devon held the woman he was falling in love with and let himself believe that maybe, just maybe, they could have this. Could build something real and lasting despite everything working against them.

He just hoped whoever was targeting her would give them the chance to find out.

Nine

The morning sun beat down on the vineyard rows, already warming the October air to an uncomfortable degree. Devon walked between the vines with Bryson on his left and Gabe on his right, the dry earth crunching beneath their boots as they moved deeper into the property where conversation wouldn't carry back to the main house —or the guesthouse.

Gabe had been reluctant to leave the production facility when they'd shown up asking him to go for a walk. Now, he moved with the kind of tension that suggested he knew exactly what this conversation was about.

From the moment Gabe had been hired, he'd been a quiet, reflective man. Reserved. He kept his head down and worked hard. He asked questions when he didn't understand something or needed clarification. He gave his opinion, though often reluctantly, and through the gentle nudging of Sean Callahan.

God, Devon missed that man.

For the first two years Gabe worked at Stone Bridge

Winery, he'd carried the weight of his family's history like it was a brick tied to his ankle. As if the past was a snake hidden under the tall grass, just waiting for a stray foot to land close enough to strike without too much effort.

The secrets and folk tales that had built Stone Bridge did come out on occasion, but faded into the background quickly, like the fog burned off with the rising of the morning sun. And soon enough, Gabe learned that the shadows lurking in dark corners couldn't hurt him. He wasn't his grandfather, and that didn't have to be his legacy.

Gabe stuffed his hands in his pockets as he listened and nodded in response to Bryson.

"Winston cornered you at the funeral," Devon said finally, cutting through the small talk about soil moisture levels and irrigation schedules. "We saw it. Looked heated and looked damned uncomfortable."

Gabe's jaw tightened, his gaze fixed on the horizon. "It was nothing."

"Didn't look like nothing," Bryson said. "You looked ready to throw a punch at a cemetery." He shifted his weight, angling his body toward Gabe's in unwavering support. "We were ready to jump into action if necessary."

"Winston has that effect on people," Gabe said.

Devon stopped walking, forcing the other two to halt as well. "We're not trying to pry. We're worried about you. Whatever Winston said, it clearly upset you."

For a long moment, Gabe said nothing. He stared out at the vineyard, his expression carefully blank, a look he'd perfected over the years, but Devon could see the war playing out behind his eyes. Finally, his shoulders sagged slightly. "Someone sent Winston a photo," Gabe said quietly. "Of my mother and David. Together, when they were young. Not the same one I have but similar. Showed them hanging out, looking close. Arms draped around each other. They appeared intimate."

Devon exchanged a glance with Bryson. "Who sent it?"

"Anonymous. Came with a note saying the sender knows who the third heir is." Gabe's voice was tight. "Winston thought I sent it. Thought I was making some kind of play for the Callaway inheritance."

"Jesus," Bryson breathed.

"He accused me of playing games. Said there was no way I could be David's son, that I was delusional if I thought I had any claim to the Callaway legacy." Gabe's hands curled into fists. "Told me that on the off chance we were actually related, he'd do whatever was necessary to make sure I got nothing." The bitterness in his voice cut through the morning air like a blade.

Devon understood where the bitterness had been born from. The story was long and complicated. But it had nothing to do with Gabe and everything to do with Winston holding a grudge on behalf of men who'd been dead for decades.

But Winston—much to his father's dismay—had idolized his grandfather. They exchanged letters while his granddad was in prison prior to his death. His grandpa had painted a glorified picture of what happened all those years ago when his muscle—Cote Maxwell—murdered his brother in cold blood.

However, there was more to that story. EJ Callaway, who cooked the books for his brother Jasper, was also in a relationship with Cote's sister, Annabelle. But Annabelle went missing. Her body was found three weeks later. She'd been beaten and raped. Cote went crazy, knowing in his heart that EJ had killed his sister. So, Cote turned a gun on EJ, shooting him twice in chest at point blank range. Sources say, Cote didn't bat an eye. That he had no remorse. Just set his gun down, walked into a bar, and ordered a drink as if nothing happened.

For more than a decade, no one could prove that EJ had been the one to murder Annabelle until new forensic and DNA evidence had been introduced, proving EJ had committed the crime.

It didn't exonerate Cote. He'd still spent the rest of his life behind bars. However, it certainly changed the way some people viewed what he did.

"But that's not all," Gabe continued. "He wanted the guns back. Said the collection belonged to the Callaways, that David shouldn't have left them to me. Offered to pay for them—a substantial amount."

"How substantial?" Bryson asked.

"Millions." Gabe ran a hand over his mouth.

"That feels like a payoff," Devon said.

"Exactly." Gabe started walking again, his pace faster now, agitated. "Which made me think—maybe Winston does believe we could be half-brothers. Maybe that's why he's so desperate to buy me off, to make sure I have no reason to stake a claim."

"Do you want to?" Bryson asked carefully. "Stake a claim if you are related?"

"No. Yes. I don't know." Gabe ran a hand through his hair. "Just the other day, between talking with Emery and my wife, I'd made peace with not caring. With letting it be whatever it was and moving on with my life. But now, Winston's acting like I'm a threat, like there's something to be threatened by, and it's fucking with my head."

They walked in silence for a moment, the only sounds their footsteps and the distant call of hawks circling overhead.

"There's more," Gabe said. "Winston gave me a warning. About Emery."

Devon went very still. "What kind of warning? Like a threat?"

"He said no one knows the full story about her past. About her father who was going to end up in prison." Gabe's voice was careful now, measured. "Said history was going to repeat itself and take the Boones down with it."

"That's ridiculous," Bryson said immediately. "Emery's father was never charged with anything. The accusations are just that—accusations."

"I know that." Gabe stopped walking again, turning to face them, his expression tortured. "But Winston was very specific. Very certain. Like he knew something we didn't."

Devon's pulse started to race. Dread coiled in his gut. "What are you saying?"

Gabe was quiet for a long moment, clearly wrestling with something internal. "The insurance thing. The accusations against Emery's father are about accepting bribes to overlook fraudulent claims." He met Devon's eyes. "I know something about that case."

The words hung in the air like a bomb waiting to detonate.

"How?" Devon demanded.

"Because it affected my parents." Gabe's face changed.

His brow furrowed, lines carving deep between his eyes. He looked down at his feet, shoulders curving inward. "My father works in insurance fraud investigation. Has for over thirty years. Two years ago, he was brought in as a consultant on a major federal case. And my mother—she got caught up in it."

"Caught up how?" Bryson's voice was sharp.

"She worked as a senior claims administrator for one of the insurance companies being investigated. Had been there for twenty-five years, worked her way up from entry-level." Gabe's hands shook. "When the feds started building their fraud case, her name came up. Her signature was on documents that turned out to be fraudulent."

Devon's stomach dropped. "She was involved in the fraud?"

"No. She had no knowledge she was signing off on fraudulent claims. But that doesn't matter to federal prosecutors building a case." Gabe's voice cracked. "Her signature was there. Her authorization codes. On paper, she looked complicit."

"Jesus," Bryson inched out the word in a whisper.

"Can you imagine? My father gets brought in to consult on a massive fraud case, and discovers his own wife is about to be implicated as an accessory." Gabe wiped a hand over his face. "She could've faced federal charges. Prison time. All for doing her job without knowing what was really happening."

"How does Michael Tate fit into this?" Devon asked, even if part of him already knew the answer.

"Michael worked for a different insurance company, but he had connections to people caught up in the fraud. When the investigation started, his name came up, too—the feds thought he'd accepted bribes to overlook fraudulent claims." Gabe took a shaky breath. "The evidence looked damning. His signature on authorization forms, wire transfers to accounts in his name, a pattern of approving suspicious claims."

"But he didn't do it," Devon said, pieces clicking into place.

"The feds don't think so. At least, not anymore. But two years ago, when the investigation was just starting, Michael looked guilty as hell." Gabe sighed. "That's when my father really got involved. He's been working with federal prosecutors ever since, helping them build the real case against the actual perpetrators. And Michael—from what I've overheard, what I've pieced together from phone calls and documents I wasn't supposed to see—he's cooperating with the investigation, too."

"Was Micheal framed?" Bryson asked.

"Looks that way. Someone set him up to take the fall, used his credentials and access to make it look like he was the one accepting bribes and approving fraudulent claims." Gabe started pacing now, agitated energy pouring off him. "But the investigation is ongoing. Active federal case. Everyone involved—my parents, Michael, the other witnesses—they can't talk about it. One wrong word to the wrong person, and the whole case could collapse."

"So, Michael's been living under suspicion for two years," Devon said, "knowing he's innocent but unable to prove it."

"And my mother's been terrified that despite cooperating with prosecutors, she might still face charges for her unwitting involvement." Gabe's voice grew quieter. "My father's spent two years walking the line between building the case that potentially included Michael and protecting his own wife with reference to claims that bleed over. It's complicated, and I don't understand most of it. It's one of many reasons I don't want to go to them with this bullshit about these stupid pictures of my mom and David."

The morning sun climbed higher, heat pressing down like a physical weight. Sweat trickled down Devon's back, though whether from temperature or stress, he couldn't tell.

"How do you know all this?" Bryson asked. "If it's an active federal investigation—"

"I shouldn't know any of it," Gabe cut him off. "My father's never confirmed anything directly. He can't—he's bound by the investigation. But after Olivia had her first miscarriage and there was a mix-up with an insurance claim, my mother had a panic attack. I've never seen her so distraught. She's always been a pillar of strength. It freaked both me and Olivia out. That's when my dad sat me down and told me the whole sordid tale. All of it." He stopped pacing, turning to face them. "Olivia doesn't know. I've never lied to my wife before, but my dad and I came up with a story about how Olivia's loss affected her so deeply and oddly, that helped pull Olivia out of her emotional distress."

"Your dad took a big risk in telling you all that," Bryson said.

"Maybe, but at the time, he thought, who the hell was I gonna tell?" Gabe raised his palms toward the sky, then dropped them to his thighs. "How was my dad supposed to know that Emery would be publicly humiliated and then land a job here."

"Is that why you didn't want us to hire her?"

"Yes and no," Gabe admitted. "I was worried about the optics. That's true. But I also worried about the information I'm carrying that I definitely can't share."

"Emery desperately wants to believe her father's innocent," Devon said, his voice tight. "But he's always telling her to let the wheels of justice work. Could she know the feds are involved?"

"You know her better than I do," Gabe said. "But I doubt Michael would tell her anything, so I don't think so." Gabe met Devon's eyes. "Even if she did know, she couldn't talk about it. *I* shouldn't even be talking about. If my dad knew, he'd flip."

"So, when that article mentioned her father's scandal..." Devon felt sick.

"It referenced real accusations, real allegations. The federal investigation is public record—anyone can look up that Michael Tate is under investigation for insurance fraud." Gabe planted his hands on his hips. "What's not public is that he might be innocent. That he's helping federal prosecutors catch the real criminals. That he might have been framed to protect whoever's actually guilty."

"And that's information that can't get out," Bryson said.

"Not without destroying two years of investigation. Not without potentially letting the real criminals walk free. Not without exposing every cooperating witness—including my mother—to retaliation or legal jeopardy." Gabe's voice rose. "Do you understand what I'm saying?

The truth that could vindicate Emery's father and restore his reputation—that truth is locked away in a federal case that might not conclude for years—and it seems, based on my conversation with Winston, that he might be digging where he shouldn't , use it as leverage to keep me from making a claim while that clock ticks down for the next three months."

The magnitude of it settled over Devon like suffocating smoke.

"Your mother," Devon said. "If this case goes to trial..."

"She'll have to testify. So will my father." Gabe's voice cracked. "But if someone exposes their involvement before the case is ready, if details leak that compromise the investigation, the whole thing could fall apart. The real perpetrators could walk free with the best lawyer's money can buy, and everyone who cooperated—including my mother, including Michael—could still face charges for their unwitting involvement because prosecutors can't prove their innocence without the full case."

"Jesus, this is a lot to take in," Bryson said.

"You're telling me. Federal witnesses in an active investigation—they're all bound by secrecy. One wrong word to the wrong person, one detail that gets back to defense attorneys or the press, and years of careful work collapses." Gabe looked between them desperately. "I'm already betraying my parents' trust by telling you this much. If they knew, if federal prosecutors discovered information leaked..."

Devon's phone buzzed in his pocket. He pulled it out, saw Emery's name on the screen, and felt his chest tighten.

Emery: *Good morning. You snuck out of bed early. Coffee?*

Such a simple text. Such ordinary normalcy. She had no idea of the size and ferocity of the storm gathering around her.

"What do you believe Winston knows based on what he implied?" Bryson asked quietly.

"I don't know. He was vague. Even his threats were vague, but he still launched them like a bottle rocket. Whatever he knows, whatever he thinks he knows—he's using it as leverage." Gabe's hands opened and closed at his sides, and he turned away to stare at the vineyard rows stretching toward the hills. His shoulders hunched forward as if he were hauling a sack of rocks. "At the funeral, he made it very clear he had information about Michael's case. Information that could destroy Emery's reputation even if her father is ultimately exonerated."

"Because the investigation is ongoing," Devon said, understanding dawning cold and terrible. "Even if Michael's innocent, even if he's cooperating with the feds to catch the real criminals, publicly it looks like he's under investigation for fraud. That's what Winston can use—the appearance of guilt while the truth is locked away in a federal case that might not conclude for years."

"Exactly." Gabe's voice dropped to barely above a whisper, and he looked away toward the distant hills. His jaw worked like he was grinding his teeth. "That article that came out about Emery, the piece about her dad was a side note. It focused more on her and what happened with Harold, and the fact she might be sleeping with her new boss. No one is talking about her dad. But if Winston spreads that around the valley, tells collectors and auction houses that Emery's father is being investigated for federal fraud charges, that the case is ongoing and serious..."

"It destroys her credibility before she even has a chance to build it," Bryson finished. "No one will want to work with her. No one will trust her authentication. Everything we're trying to build with the premium wine program—it all collapses under the weight of her father's apparent guilt."

"So, Winston believes you're his brother. He tries to buy you off, because everyone knows you don't want those guns, and he threatens you with what might happen to Emery because if she goes down, so will Stone Bridge Winery, and he knows your loyalty lies with this family." None of this should surprise Devon. Both Winston and Callie grew up believing they were better than everyone. As kids, both of them thought the people around them should bend to their will because of who their father was and what their family meant to this Valley. "That's a pretty convoluted plan, and it means he's had to have known about a sibling long before the reading of that will, because this isn't something you just slap into place."

The three of them stood in the vineyard, trapped in an impossible situation.

Devon's phone buzzed again.

Emery: *Everything okay? You didn't respond to my last text.*

He stared at the message, his mind reeling. How did he answer this? How did he look her in the eye knowing her father might be innocent but unable to say so without destroying a federal investigation?

"There's something else," Gabe said quietly. "Something that's been bothering me since Winston's warning."

"How could there be more?" Devon looked up.

"Not more, but a question. How does Winston know any of this? And what exactly does he know, because some things aren't public record." Gabe's hands curled into fists, then released, then curled again—a rhythm that matched his quickening breath. "This information isn't just confidential—an active federal investigation seals it—that's not information you can just Google or hear through valley gossip."

"So, either Winston has connections to federal prosecutors," Bryson said slowly.

"Or someone with inside knowledge is feeding him information," Devon finished, ice flooding his veins.

"He could've hired a private investigator." Gabe met Devon's gaze. "But I have to ask myself why. Because if I'm the heir named in this will —which honestly I struggle with, given the timing of that—let's say it's true. Why come to Emery to get me out of the picture? Why not just ruin me?" Gabe held up his hand when Devon opened his mouth. "Harold has never had an issue with a forged vintage. Never. And while I don't know Emery well, I've spent a full week working with her. Watching her. She's even more detail-oriented than I am, and that's hard to do."

"We thought maybe the break-in had something to do with her dad," Devon said. "But everything you're saying changes my perspective on that. However, she's still being targeted."

"I wonder if Gabe does exactly what Winston wants, if the attacks on Emery stop?"

The implications were staggering. This wasn't just Winston being vindictive or competitive. This wasn't small-town gossip or business rivalry. This had turned into something entirely different.

"We're forgetting one thing," Devon said. "This all started when Harold fired her. What does that have to do with Gabe possibly being a long-lost son to David? And how could Winston know we'd hire her? I literally came up with that idea sitting in the bar while she got hammered."

"Could be Winston taking advantage of a situation that landed in his lap," Bryson said.

"Maybe, but that would mean there's still someone else out there who wants to destroy Emery. And that means we're dealing with two separate problems." Gabe ran his fingers through his hair. "I'm not buying that."

"Yeah, me neither," Bryson said.

Devon turned and faced the direction of the main house. All he could see was a portion of the rooftop in the distance. "I can't lie to the first woman I've actually got real feelings for. It will ruin this before it ever had a chance."

"What truth are you suggesting we tell her?" Gabe's voice rose like a high-pitched teenage boy. "That her father's working with the feds? That I could be an heir to something I want nothing to do with and she's being used as a pawn to keep me away?"

"She deserves to know someone's using her father's case against her," Devon said, his voice firm despite the chaos in his mind. "And that she's being used to manipulate you."

"You're putting me in an impossible situation." Gabe's breath came faster, and he took a step back, one hand rising to grip the back of his neck. His gaze darted between Devon and Bryson like he was looking for an escape route. "I'm already betraying my parents' trust by telling you this much.

If it gets back to them, if federal prosecutors find out information leaked about their witnesses..."

"We won't tell her how we know," Devon promised. "But we have to warn her. She needs to be prepared. This affects her too, and I seriously can't lie to her."

"There's no good outcome in telling Emery anything. Either we stay silent and do the best we can to deal with whatever is tossed at us, and her, or we speak up and potentially destroy the federal case that might eventually clear her father's name and protect my mother."

The impossible choice hung between them like a guillotine blade.

Devon looked down at his phone, at Emery's increasingly worried messages, and felt something break in his chest. He was falling in love with this woman. And now he was holding information that could either save her or destroy everything, and he had no idea which path would do which.

"I need to know something," Devon said, looking up at Gabe. "Your dad, he knows Michael is innocent, right?"

"One hundred percent," Gabe said.

Devon's phone buzzed one more time.

Emery: *I'm coming to find you. Something's wrong, I can feel it.*

"She's coming here," Devon said, looking up sharply. "We need to decide right now what we're telling her."

"Nothing," Gabe said immediately, his voice firm. "Not until I speak with my dad and maybe not even then. I think we need to understand how Winston got access to sealed federal investigation details."

"She deserves—"

"She deserves to have her father's innocence proven in court, not compromised by premature disclosure," Gabe interrupted, his expression fierce. "This isn't just about me and my family. This case is massive. I could care less about my reputation, but I do care about my mom, about this winery, and about Emery. We need to play this smart."

"We need to at least need tell my dad," Devon said, succumbing to the fact he was going to lie to his girlfriend.

"I can live with that, but let's do it after I've spoken to my father." Gabe's voice cracked slightly on the last word, and he looked between them with wide eyes. His hand moved toward his phone pocket, then stopped halfway, fingers trembling. "I'll call him on my way back to my office."

They stood in tense silence, the weight of secrets pressing down like a physical force. Near the break in the vineyard rows, Devon could see a figure approaching across the vineyard—Emery, moving quickly between the rows, her expression concerned even from this distance.

She had no idea she'd walked right into a trap that had been set two years ago—only the jaws hadn't snapped shut yet.

And the worst part? Devon had no idea how to save her without potentially destroying the very thing that might prove her father innocent.

The woman he loved was being hunted with weapons she couldn't see, attacked with truths she couldn't speak, and defended by a federal case she didn't even know existed.

And he was standing here, holding pieces of information that could either save her or condemn everyone involved, with no clear path forward.

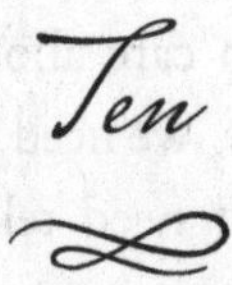

Ten

The Boone family room sprawled across the back of the main house like an invitation to relax. Oversized leather sofas faced a stone fireplace tall enough for Emery to stand inside, and floor-to-ceiling windows overlooked the vineyard beyond. Afternoon sunlight poured through the glass, warming the hardwood floors with a honied glow and catching dust motes that drifted like lazy snowflakes.

It was the kind of space that made you want to kick off your shoes and stay awhile. The kind of place where family gathered, where roots ran deep, where people belonged. Emery wanted that—wanted to sink into this warmth, to trust it, to believe she could be part of something like this. But her father's shadow followed her everywhere, and her own scandal sat like a stone in her chest. How could she let herself belong here when everything she touched seemed to crumble?

Emery perched on the edge of a sofa, Riley's tablet balanced on her knees, while the Boone women arranged themselves around her in a protective circle. Brea claimed the armchair nearest the fireplace, her reading glasses perched on her nose as she reviewed notes. Riley sat beside Emery, occasionally reaching over to swipe through documents. Ashley sprawled on the floor, her back against the ottoman, legs stretched out as if she owned the place. Hasley had claimed the window seat, one knee pulled to her chest, wine glass in hand, despite the early hour.

"Okay," Riley said, tapping her tablet. "Let's run through the key talking points one more time. Your background in art history and chemistry, how that led to wine authentication, your qualifications—"

"She doesn't need to recite her resume," Brea interrupted, looking up from her notes. "The reporter already has all that information. What she needs is to be human."

"Being prepared is being human," Riley protested.

"Being prepared is being robotic." Brea set her papers aside with a delicate touch. She was regal for a woman barely approaching sixty, yet remarkably down-to-earth. It was a contradiction that made her both unique and fascinating. "Emery, sweetheart, have you ever watched a political debate where the candidate answers every question with talking points?"

"Yes?" The word came out hesitantly, but understanding dawned as soon as she said it. Those debates were painful to watch—all performance, no substance. Brea was telling her not to be that. To be herself, messy and imperfect and real.

"Boring as hell, right? Makes you want to throw something at the TV." Brea leaned forward, her eyes danced with mischief. "That's what happens when you're too politically correct, too careful, too focused on saying the right thing instead of the true thing."

"Mom—" Ashley started. "You're insulting Riley."

"Let me finish." Brea waved her hand. "Riley, you're brilliant at this social media stuff, and I agree with most of your strategy. But dancing around certain topics, answering questions by being vague or pivoting to safer subjects—that only adds fuel to a fire the whole town is already speculating about. We can't stop gossip, but like you always say, we can control the narrative.

Emery sat frozen, absorbing every word. They were so sure—Brea, Ashley, Riley—like this was just another problem to solve. Like Emery's reputation could actually be salvaged. She wanted to believe them. God, she wanted to sink into their confidence and let it carry her. But they didn't understand what it was like to be her right now. To have every mistake catalogued online, every relationship dissected, her father's crimes attached to her name like a brand she couldn't scrub off. Being "authentic" sounded lovely in theory. But what if authentic wasn't enough? What if the real Emery was exactly as disappointing as everyone already thought?

Riley leaned back, fingers resting on the side of the tablet. "Yes, but we don't want to feed the beast. The relationship angle is sensitive."

The relationship. Right. Because that's what everyone would focus on—not her credentials, not the authentication process, but who she was sleeping with. Emery's stomach twisted. She'd worked her entire career to be taken seriously, and now she was about to do an interview where her relationship with Devon would be the headline. Again.

It didn't matter that what she felt for him was real, that he made her feel safe in a way she'd never experienced. All anyone would see was another scandal.

"It's only sensitive if we act like it is." Brea's voice was firm but not unkind. "Listen, future daughter-in-law—"

Riley's face flushed. "I'm not—we're not—"

"Oh, please." Brea's smile was so wide, and her light blue eyes sparkled in the sunlight. "It's only a matter of time before Bryson proposes. That boy's been carrying his grandmother's ring around in his pocket for two weeks. I know because I found it when I was doing his laundry."

"Since when doesn't he do his own laundry?" Riley asked.

"He brings it here sometimes after staying at your place for five days, and I just can't help myself." Brea shrugged. "Now, would you say no if he asked?"

Riley opened her mouth, closed it, then sighed. "You all know I wouldn't."

"Exactly. So, future daughter-in-law it is." Brea turned back to Emery. "My point is this—you're dating Devon. That's not a scandal. That's life. It's new, it's private, and it doesn't affect your employment any more than Riley's relationship affects hers, or the fact that family members run all major departments at this winery."

Emery's throat closed. She'd braced herself for judgment, for the subtle distance that came when families realized their son was involved with someone complicated. Someone damaged. But Brea wasn't pulling back—she was leaning in, reframing Emery's entire situation like it was nothing more than two people falling for each other. Like Emery was already part of this family, worth defending, worth normalizing. The acceptance of it—the fierce, unapologetic way Brea claimed her as Devon's—made Emery's eyes burn. She blinked hard, trying to hold it together.

"Except Gabe," Hasley added from the window seat. "But he's basically family at this point."

"Exactly." Brea tapped her perfectly polished nails against her slacks. "This is a family business. If the world wants to call out the Boones for mixing personal and professional, they'd have to call out half the valley. The Meadowbrook sisters run their place together. The Chen family at Red Oak has three generations working side by side. The Pattersons at Hillside View are all married to people they met through the business. And let's not forget the Callaways."

"That's actually a good angle," Riley admitted, making notes on her tablet. "If it's pushed as nepotism, we can frame it as industry standard rather than an exception."

"It's not an angle, it's the truth." Brea stood, moving to pour herself coffee from the carafe on the side table. "When this reporter asks about you and Devon—and she will ask—don't dodge it. Don't get defensive. Just own it. You're two adults who developed feelings for each other while working together. It happens. What matters is that you're both professionals who keep business separate from personal."

"Are we though?" Emery asked quietly. "Keeping them separate? Because right now it feels like everything's tangled together."

"Of course it's tangled," Brea said, returning to her chair with fresh coffee. "Life is tangled. Relationships are messy. Work bleeds into personal and personal bleeds into work, especially when you care about what you're doing and who you're doing it with." She settled back, cradling her mug. "The key is being honest about that while maintaining boundaries where it counts."

"Like what?" Emery felt like she was drowning in advice and strategy, all of it well-meaning but overwhelming.

"Like not letting your relationship influence authentication decisions," Ashley said from the floor. "If Devon brings you a wine and says it's legit, but your research shows it's questionable, you say so. That's the boundary."

"But having coffee together in the morning? Holding hands at the farmers' market? That's not crossing any lines." Hasley took a sip of her wine. "That's just being human."

"The town's going to talk no matter what you do," Brea added. "They talked when Riley came back. They talked when Ashley dated that sommelier from Meadowbrook. They talked when Hasley cut her hair short and started wearing blazers to wine events."

"Why did they talk about my hair?" Hasley asked. "That seems like a dumb thing to gossip about."

"Because you looked hot and it confused all the men who'd been hitting on you." Ashley grinned. "Best decision you ever made."

"Can we focus?" Riley tapped her tablet. "The interview is in less than an hour."

"We are focused." Brea's voice was gentle but firm. "We're making sure Emery understands that authenticity matters more than perfection. Sarah Martinez is a good reporter, but she's not looking for robots. She's looking for a story. Let's give her one, but one that we can be on board with."

"I'm not sure I like this," Emery said. "It feels like a game, and games can backfire."

"We're using the truth to our advantage instead of letting someone else distort it to make it something ugly." Brea met her eyes steadily. "You're a brilliant authenticator who got publicly humiliated by a mentor who threw you under the bus. You found a second chance with a family who values expertise over scandal. You're building something meaningful here, both professionally and personally. You're human, not perfect, and you're not apologizing for either."

"Sometimes, future mother-in-law, you're perfectly magnificent." Riley set her tablet aside. "Maybe you should be doing my job."

"Good heavens, no." Brea laughed. "I'll stick with fundraising, charities, and taking care of all of you."

Emery let Brea's words settle in her mind. She'd been so focused on saying the right things, avoiding the wrong topics, protecting everyone's reputations, that she'd forgotten the power of simple honesty. That hiding never did anyone any favors—except make them look guilty, and that brought her to another painful topic.

"What if she asks about my father?" The question came out smaller than Emery intended. She sat up taller. "Because I can't imagine they will let that one go unnoticed."

The room went quiet. Riley snagged her tablet, her fingers dancing across the screen. Ashley stopped playing with the ottoman's fringe. Even Hasley set down her wine glass.

"Battle everything with the truth. It's what Walter has always done," Brea said.

"But what if they ask the question that most people are afraid to ask?" Emery's heart pounded.

"And what's that?" Riley glanced up."

"If I believe my father's guilty of the crimes he's been accused of."

"That's an interesting question." Riley glanced between Emery and Brea. "There is that saying, *innocent until proven guilty in a court of law,* something to which I know a little bit about since my mother keeps tossing it around like confetti. When she's been asked, 'why'd you do it', or 'did you do it', she gives vague answers, like the truth will come out when I get my day in court. But when my siblings and I are asked, we all say the same thing."

"And what's that?" Emery asked.

"That we believe she put that poison in our father's coffee, handed it to Grant, and that led to our father dying. That she purposefully, and with intent, killed our dad. No question."

"Yeah, but people in this town always think something," Hasley said. "Unfortunately, not enough time has passed since Sean was murdered, and there are a few idiots who whisper that maybe it wasn't Elizabeth. That may be something else happened."

"It's ridiculous," Ashley added, "half the people talking probably have family members with secrets. Everyone's got something. The difference is whether you own it or let it own you."

"The problem is I don't know what to believe when it

comes to my father." Tears welled in Emery's eyes. She hated herself for even having one single doubt, but she had plenty. Her dad never once publicly defended himself. He had a team of lawyers, but all he said was that time would fix everything. And to her, that sounded like a guilty person. "If asked, I worry I'd stumble over the question, giving that reporter something to chew on, to twist and distort, and the next thing that would happen is my poor dad would be watching on YouTube how I think he's guilty."

Riley was typing furiously now. "Thing is, you can't comment on what you don't know, and we can use that. It's an ongoing investigation. Simple."

"Now, what about the Harold situation?" Emery asked. "We know that's going to keep coming up, and I'm honestly tired of dodging the question."

"What do you want to say about it?" Riley asked.

Emery thought about the humiliation, the betrayal, the three months of carrying shame for something she didn't do. "I want to say he's a lying snake who destroyed my career for—and that's the problem. I don't know why he did it."

"Perfect. Say that." Brea shrugged.

"Mom." Riley's voice rose. "You know she can't say that."

"Maybe not those words, but no reason she can't be honest." Brea smiled. "Emery didn't do it. And you called me mom."

"It just slipped out." Riley sighed. "Right now, we need Emery to sound professional, not vindictive."

"Why can't she be both?" Ashley asked. "Professional people can be righteously pissed when they're wronged.

Emery looked around the room at these women—Devon's mother, his sisters, his brother's girlfriend, who was practically family already. They were strong, opinionated, and unafraid to speak their minds. They weren't asking her to be perfect, polished, or politically correct.

They were asking her to be real.

"It sounds like I'm fighting back," Emery said quietly.

"I like it, but we should make sure Walter's on board," Riley said."

"He'll agree. I'll make sure of it." Brea's voice was warm with approval. "But we have to be smart. Don't sink to Harold's level. Don't make wild accusations you can't support. Just tell your truth and trust that people who matter will see it for what it is."

"And the people who don't?" Emery asked.

"Fuck them," Hasley said cheerfully.

"Language." Brea's tone held no real censure.

"What? You were thinking it." Hasley laughed.

"I was thinking it more diplomatically." Brea raised her coffee cup and sipped, with her pinky sticking out.

The room erupted in laughter, the tension breaking like a burst bubble. Emery felt something loosen in her chest—anxiety giving way to something that felt almost like confidence.

"Okay," Riley said, still smiling as she composed herself. "Let's go through a few more potential questions. I'll ask them like I'm the reporter." She cleared her throat. "Emery, what drew you to wine authentication specifically?"

"The intersection of art and science," Emery answered. "I've always been fascinated by provenance—how you trace an object's history, verify its authenticity, build a narrative from fragments of evidence. Wine authentication combines chemistry, art history, detective work, and storytelling. It's like solving a puzzle where the pieces span centuries."

"Perfect," Riley said, typing. "That's exactly the kind of answer that shows your passion and expertise. Now, what about—"

"Riley, sweetheart, she's got this." Brea interrupted gently. "Stop drilling her like she's preparing for a deposition. Let's talk about something else for a few minutes. Give her brain a rest."

"Oh, no. Don't. I beg of you." Riley set the tablet down. "I've known this family my entire life, and it was hard on me coming back in. Imagine how overwhelming it's going to be on her."

"Her is sitting in the room, and frankly, I'm getting a little tired of everyone speaking like I'm not here," Emery said, turning her attention to Brea. "Whatever you want to chat about, I'm good with."

"Let's discuss the fact that Devon's been staying at your place since the break-in." Hasley's grin was wicked. "How's that going?"

Emery felt her face heat. "It's... he's being protective."

"I'm sure he's being very protective," Ashley said, her tone suggestive. "And from the way you two look at each other, I'd say the protection is mutual—and hopefully being used, unless you want to beat Riley into parenthood."

"That's not funny," Riley said. "I can't even get your brother to understand all the hints I've been dropping since I learned about that engagement ring. If he doesn't do it soon, I might be the one dropping to one knee."

"Well, that's a revelation." Brea clasped her hands together and rubbed vigorously. "And while I'd love to sit and discuss that for hours, because you know I've got ideas, we were discussing Emery and Devon's... living situation."

"We're not living together. He's just staying there because of the break-in," Emery stammered.

"But you are dating and sharing a bed." Brea winked.

Emery opened her mouth, but absolutely nothing came out. She closed it then tried again. "Are you always this blunt?"

"It's my superpower," Brea said. "Biggest thing I've learned about being like that is blunt gets blunt back, and I value that. Sure, I've got some opinionated children because of it. But look at the kinds of partners they choose."

"Um, Bryson married Monica and Devon dated Callie," Ashley said. "Until recently, they've both had shit taste in women."

"We all make mistakes." Brea waved her hand like she shoved a bee out of the way. "A lot is going on right now, and some of it sucks. But you and Devon are good. It's new and exciting. Enjoy it while it lasts."

"That sounds ominous," Emery said.

"Not ominous. Realistic." Brea's smile was gentle. "The beginning of a relationship is intoxicating. Everything's heightened—the attraction, the connection, the feeling that you've found something special. Savor that. Because eventually it settles into something deeper but less dramatic. Still wonderful, just different. I don't want all this outside drama to take that away from you."

"Mom's being philosophical because she and Dad just

celebrated their anniversary," Hasley explained. "She gets nostalgic."

"I'm not nostalgic, I'm practical." Brea sipped her coffee. "I'm saying that right now, Emery and Devon are in the honeymoon phase. Everything feels urgent and intense. That's normal. But it doesn't mean it's not real."

"How do you know the difference?" Emery asked before she could stop herself.

"Between infatuation and love?" Brea considered the question. "Time, mostly. Infatuation burns hot and fast. Love builds slowly and lasts. But here's the thing—every lasting love starts with infatuation. You can't skip that part. You just have to be willing to see what's underneath once the intensity fades."

"That's actually kind of beautiful, Mom," Ashley said.

"I have my moments." Brea looked at Emery. "My son cares about you. I can see it in how he looks at you, how he talks about you when you're not around. Whether that becomes something lasting—that's for you two to figure out. But don't let fear or doubt or other people's opinions rob you of that exploration."

"Easier said than done." Emery smiled, even if her insides were rolling around like they were tossed out on the ocean in a dinghy during a Category 5 hurricane.

Brea set down her coffee mug. "Now, let's talk about something important. Have you thought about what you're wearing for this interview? Because I have a closet full of clothes for special occasions. You know, like when you want to destroy someone."

"You should've seen the dress Mom lent to Riley for the

garden party." Hasley twisted her hair. "Monica's jaw was on the floor."

Emery glanced down at her outfit. A modest top. Cream, not white. It didn't cover her neck, but it wasn't revealing. And a pair of slacks. Very professional. "I was just going to wear this?"

"Absolutely not." Hasley stood from the window seat. "You're wearing black pants and a cream sweater. You look like you're going to a funeral."

"What's wrong with cream?"

"It washes you out," Ashley said. "You need color. Richness. Something that says, 'I'm confident and professional' without looking like a corporate clone."

"I have a burgundy blouse in the guesthouse—"

"Burgundy says wine industry without being too on the nose. And it'll look great on camera, but I think that cabernet colored blouse I just bought last week and my dark skirt with the slit would look stunning."

"Oh, I totally agree. And the lighting in here would catch the colors perfectly," Riley said.

"I'll go snag them and bring them to the bathroom down here." Hasley jumped to her feet and raced off.

Emery could hear male voices from the den down the hall—Devon, Bryson, Walter, probably Gabe. They were being kept separate intentionally, Riley had explained, so that the women could prepare Emery without male opinions cluttering the strategy.

"You're going to do great," Riley said, reaching over to squeeze Emery's hand. "I know this feels overwhelming, but you're stronger than you think."

"I hope you're right."

The doorbell chimed, echoing through the house.

"That'll be Sarah," Riley said, checking her watch. "Right on time."

Emery felt her stomach drop. This was it. The interview would either help rebuild her reputation or cement her as the woman from the scandal.

"Breathe," Ashley said, standing and offering her hand. "You've got this."

"Remember," Brea added, "authenticity over perfection—truth over polish. And if in doubt, just be yourself. That's more than enough."

Hasley appeared with the new outfit. "Quick change in the powder room, then showtime."

Shaking, Emery took the clothing and headed for the hallway bathroom. In the mirror, she saw a woman who looked terrified and determined in equal measure. A woman who'd been knocked down but hadn't stayed down. A woman who was tired of hiding and ready to fight back.

She changed quickly, smoothed her hair, and took one last steadying breath.

Then she walked back to the family room to face whatever came next.

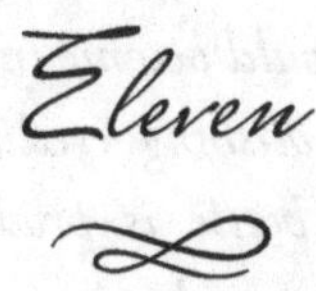

Eleven

The den felt smaller than usual with four grown men crammed around the flatscreen monitor Walter had set up on his desk. Devon stood closest to the screen, arms crossed, every muscle tense as he watched Emery sit composed and professional across from Sarah Martinez in the family room, one wall away.

The recording had started twenty minutes ago, and so far, Emery was handling herself beautifully. Poised but not stiff, honest but not oversharing, exactly the balance his mother and Riley had coached her toward.

"She's good at this," Bryson murmured from Devon's left. "Natural."

"Better than I'd be," Gabe added quietly from the leather chair behind them. "I'd have stumbled over the first question."

Walter said nothing, but Devon caught his father nodding in approval as Emery explained her authentication methodology, with a passion that lit up her entire face.

On screen, Sarah leaned forward with interest. *"So, your*

work at Stone Bridge involves not just authenticating current vintages, but building documentation for potential collector pieces?"

"Exactly. We're creating comprehensive provenance records for wines that could become investment-quality in the future. It's about establishing credibility and traceability from the moment a bottle is produced." Emery's hands moved as she spoke, her enthusiasm evident. *"That level of documentation is rare in the industry, but it's what serious collectors demand."*

"And your personal relationship with Devon Boone—how do you maintain professional boundaries while working so closely with someone you're dating?"

Devon tensed, but Emery didn't flinch.

"The same way any professional couple does. We have clear delineations between work and personal time. If I'm authenticating a wine, my assessment is based solely on research and evidence, not on whose family produced it." She smiled slightly. *"Devon knows better than to try to influence my professional judgment. I'm particularly good at saying no."*

That earned a chuckle from Bryson. "She's got your number, brother."

"Shut up," Devon muttered, but he was smiling.

Sarah nodded, making notes. *"Let's talk about your father's situation. Michael Tate is currently under federal investigation for insurance fraud. How do you respond to critics who say questionable ethics run in your family?"*

Devon's hands clenched into fists. This was the question they'd all been dreading.

But Emery's expression remained calm, steady. *"My*

father's situation is a separate legal matter that's still under investigation. I can't legally comment on ongoing federal proceedings, but I can say that I have complete confidence in his integrity and in the judicial process. What I can comment on is my own work—I've never compromised my professional standards, and I never will."

"Damn," Walter breathed. "She's good."

"Riley trained her well," Bryson said with evident pride.

Sarah pressed forward. *"But given the appearance of impropriety in your father's case, and the scandal at Pemberton's Auction House, don't you think it's fair for people to question your judgment?"*

"I think it's fair for people to question anyone's work based on evidence and results." Emery's voice was firm but not defensive. *"What's not fair is conflating my father's investigation with my career, or assuming guilt by association. I didn't do what Harold Pemberton accused me of doing. I've never forged documentation or authenticated wines I knew were fraudulent."*

Devon felt pride surge through his chest. This was the first time she'd publicly denied the accusations. The first time she'd stood up and said clearly, definitively, that she was innocent.

"That's a strong statement," Sarah observed.

"It's the truth. I wish I understood why Harold did what he did—why he destroyed my career and reputation. But I know I didn't do what he accused me of, and I'm doing my best to move forward while hoping someday the full story comes to light."

"Perfect," Gabe murmured. "She owned it without making accusations she can't prove."

For several more minutes, the interview continued smoothly. Sarah asked about Stone Bridge's expansion plans, about Emery's vision for the authentication program, and about how she was settling into the valley. Emery answered each question with the kind of genuine enthusiasm that would make any viewer want to meet her, work with her, and believe in her.

Devon was just beginning to relax when Sarah's expression changed.

"I want to circle back to your role at Stone Bridge Winery for a moment," Sarah said, her tone shifting to something more pointed. *"Specifically, your authentication work on vintage bottles."*

"Of course," Emery said, though Devon caught the slight tension that entered her shoulders.

"I received some documentation from a source—documentation that raises questions about your methodology." Sarah pulled out a manila folder and extracted several pages. *"These appear to be authentication records for vintage wines in Stone Bridge's collection. The source claims you're fabricating provenance, making up historical details to inflate the value of ordinary bottles."*

The blood drained from Emery's face. *"What? That's—can I see those?"*

Sarah handed over the pages, and even on the monitor, Devon could see Emery's hands trembling as she reviewed them.

"These aren't mine," Emery said, her voice shaking. *"I mean, they are, but this documentation has been altered. I never—"*

"But they have your signature," Sarah pointed out. *"Your initials on each page. Your authentication stamp."*

"Then someone forged them, because I didn't create these." Emery looked up, her expression stricken. *"This is exactly what happened at Pemberton's. Someone created false documents with my signature to make it look like I approved fraudulent—"*

Devon was already moving. He burst through the door into the family room with Bryson and Gabe right behind him, all three of them clearly startling both Emery and Sarah.

"Stop the recording," Devon said, his voice tight with fury. "Stop it right now."

"Devon—" Emery started.

"Those documents are fake," Gabe said, already reaching for the pages in Emery's hands. "Let me see them."

Sarah looked between them, clearly thrown by the sudden interruption. "Gentlemen, we're in the middle of—"

"I know exactly what you're in the middle of, and it's character assassination based on fraudulent documents." Devon's voice was stern. "We need to see those papers. Now."

Walter appeared in the doorway—his expression carved from stone. "Sarah, I'm going to have to ask you to pause the recording. This is a serious accusation, and we need time to review the evidence before proceeding."

Gabe was already examining the pages, his expression growing darker with each one he reviewed. "These are forgeries. The formatting is wrong. The authentication codes are outdated because we changed our system three weeks ago. Emery couldn't have created these recently because we're not using this template anymore."

"How do you know?" Sarah asked.

"Because I'm Operations Manager. I oversee all documentation protocols." Gabe looked up, his jaw tight. "And I have copies of the actual authentication records Emery's been working on. They're in my office. Give me five minutes."

He was already heading for the door.

"Devon," Walter said quietly. "Call Sandy."

Devon pulled out his phone, his hands steadier than he felt. This was it—proof that someone was actively sabotaging Emery, creating false evidence to destroy her credibility. But who? He pulled up Sandy's contact information and tapped her personal phone number, knowing she was probably off-duty, or about to be.

Sandy answered on the second ring. "Kane."

"We need you at the main house. Now. Someone just tried to sabotage Emery during an interview with forged authentication documents."

"On my way." The line went dead.

In the family room, Brea had appeared with Riley, both women flanking Emery like protective guards. Emery looked pale, shaken, her hands still trembling as she stared at the forged documents. "The night of the break-in," Emery whispered. "I was working on these." She glanced up, catching Devon's gaze.

So, that's what the intruder was doing.

"Who gave you these?" Devon asked Sarah, keeping his voice level with effort.

"A source. Someone who claimed to have insider

knowledge about authentication fraud at Stone Bridge Winery." Sarah pulled out her phone. "I have the email chain if you want to see it."

"Please." Walter stepped forward

Sarah pulled up her email and scrolled to a thread with several messages. Devon leaned in to read, and his stomach dropped as he stared at the source's name.

"Gabriel Maxwell is your source?" Devon blinked, scrolling through the conversation, reading the words, but not really comprehending them.

"That's what the email says."

"What emails from me?" Gabe asked as he stepped through the doorway.

Devon held out the phone.

"That's not from me," Gabe said, tucking several folders under his arm. "I never sent those emails."

"But it has your name," Sarah said, confusion evident. "Your email address—gmaxwell.stonebridgewinery@gmail.com."

"That's not my email," Gabe said flatly. "My work email is gmaxwell@stonebridgewinery.com. I don't have a Gmail account. My wife does, but that's in her name. Someone must have created a fake account using my name."

He spread the folders on the coffee table, pulling out authentication records with Emery's actual signature and comparing them to the forged documents. Even to Devon's untrained eye, the differences were noticeable—different paper stock, different formatting, subtle variations in the signature.

"These are the real authentication records," Gabe said, pointing to his documents. "Note the watermark on the paper—Stone Bridge custom stock. Note the authentication codes in accordance with our new protocol. And here —" he pointed to Emery's signature, "—the real signature has a distinctive loop in the 'y' that the forgeries are missing."

Sarah stared at the documents, her professional composure cracking. "I don't understand. Why would someone set me up like this?"

"Correction. Someone set up Emery. You're just the delivery person," Devon said.

The doorbell rang, and moments later, Sandy appeared in the family room, still in uniform, her expression all business.

"Someone want to tell me what's going on?" she asked.

Devon gestured to the documents spread across the coffee table. "Someone created forged authentication records with Emery's signature, then sent them to Sarah Martinez, claiming Emery was fabricating provenance for Stone Bridge wines. They used a fake email account with Gabe's name to make it look like he was the whistleblower."

Sandy pulled on gloves and began examining the documents without touching them directly. "Who had access to Emery's signature? Her authentication stamp?"

"Me, Bryson, Devon, and Walter," Gabe said. "We keep records in a shared filing system. The authentication records are duplicated. I always have a copy in the production facility, and Walter keeps a copy in the home office."

"I moved my stamp," Emery said quietly. "It's locked in a cabinet. I did that after the break-in."

"Smart," Sandy said. "But someone could have copied it before then."

"These documents were in the guesthouse the night of the break-in," Devon said.

Sandy turned to Sarah. "I'm going to need those emails. All of them. And any other communication you've had with this supposed source."

"Of course." Sarah was already forwarding everything to Sandy's email. "I should have verified the source more thoroughly. I just—the documentation looked legitimate. Professional. And the source claimed to have worked closely with Ms. Tate."

"How and when did they contact you initially?" Sandy asked.

Sarah scrolled through her emails. "Three days ago. Said they had information about fraud at Stone Bridge Winery, that they couldn't stay silent anymore after watching authentication records being fabricated. They sent samples of the forged documents to prove they had access."

"And you didn't think to call us first?" Walter's voice was calm but carried an edge.

"I was trying to protect my source and get the full story before approaching you," Sarah admitted. "In hindsight, that was a mistake."

"In hindsight, you almost destroyed an innocent woman's reputation," Bryson said.

Sandy held up a hand. "We'll sort this out. Sarah, I'm going to need you to forward any future communications from this person directly to me. Don't respond, don't engage, just forward."

"What if they don't reach out again?" Sarah asked.

"They will," Sandy said grimly. "Because when you

don't publish those forged documents, they're going to want to know why. That's when we catch them."

"Are you going to finish the interview?" Brea asked.

Sarah looked at Emery, genuine regret in her expression. "If you're willing. We can edit out the section on the forged documents and keep everything else. You handled yourself beautifully before that ambush."

Emery was quiet for a long moment, looking down at the forged documents that bore her signature but not her work. When she looked up, her jaw was set, her spine straightening as she squared her shoulders.

"Yes. Let's finish it. But I want to say something first, on the record."

"Okay," Sarah said slowly.

"Someone is actively trying to destroy my reputation and career. This isn't paranoia or defensiveness—it's fact. Someone created forged documents, used a fake email to impersonate a Stone Bridge Winery employee, and attempted to use a respected journalist to spread lies about my work." Emery's voice rang steady and strong. "I don't know who's doing this or why. But I'm not running. I'm not hiding. And I'm not letting fear stop me from doing the work I love."

"That's good," Sarah said, already making notes. "That's really good. Can I use that?"

"Please do." Emery glanced toward Devon.

He smiled. What else could he do? She was the total package, and she'd stolen his heart.

They reset the interview, with Sarah asking follow-up questions about Stone Bridge's vision for the premium market and Emery's goals for the authentication program.

The earlier sections had been good, but this final portion was powerful—Emery speaking with the kind of conviction that came from having survived an attack and deciding to fight back.

When it finally ended, Sarah packed up her equipment, promising to send a link to the video for review before final production and to keep Sandy updated on any contact from the fake source.

After she left, the family room emptied quickly—Walter and Brea heading to the kitchen to start dinner preparations, Bryson and Riley disappearing toward the vineyard for a walk, Gabe returning to his office to document everything for the investigation.

Devon and Emery were left alone in the quiet family room, surrounded by the evidence of someone's attempt to destroy her.

"I'm okay," Emery said before he could ask. "Shaken, but okay."

"You were incredible." Devon closed the distance between them, pulling her into his arms. "The way you handled that, the way you stood up and said you weren't running—"

"I didn't have a choice." Her voice muffled against his chest. "Running hasn't worked. Hiding hasn't worked. Fighting back is all I have left."

"You have me." Devon pulled back enough to cup her face in his hands. "You have this family. You have people who believe you and will fight with you."

"I know." Tears gathered in her eyes but didn't fall. "That's the only reason I was able to do it. Knowing I wasn't alone."

He kissed her then, soft and careful—more promise than passion. When they pulled apart, Emery rested her forehead against his.

"Whoever's doing this," she said quietly, "they're not going to stop. The break-in, the articles, now this—it's escalating."

"I know." Devon felt cold certainty settle in his gut. "But we're going to find out who it is. And when we do, they're going to regret ever targeting you."

"Very protective caveman of you."

"I'm serious."

"So am I." She looked up at him, and despite everything, there was a hint of humor in her expression. "But I appreciate the sentiment."

They stood together in the fading afternoon light, holding each other while the evidence of someone's malice lay scattered across the coffee table. Somewhere out there, someone was watching, waiting, planning their next move.

But for now, in this moment, they had each other.

And that would have to be enough.

Twelve

The Copper Vine nightclub sat on the edge of Main Street like a beacon of normalcy in a week that had been anything but. Warm light spilled from its windows onto the sidewalk, and the sound of laughter and clinking glasses promised a few hours of forgetting about forged documents, federal investigations, and whoever was trying to destroy Emery's life.

Ashley pushed through the door ahead of her, immediately scanning the crowd with the practiced ease of someone who'd grown up in this town and knew everyone in it.

That thought amused Emery, considering she'd also grown up in this town. It wasn't that she'd felt like an outsider as a teenager, because she hadn't. It was more like she didn't know where she fit in. Her sister, while not wildly popular, had her group of friends. Emery spent her youth with her nose in a book and her body in the chemistry lab.

"Corner booth," Ashley said, already heading toward a

high-backed wooden seat near the bar. "Best view of the room, hardest to eavesdrop on."

Emery slid into the booth across from Ashley, grateful for the semi-privacy. Even here, she could feel eyes on her—curious stares, whispered conversations that stopped when she looked up. The interview had aired online this morning, and apparently, half the valley had watched it. She wasn't sure if that was a good or bad.

A man with a baseball cap leaned against the far railing. He glanced in her direction. He seemed to look past her, but something about the way his gaze glossed right over her made her insides jittery. She was in a room full of strangers in small-town America. Someone was bound to notice her. To figure out who she was. However, between his baseball cap—which didn't fit the vibe of the nightclub—his casual demeanor, and the fact he didn't appear to be chatting with anyone, set Emery's nerves on fire.

A server appeared at their table and Ashley ordered two margaritas. Not generally Emery's adult beverage of choice, but it would be a nice change of pace.

"So," Ashley said, leaning back against the booth with a satisfied smile. "How does it feel to be Stone Bridge's newest celebrity?"

"Terrifying." Emery pulled off her jacket. "People keep staring." The man with the baseball cap had moved to the corner. His brim covered his eyes, and she couldn't tell if he was looking at them, or at the two hot chicks, wearing next to nothing, standing near the far end of the bar looking like they might pounce on the first man who spoke to them.

"Let them. That interview was brilliant. You came across as smart, honest, and tough as hell." Ashley's eyes sparkled with mischief. "Plus, the way you called out whoever's targeting you? Chef's kiss. Bryson said he's had one call and two emails from people in the biz wanting to know more about our future plans."

"Devon told me, but I can't help and wonder if that's real, or idle curiosity?"

"I'd say it's people respect someone who fights back." Ashley paused as the waiter returned with their drinks, sliding oversized margaritas across the table. "Now, more importantly—I need your completely unbiased, outsider opinion on something."

"Okay?"

"What are the odds that Bryson asks Riley to marry him tonight?"

Emery smiled, grateful for a topic that had nothing to do with her and had a happy spin. "I don't know. Devon says he can't tell if Bryson is really that nervous, or if he's simply waiting for harvest to be over. It's not like she's going to say no."

"I know, right?" Ashley took a long sip of her drink. "Ever since Bryson divorced Monica, he overthinks everything. I get he wants it to be perfect and memorable. But it's only one part of the bigger picture, and he's gonna end up making a total ass of himself if he doesn't just do this thing."

Emery leaned forward, curling her fingers around the stem of her glass. Some of the week's tension eased from her shoulders. This was exactly what she needed—everyday conversation and the kind of friendship that didn't require constant crisis management.

"What about you?" Emery asked. "Any romantic

prospects on the horizon?"

"God, no. Stone Bridge men are either taken, related to me, or—" Ashley's words cut off abruptly, her gaze locked on something across the bar. She groaned. Loudly.

Emery turned to follow her line of sight. A man stood near the entrance, tall and dark-haired with the kind of confident posture that suggested he owned whatever room he walked into. He was handsome in an almost aggressive way—strong jaw, intense eyes, expensive clothes that somehow looked casual.

And he was staring directly at Ashley.

"Who's that?" Emery asked.

"No one." Ashley's voice had gone tight. "He's not important."

"Okay, but he's definitely checking you out."

"Ignore him." Ashley lifted her drink, but she didn't sip. She just stared into it as if it might magically transport her somewhere else.

"I can do that, but only if you tell me who he is, because he looks vaguely familiar."

"Ethan Blackwell." Ashley took a long drink. "And he needs to stop staring before I throw something at him."

"Blackwell? Like Blackwell Estates?"

"The same. His family owns the vineyard on the other side of our property." Ashley's fingers drummed against her glass. "They sold off most of their land years ago."

Emery watched Ethan navigate through the crowd, his gaze never leaving Ashley. "He doesn't look like nobody important. He looks like someone you have history with."

"We don't have history. We have... past unfortunate proximity."

"That's not a real phrase."

"It is now." Ashley drained half her margarita in one gulp. "Can we talk about something else?"

"Why? Because you can't stand him? Or do you have feelings for him?"

"Definitely the former."

"Then why can't you stop staring at him?"

Ashley's head snapped back to face Emery. "I'm not—"

"You absolutely are. And unless I'm reading this completely wrong, he's drooling over you too."

"He's not drooling. Ethan Blackwell doesn't drool over anyone. He's arrogant and insufferable and thinks he's God's gift to women."

"Is he?"

"What?"

"God's gift to women?" Emery hid her smile behind her glass. "Because from where I'm sitting, he looks pretty gifted."

Ashley made a sound somewhere between a laugh and a groan. "You're terrible. And no. Well—maybe. But that's not the point. The point is, he's never looked at me as anything other than Walter Boone's annoying daughter."

"He's looking at you now."

"Because he's shocked to see me here. We don't exactly run in the same circles, anymore."

"Why not?"

Ashley's expression turned complicated. "There's bad blood between our families. Pre-dates me and Ethan, goes back to our fathers. Ethan's dad claims my dad stole fifty acres from the Blackwell estate years ago, and that the loss of that land started their financial downward spiral. It's ancient history and probably not even true, but it's a well-fed grudge."

"That sounds dramatic."

"Welcome to Stone Bridge. We specialize in multi-generational feuds and wine." Ashley glanced toward Ethan again, then quickly away. "Besides, it doesn't matter. Ethan left two years ago. Just vanished without a word. I was..." She stopped herself. "It doesn't matter."

But Emery caught the hurt beneath the dismissal. "You had something with him."

"A summer fling. Nothing serious. Secret because of the family drama." Ashley's voice was casual, and she waved her hand around as if she didn't care. Only, the gesture proved she did. "Then he disappeared. No goodbye, no explanation. So yeah, I'm curious why he's back, but not curious enough to care."

"Liar."

"Shut up and drink your margarita."

Emery was about to press further when Ethan started moving toward their booth. Ashley's spine went rigid, her entire body shifting from relaxed to battle-ready.

"Ashley Boone." Ethan's voice was deep and warm, with an edge of amusement. "Still the prettiest girl in the valley."

"And you're...." Ashley's tone was cold as a glacier. "Still the biggest disappointment."

"Ouch." But he was smiling, unfazed by her hostility. "Mind if I join you ladies?"

"Yes," Ashley said.

Ethan slid into the booth next to Emery, his attention never leaving Ashley. "How have you been?"

"Wonderful. Thriving. Living my best life without you in it."

"That's good. You look great."

"I know." She flicked her hair over her shoulder and smiled as big and wide as she possibly could.

Emery covered her mouth. This was not a side of Ashley she'd ever seen before.

The tension between them made the air feel thin, harder to breathe. Emery suddenly felt like a spectator at a tennis match, her head turning between them as they volleyed barbs disguised as pleasantries.

"I should go," Emery said, recognizing a private conversation when she saw one forming. "Give you two a chance to catch up."

"Don't," Ashley said quickly, her eyes pleading.

"Stay," Ethan agreed. "I'd love to hear how you're settling into Stone Bridge. That interview was impressive."

"You watched it?" Emery asked.

"Everyone watched it. You're the talk of the valley." Ethan's smile appeared genuine. "Takes guts to stand up and fight back like that."

"Or stupidity," Emery said. "Jury's still out."

"No," Ashley said, her voice softening slightly. "It was brave. And it's working—people are talking about your strength, not your scandal."

"See?" Ethan gestured toward Ashley. "Even she agrees with me. That's how you know it's true because we don't agree on much."

"I can agree you're a pain in my ass," Ashley said.

"I have so much I could say to that." He lifted his hand and motioned to the waiter for a drink.

"But you won't, since my pointy heel is positioned nicely to do some serious damage."

He shifted in the booth.

Regardless of the banter, there was heat beneath the words, something electric and dangerous. Emery recognized chemistry when she saw it, and whatever was happening between Ashley and Ethan could power the entire valley.

"You know what?" Emery gave Ethan a little elbow. He allowed her out, helping her to her feet. She stood, grabbing her jacket. "I'm going to head home. Leave you two to your very intense non-agreement."

"Emery—" Ashley started.

"Enjoy the night. You deserve it." Emery smiled at them both. "And Ethan? It was nice meeting you—seeing you again. I assume we came in contact with each other in high school."

"Once or twice," he said. "Get home safely."

She left them staring at each other across the table, as if they were standing in the middle of the street, hands hovering over their weapons, waiting to see who got the first shot off. As she navigated her way through the maze of people, she looked for the stranger with the baseball cap, but he was nowhere to be found.

Outside, the October night had turned crisp, the kind of cold that promised winter wasn't far off. Emery pulled her jacket tighter and started down Main Street toward the vineyard. It was only a twenty-minute walk, and the fresh air felt good after the warmth of the bar.

She'd made it half a block when a voice stopped her.

"Well, well. The woman of the hour."

Emery turned to find Callie Callaway leaning against a storefront, arms crossed, expression venomous.

"That interview was quite something." Callie pushed off the wall and moved closer. "All that talk about integrity and fighting back. Very inspiring. Also very pathetic."

"I'm not doing this with you." Emery turned to continue walking.

"Running away? How predictable." Callie fell into step beside her. "But then, running is what you do best, isn't it? Running from scandal, running from questions, running into Devon's arms like that's going to save you."

"What do you want, Callie?"

"Just to offer some friendly advice. Woman to woman." Callie's smile was sharp. "Devon's not yours to keep."

Emery stopped walking. "Excuse me?"

"You heard me. Whatever you think you have with him, it's temporary. He'll get bored—he always does. A month, maybe two if you're lucky. I lasted six months, which makes me the record holder." Callie stepped closer, invading Emery's space. "So, enjoy it while it lasts. Because soon enough, he'll be done playing hero, and you'll be alone again, exactly where you started."

"You're wrong."

"Am I? Ask yourself—has Devon ever had a serious relationship? Ever committed to anyone for longer than a harvest?" Callie's voice turned syrupy sweet. "He's a good time—a fun distraction. But don't mistake kindness for love. He felt sorry for you that night at the bar, and now he's too nice to dump you while you're still a mess."

The words hit harder than Emery wanted to admit. Because Callie was right about one thing—Devon had never been in a serious relationship. Had never committed long-term to anyone. What if this was just him being kind? What if she was reading more into it than existed?

"Stay away from me," Emery said, her voice shaking with anger and uncertainty.

"Gladly. Just wanted to make sure you knew what you were dealing with." Callie smiled. "Enjoy your walk home. Alone. You're going to need to get used to that feeling." She sauntered off, leaving Emery standing on the sidewalk with doubt curling cold in her stomach.

Don't let her get in your head, Emery told herself. *She's trying to manipulate you.*

But knowing someone was trying to manipulate you and being immune to it were two very different things.

Emery crossed toward the intersection, her mind spinning. Devon cared about her—she knew he did. But could he love her? Would he stick around when the crisis passed, and she was just... normal? Ordinary?

Headlights blazed from her left, a car accelerating from a side street. Emery's head snapped up, her body frozen in that terrible moment of recognition—she was in the street, the car was coming fast, too fast.

She tried to move, tried to throw herself backward, but her feet tangled, and the car was already there, the bumper catching her hip and spinning her around.

She hit the pavement hard, her head cracking against asphalt, and the world exploded into stars and pain and darkness.

The last thing she heard was the sound of tires squealing and the smell of burning rubber.

Then nothing.

The hospital waiting room smelled like disinfectant and burnt coffee. Fluorescent lights hummed overhead, the pitch making Devon's teeth ache. He'd been pacing the same six-foot path for forty minutes, while Bryson sat hunched forward in a plastic chair, elbows on his knees, watching Devon's circuit with resigned patience.

"You're going to wear a hole in the floor," Bryson said.

"I don't care." Devon turned, retraced his steps, and turned again. He wiggled his fingers, shook his hands, made fists, and repeated the motions. "They said they'd come get me when she was done. That was an hour ago."

"It's been forty minutes. And they said stitches, X-rays, and a CT scan. That takes time."

"She was hit by a car. Hit and left in the street like—" His voice broke. He couldn't finish the sentence.

The call had come from Officer Chen thirty-five minutes after Devon had dropped Emery and his sister at the Copper Vine. Devon had broken every speed limit between the vineyard and Stone Bridge Memorial, Bryson white-knuckling the passenger seat and not saying a word about it.

They knew almost nothing. Hit by a car at the Main Street intersection. The driver didn't stop—a witness called 911. Emery was conscious when the ambulance got there but banged up.

That was it. That was all anyone would tell him.

The waiting room doors swung open, and Sandy Kane strode in. She wasn't wearing her traditional uniform, but she'd strapped on her badge and weapon. Her expression was hard—a look that Devon had grown tired of. "Any word?"

"Nothing yet." Devon stopped pacing long enough to face her. "Please tell me you caught whoever did this."

"I wish that were the case. But we've got a partial plate from a witness, and we're running it now." Sandy pulled out her notebook. "Deputy Chen was first on scene. He was able to speak with Emery before they loaded her into the ambulance."

"What did she say?" Devon's heart hammered against his ribs.

"That she didn't see the car until it was almost on top of her. Said she was distracted, crossing the street, and the headlights came out of nowhere." Sandy flipped a page. "The car didn't appear to swerve and clipped her. Could've been worse."

"I don't see how," Devon said, barely able to form the words as a thick lump formed in his throat. "She's getting a CT scan because someone hit her with a car and drove off, but it could've been worse."

"The witness—did they see anything else?" Bryson asked.

"Actually, yes. They saw Emery arguing with Callie Callaway about five minutes before the accident. Heated conversation on the sidewalk outside the Copper Vine."

Ice flooded Devon's veins. "Callie was there?"

"According to the witness. But it couldn't have been Callie driving. The witness saw her walk in the opposite direction several minutes before the car came through."

"Are you sure?" Devon asked.

"Positive. Multiple people saw Callie leave the area on

foot, heading toward her car, which was parked two blocks away." Sandy met his eyes. "I know what you're thinking, but Callie's plate numbers don't match the partial, and neither does the description of the vehicle."

Devon wanted to argue, wanted to insist that Callie was somehow involved, but the logic didn't track. Callie couldn't have driven a car at Emery if she was on foot two blocks away. "What about Winston?"

"I can ask where he was, but I've got no reason to go any further than that."

"What about the emails?" Bryson asked. "The fake ones using Gabe's name."

"I'm working on tracing the IP address. Should have something in a few days." Sandy closed her notebook. "I'd like to speak with Emery when she's feeling up to it. Follow up regarding the argument with Callie and what she remembers about the car."

"I'll let you know when she can talk," Devon said.

"Thanks. And Devon?" Her expression softened slightly. "I know this is scary. But we're going to find out who's doing this. All of it—the break-in, the forged documents, now this. Someone's going to make a mistake, and when they do, we'll catch them."

After Sandy left, Devon resumed pacing. The rational part of his brain knew she was right—investigations took time, evidence had to be gathered, cases needed to be built. It wasn't that long ago that this family was dealing with the murder of Sean and the subsequent setup of Grant. But the irrational part of his brain, the part that had watched Emery get publicly humiliated and targeted and now hit by a car, wanted immediate answers and immediate justice.

The waiting room doors burst open, again, and Ashley rushed in with Ethan Blackwell right behind her.

Devon's vision went red.

"Where is she?" Ashley asked, her face pale and eyes wet. "Is she okay?"

"Why the hell did you let her walk home alone?" Devon's voice came out harsh, accusatory. "You were supposed to be having a girls' night. You were supposed to be looking out for her."

Ashley flinched like he'd slapped her. "Devon—"

"And what the hell are you doing here?" Devon turned his fury on Ethan. While he'd never personally disliked the man, or the Blackwells, he struggled with how easily Ethan had disappeared from his sister's life. It hadn't been the same as when Riley had left. There was a reason for that, and as painful as it had been, there had also been a goodbye. "This is family business. You need to leave."

"I was too upset to drive, and—"

"I don't care if he sprouted wings and flew you here. I don't want him anywhere near this family." Devon stepped closer to Ethan, rage making his hands shake. "I knew about you and my sister two years ago. I know you strung her along all summer and then vanished without a word. I'll be damned if I'm going to stand here and watch you waltz back into her life and hurt her again."

"That's not what's happening," Ethan said, his voice calm but firm. "I just wanted to make sure Ashley got to the hospital safely."

"We could hear her crying for weeks after you left," Bryson added from his chair, his voice quiet but cutting.

"Family feud or not, that kind of shit isn't going to help you get on our good side."

Ethan looked at Ashley, something complicated passing between them. She gave a tiny nod, and he stepped back toward the door.

"Ashley," Devon said, his voice tight. "Your shirt is on inside out and backward."

Ashley's face flushed crimson. She glanced down at the tag clearly visible at her neckline, then back up at Devon with her chin raised defiantly. "That has nothing to do with what happened to Emery."

"Doesn't it? You were supposed to be watching out for her. Instead, you were—"

"Careful," Ashley interrupted, her voice sharp now. "Before you start judging my choices, remember that I've watched you date Callie Callaway. Twice. And we could start in on the long list of girls who worked the gift shop and then quit because you broke their hearts. So maybe we don't throw stones about poor dating decisions."

"That's different—"

"It's really not." Ashley crossed her arms. "And for the record, I didn't let Emery walk home alone. She insisted. How was I supposed to know someone would—" Her voice broke.

The fight drained out of Devon. His sister looked wrecked—mascara smudged, shirt inside out, guilt and fear written across her face. This wasn't her fault. He knew that. But he'd needed someone to blame, and she was standing right there.

"I'm sorry," he said roughly. "I just—if anything had happened to her?"

"I know." Ashley's voice was small. "I would've never forgiven myself. I should've walked with her. I should've—"

Devon's phone buzzed. Gabe's name lit up the screen.

"Yeah," Devon answered.

"I heard what happened." Gabe's voice was tight with concern. "Is Emery okay?"

"Don't know yet. Still waiting to see her."

"Jesus. Do you need anything? Want me to come down there?"

"No. We're okay for now." Devon rubbed his free hand over his face. "But thanks."

"There's something else," Gabe said. "I spoke to my dad. About everything—the federal case, Emery's father, all of it. He wants to come talk to everyone in person. Tomorrow. Says there are things we need to know."

Devon's stomach dropped. "What kind of things?"

"He wouldn't say over the phone. But he sounded serious. Said he's coming whether I want him to or not, so we might as well make it official."

"Okay. Tomorrow. We'll set something up at the house."

"Devon?" Gabe's voice softened. "She's going to be okay. Emery's tough."

"Yeah." Devon's throat was tight. "Call you tomorrow."

He hung up and sank into the chair beside Bryson. The adrenaline was fading, leaving behind exhaustion and bone-deep fear.

They sat in silence, Ashley collapsing into a chair across from them. The waiting room clock ticked loudly, each second stretching into eternity.

Finally, after what felt like hours, but was probably only

fifteen more minutes, a doctor in blue scrubs pushed through the doors.

"Family for Emery Tate?"

Devon was on his feet before the doctor finished the sentence. "That's me. How is she?"

"She's fine. Banged up, definitely going to be sore for a few days, but fine." The doctor—Dr. Montgomery, according to her name tag—smiled reassuringly. "The CT scan came back clear, no sign of head trauma beyond a mild concussion. No broken bones, but she's going to have some impressive bruising on her left hip and shoulder. We put eight stitches in a laceration on her forearm."

"Can I see her?"

"Absolutely. She's asking for you, actually." The doctor gestured toward the doors. "Follow me."

Devon looked back at Bryson and Ashley. "I'll text you."

"Tell her we love her," Ashley said, fresh tears spilling down her cheeks.

The doctor led him through a maze of hallways to a room near the end. She pushed open the door, and Devon's breath caught.

Emery sat propped up on a hospital bed, wearing a gown that swallowed her small frame. A bandage wrapped around her left forearm, and an angry bruise was already blooming across her cheek. Her hair was tangled, and she looked pale and exhausted.

But she was alive. Conscious. Looking at him with those green eyes that made his chest ache.

"Hi," she said, her voice rough.

"Hey." Devon crossed to her in three strides, his hands

hovering over her like he was afraid she'd break if he touched her. "Are you—can I—"

"Yes." She reached for him with her good arm. "Please."

He sat carefully on the edge of the bed and gathered her against him as gently as he could manage. She buried her face in his chest, and he felt her shoulders shake with silent sobs.

"I've got you," he murmured into her hair. "You're okay. You're safe."

"I'm sorry," she choked out. "I should've been paying attention. I should've—"

"Don't. Don't apologize for something you had no control over." Devon pulled back enough to cup her face in his hands, careful of the bruise. "This wasn't your fault."

"Callie said—" Emery stopped herself, fresh tears spilling over.

"What did Callie say?"

"That you'd get bored with me. That I was just a distraction. Someone you felt sorry for." Her voice was barely a whisper. "That you'd leave when I stopped being broken enough to need saving."

Fury and heartbreak warred in Devon's chest. "Look at me."

She met his eyes, and the vulnerability in hers nearly undid him.

"I'm not going to get bored with you. You're not a distraction or a project or someone I'm trying to save." Devon's thumbs traced her cheekbones, wiping away tears. "You're the woman I'm falling in love with. The woman I want to wake up next to every morning. The woman who's brave enough to stand up and fight when the whole world's trying to knock her down."

"You're falling in love with me?" Her eyes grew wide, but if he wasn't mistaken, her lips twitched into a tiny smile.

"Have been for months. Was too stubborn to admit it until you almost got—" He couldn't finish. Couldn't say the words.

"Killed," Emery finished quietly. "I almost got killed."

"I know." He rested his forehead against hers, careful of her injuries. "And I swear to God, we're going to find out who is doing this. We're going to stop them. But right now, all I care about is that you're here. That you're okay."

"I'm scared."

"Me too."

They sat like that for a long moment, foreheads pressed together, breathing in sync. The hospital sounds faded into background noise—distant beeps and footsteps and overhead pages. All that existed was this room, this moment, this woman in his arms.

"Devon?" Her voice was small.

"Yeah?"

"I think I'm falling in love with you, too."

His breath caught. "Really?"

"I am." She pulled back to look at him, a watery smile on her bruised face. "Even though you have terrible taste in past girlfriends and your mother is already planning our wedding and your sisters are exhausting."

"My sisters are definitely exhausting," he agreed, relief and joy flooding through him. "Anything else?"

"I'm starving."

"I'll get a snack, but I'm sure the second Elsa hears what happened, she'll be in early and staying late trying to nurse you back to health."

"Oh, Elsa's waffles and bacon. I could be down with that."

He laughed, the sound surprising him. How could he laugh when she'd just been hit by a car? But sitting here with her, acting like this was just another normal day at the winery while she looked at him with love in her eyes despite the fear—it felt right.

Devon was going to make sure that Emery didn't have to lift a finger for the next few days. And whoever was trying to destroy her was going to learn a tough lesson about what happened when you came after someone a Boone loved.

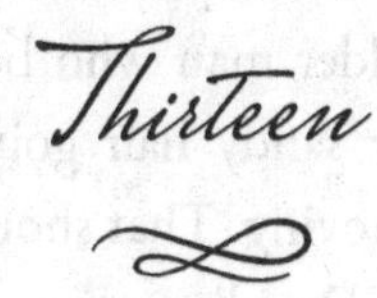

Thirteen

The guesthouse felt too quiet without Devon pacing around it. Emery shifted on the couch, trying to find a position that didn't make her bruised hip scream in protest. The TV played some mindless cooking show she wasn't really watching, but the background noise kept her from dwelling on the fact that someone had tried to kill her last night.

Or had they? Sandy seemed convinced it was a hit-and-run, an accident by a distracted or drunk driver who panicked. But the timing felt too convenient. The escalation too deliberate.

The door opened, and Emery looked up, expecting Devon to have forgotten his phone.

Instead, her father stood in the doorway.

Her dad looked older than he had just a month ago— more gray at his temples, deeper lines around his eyes. But his expression held the same gentle warmth that had defined her childhood, and seeing him now, in this moment when her world felt like it was crumbling, made her throat tighten with emotion.

"Dad?" Her voice came out small, uncertain.

"Hi, sweetheart." He stepped inside, and behind him came Gabe and an older man who bore a striking resemblance to him—same sandy hair going gray, same build, same careful way of moving. That should put an end to any rumors that Gabe was David's son.

Devon appeared last, closing the door behind them. He caught Emery's eye, gave her a look that said, 'trust me" then gestured to Gabe. "We'll give you some privacy."

Gabe and Devon slipped out through the patio doors, leaving Emery alone with her father and the stranger.

"I'm Robert Maxwell," the older man said, extending his hand. "Gabe's father. Your dad asked me to be here for legal reasons—what we're about to discuss is part of an active federal investigation."

Emery struggled to stand, her hip protesting the movement. Her father crossed to her immediately, helping her settle back onto the couch before taking the seat beside her.

"You're hurt," he said, his hand hovering near the bruise on her face but not quite touching. "Devon told me what happened."

"I'm okay. Banged up but okay." Emery looked between her father and Robert. "What's going on? I thought you couldn't talk about any of it."

Her father took a deep breath. "Under the circumstances, it's time you knew the truth. About the insurance fraud case, about why I ended up being fired, about all of it."

"Dad, you don't have to—"

"I do. You've been carrying the weight of my choices without understanding them. That's not fair to you." He glanced at Robert, who nodded. "Two years ago, I was approached by federal investigators about a massive insurance fraud operation. Multiple companies, millions of dollars in fake claims, a network of people all working together to defraud the system."

"I know all this," Emery said quietly.

"You know the public version. But what you don't know is that I was never part of the fraud. The real perpetrators set me up to take the fall." Her father's voice was steady, matter-of-fact. "By the time I realized what was happening, the evidence against me looked damning, but I had already started preparing for battle."

"The feds know you're innocent?"

"They do now. But two years ago, they weren't sure. That's when Robert got involved." Her father nodded toward Gabe's father. "He was brought in as a consultant, and he was the one who'd started finding the inconsistencies in the evidence against me. He was also the one who got the feds to examine the information I'd collected more closely."

Robert leaned forward. "The more I dug, the more I realized Michael had been framed. But here's where it gets complicated—the people who framed him weren't just after him. They'd also set up several lower-level employees at various insurance companies to look complicit. People who'd unknowingly signed off on fraudulent claims, whose authorization codes had been used without their knowledge."

"Like Gabe's mother," Emery's father said.

"Among others," Robert confirmed. "My wife was one of several people who would have been charged as accessories if the case had moved forward as originally structured. They were innocent—just doing their jobs—but on paper, they looked guilty."

"So, what happened?" Emery's chest hurt as she tried to suck in a deep breath. For two years, she wondered if her father—her hero—could've committed a crime. Could've been driven by greed.

Her father took her hand. "I made a deal with the prosecutors. I agreed to cooperate with their investigation, to help them build a case against the real perpetrators, in exchange for immunity for the employees who'd been set up. People like Robert's wife, who had no idea what was happening."

"You protected them," Emery said, her throat tight.

"I did what was right. Those people didn't deserve to have their lives destroyed." Her father's grip tightened on her hand. "But it meant living under suspicion. It meant letting people think I was guilty while the feds built their case. It meant watching you suffer because of accusations I couldn't publicly refute." Her father sighed. "I wanted to tell you so badly. Wanted to explain why I wasn't fighting back publicly. But I couldn't risk it."

Robert stood. "I should give you two some privacy. Michael, you have my number if you need anything. Emery, it was good to meet you, though I wish it were under better circumstances."

After he left, Emery and her father sat in silence. The TV still played in the background, some cheerful host explaining proper knife technique, utterly at odds with the weight of what she'd just learned.

"I thought you might be guilty," Emery admitted, the words painful to say aloud. "I tried not to believe it, but you wouldn't defend yourself, wouldn't explain, and I started to wonder."

"I know. And I'm sorry. I never wanted you to doubt me." Her father pulled her into a careful hug. "But I couldn't tell you the truth without putting you in an impossible position."

"When will it be over? When can you clear your name?"

"Soon. The feds are close to making arrests. Once the case goes to trial, the truth will come out." He pulled back to look at her. "But there's something else you need to know. The people who framed me—they're powerful, well-connected, and they don't want this case to go forward. They've been trying to discredit potential witnesses, intimidate people who might testify."

Cold understanding washed over Emery. "You think what's happening to me is connected to your case?"

"I don't know. But the timing is suspicious. You take a job that puts you in the public eye, and suddenly you're being targeted with forged documents and hit by a car?" Her father's expression was grim. "It could be a coincidence. Or it could be someone trying to get to me through you."

"That's terrifying."

"I know, which is why I'm here. I should have come sooner, should have warned you, but I thought keeping my distance would keep you safe." He took her hand again. "I was wrong. And I'm sorry."

Emery leaned against her father's shoulder, feeling like a

child again—small and scared and needing his protection. "I missed you."

"I missed you, too, sweetheart. So much." He stroked her hair. "Your mother sends her love. She wanted to come, but we thought it was better if I came alone first. Less conspicuous."

"How is she?"

"Worried about you. Proud of how you handled that interview. Furious at whoever hit you with a car." Her father's voice held a hint of humor. "You know your mother—she wanted to drive out here and hunt them down herself."

That surprised a laugh out of Emery. "That sounds like Mom."

They sat together as the afternoon light faded, talking about everything. Her mother's garden, her sister's kids, the small, mundane details that made up a life. It felt normal in a way nothing had felt normal in months.

Finally, as the sun dipped toward the hills, her father stood. "I should go. I'm staying at a hotel in town for a few days, in case you need me. But I don't want to overstay and put you at risk."

"I love you, Dad."

"I love you, too."

After he left, Emery sat alone in the gathering darkness, processing everything she'd learned. Her father was innocent. He'd sacrificed his reputation to protect innocent people. And now, someone might be targeting her because of it.

———

The den smelled like leather and old wood. The fireplace crackled quietly while Walter poured wine for the small gathering. Devon accepted a glass of Cabernet and settled into one of the wingback chairs, watching Gabe pace in front of the mantel like a caged animal.

Gabe's father, Robert, sat on the sofa with the kind of calm patience that suggested he'd spent years dealing with his son's nervous energy. Walter claimed the chair opposite Devon, his expression thoughtful as he observed Gabe's circuit.

And for some odd reason, the only thing Devon could think about was that Bryson and Riley were still not engaged.

"The floor's gonna remember your footsteps," Robert said mildly. "Sit down and tell me what's got you wound tighter than a jockstrap."

Gabe stopped pacing but didn't sit. He took a small sip of wine, set the glass down, and picked it up again. "My car was broken into yesterday."

"You reported it?" Robert asked as if it weren't a big deal.

"Of course. Sandy's looking into it." Gabe ran a hand through his hair. "But it's what was stolen that's bothering me. The gun collection—the one David left me. I'd been working with a museum curator, thanks to Emery's connections, and I had the guns in cases in my trunk. I had to run an errand for Olivia and left the car locked in the parking lot for about 20 minutes. When I came back, the trunk had been pried open, and the cases were gone."

Walter leaned forward. "When did this happen?"

"Yesterday afternoon. Before Emery was hit." Gabe's

expression darkened. "I know what you're thinking—that it's connected. But I can't figure out how—or why."

Devon's chest tightened. The guns were stolen hours before someone tried to run Emery down—that couldn't be a coincidence.

"We'll come back to that," Robert said. "What else is bothering you?"

Gabe pulled the worn photograph from his wallet and handed it to his father. "This. I need to know about this."

Robert studied the image, and to Devon's surprise, he chuckled. "Where did you find this old thing?"

"In a box in your attic when you asked me to help clean it. Mom's box." Gabe's brow furrowed. "Why did she keep it? Why keep a picture of her and David Callaway looking that... close?"

"Your mother loves pictures. Always has. She keeps everything—ticket stubs, postcards, photographs of people she hasn't seen in decades." Robert looked up at his son. "But I'm guessing that's not really what you're asking."

Gabe was quiet for a moment, his jaw working, his fingers flexing at his side. "This is going to sound crazy, and I mean no disrespect. But is there any possibility that I'm David Callaway's son?"

The room went very still.

Robert blinked once, twice, then dropped his head back and burst out laughing. The sound was so unexpected that Devon nearly dropped his wine glass.

Devon's gaze shifted between Gabe, his father, and back. One man, looking confused, conflicted, even scared. While the other laughed like he was sitting front row at a comedy show.

"Dad, this isn't funny," Gabe said, his cheeks blazing scarlet.

"I'm sorry, I'm sorry." Robert tried to compose himself, failed, laughed again, then finally cleared his throat. "I promise you—and I mean this with absolute certainty—you are not David Callaway's son. It's literally impossible."

"How can you be sure?"

"Because—" Robert stared into his drink. Humor gleaming from his eyes. He glanced at Walter and Devon, clearly amused, then back at his son. "Because one has to have sex to get pregnant, and your mother never slept with David."

Gabe's face went scarlet. "And you know this how?"

"I never thought I'd be having this conversation with my son." Robert took a large gulp. "Your mother's going to make me clean out the garage for sure after this one, but I know because your mom's first time was with me. I can assure you with 100% certainty that I am your biological father."

"Oh my God," Gabe muttered, sinking into a chair and covering his face with his hands. "I never needed to know that."

"Why would you even think such a thing?" Robert asked more gently.

Devon spoke up. "Winston cornered Gabe at David's funeral. Accused him of sending an anonymous photo and note claiming to know who the third heir is. Winston threatened him and offered to buy the gun collection for a substantial sum. He warned Gabe about Emery—mentioned her father—and mentioned taking us down, too."

Robert's expression turned thoughtful, the humor fading away like the afternoon sun. "A bribe to make him go away."

"That's what we thought," Gabe said, his voice muffled by his hands. "But now that you've thoroughly embarrassed me and confirmed I'm definitely not David's son—"

"Which I'm happy to do anytime," Robert interjected. "That is to embarrass you. But if Winston thinks it's Gabe, why steal the guns? That was his leverage. His way to buy Gabe off and make him go away quietly." Robert rubbed his jaw with his thumb and forefinger. "Unless he realized they weren't effective leverage. Maybe Winston's trying a different approach—remove the guns from the equation entirely, shift focus to discrediting Gabe through other means."

"But someone sent Winston that photograph," Gabe said. "Someone who wanted him to think I might be the heir. Who would do that?"

The room fell silent as everyone considered the question.

"The same person who sent forged documents to the reporter," Devon said slowly. "The same person who's been targeting Emery."

"Why target Emery if they think the heir is Gabe?" Walter asked. "That doesn't make much sense."

"Unless they don't think it's Gabe," Devon said, pieces clicking together in his mind like a puzzle magically putting itself in place. "Unless they're using Gabe as a distraction while they go after the real heir."

"Who would be?" Robert asked.

Devon moved to stand by the fireplace, his mind racing.

He lifted his wine glass and drained it before setting it down harder than he meant to. "Emery was born here in this valley. She told me her bio mother gave birth to her in Stone Bridge—it was a private adoption, so she doesn't know much about it. But she was born here."

"So were a lot of people," Bryson pointed out.

"She's the same age as the heir would be. The same age as Gabe." Devon turned to face them. "Someone wants her gone."

The room went absolutely silent. The only thing to be heard were their thoughts turning over and the wind rustling the vines.

Walter and Robert exchanged a long look. Bryson straightened from where he leaned against the bookshelf, his expression stunned. Gabe stared at Devon like he'd grown a second head.

"You think Emery is David Callaway's daughter," Walter said quietly.

"I think someone might believe she is. And they're doing everything they can to drive her away before anyone else figures it out." Devon's voice was steady despite the chaos in his mind. "Think about it—Harold fires her publicly. She gets blacklisted and has to leave Stone Bridge. But then we hire her, and she suddenly is being attacked from every angle. Forged documents, anonymous tips, a hit-and-run that could have killed her."

"Winston and Callie," Bryson said. "They're trying to eliminate the heir before the three-month deadline."

"Or at least make sure she leaves town and never stakes a claim," Robert added.

"But how would they know?" Gabe asked. "How would

Winston and Callie know Emery might be David's daughter when she doesn't even know herself?"

"When David had his heart attack last year, he felt his mortality. He could've told his kids about the sibling," Walter said grimly. "If I had hired someone to find the heir, and that investigator started digging into private adoptions in Stone Bridge thirty-three years ago, Emery's name might come up, private adoption or not."

"They would have had months to plan how to at least discredit her to the point that David might have second thoughts about naming a third heir," Bryson said. "David did struggle with his father's legacy."

"Harold is the key," Gabe said suddenly. "What if they paid Harold to set her up? To destroy her career and drive her away from the valley entirely?"

The pieces fit too well. Devon's stomach twisted into a tight knot.

"We need proof," Walter said, standing. "I'm calling Declan. He needs to know what we're thinking. This might change the way he investigates the situation. If anyone can connect all the dots, it's him."

"And I need to tell Emery," Devon said quietly.

"Tell her what?" Robert asked. "That you think she might be David Callaway's secret daughter? That Winston and Callie have been trying to destroy her professionally, personally, and possibly now kill her to protect their inheritance? You don't have proof. Just speculation. And that poor girl has been through enough. She's barely had any time to digest this information about her father. Piling more shit on her won't help."

"We should consider having a conversation with

Michael," Walter added. "See what he knows, match it to what Declan finds. Get facts before we say anything."

"She deserves to know," Devon argued. "Knowledge is power."

"She deserves the truth, not theories, especially with everything that's happened to her in the last few days," Walter countered. "Give it a few days. Let Declan work. Then we'll tell her everything we know for certain."

Devon wanted to argue, wanted to run to the guesthouse right now and tell Emery everything they'd just pieced together. But his father was right—without proof, this was just speculation. Dangerous, potentially devastating speculation.

"Fine," he said. "A few days. But the moment Declan has anything concrete—"

"You'll be the first to know," Walter promised. "And then you can be the one to tell Emery."

After Robert and Gabe left, Devon stood alone by the fireplace, staring into the flames. Somewhere out there, Winston and Callie Callaway might be plotting their next move against the woman Devon loved. A woman who had no idea she might be fighting for an inheritance she didn't even know existed.

And he had to stand here and keep that information from her while Declan investigated.

It felt like the worst kind of betrayal.

But it was also the only way to protect her until they knew the truth.

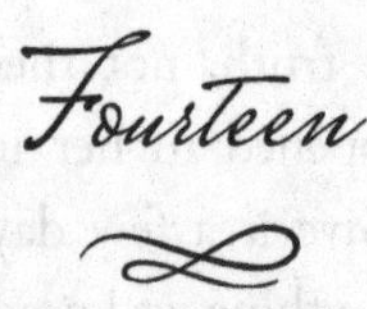

Fourteen

The production building hummed with the controlled chaos of late harvest—workers moving between fermentation tanks, the sweet-sharp smell of crushed grapes hanging heavy in the air, clipboard-wielding supervisors calling out updates on sugar levels and pH. Emery stood at a stainless-steel workstation with authentication records spread before her, trying to focus on provenance documentation while the activity swirled around her.

Gabe worked beside her, ostensibly reviewing her notes, but his attention kept drifting. He'd flip a page, stare at it without really seeing it, then flip back like he'd forgotten what he just read. His jaw was tight, his shoulders hunched, and he'd barely said three words since she'd arrived twenty minutes ago.

In a matter of twenty-four hours, the whole winery felt like—everyone was tense, conversations stopping when she walked into a room, concerned glances exchanged over her head like she was made of glass and might shatter if someone looked at her wrong.

Emery slapped her pen down on the counter. "Okay, what the hell is going on?"

Gabe's head snapped up. "What?"

"You. Everyone. The entire winery is walking around like someone died, and I'm taking it personally." She crossed her arms. "If this is about the hit-and-run, I'm fine. A few bruises don't make me an invalid."

"It's not that." Gabe set down the papers and rubbed his face. "I'm just stressed about the gun collection being stolen. Those guns were dangerous enough in locked cases. Now they're out there somewhere, in the hands of God knows who."

The explanation made sense, but something in his delivery felt off. Too rehearsed.

"Okay, I get that. But why is everyone treating me like I'm going to break?" Emery gestured toward the production floor, where two workers had been whispering, stopped mid-conversation when they saw her, and suddenly found something fascinating to inspect on the far side of the room. "People are avoiding me. Devon keeps hovering. Your dad looked like he was going to cry when he saw me yesterday—and he's the man with a sense of humor. What aren't you telling me?"

Gabe was quiet for a long moment. "It's probably just the combination of everything. Last of the harvest wrapping up—that's always stressful. Worry about your accident. And then there's Ethan Blackwell."

"What about him?"

"He left town two years ago. Defended someone accused of embezzlement, lost spectacularly, and it basically destroyed his reputation here—not that he had much of one, unless you did something that needed the kind of criminal lawyer that was known for either making decent plea deals, or winning." Gabe started stacking papers with too much precision. "He's been working as a criminal lawyer in San Diego ever since. No one knows why he's come back—though we all have ideas."

"And people think that's connected to me, how?"

"They don't. But there's speculation his return has to do with Riley's mother's case—that maybe he's here as part of her defense team or something. It's got people on edge." Gabe glanced up. "Especially Ashley, because she's in love with him, even if she thinks no one knows."

"Well, that explains a lot," Emery said, thinking of Ashley's combative behavior at the bar and the way she'd looked at Ethan like he was both salvation and damnation.

She gathered her papers and slid them into her portfolio. The harvest activity around them continued—the crush of grapes, the hiss of pneumatic presses, workers calling measurements back and forth. All of it normal, routine, the rhythm of wine production that had been happening in this valley for generations.

"I'm heading back to the guesthouse," Emery said. "Work on these authentication records somewhere quieter."

"Be careful," Gabe said, and the intensity in his voice made her pause.

"Careful of what?"

"Just... be aware of your surroundings. After the hit-and-run—" He stopped himself. "Just be careful."

Emery studied his face, seeing genuine concern beneath the stress. "Okay. I will."

She left through the main entrance, portfolio tucked

under her arm and took the path that cut through the vine-yard toward the guesthouse. The afternoon sun hung low and golden, painting the vine rows in warm light. Workers moved between the rows with harvest bins, their voices calling back and forth in a mixture of English and Spanish as they assessed the last blocks to be picked.

The vines, heavy with fruit, created a canopy overhead, leaves rustling in the breeze. Emery breathed in the earthy sweetness of late harvest—that particular scent of grapes at perfect ripeness mixed with sun-warmed soil and autumn air.

She was admiring a hefty cluster when movement caught her peripheral vision.

One of the workers—a man she didn't recognize—was running toward her. Full sprint. His face twisted with urgency. He shouted, but the words didn't register.

Emery opened her mouth to ask what was wrong.

He slammed into her like a linebacker, his arms wrapping around her torso as he drove them both to the ground.

A sound cracked through the air. Sharp. Distinct.

Pop! Pop!

They hit the dirt hard, Emery's portfolio flying from her grip, papers scattering. The worker covered her body with his, and she felt rather than heard his grunt of pain as another shot rang out.

"Stay down," he gasped in her ear. "Don't move."

Chaos erupted around them. Workers shouting, people running, someone screaming. The man on top of her—Jesus Christ, he was bleeding—his leg, she could feel hot wetness soaking through his jeans where it pressed against her side.

"You're shot," she said, her voice coming out strangled. "Oh God, you're shot."

"Better me than you," he managed, his breathing ragged.

Other workers flooded around them, creating a human shield. Someone was yelling into a phone—calling 911, calling for help. A woman knelt beside them, pressing her hands to the worker's leg, trying to stop the bleeding.

"The shots came from the production building," someone shouted. "The roof! I saw someone on the roof!"

"There!" Another voice, younger, pointing. "Running toward the access road!"

Two workers took off sprinting, chasing a shadow that disappeared into the tree line beyond the vineyard.

Then Devon was there, skidding to his knees beside her, his face drained of all color. "Emery, talk to me. Are you hit?"

"No. He—" She looked at the man who'd tackled her, who'd taken a bullet meant for her. "He saved me."

"Miguel." Devon gripped the man's shoulder. "Hang on. Ambulance is coming."

"I'm okay, boss." Miguel's smile was tight with pain. "Just my leg."

The sound of sirens wailed in the distance, growing closer. Emery's hands were shaking—no, her entire body was shaking. Someone had shot at her. *Actually* shot at her. And this stranger, this vineyard worker she'd never even spoken to, had seen it happening and thrown himself into the line of fire.

"Can you move?" Devon asked, his hands running over

her arms, her shoulders, and her legs. "Are you hurt anywhere?"

"I'm fine. I'm not hurt." But her voice didn't sound right, too high and thin. "Miguel's the one who's bleeding."

The ambulance tore up the vineyard road, followed by Sandy's patrol car. EMTs swarmed Miguel, assessing his wound, applying pressure, and loading him onto a gurney with efficient speed.

Sandy appeared at Emery's side. "I need you to tell me exactly what happened."

Emery's teeth chattered despite the warm afternoon. "I was walking. Miguel ran at me. Then gunshots. Two of them. He got hit covering me."

"Did you see the shooter?" Sandy asked.

"No. I didn't see anything until Miguel knocked me down."

"Witnesses say someone was on the production building roof. They jumped down and ran toward the access road," Sandy said into her radio, calling for backup, for additional units to search the property.

"Ms. Tate, I need to check you out." One of the EMTs —a young woman with kind eyes—knelt beside her. "Make sure you're not injured."

"I'm fine. Miguel's the one who needs help."

"They're already loading him. He's stable—bullet went through the fleshy part of his thigh, missed the femoral artery. He's going to be okay." The EMT started checking Emery's vitals anyway. "But you were in a hit-and-run two days ago. You're coming to the hospital to be examined."

"That's not necessary—"

"It absolutely is," Devon said, his voice leaving no room for argument. "You're getting checked out."

"Devon, I'm fine—"

"Someone just shot at you." His hands trembled as he helped her stand. "You're going to the hospital if I have to carry you there myself."

Sandy barked out orders, coordinating search teams. Workers clustered in groups, some still staring at the production building roof, others gathered around where Emery and Miguel had fallen. Her scattered authentication records lay in the dirt, a deputy was already collecting them with carefully gloved hands.

"This is an active crime scene, and we'll need to lock down the production building," Sandy announced to the gathered workers. "I need everyone to remain on the property. We'll be taking statements from each of you."

More patrol cars arrived, along with a second ambulance, and deputies spread out to search the buildings and the property. The ambulance doors stood open, Miguel already loaded inside, an IV in his arm and an EMT wrapping his leg wound with practiced efficiency.

"I'm riding with her," Devon told the EMTs, his tone making it clear this wasn't negotiable.

The female EMT nodded. "Fine. But we need to leave now."

Devon helped Emery into the ambulance, his hands gentle despite the urgency. She was still shaking, adrenaline and shock making her limbs feel disconnected from her body.

The ambulance doors closed, siren wailing to life as they pulled away from the vineyard. Through the back windows, Emery could see the production building growing smaller, police swarming the grounds, workers being directed into groups for questioning.

Someone had tried to kill her.

Not scare her, not intimidate her.

Kill her.

And if it weren't for Miguel's split-second decision to tackle her to the ground, they would have succeeded.

Devon took her hand, lacing their fingers together, his grip almost painful in its intensity.

"We're going to find them," he said, his voice low and fierce.

Emery wanted to believe him. Wanted to trust that the police and investigators and her protectors could keep her safe.

But right now, watching the vineyard disappear behind them while her would-be savior bled onto a gurney in another ambulance, all she could think was that someone wanted her dead badly enough to shoot at her in broad daylight.

And she still had no idea why.

The main house felt safer than the guesthouse, though Emery wasn't sure if that was actually true or just the illusion Devon needed to maintain his sanity. Either way, she'd agreed without argument when he'd insisted they stay there tonight, surrounded by family and solid walls and the kind of security that came from numbers.

Her father had arrived an hour ago, his face pale, when

he'd pulled her into a tight hug and whispered that he was sorry—so sorry this was happening. Then he'd disappeared into the den with Walter and Devon, the three of them speaking in low voices behind a closed door.

Emery sat curled on the oversized sofa in the family room, her head tilted sideways, hoping to catch a few words here and there, but it was hard over the crackle of the flames. She draped a blanket over her legs despite the warmth from the fireplace. Ashley sprawled in the armchair to her left, bare feet tucked under her, while Hasley claimed the window seat with a glass of wine that was probably her third, not that Emery was judging. She wasn't. Hasley's day had been long, and her evening not any better, considering her date had turned out to be a complete asshole.

But the girls had promised not to speak of that.

"I can't stop thinking about Miguel," Emery said, breaking the silence that the family seemed to bask in. "The way he just ran at me without hesitation and tackled me like he was willing to die for me. Who does that?"

"Someone braver than most," Ashley said. "I talked to his wife earlier. She said Miguel saw the glint of the rifle scope on the production building roof and didn't even think. Just moved."

"He took a bullet for me." Emery's voice cracked. "I've never met anyone so selfless. I consider myself a compassionate person. I have empathy. But I'm not sure I could do that."

"He's not a stranger anymore," Hasley said gently. "And he's going to be fine. He'll be back on his feet in a few weeks."

"With a hell of a story to tell," Ashley added. "And

probably a promotion. Dad's already talking about making him a crew supervisor. Not to mention we'll pick up any medical bills that insurance doesn't pay for, give him a few bonuses, and probably buy his wife a new car and donate to their family home addition."

"I'd donate my first paycheck to that." Emery pulled the blanket tighter. "I just can't believe Sandy dragged Gabe down to the station for questioning like he's a suspect."

"She has to follow procedure," Hasley said. "The gun was his—even if it had been stolen. The shots came from where he was working. She has to ask questions. Besides, maybe he saw something, but had no idea if it was important or not. Sandy picks up on that kind of stuff better than anyone. She always has."

"But he didn't do it. The idea that Gabe would take a shot at me is insane." Emery shook her head. "He's been nothing but kind since I got here. Helpful and patient and —there's no way."

"We know that," Ashley said. "Sandy knows that. But she still has to build a case, eliminate possibilities. Unfortunately, it's not the first time Gabe's been questioned. When he first came to work for us, Winston didn't like it. There was an incident with Callaway's harvest, and Winston pointed his crooked little finger at Gabe. He'll take it in stride."

"Will he? Because he looked pretty shaken when they took him."

"He'll be fine," Hasley assured her. "Sandy's fair. She'll clear him once she reviews everything."

The conversation drifted into easier territory—speculation about when the harvest would fully wrap, plans for the upcoming holiday season, and the elaborate Thanksgiving dinner Brea was already planning despite it being over a month away.

"So," Hasley said, her tone shifting to something playful as she turned her attention to Ashley. "Ethan Blackwell. Want to talk about it?"

Ashley's face turned hard. Her gaze narrowed and her jaw tightened. "There's nothing to talk about."

"That's not what our brothers say," Hasley said.

Ashley rolled her eyes. "Those two are morons."

"I'm offended on Devon's behalf," Emery said. "But I have to admit, I'm honestly more than curious about the history with Ethan."

"It's simple. He's my Monica. My Callie. My mistake." Ashley picked at the arm of the chair. "A really hot mistake that's good in bed, but still a mistake, and I can't forget that."

"Why?" Emery asked.

"Because he left once already, with no explanation, and he still hasn't given me one. That means he'll break my heart again." Ashley stared into her wine. "I know I'm young. I know I have plenty of time to find the right man, but I want to get married. Have kids. Jumping back into something with the likes of Ethan Blackwell would be stupid."

"Maybe he's changed," Hasley suggested.

"Maybe he hasn't. Maybe he's just here temporarily for whatever legal thing he's working on for the new big firm with law offices all over the state, and he'll leave again the second it's done." Ashley lifted her drink, tipped her head back, and gulped her wine like a shot of whiskey. "I can't do it. I won't."

"But you want to," Hasley said.

"Wanting something doesn't make it smart." Ashley sighed.

"No," Hasley agreed. "But it makes it worth considering. Life's too short to avoid things because they might hurt. Sometimes the risk is worth it."

"Says the woman who hasn't dated anyone seriously in three years," Ashley shot back without heat.

"Exactly. I'm living proof that playing it safe doesn't make you happy." Hasley raised her glass. "Take the risk, little sister. Or spend the rest of your life wondering what if."

The conversation shifted again, this time to Bryson and Riley. How long has he been carrying that ring? Whether tonight might finally be the night he popped the question—or if he'd put it off again because of everything that was going on.

"I give it another week," Ashley said. "He's overthinking it. Probably has seventeen backup plans, and we all know how sensitive Bryson can be. He's not going to do anything while this house is in turmoil."

"I hate that I'm responsible for that." Emery fiddled with the blanket.

"It's not just you. It's everything. But he should just do it," Hasley said. "Riley would say yes if he proposed in a parking lot. All this elaborate planning is just a little residual fear from years ago and maybe his marriage with Monica."

Emery listened, contributing when appropriate. But her body felt heavy, exhausted from adrenaline crash and fear and the constant strain of being a target. She stood, stretching her legs, needing to move before she fell asleep on the sofa." I'm going to grab some water," she said. "Anyone need anything?"

Both sisters shook their heads, already debating whether Bryson would stick with proposing at the tree or somewhere more elaborate.

Emery padded into the hallway, heading toward the kitchen. But voices from the den stopped her mid-step.

"I don't agree." That was Devon, his voice tense. "We need to tell her. I'm tired of keeping this from her."

"It's just a little while longer." Her father's voice was firm.

"The adoption records Declan found—they match the timeline exactly. Private adoption, sealed records, handled through a now-defunct agency that specialized in discretion," Devon said.

"Discretion or illegality?" Walter asked.

"Both, probably. The adoption was closed. And we have the paperwork, but we both knew it wasn't necessarily legal. We didn't have to jump through the same hoops as we did with her sister." Her father sighed. "But that doesn't prove anything. Just because the adoption was questionable doesn't mean Emery is David's daughter."

Emery's hand found the wall, steadying herself. Adoption records. Black market. David's daughter.

"The timeline fits," Devon said. "She was born here, same month and year as the heir would have been. Private adoption through shady channels. Her birth mother—"

"We don't know who her birth mother is," her father

interrupted. "That's my point. Yes, Declan found records of a private adoption in Stone Bridge thirty-three years ago. Yes, it matches Emery's birthday. But that's circumstantial. There could have been multiple private adoptions that year."

"How many babies do you think were born and adopted five weeks later through black market channels in a town this small?" Walter's voice was gentle but pointed. "I understand you don't want this to be true—"

"It has less to do with that and more to do with her being crushed over speculation," her father said, his voice rising. "

Oh, it more than crushed her. The words were like a bomb exploding in her heart.

"But if it's true—" Devon started.

"If it's true, she deserves to know," her father finished. "But not yet. Not until we have proof. Real proof, not just timelines and sealed records. She's been through enough. She doesn't need this on top of everything else."

Emery's breath came in short gasps. David Callaway's daughter. The heir everyone was looking for. The reason someone was trying to kill her.

"Devon, I know you want to tell her." Her father's voice softened. "I know keeping secrets from her feels wrong. But trust me on this—telling her now, with no proof, while someone's actively trying to kill her? That will destroy her. Let Declan keep digging. Let's find something concrete before we turn her entire world upside down."

"How long?" Devon asked.

"A few more days. Maybe a week. Declan's tracking

down the lawyer who handled the adoption, trying to find the birth mother's identity. Once we have that—"

"Once we have that, we tell her everything," Devon said. "No more delays. I can't keep lying to her."

"I understand. I did it for two years. It sucks," her father said.

Emery pressed her hand to her mouth to keep from making a sound. Her vision blurred with tears—anger, betrayal, confusion swirling into a toxic mix that made her want to scream.

They had suspicions. They withheld information. They lied.

Devon had held her, kissed her, told her he was falling in love with her—all while keeping this secret. He was willing to risk whatever was growing between them to keep a truth hidden in the name of protection.

Her father had comforted her about the attacks, about the danger, while knowing exactly why someone might want to ruin her career and possibly want her dead. And this wasn't the first time her father had done this.

Jesus, she could be David Callaway's biological daughter.

The words echoed in her mind like a death sentence.

She inched closer toward the den. Her body trembling. Her mind jumbled with words that she could put together into a coherent thought. Her heart bled with crushing pain. Curling her fingers around the knob, she pushed open the door. A rage roared through her as if lightning struck, filling her body with electricity.

The men turned and stared at her, their expressions shocked, confused, and guilty.

"Emery," Devon spoke softly. His brow pulled together in a tight formation. His eyes pleaded with her to understand. To forgive.

"You lied to me," Emery managed. "You fucking lied. All of you. Every single one of you betrayed my trust when I needed that more than I needed anything else."

"Sweetheart." Her father set his glass down, stood, and took a step.

She pushed out her hand. Her heart pulsed in her throat. "Leave me alone. I can't stand looking at any of you." Turning on her heels, she raced out of the room and made a beeline for the back stairs. As she took the steps two at a time toward the bedroom she and Devon were now sharing, she could hear him and his sisters calling after her.

Once inside the room, she slammed the door shut, locked it, and sank to the floor, covering her face, and sobbed. Everything she thought about herself, who she believed she was, changed in a second.

She barely had a chance to let the tears fall, to purge it, when someone rattled the door—then pounded.

"Emery." Devon's voice was rough with emotion. "Let me in."

She stayed silent as she rose.

"Come on. I know you're upset, but please, let me explain."

"Go away."

"No. I'm not leaving until you hear me out. I'll sleep in the hallway if I have to."

One thing she knew about Devon was that he could be one of the most stubborn men on the planet. It was a Boone trait.

"You lied to me." She pressed her hand against the door.

"I know. But I didn't know how to tell you something I wasn't sure was true. We don't even know if it's real. It's speculation, that's all. Circumstantial evidence and timelines that match but don't prove anything."

"You should have told me."

"I wanted to. God, I wanted to tell you about it when the thought first occurred to me. And even more, the second Declan found those adoption records. But my dad said to wait. Your dad said to wait. They didn't want you worrying about something that might not even be true, especially after you were shot at. I was trying to protect you."

"By keeping secrets?"

"By not giving you one more thing to be terrified about." His words came out ragged, breaking on the last syllable. Something thudded softly against the door - his hand, maybe, or his whole body sagging against it. "Someone's trying to kill you. And if you knew—"

"I deserved to know." Tears streamed down her face. "It's my life. My adoption. My possible inheritance. You don't get to decide what I can handle."

"You're absolutely right." He paused for a moment. "I'm sorry. I love you so much, and I thought I was protecting you, but I was just being a coward. I was scared of what it would do to you, scared of adding more weight to what you're already carrying. I've never been in love before, and while the feeling doesn't scare me, doing or saying the wrong thing does. I'm constantly wondering if every action I take is going to be the one that makes you leave."

Emery stood with her forehead pressed against the

door, her hand flat against the wood. On the other side, she could hear Devon's ragged breathing. His confession was so utterly honest. So raw. Their romance hadn't been conventional. They hadn't really dated. They had sex a few times. A couple of good laughs when they'd run into each other. A bunch of fun, flirty texts.

But that wasn't a relationship. It hadn't grown into that until recently, and it scared her, too. It just happened too fast. And at a time when her world had been thrown into a meat grinder.

"I love you," he said again, softer. "And I swear, I will never keep anything from you again. No more secrets. No more protecting you from truths you have a right to know. Please let me in."

His words settled over her like a blanket, warm and solid and real. No more secrets. No more half-truths. Just honesty, even when it hurt. Especially when it hurt. That was what she needed. What they both needed. And standing here, separated by wood and her own fear, suddenly felt like the biggest mistake she could make.

She unlocked the door, twisted the knob, and pulled open the door.

Devon stood in the hallway, his face wrecked—eyes red, jaw tight, hands shaking. He looked like he'd aged ten years in the past hour.

"Come in," she whispered.

He stepped inside, and she closed the door behind him. They stood facing each other in the dim light from the bedside lamp.

"Promise me," Emery said. "Promise me you'll never lie to me again. Not to protect me, not because you think you know what's best. I need to look in your eyes and hear you say it."

"I promise." He reached for her hands, gripping them as if they were a lifeline. "No more secrets."

She searched his face, looking for any sign of deception, any hint that he was just telling her what she wanted to hear. But all she saw was love and regret and absolute sincerity.

"I'm terrified," she admitted. "If this is true—if I really am David's daughter—"

He pulled her closer. "Whatever it means, whatever comes next, I'm right here. I'm standing with you." He cupped her chin. "But right now, in this moment, I just need you to know that I love you. That I'm sorry. That I will spend every day earning back your trust if that's what it takes."

"I love you, too." She wrapped her arms around his body, dropping her head to his chest. A million things raced through her mind. Questions about who'd been threatening. How and why Gabe could be involved, because that just didn't make sense. Her father's insurance fraud, and could they have it wrong, and the attempt on her life be related to that?

And the last thought that seemed to linger the longest, and made her feel like a crazy person, was what if she was David's biological daughter, and she took her stake in the Callaway Wineries? What would that mean for her position at Stone Bridge Winery? And more importantly, how would it change her relationship with the man she'd just declared her undying love for?

Fifteen

The Stone Bridge Café smelled like fresh coffee and warm, freshly baked apple pastries with cinnamon and a hint of nutmeg. It was the kind of comforting normalcy that felt wildly out of place given the chaos of the past week. Devon sat in a corner booth, nursing his second cup of black coffee and watching the door as the sun struggled to lighten the dark morning sky.

Gabe arrived ten minutes late, looking like he'd been dragged through hell backward. Dark circles shadowed his eyes, his usually neat hair stuck up at odd angles, and his shirt was wrinkled like he'd slept in it.

"You look like I feel," Devon said as Gabe slid into the booth across from him.

"Thanks. That's exactly what I wanted to hear at six in the morning after spending five hours at the police station and then another two trying to calm down my wife while she cried, yelled, and threatened to beat someone up, only she had no idea where to direct her anger. Most of it landed on the Callaways." Gabe flagged down the server, ordered coffee, and didn't bother with food.

"That bad?"

"Worse." Gabe scrubbed his hands over his face. "Sandy grilled me for hours. I had Harlan there, thanks to your dad, and I was grateful because it got intense. Honestly, I've never been so scared in all my life."

"Define intense." Devon had watched Grant go through a few rounds with Sandy three months ago, and he understood that when Sandy flipped the cop switch, the badge was front and center. Grant said it was as if she was an entirely different person than the all-smiles, fun-loving chief who walked around the streets of Stone Bridge, waving at everyone in the community she was elected to protect, which just weirded Devon out.

"She started with basic questions. Things that felt normal in a situation like this, as crazy as that sounds. But her demeanor began to shift. She leaned across the table. Stared at me with a blank expression. It made me shiver."

"I've seen that look before when Grant was going through it. Even Mason says it's a little creepy, and he's married to her."

"The questions weren't hard—easy enough to answer, actually. But the way she asked them..." Gabe leaned back, draped his arm over the booth, and shifted his gaze around the cafe like he didn't know where to turn. "She practically accused me of filing a false report about the guns being stolen."

Devon set his cup down. "What?"

"The guns were found. In a storage unit rented in my name." Gabe's laugh came out low, almost strangled sounding and more than a little caustic. "A storage unit I never rented, at a facility I've never been to. And inside that unit, Sandy says there's evidence that makes it look like I've been systematically stalking Emery. Targeting her."

"That's insane. Why would you do that? You literally have no reason."

"I wouldn't. But someone's doing a damn good job of making it look like I'm the one behind everything." Gabe accepted his coffee from the server with a nod of thanks. "I laughed when Sandy suggested I was behind the attacks. I asked her, point-blank, what could possibly drive me to do all this. You know what she said?"

"What?"

"Jealousy. That Emery got the authentication program at Stone Bridge Winery, and I wanted to run it myself. That you all had overlooked my hard work, brought in an outsider, one you were sleeping with, no less, and I lost my shit." Gabe took a long sip of his coffee.

"I can't believe she said that."

"Neither could I. But I pointed out that if I was jealous of her job, why would I sabotage her work with Harold before she even got here? That makes no sense."

Devon's hands tightened around his coffee cup. Jealousy? That was Sandy's theory? Gabe had been the one pushing for premium wines and authentication from the beginning, had spent years building toward that program. However, he'd even admitted two years ago that he was spread too thin and they'd need to hire someone.

But he'd also been vocal about his concerns when they'd hired Emery—worried about her reputation, the optics, the risk to Stone Bridge Winery. Devon had seen that hesitation firsthand. Still, concerned wasn't the same as homicidal. And the idea that Gabe would orchestrate attacks meant to get rid of, or kill Emery, all over a job he'd never wanted for himself anyway? Absurd. But someone had planted evidence knowing exactly how it would look— methodical, damning, designed to make Gabe the perfect suspect.

"What did Sandy say?" Devon asked.

"She said perhaps I didn't anticipate that you'd risk hiring her, and I had to inform her that you hadn't even thought about it until that night." Gabe's jaw tightened. "Then I made a mistake. I told her about the David Callaway thing. About Winston thinking I might be the heir."

Devon went very still. "Not sure that's a mistake, but I'm sure it means she'll be coming by the house today and asking a bunch of questions that we don't have answers to. And then there's the questions she'll want to ask the Callaways. We aren't prepared for that."

"I had to give her some kind of alternative motive to investigate. I felt trapped. Like she'd shackled my wrists and ankles. I just blurted it out." Gabe rubbed his temple. "I know you're not thrilled about that. But Sandy had nothing else to go on except evidence that's been planted to make me look guilty, and that's a horrible feeling, man. Worse in a town full of people who like to remind me that my grandfather was a murderer."

Devon wanted to be angry, wanted to point out that bringing the Callaway inheritance into an official police investigation complicated everything. But one look at Gabe —exhausted, desperate, barely holding it together—killed the impulse. "What did she say about the Callaways and Emery?"

"Asked a lot of questions about the will, the timeline, Winston's behavior at the funeral. Took notes. Said she'd look into it." Gabe hunched over his coffee. "But here's the thing—there were no prints on the gun they found. Wiped completely clean. And Sandy mentioned they have video from the storage facility, but she wouldn't share what was on it. Just said she'd be reviewing it more closely."

"But it wasn't you, right?" The question came out before Devon could stop it, and the look Gabe shot him made Devon want to take it back immediately. Of course, it wasn't Gabe. Devon knew that. Had known Gabe for years, worked beside him, and trusted him with his family's winery. But someone had gone to extraordinary lengths to make it look like Gabe—planting evidence, creating paper trails, manipulating timelines. And for just a fraction of a second, doubt had crept in. Not real doubt, not the kind that changed what Devon believed, but the insidious kind that whispered what if everyone else believes it? What if the evidence is too convincing? What if Sandy arrests him anyway? "I'm sorry. I shouldn't have asked that."

"It's fine. I might have done the same thing if the tables were turned." Gabe pushed his mug aside.

"I get why the Callaways would want Emery out of the picture. But who would benefit from destroying you?"

"The same person who benefits from Emery being driven away or killed. The same person who doesn't want the real heir found." Gabe ran a hand over his mouth. "Winston and Callie. They've always taken issue with me being in the Valley. As if my mere presence has tainted Napa's reputation more than anything their grandfather has ever done." Gabe tapped his finger on the table. "And don't try to tell me it's ancient history. I heard some of the shit Callie had to say about me when you were dating her. Both times. She doesn't like me, and she believed that I was damaging your winery's reputation."

"I won't deny that." Devon grimaced. "One of the many reasons we broke up."

"Until Emery, I never understood your taste in women." For the first time since sitting down, Gabe's lips twisted into a slight smile, and he chuckled, before growing somber again. "When I left the station, Sandy told me to stay in town, don't do anything stupid, keep a low profile, and stay away from the Callaways." Gabe tilted his head. "She emphasized it. She told me to stay close to home and that she'd increase patrols around my house. Which made me wonder if she thinks Oliva's not safe. So, my dad decided to stay a little while longer."

"That's "a good idea." Devon glanced around the Cafe as the morning crowd filled in. "I'm sure my folks would be okay if you all moved into the main house for a bit. It's not like we don't have room."

"I'll ask Olivia. She might enjoy the company, and it might keep me from doing something stupid, and confronting Winston and Callie." Gabe reached for his cup, raised it, glanced inside, set it down, and pushed it away again. "This is so messed up. My grandfather's guns were used in a shooting. Evidence has been planted to make me look like a stalker. And I have no idea how to prove I'm being framed."

Devon's phone buzzed. Emery's name lit up the screen.

"Hold on," he said to Gabe, answering immediately. "Hey, you okay?"

"I'm fine. I'm at the main house with your mom." Emery's voice sounded strange—excited but cautious. "I've got a visitor. A strange one."

"Who?"

"Vanessa Wright. The woman who works with Harold." Emery paused. "And she has something very interesting to say."

Devon exchanged a look with Gabe across the table. "I'll be there in ten minutes."

"We'll be here," Emery said.

He hung up and stood, tossing bills on the table. "Vanessa Wright's at the house."

"Harold's assistant?" Gabe was already standing. "What does she want?"

"Don't know." Devon headed for the door. "But if this is about Harold and the forgeries, you might want to tag along."

They left the café together, the morning sun just breaking over the hills, painting the valley in shades of gold. Somewhere out there, someone was orchestrating an elaborate frame job, planting evidence, destroying lives.

But maybe, just maybe, Vanessa Wright was about to give them the first real break in figuring out who.

———

The kitchen at the main house smelled like fresh hazelnut coffee and Brea's cinnamon rolls—the go-to breakfast when Elsa wasn't around, but Emery's stomach was too tight to even think about eating. She sat at the large island with Devon on her left, Riley on her right, while Bryson leaned against the counter, Gabe stood near the window with his arms crossed, and Walter claimed the head of the island like this was a board meeting instead of something that might blow apart everything they thought they knew.

Vanessa Wright perched on the edge of her stool across from them like a bird ready to take flight at the first sign of danger. She was a few years older than Emery—early forties maybe, with mousy brown hair pulled back in a severe ponytail. A manila folder sat on the table in front of her, and her hands kept reaching for it, then pulling back, like she couldn't decide if she was making the biggest mistake of her life.

"Now that we're all here," Walter said, his voice warm but businesslike. "Emery mentioned you had information about Harold's auction house?"

"About Harold, yes. And maybe about what happened to Emery." Vanessa's voice was barely above a whisper. She cleared her throat, tried again. "I've worked for Harold for nearly ten years. Started as a cataloger and worked my way up to his assistant. I've always been loyal. Always did what he asked, no questions."

"Has he asked you to do questionable things?" Devon asked

"No, but as Emery can tell you, Harold can be difficult to work for. He's big on loyalty. Big on things being done his way," Vanessa said.

"And he doesn't like to have his authority questioned." Emery stared at Vanessa. She'd always been a kind but quiet person around the office. Always greeted people with a smile. She never minded going the extra mile for a client. Emery had enjoyed working with Vanessa until about two weeks before the incident. That's when things had gotten weird. When Vanessa had become cold.

"I think Harold enjoys the idea that people are intimidated by him." Vanessa lifted the spoon off the plate, swirled her coffee, set the spoon back down, but didn't take a sip. "It took a few years for me to learn that he also enjoyed it when people challenged him. But not arrogantly or aggressively. More like willing to stand up for what they believed and knew to be true."

"But he never let me defend myself." Emery rested her arms on the island and leaned forward. "He wouldn't hear a word I had to say, and frankly, neither would you."

"I was instructed not to," Vanessa said. "But hearing someone shot at you..." Vanessa's hands trembled as she opened the folder. "That's when I knew this had gone too far. When I realized I couldn't keep quiet anymore. That whatever I was sitting on wasn't some childish revenge or... I don't know. But it got too real."

Emery's chest tightened. Her pulse raced. Vanessa might have been quiet, but she'd been loyal to a fault when it came to Harold. Whatever was in that folder had to have been really bad. Otherwise, Vanessa wouldn't risk her career, her reputation, or the wrath of Harold to divulge it.

"What do you have?" Walter asked.

Vanessa pulled out a document and slid it across the table. "This is a copy of a personal check made out to Harold. From Winston Callaway. For a million dollars."

The number landed like a physical blow. Emery blinked. Her lungs burned. She scanned her brain for every deal that Winston had made regarding vintage wines—not one collection came close to that number.

"I've seen Winston at Pemberton's Auction House many times," Gabe said. "I'm sure he's purchased numerous vintage collections and premium wines from a wide variety of sources. He's always bragging about his private cellar."

"He's never bought one for that dollar amount. At least not while I was working with Harold," Emery said. "And I'd know. I logged all the sales."

"And I filed them." Vanessa held her gaze. "She's right. That check wasn't for wine."

Devon leaned forward, studying the check. "When was it dated?"

"The week before the auction. The one where Emery was—" Vanessa's voice broke. "Where Harold fired her publicly."

"Would there be another reason for Winston to be writing that large a check to Harold?" Riley asked. "A purchase, a consignment fee—"

"If it were for say a hundred grand, I might not have thought anything of it," Vanessa interrupted. "But it's too large to be something like that." She pulled out another document. "This is an email from Harold to his accountant, marked confidential. It references 'compensation for services rendered re: E. Tate and notes the funds as 'consulting fee—non-itemized.'"

"What does that mean?" Bryson asked.

Emery flattened her hands on the cold granite. She focused on taking in long, slow, calculated breaths. In through her nose, out through her mouth.

Gabe pushed off from the window, moving closer to the table. His jaw was tight, his hands curling and uncurling at his sides.

Emery couldn't think. Harold had been paid. Paid to fire her. Paid to humiliate her in front of the entire industry. Paid to destroy her career and reputation.

By Winston Callaway. "Why?" The word came out strangled. "Why would Winston pay Harold to fire me? What have I ever done to him?"

Vanessa shook her head. "I don't know why. But there's more." She pulled out additional papers and spread them across the table. "I know for certain that Winston, Callie, and Harold had a meeting two weeks before the auction. I scheduled it myself, though Harold told me to keep it off the official books. Said it was a sensitive matter."

"What kind of sensitive matter?" Walter asked.

"I don't know. I wasn't in the room. But I heard raised voices through the door. Harold saying something about it being too risky, that he had a reputation to protect." Vanessa's voice trembled right along with her hands. "Then they had a second meeting a week later. That's when this check was written. And that's also when Harold suddenly had the guarantees to purchase two major collections—the Harmon estate wines and the Morrison vintage portfolio. Both from Callaway family connections."

"He sweetened the deal," Devon said, his voice hard.

"Exactly. These are copies of the purchase agreements." Vanessa pointed to the documents. "Both collections are worth easily half a million. Harold's commission on those sales would be substantial."

Emery stared at the papers. This wasn't just a

payment. This was a business arrangement—an orchestrated plan to destroy her while enriching Harold. Potentially, holding him hostage for what he'd done, but in the same breath, ensuring they had an ongoing business relationship that benefited the Callaways and greased Harold's palms.

"What about the forgeries?" Gabe asked. "The authentication records that got Emery fired—were those created by Harold?"

"I can't prove Harold created them, but I can prove they're fake." Vanessa pulled out a thin stack of photographs. "These are copies of the authentication records Harold submitted to the auction board when he fired Emery. The ones with her signature approving the fraudulent bottles."

Devon took the photos, and Emery leaned in to look. Her stomach dropped, a dizzying sensation like falling. She recognized the format, the layout—these were supposed to be her authentication records. Her work. Her signature.

But they weren't.

The signatures were wrong. Close, but not quite right. Someone had studied her handwriting, practiced the loops and curves, gotten it almost perfect. But the 'y' was off. The pressure was different. These were fake documents claiming she'd approved the sale of counterfeit wines.

Harold had done this. Had created false evidence with her forged signature and used it to destroy her in front of everyone she'd ever worked with. Had looked her in the eye while he fired her, had let her walk out of that auction house believing she'd failed, thinking she'd somehow missed obvious forgeries—

The room tilted slightly. She gripped the edge of the island, her breathing coming too fast.

"Emery?" Devon's hand was on her back, warm and steady.

She couldn't speak. Could only stare at the photos of documents, bearing her name, destroying her reputation, all while Harold pocketed a million dollars and lucrative business deals.

"I'm fine." She caught Devon's gaze. "Really. I'm good. Let's keep going."

Gabe reached for the photos and studied them. "The timestamps on these records don't match the provenance. I know this because Devon and I were discussing these wines at the auction before the public shaming."

"I compared these to the actual authentication records," Vanessa said. "The ones still in our system, the ones that were never submitted to the board. What's interesting about it is that I know Emery submitted the original paperwork on this, and that timestamp is the proof." Vanessa tapped her finger on one page, flipped it over, and ran her finger across another one. "That's the forgery, the one that was submitted to the board. Same timestamp, bad autotoxication code and the misinformation that Emery supposedly documented."

"He set me up," Emery whispered. Fire exploded in the center of her belly. It radiated to every part of her body like hot molten lava creeping down the side of a volcano. Slow, but deadly. "I knew it."

"These are the same inconsistencies I found in the documents sent to that reporter," Gabe said quietly. "Same signature errors, same formatting problems."

Walter studied each document with careful attention. "May we keep these? Make copies for our attorney and the police?"

"You can keep them. I made copies." Vanessa's hands were steadier now, though her voice shook with every syllable. "I've been documenting things for weeks. Ever since I overheard Harold on the phone with Callie right after David's funeral."

"Callie?" Emery asked.

Vanessa met her eyes. "He was worried. Asking if they were sure this was going to work, if they were certain Emery wouldn't fight back. And Callie—" She paused, swallowing hard. "Callie told him not to worry, that they had 'contingencies in place' and that Emery would be taken care of."

Emery felt Devon's hand find hers under the table, squeezing tight.

"That's when I knew I had to do something," Vanessa said. "I told myself maybe I misheard, maybe it was about something else. But then I heard someone shot at her in broad daylight. That's when I couldn't pretend anymore."

Emery wanted to cry, wanted to scream, wanted to storm over to Pemberton's Auction House and demand answers. But all she could do was sit there, staring at the evidence of her mentor's betrayal.

"There's one more thing," Vanessa said quietly. She pulled out a final document—a printed screenshot of a text message exchange. "This is from Harold's phone. I shouldn't have access to his messages, but he uses the same computer I do for backups, and I found these in his cloud storage."

Riley took the paper, her face paling as she read. She

handed it to Walter, who closed his eyes briefly before passing it to Devon.

Devon read it, and Emery felt his entire body go rigid beside her.

"What?" Emery asked. "What does it say?"

Devon handed her the paper silently. Gabe moved to read over her shoulder.

The exchange was between Harold and an unknown number, dated two days after Emery had started working at Stone Bridge:

Unknown: *I need you to recreate a set of forged documents.*

Harold: *I did what you asked. It was a one-time thing.*

Unknown: *If you don't do it, business goes away, and maybe things get leaked.*

Harold: *Are you threatening me?.*

Unknown: *I'm telling you that I need one more favor. It's a simple one—same forged document. C and I need her gone. C will resort to drastic measures if she's not. C's already talking crazy shit. Just do it.*

Harold: *Fine. But this is the last time.*

Emery's hands shook so badly the paper rattled.

"C," Gabe said. "I'm thinking that's short for Callie?"

"We don't know that for certain," Walter said carefully.

"Who else would it be?" Bryson asked. "That's got to be Winston. I'm sure a good IT forensics guy could figure out who that unknown caller is. It's so easy these days to mask your phone number, or even have it flash a different one, but IT can still trace it."

"One thing that reporters learned the hard way was to do more diligent checks on whether things are real or not instead of jumping into a juicy story," Riley said. "Proving those are real, having them authenticated, and then how we got them, that all might be an issue."

"I know they're real. I can show you the cloud backup, the metadata, everything. And I'm allowed access, so I'm not violating anything. Or at least, I don't think I am." Vanessa reached up and grabbed a lock of her hair, twisting it through her fingers.

"I don't mean to be rude, but you've known about this for a long time. Why did you wait?" The question burst out of Emery harsher than she intended. "You could've stopped this. Or at the very least help save an innocent man."

Vanessa dropped her hands to the table and her shoulders hunched forward. "Winston and Callie scare me. They have powerful friends. And coming forward would end my career. I need this job. I have two little kids. My husband recently lost his job, and it's been hard for him to find work. And if Harold would do that to you—someone he thought so highly of--for money. I can only imagine what he might be willing to do to me." She looked down at her hands. "I told myself it wasn't my business, that maybe there was a legitimate reason. But when I heard you'd been shot at— that someone actually pulled a trigger—I realized I'd been complicit through my silence."

Emery wanted to stay angry, wanted to hold onto the rage. But looking at Vanessa's tear-streaked face, her trembling hands, the obvious terror in her eyes—Emery couldn't sustain it.

"Thank you," Emery said quietly. "For coming forward."

"It's not brave. It's the bare minimum." Vanessa wiped

her eyes. "I'm sorry I didn't do it sooner. But I'm here now. I just worry what will happen to me."

"For right now, you don't say anything to anyone," Devon said. "No one needs to know you came forward. But I'm sure Sandy will need to speak to you."

"I'll do whatever it takes." Vanessa sat up taller.

Walter gathered the documents carefully. "I'll call Sandy and Harlan. You'll need an attorney, and he's the best."

"What do we do until then?" Emery asked. So many things still didn't make sense.

"We stay together," Devon said. "We stay vigilant. And we wait for the police to do their job."

After Vanessa left, promising to remain available for questioning, the kitchen fell into heavy silence. Emery sat, staring at the documents spread across the table—proof of Harold's betrayal, evidence of conspiracy, text messages discussing her elimination as if she were nothing more than a problem to be solved.

"I can't believe Harold sold me out," she said finally. "For money. Harold sold me out for money and business deals."

"I'm sorry," Devon said, pulling her closer. "I'm so sorry."

"And someone's still out there. Whoever Harold was texting. Whoever's been doing the actual—" She couldn't finish the sentence.

"We'll find them," Gabe said quietly. "Sandy will find them. It's only a matter of time.

"I'm scared," she whispered.

"I know." Devon's arm tightened around her. "I am, too."

And somehow, his admission made her feel less alone. Less like she was crazy for being terrified. Because she should be terrified. Someone wanted her dead. Had wanted her dead for months. And now, they had proof of the conspiracy, but not the person pulling the trigger.

Walter stood, phone already in his hand. "I'm calling Sandy, now. Bryson, take these documents and make copies—multiple copies. Riley, document everything Vanessa said while it's fresh."

They moved into action, purposeful and organized. But Emery couldn't move. Couldn't think past the words in that text message.

Devon stayed beside her, his hand in hers, solid and warm and genuine. The only thing keeping her grounded while her world continued to splinter apart.

Sixteen

The kitchen clock read 5:03 AM. Its soft ticking was the only sound in the sleeping house. Emery sat at the island with her hands wrapped around a mug of chamomile tea that had gone lukewarm while she stared at nothing. Sleep had been impossible—every time she closed her eyes, she saw Harold's forged documents, Winston's check, and those text messages.

Devon and Bryson had been out most of the night to help with the final harvest push. The last blocks needed to be picked before the rain moved in tomorrow, and even at four in the morning, the vineyard crew was working under portable lights. Devon had kissed her forehead before leaving, made her promise to stay inside with the doors locked, unless she was specifically told otherwise.

She'd promised. And she'd meant it.

But now, the house felt too quiet, too empty, too much like a tomb. She'd texted Devon twice since she'd gotten out of bed—but hadn't heard anything in response. That didn't surprise her, considering he was most likely knee deep in dirt, vines, and grapes.

She took a sip of her beverage and grimaced. Nothing worse than cold tea. Emery stood, dumping it in the sink, and filled the kettle again. The small domestic task gave her something to focus on besides the fear coiled tight in her chest. She pulled a fresh tea bag from the canister and went through the motions of normalcy while her mind raced in circles.

Someone wanted her dead. Someone who was still out there, still planning, still waiting for the right moment to execute their plan.

The kettle began to whistle softly. Emery lifted it before it could reach full volume, not wanting to wake anyone else in the house —a thought that should have made her chuckle, considering how large the Boone estate was. Brea and Walter were in what was called the master wing. Ashley and Hasley were in their wing. Riley had stayed over in Bryson's wing. Her father was down the hall from Devon's old room, which also had its own hallway—or wing, which consisted of three bedrooms, like all the other wings, except the master. The house was full of people, but at this hour, Emery felt utterly alone.

She poured the hot water over her tea bag, watching it steep as the water turned amber. Steam rose in lazy curls, and she breathed in the chamomile scent, trying to calm nerves that felt stretched to breaking.

A shadow carrying a light in the vines caught her attention.

Emery set down her mug, her heart rate picking up. She moved toward the back door, peering through the window.

The porch was dark. Beyond it, the vineyard stretched away into pre-dawn darkness, the portable work lights visible in the distance like earthbound stars.

Her cell vibrated on the counter. She lifted it and her heart fluttered as a message from Ralph, one of the production workers flashed on her screen.

Ralph: *Hey, this is Devon. My phone died. Bryson wants a decent, hot, cup of coffee and you know him when it comes to his brew. I told him I'd get it since I wanted to check on you. Mind meeting me by the edge of the vines with it?*

Emery: *I'll be out in five.*

She set her phone down, snagged a mug, and set it under the fancy machine before digging through the coffee pods for the blend that Bryson liked. She'd never met anyone so particular about the flavor and temperature of coffee. Tapping her fingers on the counter, she waited for the machine to heat up and spit out the brew. Once it was done, she headed for the back door and pulled it open.

The October air was cold, sharp enough to make her wish she'd grabbed a jacket. She pulled her cardigan tighter, scanning the darkness. A shadow appeared between the rows of neatly aligned grapes.

"Devon, is that you?"

The silhouette stepped into the clearing, the light pointed toward the ground, and an arm raised—waving.

She moved down the deck steps, a travel mug in hand, her bare feet cold against the wood.

"Is everything okay?" she asked, walking across the lawn toward the figure. "Why didn't you answer?"

The light disappeared, and a shadow moved closer. Something in Emery's chest went cold.

Something was wrong.

The build was wrong. The movement was wrong. This wasn't Devon.

She stopped, her body understanding before her brain caught up. The figure was still approaching, faster now.

The travel mug slipped from her fingers, hitting the grass with a dull thud. She spun toward the house, adrenaline spiking through her veins.

Run. She had to run.

Her feet found purchase on the grass, and she launched herself toward the deck, toward the open door and safety and—

Arms closed around her from behind, iron-strong, lifting her off her feet. She opened her mouth to scream, but a hand clamped over it, cutting off the sound before it could form.

She fought. God, she fought. Kicking backward, thrashing, trying to bite the hand over her mouth. Her nails found skin, and she dug in, felt flesh tear beneath her fingernails. The man grunted but didn't let go.

"Stop fighting," a voice growled in her ear. Male, unfamiliar, cold. "Make this easy on yourself."

Easy? Nothing about being dragged backward into the darkness while her heart hammered and terror flooded every nerve was easy.

She kept fighting. Drove her elbow back into his ribs.

He grunted again. His grip loosened just slightly—

Something hard connected with the side of her head.

The world exploded into white light and pain. Her legs went weak, and her vision blurred. She tried to hold onto consciousness, tried to keep fighting, but her body wasn't responding anymore.

"Told you to stop," the voice said, distant now, like it was coming from the end of a long tunnel.

Darkness crept in from the edges of her vision. She could feel herself being carried, could feel the cold morning air on her face, but couldn't move, couldn't scream, couldn't do anything but sink into the blackness that was swallowing her whole.

Her last coherent thought was of Devon. Coming back to find her gone. The open door. The dropped mug on the lawn.

He'd know. He'd know something was wrong.

But would he know in time?

The darkness took her before she could answer.

The vineyard was finally quiet. The last cluster loaded into bins and hauled to the production facility. Dawn was approaching, but the portable lights illuminated the picked rows with harsh brightness, workers moving between them with the tired efficiency of people who'd been at it all night.

Devon pulled off his gloves and shoved them into his back pocket. His shoulders ached, and all he wanted was to get back to the main house and climb into bed with Emery for a few hours of sleep before the day really started.

Bryson appeared from the next row over, looking equally exhausted. "That's the last of it. Thank God."

"We've only finished harvesting," Devon said. "The work's really just beginning."

"Don't remind me." Bryson fell into step beside him as they headed toward the path that would take them back to the main house. Bryson stretched his arms overhead, his back cracking audibly. "I'm going to finally do it."

"Do what?"

"Propose to Riley."

Devon stopped walking. "Why have you waited this long? We could all use some positivity around here."

"I could name a dozen reasons, but the biggest one is everything that's going on with Emery. It just doesn't feel right with this crap hanging over her head."

"She's not your girlfriend—she's mine—so that's a dumb reason."

"I bet if the tables were turned, you'd do the same thing." Bryson nudged Devon's shoulder. "You're good together. I'm glad you finally found someone who makes you stupid happy."

Devon felt warmth spread through his chest despite the exhaustion. "She does."

"I can tell. You smile more. Stress less." Bryson paused. "Well, you did until someone started trying to kill her. But before that, you were downright pleasant to be around."

"I'm always pleasant."

"You're tolerable. There's a difference."

They walked in silence for a few minutes, boots sinking into the dirt, the vineyard slowly giving way to the manicured lawn as they approached the main house. The sky was lightening at the edges, stars fading into pre-dawn gray.

Devon's phone buzzed in his pocket. He pulled it out, expecting maybe a text from his dad asking about harvest numbers.

Instead, he had an email. From Emery. It was strange. Texting was their standard form of communication unless it was work-related.

Except it wasn't her Stone Bridge email address. It was a Gmail account he didn't recognize.

His steps slowed. Bryson walked a few paces ahead before realizing Devon had stopped.

"What's wrong?" Byson asked.

Devon opened the email, his stomach already tightening. Something was off.

Devon,

I need time and space. All this talk about me possibly being David's daughter is too much. And with everything else going on—the attacks, the danger—I don't want to put anyone else at risk. I need to get away for a while and figure things out. Coming back to Stone Bridge might not have been the right decision.

Please don't reach out. I'll be in touch when I've had some time to think.

I'm sorry.

Emery

Devon read it twice, his heart rate picking up with each word. Then he looked at Bryson, who'd walked back to stand beside him.

"What?" Bryson asked.

Devon handed him the phone silently.

Bryson read, his expression darkening. "This doesn't sound like her. She wouldn't just leave. Not with her father here. Not with everything that's going on."

"It's not her." Devon's voice was flat, certain. "She

wouldn't—" He took off running. His gaze focused on getting to Emery. Everything else was just a blur.

Bryson was right behind him, both of them sprinting across the lawn toward the main house. Devon's lungs burned, his legs pumping, the distance that had seemed so short a moment ago now stretched impossibly long.

The back door stood open.

Devon's heart stopped. It had been locked when he left. She'd promised to stay inside, to keep everything secured.

He took the deck steps two at a time and burst through the door into the kitchen.

The kettle was on the stove. Everything looked normal, undisturbed.

Except for the open door.

"Emery?" Devon called, his voice echoing through the quiet house. "Emery!"

No answer.

Bryson moved toward the front, checking rooms. Devon raced upstairs, taking the steps three at a time, his boots thudding on hardwood.

Their bedroom door was closed. He threw it open.

Empty. The bed disheveled as if she might get back in it. He opened the closet. All her clothes were in there. Yanking open the bathroom door, he checked for her hairdryer, makeup, shampoo. All still there.

He knew with cold certainty that Emery was gone. But she hadn't left because she'd wanted to. Someone had taken her. His heart dropped to his toes like a brick. He couldn't suck in a deep enough breath. He loved Emery, and the thought of anything happening to her crushed his soul so completely he wasn't sure it was something he could come back from.

He thundered back downstairs. Bryson was in the kitchen on his phone, his face pale. He'd flipped on all the outside lights. The backyard looked like a midnight party.

"Sandy's on her way," Bryson said. "I'm calling Dad and—"

"There." Devon pointed out the back door at something glistening in the bright lighting.

In the grass, maybe twenty feet from the deck, a mug lay on its side. White travel mug against dark green grass, impossible to miss once he saw it.

Devon pushed open the door and raced down the steps, crossing the lawn in long strides. He bent over and examined the mug—coffee soaking into the ground beside it.

She'd been here. Right here, twenty feet from the house, and someone had—

His vision tunneled. His hands shook so badly he nearly dropped the mug.

"Devon." Bryson's voice was calm despite the situation. "Come back inside. We need to search the house, make sure—"

"She's not in the house." Devon's voice didn't sound like his own. It had grown dark. Distant. Empty. "Someone took her. Someone lured her out here and took her."

Lights flickered through second-floor windows. Voices called out, confused and alarmed.

Walter appeared in the doorway in his robe. "What's going on?"

"Emery's gone," Devon said. He stared out into the vineyard. The sky gave way to the faint glow of the morning rays peeking over the horizon. There was so much movement on the property during harvest. People milling about day and night. Motion detectors in specific locations had been turned off. "Someone took her. Someone who knew which blocks we'd be working on. Someone who had a basic understanding of our security system."

"What?" Walter descended the steps, Brea right behind him in her nightgown and robe. "What do you mean someone took her?"

Devon held up his phone, showing the email. "This came ten minutes ago. It's not from her. It's fake. She's gone. Taken."

Brea took the phone and read quickly. Her hand went to her mouth. "Oh my God."

Riley appeared next, followed by Ashley and Hasley. Then Michael Tate, Emery's father, his face draining of color as he took in the scene." How did this happen?" Michael demanded.

"I don't have that answer." The words tasted like ash. "I left her here—I thought she'd be safe—there were people in the house—"

"You can't go down that road." Walter's voice cut through the spiral. "This is not your fault."

"I left her alone." Devon's pulse continued to increase. His chest tightened as if a wrecking ball had crashed into it, pinning him to a wall.

"The house was full of people," Brea said firmly. "We were all here. How could anyone have known—"

"Because they've been watching." Devon's hands curled into fists. "They knew the harvest schedule. Knew I'd be in the vines. They knew how to get to her."

Michael moved past them, out onto the lawn, his eyes scanning the ground. "No signs of a struggle here. She must have dropped the mug and tried to run, or—" He stopped, bending down. When he stood, he held something between his fingers. "Blood. On the grass. Not much, but some."

Devon felt bile rise in his throat. Blood. Emery's blood.

"Sandy's five minutes out," Bryson said, still on his phone. "She's bringing backup. They'll search the property, set up roadblocks—"

"Whoever took her, they had this planned. They're not stupid enough to stick around," Devon said. "And we have no idea where they went. What direction. We have nothing."

Riley was typing furiously on her phone. "I'm checking security footage and texting a few neighbors, asking if they can check Ring cameras, anything. If they took her in a vehicle—"

"Then they'll be long gone before we find anything." Devon wanted to hit something, wanted to destroy something, wanted to do anything but stand in his parents' home feeling helpless while Emery was out there with someone who wanted her dead.

Walter gripped his shoulders, tight. "We will find her. We will get her back."

"What if we don't?" He let his gaze drift to the vines. The scent of freshly picked grapes whispered in the wind. Harvest had always been a mixture of excitement and dread. The anticipation of making a new year of wine. New blends. Perhaps a new flavor. But the work was hard. The hours are long. And he looked forward to when it was over.

But this year, all the harvest had brought was a litany of lies. "What if we're too late?"

"Don't." Michael's voice rang out sharp. Strong. "My daughter is smart and fierce and a fighter. Whoever has her is going to regret it." But his eyes said what his words didn't. He was terrified, too.

Sirens wailed in the distance, growing closer. Sandy's patrol car flew up the driveway, followed by two more units. She was out of her vehicle just as it jerked to a stop, striding toward them with purpose. "Talk to me," she said. "What happened?"

Devon handed her his phone and showed her the email. "It's fake. Emery didn't send it. Someone took her from right here—" He gestured to where the mug had been found. "I don't know how long ago, but I got that email fifteen minutes ago."

Sandy read the email, expressionless. All cop. Something that Devon had grown to resent, but in this moment, he appreciated the sense of urgency. "I'll need a copy of this, and I can have IT check it out." She glanced up. "So, I had enough to bring in Winston and Callie for questioning last night, but not enough to keep them. Not to mention, they lawyered up the second they came into the station. But it was insightful."

"What does that mean?" Devon asked.

"You're going to have to trust me." Sandy handed the cell back to Devon. "I'm still waiting for IT to get back to me on the email chain that was sent to the reporter. They promised I'd have it by morning."

"How are Gabe's fake emails connected to this, exactly?" Devon glared.

"We have reason to believe that someone was trying to make it look like Gabe and Emery were working together to do two things. I can't get into what that is, or how I know that." Sandy turned and faced one of her deputies. "I want a full search of this property. Look for signs of a vehicle, tire tracks, anything that shows how they got her off the premises."

The deputies scattered, moving with practiced efficiency. Riley was already on her laptop, fingers flying across the keyboard. Ashley and Hasley stood huddled together on the deck, both pale and shaken.

Sandy turned her attention back to Devon. "I need access to your security cameras."

"Not a problem," Walter said.

Devon couldn't move. Couldn't think past the image of Emery being dragged away in the darkness, scared and hurt and wondering why no one had come to help her. He'd failed her. "I should have stayed," he said. "I should have been here."

"You can't be with her every second," Walter said quietly. "No one can."

"But I promised. I promised I'd keep her safe."

"And you did everything you could." Brea pulled him into a fierce motherly hug. The kind of hug she'd given him as a small boy when he'd been hurt or didn't feel well. But this time, it didn't ease the torment. "This is not your fault. Do you hear me? This is not your fault."

"It's hard not to blame myself." He kissed his mother's cheek and pulled away.

Michael stood apart from the group, staring out at the

vineyard like he could see something the rest of them couldn't.

"I'm sorry," Devon said, moving to stand beside him. "I swear to God, we'll get her back."

"If anything happens to my daughter, there won't be enough police in this valley to stop me from tearing apart whoever took her."

Devon understood the sentiment. Felt it in his bones.

Someone had taken Emery. Had lured her out of the house and disappeared with her into the pre-dawn darkness.

And when Devon found them—when, not if—they were going to regret they'd ever been born.

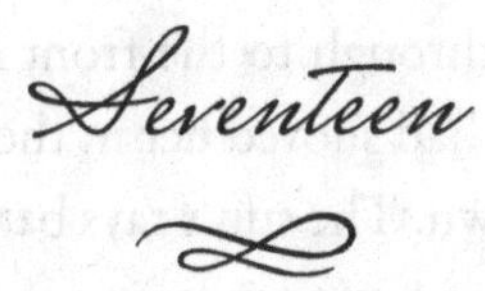

Seventeen

Pain radiated through Emery's skull in waves, each one making her stomach lurch. Her eyes felt glued shut, and when she finally forced them open, the world swam in sickening circles.

She blinked.

It wasn't dark. But it wasn't bright. And she was moving. In a vehicle. The engine hummed beneath her, vibrations traveling through her body where it pressed against carpet that smelled like mildew and motor oil.

She tried to move her hands and couldn't. Her wrists were bound behind her back, zip ties cutting into skin. Her ankles were tied too—she could feel the bite of plastic when she tried to shift her legs.

Panic flooded through her, sharp and immediate. Where was she? How did she—

The man. The shadow in the vineyard. Arms around her. Something hitting her head.

Oh God.

Emery wiggled, struggling against her restraints,

fighting to get upright. Her shoulders screamed in protest, muscles cramping from being twisted behind her. But she managed to roll onto her side, then wedge herself up against the side of the vehicle.

She could see through to the front seat. She was in an SUV, and the man had shoved her in the cargo area with all the seats folded down. The sun's rays barely peeked over the horizon as night gave way to morning.

A man sat in the driver's seat—with a baseball cap. The same cap she'd seen that night she went out with Ashley. The night she'd been hit by a car.

It couldn't be.

"Where are you taking me?" Her voice came out hoarse, raw. "What do you want?"

"Be quiet." The man turned his head. The cap had the same logo. It was distinctive. And she remembered it.

"Please, just tell me what's going on. I don't understand—"

"I said, be quiet. Or I'll shut you up, again. Your choice."

Emery's head throbbed where he'd hit her. Bile rose in her throat at the threat of being knocked unconscious again. She bit her lip, tasting blood, and tried to think through the panic.

They were on a highway. She glanced out the window, looking for signs. There was one up ahead. They were headed north. She shifted her gaze toward the dashboard. It was 5:32. It hadn't been that long since she'd been snatched.

Would Devon even know she was gone?

A phone rang—the driver's phone, lighting up where it

sat in a cup holder. He grabbed it, answered with a clipped, "What?"

Emery strained to hear the other side of the conversation but couldn't make out any words. Just muffled sound, the cadence of someone—a female—speaking urgently.

"No." The driver's voice rose, agitated. "I'm not going to meet you. I have to get out of town. This whole thing's blown up—"

More muffled speaking on the phone.

"I can't dump her here. I can't even do it, California." He was getting angrier, his free hand gripping the steering wheel until his knuckles went white. "Stopping is too risky, and I'm not doing it for any amount—"

The voice on the other end cut him off.

"Fine." The driver bit the word off. "But you're going to have to pay me double, and you better bring it."

He ended the call and tossed the phone back into the cup holder.

Emery's heart hammered against her ribs.

They were going to kill her. Take her somewhere remote and kill her.

"Please." The word came out small, desperate. "Please, I'll give you whatever you want. Money. I have money—my boyfriend will pay whatever you ask. Just let me go."

"Your boyfriend." The man laughed, harsh and without humor. "Yeah, I'm sure he'd pay. Right before he killed me himself. No thanks."

"Then what do you want? Why are you doing this?"

"I was paid to do a job. Nothing personal." The man reached into the passenger seat, and when his hand came back, he was holding a gun. He didn't point it at her—just held it where she could see it, the metal catching ambient light from passing cars.

"Hush," he said quietly. "Or I'll hush you myself. We clear?"

Emery looked at the door, then shifted her gaze to the dashboard, contemplating what might happen if she managed to open that door and try to jump at seventy miles an hour.

Probably not a good idea.

"Good." He set the gun on the passenger seat within easy reach. "Now shut up, and let me drive."

The car merged onto what felt like an off-ramp, the smooth highway giving way to rougher road. They were leaving the interstate. Going somewhere more isolated.

Somewhere no one would hear her scream.

Emery pressed her back against the side of the cargo area, her bound hands aching, her head throbbing, terror making it hard to breathe. She thought of Devon's face, the way he'd kissed her forehead before leaving for the vineyard—the promise she'd made to stay safe, to keep the doors locked.

She'd broken that promise by opening the door. By thinking the shadow was him.

And now she was going to die because of it.

The backyard felt too small for the rage building in Devon's chest. It expanded like a balloon, growing to full capacity and dangerously beyond, close to the breaking point. He paced from the deck to the edge of the lawn and back again, his phone clutched in his hand like a life-line. Every thirty seconds, he checked it. No calls. No texts. No miraculous email from Emery saying this was all a mistake.

Just silence.

The sun had climbed higher, warming the October morning, but Devon felt cold all the way through to his bones like ice was forming in his bloodstream.

The back door opened, and Bryson stepped out, his expression careful.

"Mom made breakfast," he said. "There's food on the table if you want—"

"I can't eat."

"Devon—"

"I can't sit in there and eat pancakes while Emery's out there with whoever took her." Devon glanced at the time. "It's been almost an hour, and I can't pretend everything's normal. I can't—"

"Nobody's pretending anything's normal." Bryson moved closer, his voice calm and presence as big as their bond. They'd been best friends since they were kids. Of course, there'd been brotherly rivalry, but they were always there for each other. Always willing to be the pillar of strength for the other. Bryson was the one person he could always count on not to judge or scold but who'd also be brutally honest when he needed it the most. "You need to eat. You need to do something other than concentrate on something you can't control."

"What I need is to be out there looking for her."

"The police are looking. Sandys got every unit in the valley searching. She's called state, and I think she even called in the Feds. Roadblocks on every major route out of town and the valley. They're doing everything—"

"It's not enough." Devon hurled the words at his brother like a grenade. "She's been gone for an hour, and the cops don't have a single clue. And we're sitting here doing nothing."

"We're doing what we can. Staying here in case she comes back or contacts us." Bryson stared at him with sheer determination and resolve. "I get it. I understand why you feel powerless. But running around without a plan isn't going to help her."

Devon wanted to argue. Wanted to get in his truck and drive every road in the valley until he found her. But he knew Bryson was right. Knew that leaving meant possibly missing a call, missing information, missing something critical.

"Just come inside," Bryson said. "It's not good for you to be out here, alone. Come be with family."

"I need a few more minutes." Devon turned away, looking out at the winery. "I'll be along in a bit. I just need to clear my head."

Bryson was quiet for a moment, then sighed. "Okay. But if you're not inside in fifteen minutes, I'm coming back out."

After he left, Devon resumed pacing. He kept replaying the scene—the open door, the dropped mug, blood on the grass.

He snapped his head up at the sound of tires on gravel. A car was coming up the driveway.

Sandy? Please let it be Sandy with news.

Devon raced around the side of the house, his heart

hammering. But the vehicle pulling to a stop wasn't Sandy's patrol car.

It was Callie Callaway's silver Mercedes.

Devon reached for his phone, pulling it out to text his family. But before he could type a word, Callie was out of the car, striding toward him in designer jeans and a cashmere sweater as if this were a social call.

A million things ran through his brain like an electric current. But only one popped like a firecracker.

Why wasn't Callie in custody? Or at the very least, being detained for questioning. So many things pointed to her. She'd been jealous the last time they dated. And while he'd never experienced her vindictiveness, he knew other people who had.

"What are you doing here?" Devon demanded. Heat filled his muscles. It worked its way through his body like a drug.

"I heard about Emery." Callie tilted her head and gave him a half smile, as if she cared. As if that concerned expression meant something. "I'm so sorry. I wanted to check on you."

"What are you talking about?" He heaved in a breath and took a step back.

"She left town. I know you must be devastated." Callie moved closer, invading his space. "I saw her, actually. Early this morning. She stopped for coffee. She looked upset. I asked her if she was okay, and she told me she didn't want to talk about it, and that she was leaving—for good."

Devon went very still. "You saw her."

"Yes. I was getting pastries and coffee better than I can brew for the harvest crew." Callie inched closer and touched his arm. "I'm here for you. If you need anything at all—"

"You're lying." The words came out low, harsh, and dangerous. "You didn't see her. And if you did, then you did something to her. Which is it?"

Callie's eyes widened. "What? I don't know what you're talking about. I just stopped by because I was worried about you."

"Bullshit."

"We might be business adversaries, but we've been friends." Her voice took on a wounded quality. "I care about you. I always have. And I'm sorry Emery's gone, but maybe it's for the best—"

"I'm calling the police." He pulled out his cell. His finger hovered over the screen.

Callie backed away, her expression shifting from concerned to cold in seconds. "I don't even know who you are, anymore." She climbed into her Mercedes, slammed the door, and peeled out of the driveway fast enough to spray gravel.

He strode toward the house, yanking open the back door. He swiped on the screen, pulling up Sandy's personal cell, but then realized maybe he should call 9-1-1.

The family was gathered in the kitchen—Walter, Brea, Riley, Ashley, Hasley, Michael, Bryson. All of them turned when he entered.

"What was that about?" Walter asked. "We heard voices."

"Callie just showed up."

"What?" Brea stood. "What did she want?"

"To tell me she's sorry Emery's gone. That she saw her leaving town this morning." Devon's hands curled into fists.

"She's trying to find a way into your life," Michael said, his voice hard. "Why did you let her leave?"

Before Devon could respond that he hadn't and was about to call the authorities, Sandy's patrol car pulled into the driveway.

Devon was out the door before she'd fully stopped, meeting her halfway across the lawn. "Tell me you found something. Tell me you pulled Callie over, and someone is taking her in."

"She's not getting far," Sandy said. "I've got people on her, don't worry."

"I'm beyond worried." Devon ran his fingers through his hair.

"I came by to tell you the IT department got back to me about that fake email." Sandy pulled out her notebook. "It was sent from the Callaway estate. Same IP address as the other fake emails sent using Gabe's name."

"So, it *was* Callie."

"Or someone at the estate." Sandy looked past him toward the house. "Is Gabe here? His wife said he was helping with the investigation."

"He's inside."

"I need to update him. And everyone else." Sandy headed for the house, Devon following. Once inside, she addressed the room. "We're bringing in Winston and Callie Callaway for formal questioning. The evidence is strong enough for arrest warrants on conspiracy charges."

"Callie was just here," Devon said. "Five minutes ago. She drove up, told me she saw Emery leaving town."

Sandy's expression darkened. "She's fleeing. Or about to. We need to move now." She keyed her radio, calling for backup. "All units, suspect Callie Callaway just spotted at the Boone residence. Consider her a flight risk. Proceed with arrest."

"There's more," Sandy continued. "We got a hit on that partial plate from the witness who saw the car near your property this morning. Vehicle's registered to Jim Webb. He's been staying at the Valley Inn for the past week."

"Who is he?" Walter asked.

"That's what we're going to find out. Deputies are heading to the Valley Inn to pick him up now." Sandy looked at Devon. "I know you want to be out there. But the best thing you can do is stay here. If Emery gets free, if she calls, you need to be available."

"She's been gone for over an hour," Devon said, his voice breaking on the words.

"I know. And we're doing everything we can to find her." Sandy gave him a weak smile. "Hang tight. I'll update you as soon as I know anything."

After she left, the kitchen fell into heavy silence. Everyone standing around, helpless, waiting for news that might never come.

Devon sank into a chair, his head in his hands. Callie showing up here, taunting him. Some stranger named Jim hitting her with his car—fake emails from the Callaway estate.

They had pieces. But they didn't have Emery.

And every minute that passed made it less likely they'd get her back alive.

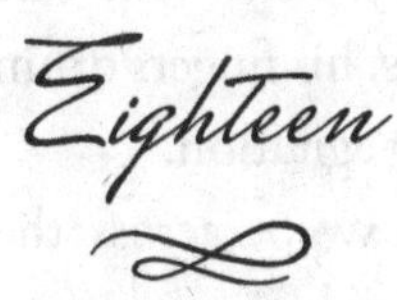

Eighteen

The man slowed the SUV and pulled off the highway. He made a right turn, then a left, into the truck stop parking lot.

It was one of those nameless places that existed purely for function—gas pumps, a convenience store with flickering neon, a handful of eighteen-wheelers parked along the perimeter. The man—she still didn't know his name—drove past the main parking area and around to the back, where the asphalt gave way to gravel and weeds and the kind of shadows that swallowed secrets.

He put the SUV in park but left the engine running.

They sat in silence. Emery's wrists ached from the zip ties, her head still throbbing. She shifted, trying to find a position that didn't make everything hurt worse.

"How long are we waiting here?" she asked.

"Shut up."

"I just want to know—"

He raised his hand, his fingers curled around the butt of the gun. He turned, his gaze meeting hers with a coldness that made her shiver. "I said shut up. One more word, and I'll make sure you can't talk at all. We clear?"

Emery pressed her lips together and nodded.

Minutes ticked by. Five. Ten. The man kept checking his phone, his mirrors, his fingers drumming on the steering wheel with increasing agitation.

Then headlights swept across the gravel lot. A silver Mercedes pulled in beside them.

She knew that car. Worse, she knew the owner.

The man got out, circled, and yanked open the rear hatch where Emery sat bound. "Don't even think about screaming."

Emery's heart hammered. Her body trembled. Her mouth grew dry. But heat burned through her veins. The kind of rage that wanted blood. That demanded she rip something apart with her bare hands.

The Mercedes door opened, and Callie Callaway stepped out.

Emery's breath caught. Not from shock—they'd suspected Callie was involved, had known from those text messages that C meant Callie. But seeing her here, seeing her walk toward the SUV in her designer clothes and perfect makeup like this was just another business meeting, made it real in a way that flipped a switch in Emery.

All this to silence her. To make sure a third heir never made a claim on the Callaway estate, regardless of what David Callaway had wanted.

Callie had the audacity to smile. And not just any smile. It was wide, sweet-looking, and almost genuine. She eased into the trunk of the SUV, settling in like she owned the space.

"Well, well, well," Callie said, in a sing-song voice. "You've been a thorn in my side for far too long."

"You're behind this," Emery said. Not a question. A statement.

"It depends on what *part* you're referring to." Callie picked at the side of her nail, then lifted her gaze with deliberate slowness. "My brother was the mastermind behind getting Harold to humiliate you. That was all Winston—and while it was a good plan, I did worry it wouldn't be enough. I warned him that you and Devon had this thing. So, I made sure I was prepared with a contingency plan." Her manic smile widened. Her eyes lit up.

"You tried to discredit me a second time, and you used Gabe to do it. Why?" Emery wanted answers. She needed them. If she was going to die, she was going to leave knowing.

"That was only partially me." Callie sighed. "My brother had this strange idea that if Gabe either got fired from Stone Bridge Winery or was somehow involved in a scandal, we'd be able to scoop him up, and he could be our vintner. I thought that was ridiculous. Gabe would never. He'd become a garbage collector before that happened. I came up with the idea that you were working together. Scamming us for the inheritance. Scamming the Boones with forgeries."

"That's insane." Emery couldn't believe what she was hearing. It had to be the most convoluted story she'd ever heard. It was absurd. It bordered on lunacy.

"Is it, though?" Callie leaned closer, pressing her hand on the carpet of the SUV. "This entire valley is built on family legacy. My family's winery, the Boones', they go back three generations, as do others. Gabe's grandfather was a criminal. Hired muscle who murdered one of his employers over gossip." She tapped her fingers against the carpet. "Your father is being investigated for fraud. It's only a matter of time before charges are brought. Both you and Gabe are simply repeating history, and all it takes is a few whispers in the vines to make it true."

Callie had come unhinged. She'd lost her mind.

Emery's breath came in shallow pants. Her heart raced. Her mind played all the events like a movie loop—in fast forward. They whizzed by, only allowing her to catch glimpses of the horror.

But it was enough to remind her that Callie was not only nuts but also dangerous.

"You tried to kill me."

"That wasn't me." She jerked her thumb over her shoulder. "That was him. Turns out, you're surprisingly hard to kill."

"And this conversation needs to end." The man who had been leaning against the car, with his arms folded, saying absolutely nothing, had pushed from that position and stood at the opening of the SUV. "I need to get me and her out of here, or she becomes solely your problem."

"Just a few more moments," Callie said in that sweet, but annoying voice that was one octave too high to be anything other than fake.

"You've got five minutes," the man said. "I'm not risking my freedom for this paycheck."

Callie shifted her gaze back to Emery. "I've been trying to figure out what you have that I don't, because it doesn't make sense."

"What are you talking about?" Emery asked.

"You and Devon," Callie said, as if the words tasted bitter, and she needed to spit them out. "He doesn't do drama. He hates it. Avoids it all costs. So, why is he still with you? It's not your good looks, because you're average. You don't have money, though, he doesn't need any. I can't imagine you're all that great in bed."

"This is about Devon?" Emery's wrists burned where she pulled against the zip ties. "Not about me possibly being an heir?"

"Winston only wanted you gone. All he cared about was making sure the three months passed for the heir to be made known. After that, he didn't care what you did or where you worked. But the problem was we didn't know our dad was going to die or that you'd come back to Stone Bridge. Once that happened, your adoption, your birthday, your connection to this valley—it was only a matter of time before someone put it together." Callie scooted to the edge of the hatch and stood. "And there is no way I'm letting you take even a portion of my family fortune. Being the bastard kid of my father's indiscretion doesn't make you an heir. It makes you a mistake that should have stayed buried."

"Your mother hired an investigator—"

"My mother's a sentimental fool who thinks family is more important than money. She wanted to find you, to welcome you with open arms, to split everything three ways like we're all one big happy family." Callie's voice dripped venom. "But I'm not sharing the Callaway fortune. Not with you. Not with anyone." Callie's expression shifted, something predatory sliding across her features. Cold. Calculating. Malicious. "And Devon's mine. Always has been, always will be. You were just a distraction. But once you're gone, once you've 'disappeared' after sending that sweet little email about needing space—I'll be there to help him pick up the pieces. Console him. Remind him that I'm the one who's always been there."

"You're insane."

"I'm practical." Callie sat back. "You disappear. The will's clock runs out. Winston and I split everything. Devon eventually moves on—with me. Everyone wins."

"They're onto you," Emery said. "The police, Devon's family, everyone. Even if you kill me, you're going down for this."

"Am I?" Callie's smile didn't waver. "Thanks to my brother, all the evidence points to poor, jealous Gabe. His guns, his emails, his motive."

"I don't understand. You said you tried to make it look like we were working together." The question burst out.

Callie leaned closer, and Emery could smell her perfume—expensive, cloying. "We had to give my mother a distraction. She was salivating over the possibility that he was an heir when that photo surfaced. But then we show her how he might have been sabotaging you—or maybe working with you—and she'll be ready to call off the search. Besides, I don't like Gabe. Devon listens to him too much. Respects his opinion in areas where he should be listening to me."

"You sent those emails to that reporter," Emery said as fact.

Callie shrugged.

"You're destroying an innocent man's life."

"Collateral damage." Callie shrugged. "Now, I think

we're done here. Time for you to go take your final drive with—"

Sirens. Distant but growing closer.

The man pacing in the lot paused and stared at Callie. "No. No, I'm not getting caught. I'm not going down for this."

"Drive!" Callie slammed the hatch closed. "Drive now!"

But the man was already moving, bolting into the darkness beyond the truck stop.

"You idiot!" Callie screamed after him. "Get back here!"

More sirens. Closer now. Red and blue lights flashing in the distance.

Callie's head whipped around, scanning, searching. She raced around the vehicle, slipped behind the driver's seat, and slammed the gearshift into drive.

"What are you doing?" Emery shouted.

Callie didn't answer. She gripped the steering wheel with both hands.

The SUV lurched forward, tires spitting gravel. They careened around the side of the truck stop.

Emery slammed against the side of the cargo area, her bound hands making it impossible to brace herself.

A patrol car appeared at the truck stop entrance. Then another. And another.

Callie swerved onto the highway, accelerating. The SUV fishtailed, and Emery rolled, her head cracking against something hard. Stars exploded across her vision.

"You're going to kill us both." Emery struggled to sit up, her balance impossible with her hands tied. "Callie, stop."

"I'm not going to prison." Callie glanced in the rearview mirror. "I'm not losing everything because of you."

More sirens. More lights. Coming from ahead now—state patrol cars blocking the road, forming a barrier.

Callie yanked the wheel, trying to veer off onto a side road. The SUV tilted, two wheels lifting off the pavement. Emery screamed. They were going to roll. They were going to—

The vehicle slammed back down with bone-jarring force. Callie overcorrected, and suddenly they were sliding sideways, the world spinning in a chaos of lights and sirens and Callie screaming.

Callie yanked the wheel back and forth, the SUV swerving wildly across both lanes.

A guardrail appeared ahead. The SUV sped toward it, and then suddenly, the tires squealed. Rubber burned. And the vehicle suddenly slowed.

Emery flew forward. Her shoulder slammed into the back of the passenger seat. The front airbags deployed with explosive force. The SUV spun once, twice, then came to a shuddering stop half on the road, half in the ditch beside it.

Emery's ears rang. Everything hurt. Every muscle. Every bone. She blinked, and all she saw was a combination of stars and flashing lights. Her head throbbed like a jackhammer digging into concrete and not making progress. She shifted, blinking more, as her vision slowly came into focus.

Through the cracked windshield, she could see patrol cars surrounding them, officers emerging with weapons drawn.

I'm safe. I'm safe. They're here to save me. To protect me. But Emery's pulse didn't slow.

Callie fumbled with her seatbelt, cursing. She undid the belt, shoved the door open, and tried to run.

She made it maybe ten feet before officers tackled her to the ground.

"No!" Callie screamed and thrashed. "Get off me. You don't understand. She's the one who kidnapped me. I was protecting myself."

Emery stared. She couldn't turn away. She couldn't blink. The entire scene was part of a horror movie. This didn't happen in real life.

Callie continued to plead her case as the policeman lifted her off the ground and guided her to a police car.

Another officer approached the rear of the SUV and opened the rear hatch. "Ma'am? Are you Emery Tate?"

Emery blinked up at him, dazed, still confused by the events. Rattled by the confessions. Horrified by the outcome. "Yes," she managed.

"Hold still." He pulled out a knife and carefully cut through the zip ties. Blood rushed back into Emery's hands and feet in a painful flood. "Can you move? Are you hurt?"

"I don't know." Everything felt disconnected, unreal. She reached up and gently touched the back of her head. When she looked at her hand, there was a small amount of blood on her fingertips. "The man. The one driving before. He ran."

"We saw him. Units are searching now." The officer helped her sit up. "Ambulance is on its way."

Emery, needing fresh air, inched to the edge of the cargo area and swung her shaky legs over the side. She could still hear Callie spewing lies about Emery. About what had happened. Trying to explain why she had to tie Emery up, because it was Emery trying to kill her over the fact that Devon loved Callie, not Emery.

It was pure insanity.

Emery almost felt sorry for her.

Almost.

Sandy appeared, her face tight with concern. "Emery. Jesus, we thought—are you okay?"

"The man," Emery said. Her voice sounded strange, too calm. It was almost as if she'd left her body, and someone else was speaking. Shock, probably. "He's still out there. He was hired to kill me. What if he goes after Devon? After the family?"

"We're already on it. I've got units at the main house. We know who he is—Jim Webb, hired gun with a record. We'll find him." Sandy placed a kind, warm hand over Emery's. "But right now, you need medical attention."

An ambulance pulled up, EMTs jumping out with a stretcher. Emery wanted to protest, to say she was fine, but she knew that wasn't true. And when she tried to stand on her own, her legs gave out.

The EMTs caught her, eased her onto the stretcher. One of them shone a light in her eyes, asked her questions she barely heard. Everything felt muffled, distant.

But she was alive.

As they loaded her into the ambulance, she caught sight of Callie being shoved into the back of a patrol car. Their eyes met for one, brief moment.

Callie's expression was pure hatred. But behind it, Emery saw something else.

Fear.

Callie Callaway had lost. And she knew it.

Bryson's truck had barely rolled to a stop in the ER drop off zone when Devon threw open the passenger door and hit the pavement running. His brother shouted something behind him, but Devon didn't stop, didn't slow, just sprinted toward the automatic doors.

They whooshed open, and he was inside, desperately scanning the waiting area.

"Devon."

He spun. Sandy stood near the admissions desk, exhaustion written across her face.

"Where is she?" His voice came out rough. "Is she okay?"

"She's fine. Banged up, bruised, a possible concussion. She needs stitches but otherwise fine." Sandy moved toward him. "But there's news you need to hear first."

"I don't care about the news. I need to see her."

"Jim Webb was found hiding in a drainage culvert two miles from the truck stop. He's in custody." Sandy's voice was firm, making him listen, even as his heart raced for the woman he loved. "He confessed to everything. Callie hiring him to kidnap and kill Emery. He's got a record—hired muscle, extortion, assault. This was just another job to him."

Devon's hands curled into fists—another job. Emery's life had been another job for this man.

"Winston's in custody too," Sandy continued. "And he wants to make a deal. Full cooperation, testimony against Callie, everything—as long as he gets immunity."

"Immunity?" Devon's voice rose. "He paid Harold to destroy her. He orchestrated—"

"He claims he never wanted it to go this far. That he only wanted Emery's career destroyed, wanted her driven out of the valley, humiliated, so his family wouldn't want her as an heir if and when his father decided to find her — or he passed. He says his sister always had something else in mind, and he couldn't keep her in check." Sandy held up her hand when he tried to say something. "I'm not saying he's innocent. I'm saying he's willing to testify to put his sister away for a very long time."

Devon wanted to care. Wanted to feel something about Winston's change of heart or Jim Webb's arrest. But all he could think about was Emery. Seeing her. Touching her. Knowing for certain she was alive and safe.

"Where is she?"

"Room 4, down that hall." Sandy pointed. "She was asking for you. Very brave, by the way. Kept her head through the whole ordeal."

Devon was already moving, striding down the corridor, scanning room numbers. One. Two. Three. Four.

He pushed through the door.

Emery sat on the exam table, her hair tangled, a bruise blooming across her cheek, her wrists and ankles wrapped in bandages. But she was alive. Whole. Looking up at him with those green eyes that had haunted him for hours.

"Devon—"

He crossed the room in three strides and pulled her into his arms, careful of her injuries but unable to stop himself from holding her as close as possible. She was warm and solid and real, her heart beating against his chest, her breath on his neck.

"I thought I lost you," he said, his voice breaking. "When I found that mug in the grass and you were gone—I thought—"

"I'm okay." Her arms came around him, squeezing back. "I'm okay."

He pulled back just enough to cup her face in his hands, his thumbs tracing the curve of her jaw. "I love you. God, I love you so much. I'd be lost without you. I can't—I couldn't imagine my life without you in it."

She laughed. Actually laughed. The sound caught him off guard.

"What?"

"You're coming on a bit strong." Her smile was soft, warm, everything he'd been terrified he'd never see again. "Though, I appreciate the dedication."

"I almost lost you."

"But you didn't." She reached up, covering his hands with hers. "I'm right here. And I love you, too."

He kissed her then, pouring every ounce of fear and relief and love into it. She kissed him back, her hands sliding into his hair, pulling him closer, despite her injuries and the fact that they were in a hospital room with the door wide open.

When they finally broke apart, both breathing hard, she rested her forehead against his.

"Never again," he said. "Never again do I leave you alone. I don't care if family or police or an entire army surrounds us. I'm not letting you out of my sight."

"That might get awkward."

"I don't care."

"Even in the bathroom?"

"Especially in the bathroom. Those are prime kidnapping locations."

She laughed again, and the sound loosened something in his chest that had been locked tight for hours.

Familiar voices echoed in the hallway, growing louder and louder.

Michael Tate entered first, his face flooding with relief when he saw his daughter, followed by Walter and Brea, then Riley, Ashley, and Hasley. Bryson was the last to stroll across the threshold.

"Emery." Michael pushed past everyone else and pulled her into a careful hug. "Thank God you're okay."

"I'm fine, Dad. Really."

"Don't ever do that to me again." His voice was rough with emotion. "My heart can't take it." He pulled back, cupping her face, and kissing her temple.

"I'll do my best to avoid getting kidnapped in the future."

Brea wiped a tear before pulling Emery into a warm embrace. "We were so worried. We thought—"

"I know. I'm sorry," Emery said.

"Don't apologize." Walter rested a gentle hand on her arm. "We're just glad you're safe, and that Callie and the man she hired have been arrested."

Ashley and Hasley crowded in, both talking at once about how scared they'd been, how brave she was, how they were never letting her out of their sight again, either. Riley hung back slightly, typing on her phone, probably already documenting everything for legal purposes or social media damage control.

Devon watched them all fuss over Emery, his family claiming her as one of their own, and felt his throat tighten. This was what he'd wanted. What he'd hoped for but hadn't quite believed could happen.

Emery belonged here. With them. With him.

And now that they'd almost lost her, he was never letting her go.

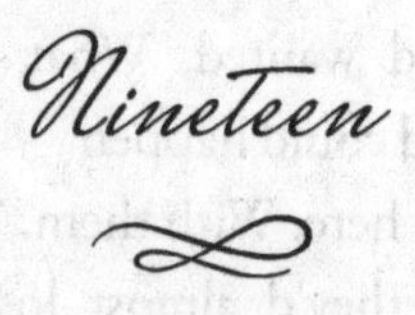

Nineteen

TWO WEEKS LATER...

The main house felt suspended in time, caught in that peculiar afternoon quiet when the world outside continued, but everything inside held its breath. Sunlight filtered through the dining room windows in dusty beams, catching on the polished mahogany table where a single manila folder sat like a verdict waiting to be read.

Emery couldn't stop staring at it.

That folder—unremarkable, standard office supply store manila—contained the answer to every question she'd asked herself since she was old enough to understand what "adopted" meant. Inside those pages lived the truth about who she was, where she'd come from, and why an eighteen-year-old girl had kept her for five weeks and then let her go.

Devon sat to her right, his presence solid and warm, his hand resting on the table close enough that she could reach for it when the ground shifted beneath her feet. Her father occupied the chair across from her, his expression already braced for impact, already preparing to catch her when she fell.

Declan, the private investigator, and Harlan, the family attorney, flanked the other sides of the table, wearing matching expressions of professional gravity. This was the look people wore when they were about to change your life. The look that said I'm sorry for what I'm about to tell you, but you asked for the truth.

"Before we open this," Harlan said, his voice measured and careful, "I want to make sure you understand what we're dealing with. What Declan learned isn't just information—it's your history. And once you know it, you can't unknow it."

"I understand." Emery's voice came out steadier than she felt.

"Declan's investigation uncovered records of a private adoption. Black market, technically illegal, but documented nonetheless." Harlan's fingers drummed once against the table, then stilled. "We have evidence that strongly suggests you're David Callaway's biological daughter. But 'strongly suggests' isn't proof."

"Which is why DNA testing is the next step," Declan added. His weathered face showed years of delivering difficult news, of being the bearer of truths people didn't want to hear. "I've already spoken with Winston Callaway's attorney. He's willing—eager, actually—to submit to testing. To establish that you and Winston are half-siblings."

"Why?" The question escaped before Emery could stop it. "Why would Winston cooperate after everything he did?"

"Because his attorney believes full cooperation is his only path to avoid real prison time," Harlan said. "Winston's willing to testify against Callie in exchange for immunity on the conspiracy to commit murder charges. He's admitted to paying Harold Pemberton. He's admitted to the scheme to destroy your career, to funding the campaign to drive you out of Stone Bridge. Everything except the actual violence."

"So, he draws a line at murder but not at destroying someone's life." Emery heard the bitterness. She tasted it when she swallowed, and she didn't give a damn.

"Apparently, that's where his conscience kicks in," Harlan said. "For what it's worth, his attorney claims Winston genuinely regrets how far things went."

"It doesn't change what he did, or how complicit he was in the whole thing." Devon leaned back, folding his arms, anger radiating from his muscles.

Emery was tired of carrying the weight of it all. Of the rage. Of the resentment. Of the fear. "And what about Callie?"

"Still in jail. Her family refused to post bail—apparently even the Callaways have limits. She's claiming innocence. However, her story has changed. Now she's claiming she was trying to save you from Jim Webb. That someone else hired him. I've heard she's hinting at some names, but I don't know who."

"That's bullshit, and I can gather she's trying to shift the blame to Gabe." Devon found Emery's hand under the table with his own, squeezing hard enough that she felt his frustration through his grip.

"We don't need to concern ourselves with Callie," Harlan said. "Jim Webb has rolled over completely in hopes of a reduced sentence. He's given detailed testimony about everything Callie hired him to do. The hit-and-run attempt. The shooting in the vineyard. The kidnapping. He's documented payments, shown text message exchanges, and provided a timeline that corroborates every single attack. This isn't his first time heading to prison for being a hired man. He knows the system, and he knows how to play the game." Harlan leaned forward. "All that matters is the DA has enough to take Callie to trial and is confident they'll win. She'll go to prison. No question."

"What about a plea deal?" Devon asked.

"That's always a possibility, but the DA won't take anything that doesn't have prison time included," Harlan said.

The knowledge should have brought relief. It should have felt like justice. Instead, it just felt heavy—the weight of all that hate, all that violence, all because Emery had committed the crime of being born.

"What about Jim?" Devon asked. "What kind of deal is he getting?"

"Unknown yet. That's up to the DA and ultimately the courts." Harlan closed his legal pad with a decisive snap. "But even with full cooperation, he's facing prison time. His endgame is to keep it as short as possible. This is his second offense, so that will be considered."

"Good," Michael Tate said quietly, the single word carrying more weight than a speech.

"Shall we move on to this?" Declan slid the folder toward Emery with careful deliberation, like he was sliding a loaded weapon across the table. "This is everything I found. Birth records, adoption papers, and correspondence between David Callaway and the adoption facilitator. Hospital records from your birth. Financial transactions. Witness statements." He paused, his expression softening in a way that made Emery's stomach clench. "It's not pleasant reading. But you deserve to know the truth."

Emery stared at the folder. For thirty-three years, she'd wondered. Had spun stories in her head about star-crossed lovers or tragic circumstances or noble sacrifices. She'd imagined her birth mother as someone who'd loved her desperately but couldn't keep her—had imagined her birth father as someone who'd ached with the loss but had no choice.

She'd never imagined this. Whatever this turned out to be.

"Do you want me to summarize?" Declan asked gently. "Or would you rather read it yourself first?"

"Summarize." The word came out barely above a whisper. "Please. I'll read the details later, but right now I just... I need to know."

Declan pulled out a document, but he barely glanced at it. "Your birth mother's name was Sarah Mitchell." He spoke slowly, giving her time to absorb each piece. "She was eighteen years old when she met David Callaway at a wine industry event in San Francisco. According to multiple witness statements I obtained, she lied about her age. Told David she was twenty-three."

Eighteen. God. Barely more than a child. But Emery had known that. Accepted it. It wasn't like she hadn't believed she could conquer the world at that age. Thought that she was more of an adult than most people twice her age. But David had been older—twenty-six maybe? And now, this just felt icky.

"They had a brief affair. Two months, maybe less. David was single at the time. But he broke off the affair when he met his current wife. A few weeks later, when Sarah discovered she was pregnant, she told David the truth. About the baby and about her real age." Declan's voice remained carefully neutral, but Emery heard the judgment underneath. "David was eight years older. Established in his career. And he told Sarah he couldn't acknowledge the baby. Couldn't risk his reputation, his position in the wine industry. And he was falling in love with another woman."

"So, he abandoned her," Devon said flatly.

"He offered to pay for an abortion. Sarah refused." Declan turned a page. "She returned to Stone Bridge—this was her hometown, she'd grown up here—and tried to make it work. She gave birth to you at the county hospital. Kept you for five weeks—and David knew all about it."

Five weeks.

Emery's throat closed. Five weeks of holding her baby. Five weeks of trying to be a mother when she was barely more than a child herself. Five weeks of hoping her child's biological father might see her and change his mind before reality crushed it.

"But she was eighteen. Alone. No family support—her parents had died in a car accident when she was sixteen, and she had no siblings. No money. No resources. No way to care for an infant." Declan's professional mask slipped slightly, showing something that looked like sympathy. "According to the notes from the adoption facilitator, Sarah contacted David again. Begged him to take you. To acknowledge you as his daughter and give you the life she couldn't provide. To step up and be a father."

"Let me guess." Her father slapped his hand down on the table, open palm. "He refused."

"That would be correct." Declan pulled out another document. "Instead, he arranged a private adoption through a facilitator who specialized in discreet placements. Black market, essentially. He paid for everything—Sarah's outstanding medical bills, her living expenses for three months, and the adoption fees. The couple who adopted you—your parents—had been contacted because they were on a long list of couples waiting for an infant, and this was one way to put them in the front. They were assured it was legal, and by all accounts, on paper, it looks that way."

Emery looked at her father. His face was carved from stone, every line etched deep, but his eyes were swimming with unshed tears.

"David paid the facilitator a quarter of a million," Declan continued. "And paid Sarah twenty thousand to sign the papers and disappear. Paid your parents the fifteen thousand in 'processing fees.'" He said it without judgment, but Emery heard it anyway. Her parents had paid for her, even if they hadn't understood that's what they'd done. "Though, it cost your parents a lot more than that."

"We would have paid a million," Michael said hoarsely. "One look at you, and we were in love."

"I've always loved being your child." Emery reached across the table, taking his hand. "I don't have any negative feelings about what you or Mom did. But I can't say the same about the Callaways."

"David walked away," Declan said quietly. "Never contacted Sarah again. Never checked on you. Never sent money or asked how you were doing. As far as he was concerned, the situation was handled. Problem solved."

"And Sarah?" Emery asked, though dread was already

pooling in her stomach. She knew from Declan's expression that this part wouldn't end well.

"Sarah struggled." Declan's voice went softer. "She tried to pull her life together. Got a job waitressing, rented a small apartment. But she'd been using drugs before you were born, and she picked up again after she gave you up. Within a year, she'd lost her apartment, lost her job. She was arrested multiple times for possession and sex work."

Emery felt Devon's arm come around her shoulders, anchoring her.

"The records suggest she was trafficked for several years. Moved up and down the coast, controlled by men who exploited her addiction and her desperation." Declan's hands tightened on the document. "She died of an overdose at thirty-five."

Jesus, that was only two years older than Emery now.

The number hit Emery like a physical blow. While she'd been finishing college, starting her career, falling in and out of love, building a life, Sarah Mitchell had been dying alone, destroyed by a choice she'd made at eighteen when a wealthy man had taken what he wanted and walked away.

The room was silent except for the grandfather clock ticking in the corner, marking seconds that felt too loud, too final.

"I'm sorry," Declan said, and he sounded like he meant it. "I know that's not the story you hoped to hear."

Emery couldn't speak. Couldn't think past the image of a girl—barely more than a child—holding her baby and trying to make it work. Couldn't process the trajectory of a life destroyed by one man's refusal to take responsibility.

Devon pulled her closer, his chin resting on top of her

head. Her father's hand squeezed hers hard enough to hurt, and she was grateful for the pain because it meant she could still feel something other than this hollow ache.

"You're a Tate," her father said, his voice fierce despite the tears now streaming down his face. "Sarah gave you to us because she loved you. Because she wanted you to have the life she couldn't provide. And we loved you from the moment we held you. That makes you ours. David Callaway's DNA doesn't change that. His money doesn't change that. Nothing changes that you're my daughter."

"I know." And she did. The Tates were her family. Had always been her family. But knowing the truth about Sarah—about the girl who'd carried her, birthed her, loved her for five weeks—changed something fundamental about how Emery understood herself.

She was the daughter of a girl who'd been exploited and abandoned. The daughter of a man who'd paid to make his mistake disappear. The daughter of desperation and privilege, of hope and cruelty, of love and devastating loss.

"What do you want to do?" Harlan asked after a moment, his voice gentle. "About the inheritance. You have a legitimate claim. With DNA evidence, we can prove you're David's biological daughter. The will is clear—you're entitled to a portion of the Callaway estate."

"How much time do I have to decide?"

"The will stipulates the heir must be found within three months of David's death. We're at two months now." Harlan consulted his notes. "But Winston's cooperation extends the timeline. If he's willing to acknowledge you as his sister and facilitate DNA testing, the courts will likely allow additional time for legal proceedings. You probably have another six months before you need to make a final decision."

Emery looked at the folder. At all the documents proving she was someone's bastard daughter. Someone's inconvenient mistake. Someone's dirty secret.

But she was also Michael and Catherine Tate's chosen daughter. The daughter they'd fought for, paid for, loved fiercely.

She was Walter and Brea Boone's employee and friend, Devon's partner and love.

She was her own person, built from her own choices, her own determination, her own refusal to be defined by other people's mistakes.

"I don't know what I want to do," she admitted, her voice steadier now. "I love my job. I love being a Tate. I'm not sure I want to be a Callaway, too. I'm not sure I want David's money or his name or any connection to the man who destroyed Sarah's life and then pretended I didn't exist."

"You don't have to decide today," her father said firmly. "Take your time. Think about what you want—not what you think you should do, not what anyone else expects. What you want."

"And whatever you decide," Devon added, his voice rough with emotion, "we'll support you. If you want to claim the inheritance and use it for something good— honoring Sarah's memory, helping people like her—we'll be there. If you want to walk away and never speak the Callaway name again, we'll be there for that, too."

Declan and Harlan gathered their materials and promised to follow up on DNA testing procedures and legal timelines. After they left, her father stood, moving around the table to kiss her forehead.

"I'm going to give you two some privacy," he said quietly.

After he left, Devon pulled his chair closer, turning her to face him. His hands found hers, holding on like she was the only thing keeping him grounded.

"How are you really doing?" he asked.

"I don't know." The truth felt too big, too complicated to articulate. "I feel angry. And sad. And guilty." The words tumbled out faster now. "Sarah gave me up so I could have a better life, and then her life became a nightmare. She died alone because she made the mistake of trusting the wrong man. And I got everything—education, opportunity, love—while she got nothing."

"None of that is your fault." Devon's hands cupped her face, forcing her to meet his eyes. "You didn't ask to be born. You didn't ask for Sarah to be exploited. You didn't ask for David to be a coward. None of that is on you."

"Then why does it feel like it is?"

"Because you have a heart. Because you care about people you've never met. Because you're the kind of person who feels other people's pain." His thumbs wiped away the tears rolling down her cheeks like a river. "But Sarah's tragedy doesn't diminish your right to exist. David's choices don't make you any less worthy of love, happiness, or success. You're not responsible for fixing what they broke."

"Then what am I supposed to do with all this?" She gestured vaguely at the folder, at the weight of information that felt like it was crushing her chest. "How do I just... carry this and keep going?"

"You don't carry it alone." Devon pulled her into his arms, holding her tight. "You let me help. You let your dad help. You let this family—this crazy, overwhelming, sometimes overbearing family—help shoulder it. And you give yourself time to figure out what it means and what you want to do about it."

They sat like that for a long time, Devon's arms around her, his heart beating steady against her ear. The grandfather clock kept ticking. Outside, she could hear birds calling to each other. Life continuing despite the ground shifting beneath her feet.

He tilted her face up, his eyes intense. "I love you. Not because of who your father was or wasn't. Not because of what you might inherit. I love you because you're brilliant, brave, and stubborn as hell. Because you fight for what you believe in. Because when the world tried to break you, you refused to stay broken."

Fresh tears spilled down her cheeks. "I love you too."

She kissed him then, pouring everything she couldn't say into it—gratitude and fear and hope and love all tangled together. He kissed her back like she was air, and he'd been drowning, his hands gentle despite the desperation she felt in the way he held her.

When they finally broke apart, both breathing hard, she rested her forehead against his.

"No more secrets?" she whispered.

"No more secrets. No more lies hiding behind the harvest. Just us. Just truth. Just whatever future we build together, one honest day at a time."

"Just us," she agreed.

And for now, in this moment, with Devon's arms around her—that was enough.

The danger was over. The secrets were exposed. Whatever came next—whatever she decided about the Callaway inheritance, whatever complications arose from being David's daughter and Sarah's tragedy—she wouldn't face it alone.

She had Devon. Had her father. Had a family who'd claimed her as their own.

She had a life she'd built through her own determination, talent, and refusal to quit.

And that, she was beginning to understand, was worth more than any inheritance David Callaway could have left behind.

Twenty

TWO WEEKS LATER...

The November afternoon had settled into that perfect golden hour when the sun hung low enough but high enough to still chase away the autumn chill. Devon stood on the main house deck, one hand wrapped around a glass of iced tea that had long since stopped sweating, the other braced against the railing as he surveyed the organized chaos unfolding in the backyard.

This was what family looked like when the storms had passed.

Grant's son, Randy, and Erin's boy, Nathan, had turned the lawn into their personal football field, complete with elaborate plays they'd clearly been planning for weeks. Randy crouched low, hands on his knees, calling out plays that made absolutely no sense but sounded impressively strategic. Nathan bounced on his toes in what he probably thought was a defensive stance, his dark hair flopping in his eyes.

"Blue forty-two! Blue forty-two! Hike!" Randy took off running, dodging an invisible defensive line, while Nathan charged after him with the kind of determined fury only boys that age could muster. They collided near the oak tree in a tangle of limbs and laughter, the football squirting free and rolling across the grass.

Willa appeared from nowhere, scooping up the ball with the confidence of someone who'd been waiting for exactly this opportunity. "I got it! I got it!"

"Hey, that's not fair." Nathan scrambled to his feet. "You can't just steal the ball!"

"I can if you fumble it." Willa clutched the football to her chest and took off running, her ponytail streaming behind her like a victory flag.

Grant stood near the first block of vines, arms crossed, watching his nephew and son chase his niece across the lawn with barely contained amusement. His wife, Kelly, sat on a blanket nearby with Erin and Walter, all three of them clearly enjoying the show.

"Twenty bucks says Willa scores," Erin called out.

"You're on," Grant shot back. "Randy's faster."

"But Willa's more determined."

"Fair point." Grant laughed.

Jessica, Grant's almost-thirteen-year-old daughter, had claimed one of the lounge chairs and declared herself far too mature for football, tag, or anything that involved running and sweating. Instead, she'd positioned herself as the centerpiece of what appeared to be an impromptu nail salon, with Hasley, Ashley, and Emery arranged around her like ladies-in-waiting attending a very particular queen.

Gabe and Olivia had claimed the picnic table under the pergola, both of them looking more relaxed than Devon had seen them in months. The investigation had finally cleared Gabe completely. His reputation had taken a bit of a hit, as there was renewed interest in his grandfather and the whole sordid affair. Gabe hated talking about it. But since the guns had been returned, and he'd successfully donated them to the local museum, his attitude about his heritage had shifted—a little.

He'd decided he couldn't change where he came from. Nor could he change the fact that Stone Bridge had been built on wine, whispers, and secrets. He might as well control the narrative, as Riley constantly put it.

Michael, Emery's father, occupied an Adirondack chair near the garden, a book open in his lap that he clearly wasn't reading. Instead, he watched his daughter laugh with Devon's sisters, a small smile playing at his lips. The terror of almost losing Emery had left its mark—Devon saw it in the way Michael's eyes tracked her movements, the way he relaxed incrementally whenever she laughed.

Emery's mom had flown in for a visit, and she sat between Michael's legs, waving at Willa as she paraded around the lawn, dancing and singing without a care in the world.

It was perfect. The kind of autumn afternoon that belonged in a painting or a memory you pulled out years later when you needed to remember what happiness felt like.

But Devon couldn't quite settle into it. His eyes kept scanning the vine rows, searching for movement, waiting. While Bryson did have some anxiety about how he'd propose, he had none about his and Riley's future. He was only concerned he'd blunder, making an ass out of himself, giving Riley—and the rest of the family—ammunition for the rest of his life because that was just the Boone way.

"What are you thinking about?" His mother appeared at his elbow, her own glass of wine in hand, her facial features soft, but she had that crinkle in her brow that she got when she worried about one of her children.

"Nothing."

"Devon Walter Boone, I raised you. I know your 'thinking about nothing' face, and that's not it." Brea leaned against the railing beside him. "For the last two weeks, you've been quiet. More reserved. What's going on?"

Devon sighed, admitting defeat. His mother had an uncanny ability to extract confessions. "I'm waiting for Bryson and Riley to come back from their walk."

Confusion filled his mother's eyes. "He can't seriously be worried he's coming out of that vineyard without a fiancée?"

"For the first time since he was born, I don't want him to do something funny so I can poke fun at him."

"Now, that's a new one." Brea's hand covered his on the railing. "But at this point, it's virtually impossible for him to screw it up."

"You don't know Bryson like I do."

"I raised him. I'm pretty sure I know him better." Brea sipped her wine. " Have a little faith. He's got this. "

Devon wanted to. Wanted to trust that his brother's carefully orchestrated proposal would go smoothly. But Bryson had a particular talent for overthinking simple things into complicated disasters while Devon waited in the wings, so he had fodder for family dinners.

Movement at the edge of the vineyard caught his attention. Two figures emerging from between the rows, hands clasped, both of them smiling.

Riley lifted her left hand high, wiggling her fingers. Even from this distance, Devon could see the diamond catching the golden hour light, throwing tiny sparks into the air.

The backyard exploded.

Ashley's shriek could probably be heard in the next county. She launched herself from her chair with such enthusiasm that she knocked over the bottle of nail polish, sending iridescent pink streaming across the patio table. Hasley was right behind her, both of them sprinting across the lawn toward Riley like their lives depended on it.

Emery jumped up more carefully, mindful of her still-wet nails, but moved just as quickly. Jessica bolted after them, her half-painted nails forgotten in the excitement.

Ashley reached Riley first, grabbing her hand to examine the ring. "Grandma's ring looks perfect on you."

"Let me see." Hasley crowded in, practically climbing over her sister.

Riley laughed, tears streaming down her face, trying to show everyone the ring while also trying to hug everyone at once.

Grant, meanwhile, had charged at Bryson like a linebacker seeing an opening. He hit his future brother-in-law with enough force to stagger them both, wrapping him in a bear hug that turned into a headlock that turned into a full wrestling match on the lawn.

"Took you long enough," Grant said.

"Get off of me." Bryson managed to break free. Both men jumped to their feet. "You know, payback is a bitch."

Bryson tackled Grant around the waist. They went down in a heap, both of them laughing like kids.

Devon watched them roll around in the grass, grinning so hard his face hurt. A year ago—hell, six months ago—Grant and Bryson could barely be in the same room without words of frustration being tossed between them like they were playing tennis. Their relationship had been difficult since childhood, marked by years of resentment and misunderstanding, thanks to pride and stubbornness, and thanks to Grant's mother, who'd constantly meddled in her children's lives.

Now, Grant and Bryson were wrestling in the backyard, celebrating together, acting like best friends.

"Look at them," Devon's mother said. "Look at all of them. Grant, Erin, and Riley have fought to be a family again, and I love them all as if they were part of our family. I worry about Grant through, with their mother's trial coming up. I can see how he's trying to be strong. Trying to hold it together for his family. But he carries so much guilt." Brea wiped a tear from her cheek.

"He'll get through it," Devon said. "He's got his sisters. He's got an amazing wife. Two beautiful children. And now, he's got all of us to support him through testifying against his mom. I think the hard part will be admitting in a courtroom full of people that he took a cup of coffee filled with poison that his mom gave him and handed it to his father, who died less than an hour later." Devon stared out at the perfect chaos in the yard. The kids had gone back to running around. Jessica leaned against her dad, head resting on his shoulder. All of a sudden. she looked less like a teenager and more like a little girl.

Bryson and Riley had taken a seat on the blanket and were in deep conversation.

"Something else is on your mind, because you're not out there busting your brother's ass," Brea said.

Devon should have known better than to think he could hide anything from his mother. "Emery got her DNA results back yesterday," he admitted quietly. "It's confirmed. She's David Callaway's daughter. Winston's half-sister. Official heir to the Callaway estate."

"I think we all knew that was coming."

"She doesn't know what to do. Whether to claim her inheritance, whether to acknowledge David publicly as her father. The only thing she knows for sure is she'd never take the Callaway name." Devon's hands tightened on the railing. "I want to help her, but I don't know how. I don't know what to say or how to make this easier."

"You can't make it easier, sweetheart. This is something she has to work through herself." Brea's voice was gentle but firm. "What you *can* do is let her digest the information in her own time. Give her space to figure out who she wants to be now that she knows the truth. And just be there for her."

"What if she decides she wants to claim everything? What if she decides she's a Callaway and that means she belongs at Callaway Wines instead of here?"

Brea set down her wine glass and turned to face him fully. "That woman loves you. Anyone with eyes can see it. She looks at you like you hung the moon and stars specifically for her enjoyment. Whatever she decides about David's money or his legacy—it won't change how she feels about you."

"How can you be so sure?"

"Because I've watched the two of you together. I've seen how she fights for you, how she trusts you, how she's built a life here that has nothing to do with money or inheritance or family names." His mom smiled that sweet, soft grin that always seemed to make things better. "She's not going anywhere. She's already chosen you. Now, you need to allow yourself to trust that choice."

Devon wanted to believe it. Wanted to trust that Emery's feelings were solid enough to withstand the weight of an unexpected inheritance and all the complications that came with it.

"Just love her," his mother said simply. "That's all you can do. Love her, and be patient while she figures out what this means for her future."

His mother kissed his cheek then headed down the deck steps to join the celebration.

Devon stayed on the deck, content to watch from a distance.

Until Emery detached herself from the group and headed toward him.

She climbed the steps with careful grace, mindful of her wet nails, her smile soft and knowing. "Why are you up here alone? You're going to give Bryson a complex."

"Maybe that's the point."

"Doubtful." She moved to stand beside him, her shoulder brushing his. "You're deep in thought. I can tell because you get this little crease right here—" She touched the space between his eyebrows. "—when you're thinking too hard about something that worries you. Want to talk about what's actually on your mind?"

"I'm not sure now is the time."

She tilted her head. "Because you said that, I'm going to hound you until you talk."

"I don't want to ruin the party, and I certainly don't want to pressure you about something you haven't had the chance to process."

"Now I get it. The DNA results," she said it lightly, but Devon heard the tension underneath.

He rested his hands on her hips. "I understand it's confusing. But we haven't really had a chance to talk about it, and I don't know how you feel about having that fact put in black and white, making it real."

Emery was quiet for a long moment, looking out at the vineyard where the vines stood in perfect rows, with gold at the edges. The place where Bryson had just proposed. The place where Devon's family had built everything that mattered.

"The only word I can come up with to describe how I feel is strange," she said finally. "It's strange knowing for certain that David Callaway was my father. That I'm related to people who tried to kill me. That I have a legal claim to money and property and a legacy I never wanted." She turned to look at him. "For the last twenty-four hours, I've been consumed by what to do about the inheritance. Harlan believes there's a possibility for an option to be bought out of everything. Right now, that feels like blood money. I'd be taking money from the very people who wanted me dead. And that, I need to think about. Get a little distance from what happened and some perspective." She leaned closer, placing her palm against his cheek. "However, I don't belong at Callaway Wines. It's not the place I want to build something."

"And where is it you see yourself?" Devon circled his arms around her body. His heart beat wildly. He considered himself a fairly confident man. He loved her, and he felt her love right through to his soul. But standing there, staring into her green eyes, holding his breath, he worried about what her answer might be.

"Stone Ridge Winery. And with you," she said it simply, firmly, like it was the most obvious thing in the world. "My career, my life, my future—it's all here."

Devon's chest loosened, and the tension he'd been carrying finally released. "You're sure? Because that inheritance is substantial. Millions of dollars. Property. History. You could—"

"I could what? Abandon the job I love? Walk away from the people who've become my family? Leave the man I'm in love with because suddenly I have access to money and a winery that I would have some control over?" Emery's voice was fierce now, passionate. "Money doesn't change who I am or what I want. And what I want is this. Us. Building something together."

"The family's going to love hearing that. They've already adopted you as one of their own."

"I noticed. Your mother cried three separate times yesterday when we were discussing wedding color schemes for Riley."

"Wait, what?"

"Riley asked for help planning. I got pulled into a three-hour conversation about whether burgundy or navy blue was more appropriate for a December wedding." Emery laughed. "Your mother kept saying how wonderful it was going to be to have two more daughters joining the family so close together."

"Two?"

Emery's smile turned shy. "She might have hinted—very subtly, of course—that she was hoping for another wedding announcement in the near future."

Devon laughed. He should've been mortified. It should've scared the hell out of him. But all it did was remind him that he was in love with the sweetest, kindest woman in the world, and he wanted everything with her. "And what did you say?"

"I said I thought burgundy was the better choice." Emery's eyes sparkled with mischief. "Why? Did you have something you wanted to ask me?"

"Maybe. Eventually." Devon kissed her nose. "When the timing's right. When—"

"I already know what I want. I want you. I want this family. I want to build a life here at Stone Bridge, authenticating wines and creating documentation that will matter long after we're gone. I want to wake up next to you every morning and fall asleep in your arms every night. I want to fight about stupid things and make up in creative ways and grow old together watching our nieces and nephews—and maybe someday our own kids—run around this vineyard."

"You've thought about this."

"I've thought about nothing else since the DNA results came back." She took his hands in hers, her burgundy nails stark against his tanned skin. "Whatever I decide about the Callaway inheritance—whether I take the money or walk away from it— won't change what I want for my future. And my future is you."

"You know, my family's a little crazy."

"That kind of crazy I can handle." She gestured toward the backyard, where Grant and Bryson were now arguing good-naturedly about something while Riley showed her ring to Jessica, who was providing very serious opinions about who Riley should choose to be in the wedding. "They're my family too now. For better or worse."

"Mostly worse," Devon said.

"Mostly better." She squeezed his hands. "I love you. I love your family, your winery, your ridiculous valley full of gossip and drama and people who care way too much about each other's business."

"I love you, too." The words felt inadequate for the emotion flooding his chest. "And I promise—no more secrets. No more lies hiding behind anything."

"Just us."

"Just us," he agreed. "And whatever future we harvest together."

"Did you really just make a wine pun?"

"I've been saving it."

"It was terrible."

"It was perfect, and you know it."

She laughed, the sound warm and genuine and everything he'd been terrified of losing. Then she kissed him—a kiss filled with promises of truth, trust, and building something real together.

When they finally broke apart, both breathless, she rested her forehead against his. "You need to go congratulate your brother before he has a panic attack about actually having to plan a wedding."

"Too late. I saw his face when Ashley started talking about guest lists."

"Then we definitely need to intervene."

She took his hand, pulling him toward the steps. Devon let himself be led, let himself be pulled back into the chaos and celebration and love that defined his family.

The harvest was over. The secrets were revealed. The danger had passed.

But the best vintage was still ahead—waiting to be created from everything they'd weathered together, from the trust they'd rebuilt, from the love that had taken root in the richest soil of all.

Devon looked at Emery, at the woman who'd survived attempted murder and betrayal and the revelation of a father who'd abandoned her, and he saw only strength. Only courage. Only the future he wanted to build.

They joined the celebration, folding back into the family that had claimed them both. Riley pulled Emery into the conversation about wedding colors. Bryson grabbed Devon's shoulder and said something about needing moral support against his sisters' increasingly elaborate ideas. The kids resumed their football game with renewed vigor.

And as the sun dipped lower, painting everything in shades of gold and amber, Devon realized this was what he'd been searching for without knowing it. Not just love, though he had that. Not just family, though they surrounded him.

But home. Real home. The kind that had nothing to do with property lines or family names or inherited legacies.

The kind of home you built with your own hands, one

honest conversation at a time, one shared moment at a time, one harvest at a time.

The kind of home that lasted.

Thank you for taking the time to read *A Harvest of Lies*. Please feel free to leave an honest review.

I hope you will check out my newest series...
The Aegis Network: The Everglades Division
Hunted in Calusa Cove
Shadows in Calusa Cove

Grab a glass of vino, kick back, relax, and let the romance roll in...

Sign up for my Newsletter (https://dl.bookfunnel.com/ 82gm8b9k4y) where I often give away free books before publication.

Join my private Facebook group (https://www.facebook.com/ groups/191706547909047/) where I post exclusive excerpts and discuss all things murder and love!

About Jen Talty

Jen Talty is the *USA Today* Bestselling Author of Contemporary Romance, Romantic Suspense, and Paranormal Romance. In the fall of 2020, her short story was selected and featured in a 1001 Dark Nights Anthology.

Regardless of the genre, her goal is to take you on a ride that will leave you floating under the sun with warmth in your heart. She writes stories about broken heroes and heroines who aren't necessarily looking for romance, but in the end, they find the kind of love books are written about :).

She first started writing while carting her kids to one hockey rink after the other, averaging 170 games per year between 3 kids in 2 countries and 5 states. Her first book, IN TWO WEEKS was originally published in 2007. In 2010 she helped form a publishing company (Cool Gus Publishing) with *NY Times* Bestselling Author Bob Mayer where she ran the technical side of the business through 2016.

Jen is currently enjoying the next phase of her life...the empty nester! She and her husband reside in Jupiter, Florida.

Grab a glass of vino, kick back, relax, and let the romance roll in...

Sign up for my Newsletter (https://dl.bookfunnel.com/82gm8b9k4y) where I often give away free books before publication.

Join my private Facebook group (https://www.facebook.com/groups/191706547909047/) where I post exclusive excerpts and discuss all things murder and love!

Never miss a new release. Follow me on Amazon:amazon.com/author/jentalty

And on Bookbub: bookbub.com/authors/jen-talty

Also by Jen Talty

Brand New Series!
The Aegis Network: The Everglades Division
Hunted in Calusa Cove
Shadows in Calusa Cove

Welcome to...Everglades Overwatch!
Secrets in Calusa Cove
Pirates in Calusa Cove
Murder in Calusa Cove
Betrayal in Calusa Cove

The Secrets of Stone Bridge
A Vintage of Regret
A Harvest of Lies

Safe Harbor Series
Mine To Keep
Mine To Save
Mine To Protect

Mine to Hold
Mine to Love

Check out LOVE IN THE ADIRONDACKS!
Shattered Dreams
An Inconvenient Flame
The Wedding Driver
Clear Blue Sky
Blue Moon
Before the Storm

NY STATE TROOPER SERIES (also set in the Adirondacks!)
In Two Weeks
Dark Water
Deadly Secrets
Murder in Paradise Bay
To Protect His own
Deadly Seduction
When A Stranger Calls
His Deadly Past
The Corkscrew Killer

First Responders: A spin-off from the NY State
Troopers series
Playing With Fire
Private Conversation
The Right Groom
After The Fire
Caught In The Flames
Chasing The Fire

Legacy Series
Dark Legacy
Legacy of Lies
Secret Legacy

Emerald City
Investigate Away
Sail Away
Fly Away
Flirt Away
Anchor Away

Hawaii Brotherhood Protectors
Waylen Unleashed
Bowie's Battle

Colorado Brotherhood Protectors
Fighting For Esme
Defending Raven
Fay's Six
Darius' Promise

Yellowstone Brotherhood Protectors
Guarding Payton
Wyatt's Mission
Corbin's Mission

Candlewood Falls
Rivers Edge
The Buried Secret
Its In His Kiss

ALSO BY JEN TALTY

Lips Of An Angel
Kisses Sweeter than Wine
A Little Bit Whiskey

It's all in the Whiskey
Johnnie Walker
Georgia Moon
Jack Daniels
Jim Beam
Whiskey Sour
Whiskey Cobbler
Whiskey Smash
Irish Whiskey

The Monroes
Color Me Yours
Color Me Smart
Color Me Free
Color Me Lucky
Color Me Ice
Color Me Home

Broken Heroes Mended Souls
Shelter for Danni
Shelter for Shay

Fallport Rescue Operations
Searching for Madison
Searching for Haven
Searching for Pandora
Searching for Stormi

Searching for Winslet
Searching for Odessa

DELTA FORCE-NEXT GENERATION
Shielding Jolene
Shielding Aalyiah
Shielding Laine
Shielding Talullah
Shielding Maribel
Shielding Daisy

The Men of Thief Lake
Rekindled
Destiny's Dream

Federal Investigators
Jane Doe's Return
The Butterfly Murders

THE AEGIS NETWORK
The Sarich Brother
The Lighthouse
Her Last Hope
The Last Flight
The Return Home
The Matriarch

Aegis Network: Jacksonville Division
A SEAL's Honor
Talon's Honor
Arthur's Honor

ALSO BY JEN TALTY

Rex's Honor
Kent's Honor
Buddy's Honor
Duncan's Honor
Garth's Honor
Hawke's Honor

Aegis Network Short Stories
Max & Milian
A Christmas Miracle
Spinning Wheels
Holiday's Vacation

The Brotherhood Protectors
Out of the Wild
Rough Justice
Rough Around The Edges
Rough Ride
Rough Edge
Rough Beauty

The Brotherhood Protectors
The Saving Series
Saving Love
Saving Magnolia
Saving Leather

Hot Hunks
Cove's Blind Date Blows Up
My Everyday Hero – Ledger
Tempting Tavor

ALSO BY JEN TALTY

Malachi's Mystic Assignment
Needing Neor

Holiday Romances
A Christmas Getaway
Alaskan Christmas
Whispers
Christmas In The Sand

Heroes & Heroines on the Field
Taking A Risk
Tee Time

A New Dawn
The Blind Date
Spring Fling
Summers Gone
Winter Wedding
The Awakening
Fated Moons

The Collective Order
The Lost Sister
The Lost Soldier
The Lost Soul
The Lost Connection
The New Order

www.ingramcontent.com/pod-product-compliance
Lightning Source LLC
Chambersburg PA
CBHW011113100726

47898CB00011B/3071